World War A

World War A

Book 1 - Chinese Trojan

CLARENCE XON

Faith Publishing

Faith Publishing
Singapore

Website: www.WorldWarA.com

Copyright © 2016 by Clarence Xon

Xon, Clarence
World War A / Clarence Xon

ISBN 978-981-09-9537-9 (Ebook)
ISBN 978-981-09-9775-5 (Printbook)

Book design by Yocla Designs

One

Los Angeles, California
2030 A.D.

The WarGames stadium at the University of California was a roaring, seething mass of humanity. It was the last match of the season; a college championship decider, or "the Big Game," as they called it.

Parents, friends, and fans jostled for their seats, peering down into the glass-domed arena and its simulated terrains, mounted laser turrets, and defensive pillboxes. Within the war zone waited two teams in black combat fatigues, their faces tipped toward the umpire's box. The game would soon begin.

Around the field, 3D conglomerate advertisements burst atop the helmets of the players, each cutting-edge animation vying to be the biggest, brightest, and most explosive. In recent years, Chinese companies like Haier, Alipay, and Xiaomi had begun to crowd out the smaller advertisements put up by Pepsi-Cola, McDonald's and Apple, but the home crowd didn't care; their eyes were glued to the young men and women before them as "The Star-Spangled Banner" rumbled through the speakers.

Kaden Sun stood within a two-story observatory tower—the team headquarters. It was shaped like the bishop piece from a chess set, its crystal top offering a complete view of the arena. He licked his lips—still cracked from an early jog into dawn wind—and scanned the faces of his group below. Some were lost to anxiety, others were simmering with hunger for the fight ahead. Kaden was sick with nerves and glad that no one's eyes were directed at him.

His team's chief strategist, Kaden waved a palm over the dashboard and instantly conjured a holographic topography of the ground below, including the opposing team's tower, located at the far end of the stadium. Upon his chest was stitched the small blue-and-gold square that everyone wanted. The object of the game was simple: get the flag, win the championship. But that was where the simplicity ended.

"Speed up, Zac. Five minutes and counting," Kaden said, frowning at the half-finished barricade below.

His best friend's voice returned through his earpiece, so clear he might have been standing at Kaden's shoulder.

"This is crazy," he grumbled. "Championship game and half our team's out with gastro…It's gotta be rigged."

"Obviously," cut in their manager, Johnson, who was seated in the VIP box but had his own comm system. "No one's heard from the cook since breakfast; he's probably halfway to Mexico by now."

This was met with a loud sigh, and Kaden could see Zac shaking his head below. "You sure you want us to go ahead with this, Kay? Surely it's better to forfeit, than lose?" Zac asked.

Kaden's eyes scanned the multitude of offensive and defensive formations he had tirelessly developed. "Love your fighting spirit, Zac. Now shut the hell up and focus."

The crowds were whistling as the official countdown began and Kaden delivered his preparatory instructions. Cheerleaders danced on a pavilion that hovered above the players and aerial cameras whirred their way around the contestants. The whole thing felt like flies buzzing over a carcass.

They weren't dead yet, but for all his bravado, Kaden knew they were in for a massacre.

"Jeremy, you've got the nanomirrors all sprayed up?' he asked.

"Aye, aye, Captain!"

Two minutes and counting.

"Now, listen in team." Kaden spoke in a slow, deliberate tone. "We're ten soldiers short, and they know that. They will attack with everything they have and try to punch a hole right through our front. I want you to let them."

Brief silence was quickly filled with a flurry of curses and uninvited opinions. "I thought you wanted us to fight?" said Ryker, his communications officer.

"Oh, you'll get your chance to fight," said Kaden. "Jeremy, take six to the front line. Fall back as you need to, but stagger it, and stick to the corridors of the nanomirrors. Remember that."

"Er, roger."

Kaden couldn't help but smile at the tone of his sergeant's voice. Clearly, they all thought he was mad.

"Zac, bring Ella and Mia with you on the right turrets and hold off their pincer attack. Ki, you do the same on the left with Miles and Gatwick."

"Got that, CS."

Even though the weather had cooled to a refreshing sixty degrees, Kaden had to wipe the perspiration from his brow.

As the countdown dribbled into single digits, the crowd reached a fever pitch. Kaden watched as the referee—a lumbering, bull-necked man in black-and-white stripes—pointed to a dark-suited army corpsman with a red peak cap. The soldier responded by raising his bugle to his lips, the shrill but authoritative timbre of "To Arms" jolting the players into action. They grabbed their laser guns and double-checked their equipment, giving final waves to the crowd as it roared behind the glass enclosure.

Kaden's heart pounded and, for a moment, he wondered if he might be sick. There was a large vase nearby, but he turned from it and pulled his safety googles down, adjusting his helmet and checking the laser tags on his head and chest. If they were covered up they could cost the team the game and label them cheaters.

He felt isolated in his transparent container, beading sweat as he took in the twenty thousand onlookers around him. Above him to the left was the commentator's box; the game was being beamed live to every household across the United States. Millions of others were watching, and the thought sent a fresh wave of goose bumps across Kaden's skin.

Down the field he could make out the vague outline of the opposing CS, also encased in his tower. Kaden guessed their guy was probably feeling the same way. Then again, maybe not. He was the son of China's wealthiest industrialist, a conniving businessman who was said to have cheated and bribed his way into the highest echelons of material success. Kaden had crossed paths with the son, Wang Hom, several times. By all accounts, the apple hadn't fallen far from the tree. Right now, Hom was probably fine-tuning his victory speech.

The bugle sounded again and the announcer blared: "Let the WarGames begin!" The players dashed toward their assigned positions.

"All right guys, this is it," Kaden said with a breath, but before he could even begin to deliver his launch instructions laser beams of red and blue flared across the war zone. As suspected, the opponents had massed their attack in the middle of the battlefield, right toward the heart of Kaden's defense, concentrating their firepower at the defenders stationed behind the barricades and mounted turrets.

Kaden placed his hands on the panel in front of him and leaned forward. *Gee, Hom, going straight for the kill?*

"Jeremy, try to hold your position for the next ten minutes. Zac, man the pillbox below the turret; two encroachers coming your way."

"Miles has been hit, Kaden. He's down!" Ki cried.

"Stay your course, Ki. They're massing a secondary attack on your side to draw us over and open us up."

Kaden tried to swallow and couldn't.

"Our formation's breaking up," Jeremy's urgent voice came through. "They're all over us. We're going to have to move."

Kaden narrowed his eyes at the action unfolding before him. "Jeremy, deploy a man over to Ki and retreat along the preassigned pathway. The nanomirrors will confuse them. Do you read me?"

After a tentative pause Jeremy responded, "Roger, proceeding."

"Zac, push Ella and Mia behind the advancing enemy, and don't attack unless they fall back," Kaden said, his voice rising.

"What? I should be out there with them, instead of being stuck in this turret. There's no one coming our way!" Zac exclaimed.

"Stay." Somehow his voice was firm, even as the endless barrage continued. "Jeremy, invite them in along the mirrored corridor; staggered retreat. Ki, you must hold off their attack—do not let them break through."

"There are too many!" Ki cried. "I can hold them for five minutes, tops."

Kaden pressed his lips together. If Ki's position became compromised, Hom would be able to overrun them before they could launch their own strike. Kaden checked his screen: fourteen blue enemy blips in front of Jeremy's position and streaming in. Seven surrounding Ki's defensive pillbox. With only one fighter held in reserve, it was clear Hom was not out to entertain the fans with a full hour-long spectacle. He simply wanted to win and as quickly as possible.

"Okay, guys. They think they've got us cornered like rabbits. Jeremy, fall back to your target destination, *now*. Encircle the corridor exit and wait for their frontal assault unit. Ki, if you must, retreat to Jeremy's assembly point and defend from there. Ella and Mia, there's one bogey at the ridge just north of you. He's the enemy's reserve and a sniper—track and kill! Zac, get ready. I'm coming in."

"You're what?" Zac stammered. "You can't expose the flag like that!"

The adversary pack was beelining into the marked passageway like a school of fish in a narrowing net. The mirrors disoriented the attackers and veiled the locations of his defenders. Kaden glanced at his screen again. He allowed himself a half smile. Once the bulk of them had moved into the most exposed section, Kaden issued his order. "Jeremy, fry the fish."

A flash of red beams from Jeremy's troops sent the enemy falling like pins in a bowling alley. Each laser contact short-circuited the victim's nerve impulses, causing a temporary muscle malfunction that left them immobilized. The crowd exploded in rapturous applause as the bodies flopped atop one another on the big screen.

"Ella and Mia reporting in. Bogey is down."

Kaden grinned. "Great work, ladies. Now get back and finish off anyone trying to retreat from Jeremy's bottleneck."

"The raiders are through!" Ki yelled. "They're coming for you!"

"Keep them engaged," Kaden calmly replied, picking up his weapon and moving to the stairwell. "I want their CS to think we're defending our HQ to the last man." He jogged down the steps, hand pressed to the flag on his breast. Pausing a moment at the bottom, he took a deep breath before swinging the door open and running out to his right. "Zac," Kaden called, "I'm beside your bunker. Come out and cover my ass."

Zac's head popped out of the turret just meters above, his face creased into a smirk. "About time you let me see some action."

The pair moved carefully, Zac guiding the way as Kaden checked his wrist map to scrutinize the little blue and red dots swarming across the screen.

"Their CS is probably choking after losing his advantage," panted Kaden. "He's alone in his fort. I'm going in, so you cover me from here." Neither CS player wore a tracker—the risk of leaving the tower too great to consider one necessary—so Hom would have no way of sensing his location.

"That's crazy!" answered Zac, eyes wide with shock. "Why not send the girls?"

Kaden sighed, trying not to lose patience with his friend's constant questioning.

"Because I need them to keep his soldiers off our tower. As soon as they learn it's deserted, we're toast."

A tingling sensation came over Kaden as they scrambled beneath clumps of vegetation and into the shadow of the enemy prize. Kaden looked up to see Hom stomping around, his can of sponsored Pepsi hurled against the shatterproof windows. Alone, he appeared to be screaming at his troops and both his hands were waving forward in a frantic order to advance all forces.

Kaden grinned. *One big fish, alone in his tank.*

He gripped the steel ladder alongside the structure and climbed. At the top of the observatory he pulled the handle of the makeshift paneled door and held his breath as it opened slowly, Hom's vociferous cursing loud enough to make him wince.

Kaden gripped his laser gun and aimed at Hom's back. "Careful, my friend. One wrong move and you'll be on the ground, writhing like a worm."

Just like that, the howling stopped.

Hom turned and faced Kaden, eyes widened in shock—and anger.

"Think you got me, Sun?"

Kaden's mouth curled in bemusement as he nodded. "Yup, fair and square."

"But the real world doesn't play by a rule book." He tapped a button on his wrist comm, cunning eyes narrowed in satisfaction.

Kaden squared his shoulders. "Who's gonna stop me, Hom?" He waved his hand toward the outfield. "Game's over, we won. Blame it on the home crowd advantage."

Hom smiled thinly. "The advantage is all mine," he said, eyes moving beyond Kaden. "You just don't know it yet."

Two

"**G**ame's over for the Bruins," boomed an authoritative voice. The man stood in the open door, arms braced against the frame as if to keep anyone from escaping. He was tall, square-jawed, and with closely cropped hair that was instantly recognizable. The umpire.

"Technical foul," he said, frowning at Kaden. "You lose on penalty."

"What?" Kaden's voice shook at the absurdity of the remark. "What foul?"

"You left your tower. It's against regulations."

"And which rule book is that in? China's?" he shouted, clenching his hands to keep them from trembling. The glory he'd held so assuredly began to collapse before him, flimsy as a house of cards. The season of straight wins, tireless training, sleepless nights…

The umpire sneered. "The CS stays in the enclosure, as is the norm, and you know that."

"*The norm* is hardly a rule—"

"I call the rules in play as I see fit, that's my job," the man barked. "And right now, you're out of line."

Hom's smug face burst into a laugh that set Kaden's blood to boil.

"You greasy rat," he spat at the ref, eyes narrowing to slits. "How much did they give you?"

"You're out of the games, Sun! Manager Johnson!" Face beet red, he screeched into his comm, "Get your CS out of this tower before I shoot him myself!"

Kaden no longer cared about fouls, or red cards, or even the millions of TV viewers who must be cursing him for losing the match. The game had ended the moment the pig in front of him accepted his small, brown envelope. He turned on the man, his hands clenched into fists.

The umpire didn't stand a chance.

Kaden charged like a wasp-stung goat, his broad shoulders ramming right into the fat abdomen. There was a sharp "*Oooof!*" as the heavy body flew backward and slammed into the doorway, splintering the crystal frame. In the distance, Kaden could hear the cries of the onlookers and outraged commentary. He'd done some pretty reckless things in the past, but this little stint would make international news. Which meant he might as well make the most of it.

"Hope the money was worth it, scum," he snarled.

The umpire struggled to get up, plump arms waving around madly as Kaden ground his knee into the guy's chest. He was about to deliver a nice, open-palmed slap when the next thing he knew every nerve in his body was being ripped at, the hot current passing through his system in milliseconds. Limbs spasming, he collapsed on the ground, helpless. Above, Hom lurched into view, his laser gun pointed at Kaden's helmet.

"You might be smart, Kaden Sun, but you're stoo-pid, too."

And with that, a final blue flash sent Kaden into the darkness.

He slowly came to, the silence informing him the games had ended. Pulling himself to his feet, he scrambled over to the scoreboard to see the UCLA logo branded with the large red words—still smoking—that read, *Technical Penalty*. Turning, he found Zac Koby standing quietly at his side. Hom and the umpire were gone.

The real world doesn't play by a rule book. Hom's sneering words echoed in his mind. Kaden stared blankly at the WarGames logo on his laser gun: a fist clenching a flag, all in the red, white, and blue of Uncle Sam. Or perhaps it was in tribute to Pepsi-Cola, one of the founding sponsors.

Kaden and Zac were the last to leave the field, heads bowed as they picked their way through mud and boulders, all carefully shipped in to create the pretense of something real. Of course, it was nothing but farce.

They headed toward the change rooms, taking off their helmets and unbuttoning their fatigues. Before they could reach the sanctuary of the players' quarters, a half-chewed hotdog splashed across Kaden's inner shirt. They lifted their eyes to the spectator stands.

"Thanks for screwing our season, Sun!"

"Yeah, slanty eyes," another voice joined in. "How about'cha go play ping-pong next time! Give him another one, Jones."

A second hotdog sailed through the air, Kaden neatly stepping to one side only to leave Zac wide open, the mustard bright yellow in his toffee hair. Kaden's body tensed, overwhelmed with the desire to climb into the stands and show them what one slanty-eyed bastard could do. Jones and his goon jocks were a constant pain in Kaden's ass, and someone needed to teach them some manners.

Zac stretched an arm across his front. "Forget it, they're drunk."

He gave a short, bitter laugh. "That's what you say every time."

"So don't take it so personal."

He shook his head, giving the louts a finger as they passed into the safety of the corridor. "I'm all American, third-generation," he snapped. "Feels pretty personal to me."

Zac smiled, slinging his arm around Kaden's shoulder. "I know, man. Beers are on me, okay? Let's shower and head to Orb's."

Kaden's posture remained rigid, but Zac's easygoing Texan drawl always succeeded in calming him down. He was too damn happy to argue with.

The boys entered a small passageway only to find two cheerleaders waiting at the doors to the showers. They were wearing the all-purple of the opposing Bradford Bulls.

Kaden shifted his large frame to pass them. "Excuse us, ladies."

The girls giggled and blocked his path. Both of them had shapely figures, the tight-fitting spandex leaving little to the imagination. One had scarlet red hair, the other long brown tresses that framed a pair of large, almost childlike eyes.

"Oooh, I love Orientals," the scarlet one said. "Especially big, strong ones."

As she ran her hand up his torso, he blinked at Zac in wonder. Kaden's half-Chinese heritage usually chafed him, but there were moments when being considered exotic had its perks.

Kaden brushed a hand through his wavy, jet-black hair and straightened up to fill his full six-foot-two potential. The more voluptuous girl pouted at her friend and said, "I saw him first, Veronica. The least you could do is share." Brushing her fingers down the length of his arm, she murmured, "Every player has a bad day. But if you need help with scoring, we can show you how it's done, handsome."

It wasn't unusual for excited girls to fawn over them, even ask for signatures on occasion, but these girls were acting like they were rock stars. Kaden felt his brain begin to cloud as his libido took over. Zac could take the redhead, but her little brunette friend was all his.

"Hey, uh, ladies, we've got matters to attend to," Zac said, shouldering his way between them. "Some other time?"

Kaden watched in disbelief as Zac removed the girls' hands from his body and proceeded to drag him into the showers.

"Oh we get it, team Bruin. You prefer to play with boys, on and off the field." Their giggles were stifled by Zac slamming the door, hard.

"What did you do that for?" Kaden said, staring at the door as if it might magically reopen. "Those girls were all over us."

"Exactly," Zac said. "Stay away from them, they're toxic." Lips pressed tightly together, he threw his gear onto the bench and stripped off his shirt. He was slightly smaller than Kaden, but just as toned, and knew exactly how to play the Texan angle to his advantage when it came to chasing tail. A pair of cornflower blue eyes didn't hurt, either.

"Toxic?" Kaden shrugged. "Whiskey is toxic, but that's never stopped you."

"They're entrepreneurs," Zac said, narrowing his eyes as if to say, *you know what I mean.*

"What, you mean they're prostitutes?"

"Come on, man," he sighed. "You didn't see the black necklace on the brunette's chest?"

"I saw her chest," Kaden answered, laughing.

Zac gave a small grunt of displeasure. "You were spellbound, dude. That was a wireless video cam. You were being streamed live—those girls entice guys back to their rooms and make a fortune filming what happens next. I just saved you, dude, never mind your scholarship, or your father…"

Kaden stood there, speechless, as Zac continued.

"They usually go for high-profile players. Maybe they've been drawing blanks tonight and got desperate." Zac winked, ducking as Kaden pretended to punch him.

His best friend was an orphan from one of the poorest parts of San Antonio, and while he didn't like to talk about his past, he had an air of quiet dependability that made the biggest disasters somehow bearable.

"Tough day at the office," Kaden groaned, reaching for his comm device and strapping it to his wrist. As soon as it made contact with his skin, a holographic image of his father beamed above it. Four missed calls.

"He probably wants to talk to you about the game," Zac said, patting him on the shoulder.

"Not sure 'talk' is the right word there, bro. 'Chew' maybe."

Zac laughed. "Nothing a beer can't fix."

Three

The Tipsy Orb
Los Angeles, California

After several downed lagers and a whiskey chaser, Kaden's mood had risen a couple of notches— from rock bottom to hovering somewhere below a snake's belly. The mood around him was both exhilarating and contagious. The Tipsy Orb was full of LA's latest generation of sun-bronzed college students and young professionals. When the band started singing the classic tune "Party in the USA," everyone sang and clapped along.

"Time for shots!" Zac hooted as a 'nurse' appeared beside the boys. She took out a large, glowing plastic syringe and pointed it at Kaden, smiling.

"Ready for your prescription?" she asked chirpily.

Kaden leaned back in his seat, tipped his head, and closed his eyes. "Doctor's orders?"

A moment later he felt a cool, sweet alcoholic syrup travel down his throat, reminding him of the Jell-O his mother had used to make, minus the ethanol. Her favorite flavor had been raspberry, but that was before—

"Awesome!" Zac cried out, banging the table with his fist. "Dose me up, sistah!"

Kaden watched as the nurse poised the shot over his lips, the barrel lighting up as it emptied out. Halfway through, Zac began to cough, sitting up and spluttering the bright liquid all over the nurse's pristine ensemble.

"Gaargh…" he spluttered, grasping at his beer.

"I thought you didn't need your bib anymore," Kaden chuckled as the nurse walked off in a huff.

"Next time, I'll hold her hand and guide her," Zac said, hacking up a final time. "I'll betcha a girl like that would love…"

Kaden patted his friend on the back, but was no longer listening. On the stage sat a lone girl with a guitar, the name 'Katy Collins' flashing up on the screen behind her. In the distance, he detected Zac complaining and pushed his voice away to concentrate fully on the song floating over him. There was something about her, sad and yet eternally hopeful.

"Seriously, dude?" Kaden felt a sharp tug at his elbow. "What is it with you and girls today?"

"She's not a girl, she's a goddess," Kaden whispered, swaying to the song.

"I've heard that before," Zac said, wiping the remaining Jell-O from his mouth.

"This is…different," Kaden said, eyes flicking over to a guy near the stage who had called out for a more upbeat tune. Somehow, he hated the unknown drunkard even more than the umpire who had just destroyed his perfect season. "Oh yes, this is different."

When the song ended Katy took her bow and a moment later some pumping electro came on instead. Apparently, the club agreed it was not the time for ballads.

Zac waved his hands in exasperation. "Make it happen, man. I hate to see inaction here."

"I can't," Kaden said, turning back to his beer and finishing it in a single gulp.

"What do you mean you can't?"

He paused for a moment to burp, then shook his head in resignation. "I can't."

"Did that umpire steal your manhood, as well as your pride?"

Kaden slumped onto his barstool, refusing to take the bait. "I don't know what it is, but I'll have a complete meltdown if I try to speak to her."

"Kaden Sun, choking up in front of a girl? Now that's a new one."

He thumped his hand on the table, silencing his friend. "It's not the first time I've seen her, Zac. She's been here before and for some reason she scrambles my brain. I feel like I'm having a heart attack."

Zac shook his head. "Wow, maybe you got it bad, after all."

Suddenly, there was a break in the atmosphere and tension rippled through the crowd. The music continued to play, but talk descended into whispers as Kaden and Zac scanned the floor in search of the disturbance.

"Where are the beautiful girls in this joint?" shouted a heavily accented voice. "Free drinks if you bring them to our boss here!"

Kaden watched as a group of Chinese thugs pushed their way toward the private booths. Behind them, three men dressed in suits were accompanied by an escort of girls in sequined miniskirts.

"Looks like they're all dogs here, boss," said the loud, wiry thug, before nodding at one of the bouncers. To Kaden's surprise, the bouncer nodded back.

"Suck yourself dry and go home!" a young guy hollered from a group at the bar. The club rippled in laughter.

"Funny guy, huh?" the man responded. "We like that. Come on over, let's make some new friends."

The gangsters barged their way to the bar, the crowd parting nervously to reveal a group of barely legal jocks, cheeks flushed with drink. Without warning, one of the thugs put his hand at the back of the guy's head and smashed it into the bar.

"Jesus," Kaden said, watching the violence erupt. "No one's doing a damn thing to stop them."

"Money talks," Zac said, screwing his face in displeasure. "The Chinese are buying up the railways, mines, hotels. Now it looks like they've got their eye on the Orb, too."

The businessmen had avoided the kerfuffle, arranging themselves in a lounge located behind a red velvet rope. They were young, probably in their early twenties, and surrounded by armed bodyguards. The cockiest-looking one sported a deep blond hairstyle, with a sparkling two-carat diamond earring to match. They nursed their cigars and drank from brandy balloons, laughing as the girls did their best to entertain them. Beyond the dance floor, bouncers were busy accompanying the defiant locals out of the nightclub, one dragged by his two friends. Some of the patrons booed and others left the bar in disgust. A moment later the music started up again, but the atmosphere remained subdued.

"Let's go. We've got class in the morning," Zac said.

Kaden nodded, but his heart felt unsettled. He looked earnestly around the stage, but Katy Collins was gone.

Four

US Department of the Treasury
Washington, D.C.

The secretary's face was somber and creased. In twenty-nine years in the global markets, he'd never felt so powerless.

He stared at the data for a fifth time and rubbed his eyes. It just couldn't be true. The bastards had masterfully hidden their dealings, even after all the official threats of perjury.

How could he face the president now?

With this report, confidence in the country's anemic financial system would surely collapse. There would be a run on banks and that would lead to damage even the world's second-largest economy would be unable to weather. He rubbed his face, wondering how the biggest bank in the Western world had escalated a leveraged loss of a trillion dollars, when the government had installed vigilant supervision since the last financial crises. This sure as hell wouldn't be the only one to have slipped through the cracks. How had the Dodd-Frank Banking Reform and Basel Capital Accord missed it?

Impossible.

But no, the numbers glaring up at him refused to be disputed. Row after row in the list revealed highly leveraged assets, hidden within tiered capital and sleeper hedge funds. His eyes retraced their path across the data and narrowed into slits. It seemed so… calculated. And what if this blight was only the tip of the iceberg? It would lead to the destruction of the entire banking system—a Titanic sinking of the US economy, on his watch.

Secretary Dowd unlocked the small drawer at the base of his desk. Inside it lay a pistol and a 1972 whiskey he'd been saving for the birth of his first grandchild. He glanced at the gun but picked up the whiskey, ripping off the wax seal and taking a few, deep slugs. Then, placing the bottle softly upon his desk, he touched a finger to the comm panel.

"Julie, get me a meeting with the president. Now."

Five

El Mirage Dry Lake, California

The morning had been…difficult. After Kaden had failed to submit his essay on Asian politics, the professor had targeted him throughout his lecture, directing his most difficult questions at the sophomore and meeting each answer with derision. It was as if the faculty had colluded against him in retribution for his blunder at the games. But here, in the wide expanse of the desert on his dirt bike, Kaden felt free.

"Keep up, ladies," he called into his headpiece, his helmet discarded at the rental shop. "Let those engines sing and feel the wind. *Whoowee!*"

"We're doing ninety already," Zac Koby shouted over the roar of the engines. "Go push yourself, ace. You don't need us."

"Woah, steady on!" Chet Wakana sounded as if he were trying to rein in an unruly horse. "Zac's right. The world cannot lose a future Nobel laureate to some juvenile motorbike crash. Though it does have a certain poetry to it."

Kaden glanced back and grinned. His Hawaiian friend was gripping his bike for dear life, black hair splayed out beneath an oversized helmet. A round belly protruded beneath hunched shoulders, hands clenched white as he throttled the ungainly vehicle across the terrain. "My quantum access system is going to revolutionize the—Christ! I almost hit those rocks…I can't see a thing through Kaden's dust…"

He was only too glad to clear the air for them. "Okay, boys, see you later."

Kaden pressed forward, his old bike pushing past one hundred miles an hour. The cool, dusty breeze felt good across his cheeks and he tipped his head back, imagining the bike lifting from the dirt and sailing through the sky. He gunned the accelerator further, the engine screaming in response. "Come on now, how much muscle have you got?"

The bike shuddered as the wheels bounced over the harsh topography. Speeding down a highway was one thing, but across the pitted desert was madness. Problem was, acting mad was the only time Kaden felt truly sane.

"Bro, slow down," came Zac's voice. "You're gonna hit some…"

The warning was swallowed by static as the distance between the friends increased. He smiled and pushed his head down, rolling the accelerator back as far as it would go.

"Ka..den…" Zac was cutting in and out, distracting him from the peace and emptiness of the endless sand before him. He lifted a shaking hand to mute the tiny ear device when Zac's voice returned, filled with panic. "Nightmare…behind you. He's coming in…"

Out of the blue, a gleaming bike flashed past him, cutting straight into his path. Kaden swerved to avoid the rider and almost lost control as his wheels wobbled at speed. He cursed under his breath as the jerk zigged and zagged before him, forcing him to slow.

Eventually, both bikes stopped in a cloud of dust and gasoline fumes. As Kaden squinted through the haze he heard Zac and Chet's throaty motors pull up, followed by the quieter purr of more modern bikes.

Without bothering to turn, Kaden leapt off his ride and stomped over to the moron before him. A tall figure was resting against the machine, arms folded.

"What the hell—" Kaden started, cut short by his surprise as the guy lifted his helmet to reveal a sneering expression he knew only too well.

"Why," snickered George Jones, "if it isn't Chink and his friends, the peasant and their coconut."

This was met with raucous laughter, and Kaden glanced over to see that three of Jones' goons now stood beside Zac and Chet. The last time Jones had hurled his abuse—and hotdog—he'd been protected by the distance of an empty spectator stand. This time he simply had more muscle.

"What's that you said, bonehead Jones?" Kaden's whole body was tensed. "I don't speak stupid."

Jones pushed himself off his bike, hungry for a fight. The air thickened—instantly—but as the two opposing sides began to face off, a happy chuckle floated through the air. Chet slid between Kaden and Jones, looking up and grinning.

"Now gents, let's resolve this the learned way, shall we? There's no need to—"

Chet was shoved, sprawling into the dirt, Jones propping a boot upon his body like a hunter posing atop his fallen beast. Kaden and Zac were pushing him off an instant later, and with that declaration of resistance the fight started in earnest. With Chet the pacifist it was two against four, and while the two best friends put up a valiant effort, they were soon pinned down, faces pressed into rocks and sand.

"You know," Jones said, "I still can't believe Louise left me for a rice farmer." He gave Kaden a solid kick to the ribs. "Then again, she's dumb as a post. She probably thought you were Brazilian."

"Girls hate cowards," Kaden coughed. "You always stand behind your friends, and it makes you look like a pussy."

Jones barked out a cruel laugh, though Kaden was pleased to see that his cheeks were flushed. "You mean I should be a gentleman, like you, eh?"

"Oh, the world will have ended by then..." Kaden winced, waiting for another kick, but it didn't come.

The sun beat down on them, silence stretching for seconds that felt like hours.

"Let him go," Jones finally said.

Kaden glanced at Zac in surprise, wondering if it was a trick. When no blows came, they gingerly raised themselves to their feet. Chet, panting, remained sitting in the dust until Zac hauled him up.

"You want an honest fight?" Kaden asked, smirking at the concern that flickered across Jones' face. The guy was vain as a prom queen, and Kaden knew he'd hate to mar his flawless features.

"What about a race?" Jones asked.

Kaden smiled, glancing at the gleaming chrome monster at Jones' side. "That would only prove you have a better bike," he said. "If you want to show Louise you've got balls, then I'd suggest..." He shook his head and threw Zac a sly glance. "Nah, he wouldn't go for it."

"Try me." Jones' chest puffed in offense.

"Well, how about a game of chicken?"

"Chicken?"

"Bwark!" Zac crowed. "You run your bikes head on and whoever veers off first loses."

"Sounds stupid," Jones said.

"Or it sounds too dangerous," Zac replied, shrugging.

Jones' goons seemed to be staring at everything around them, except for him.

Minutes later, Kaden found himself seated on his dirt bike, throttle flaring, as he faced his adversary five hundred yards away. Before starting, Jones had demanded that someone film his 'victory,' and one of the goons stood with his comm obediently lifted. Between them, Chet raised a red baseball cap, and Zac gave him a quick wink.

The cap seemed to drop in slow motion and as Kaden released his clutch the bike jerked forward. In the distance, a large cloud of dust announced Jones had also launched himself in Kaden's direction.

Within moments, Kaden's bike had clicked up to eighty, ninety, one-hundred miles per hour, and the target before him had turned from a dot into a looming blur of steel and leather.

Kaden gripped the handlebars, jaw tightening, as Jones' polished machine roared closer. He could see his hands now, the tight set of his shoulders, the reflections off his helmet. As they hit about thirty yards, Kaden could almost sense the whites of his eyes beyond the dark visor.

Kaden and Zac had played chicken at least a hundred times over the years, though they were usually seated atop push-bikes. Still, he knew that the secret was to keep driving straight and prepare to roll. Second-guessing the other guy was the surest way to lose.

Come on, Jones. Show me what you've got...

Jones held on for dear life longer than Kaden anticipated, but he was still the first to turn. Giving a shout of surprise, he twisted his machine to the side and slammed his brakes. The bike fell to its side, Jones sent spinning through the dirt on his back. Kaden couldn't avoid the wreck before him and the bikes collided in an explosion of steel and rubber. But it no longer mattered. Kaden had already pushed himself off and flew through the air before hitting the ground in a hard roll.

When he opened his eyes, Zac's baby blues were peering down at him. "That was a little close for comfort, bro. Dirt bikes and push-bikes are hardly the same thing."

Kaden winked. "Lock, load, and roll. Works every time."

As the boys enjoyed a triumphant ride back into town—Kaden's bike faring a lot better than Jones'—Chet beamed with pleasure. "We are the champions..." he crooned.

Zac shook his head. "Until Jones decides he wants payback."

"Then we'll teach him a new lesson," Kaden responded. He walked tentatively, trying to ignore the stickiness of his jeans as they rubbed against his bloody knee. "Right, boys?"

They returned the bikes and caught a bus to the university, heading straight for the dorms. Chet was debating the virtues of their various dinner options, which comprised two-minute noodles (easy and fast) versus frozen lasagna (easy and slow) when Zac stopped dead in his tracks and nudged Kaden's shoulder.

"I think chowtime will have to wait."

Ahead, a middle-aged man in a wheelchair sat at the bottom of a flight of stairs, his hands neatly folded in his lap.

Kaden frowned. *What is he doing here?*

Six

Kaden walked toward the lonesome figure, each sore step heavier than the last. Peter Sun was balding but remained handsome, with the same soft brown eyes as his son. Now bound to a wheelchair, he was not the imposing man he'd once been, but with quiet gravity he commanded respect.

"Hi sport, how are you?" His eyes swept across Kaden's dusty, bloodied clothes.

"Fine, I guess. What are you doing here, Dad? It's a long ways from Oklahoma."

"I was at the registrar." His tired face lightened and grew animated. "Chief Sutton introduced me to the law dean. He said he could consider your admission if you'd complete a—"

"Dad…" Kaden ran his hands through his hair and tried not to groan. "I'm not going to study law."

"Just try it, son. I'm sure—"

"We've gone through this a thousand times."

"And we'll go through it a thousand more. This is your chance Kaden. What other option do you have? A career as political analyst?" The senior Sun slapped his knee. "You were born to be a great orator. Remember the speech you made in fifth grade? The whole class was spellbound, even the teachers." His eyes glistened with the memory, and Kaden felt his chest tighten. "You're a natural, *Zaizai*. Use it to your advantage."

Kaden took a breath. "Sure, but I want to do something meaningful with my life, not be some flashy lawyer living off divorces and litigations."

"Not all lawyers are like that. There are good ones too, like Judge O'Hara."

"That's not the point. I want to be like you, to enjoy my work."

His father sighed, eyes dropping to the buckled legs before him. "And then what, end up like me?"

An uncomfortable silence prevailed, before Kaden murmured, "There's... nothing wrong with you, Dad."

"Nothing wrong? Running into burning houses might seem glorious, but look what I got for it." He swept a hand disdainfully over his knees. "And look what it did to Robbi..." He paused, as if choking on the words. "Don't follow in my footsteps, *Zaizai*. I've made arrangements—"

"Enough!" Kaden lifted his hands and backed away from him. "I will do this on my own terms. If that's not enough for you, then go back to Oklahoma and forget about me. Okay?"

Peter started to wheel himself forward. "You're just like your mother, stubborn and passionate."

"And that's why you loved her." Kaden tried to grin, but it felt hollow. "I'll see you for Thanksgiving, okay?"

"Son…"

Kaden turned and walked away, knowing that if he stayed a moment longer the old man would win. And he couldn't— *wouldn't*—let that happen.

While still alive, his mother had acted as a balm between them, encouraging one and pacifying the other. Without her, they just couldn't seem to get along. But she would have wanted Kaden to keep trying and that was the only reason he persisted, long after the memories of fly-fishing and soccer games had been replaced by endless fights and bitter words.

Upon reaching his friends, Kaden risked a glance over his shoulder. The old man was still there, watching him as he walked away.

Seven

Los Angeles, California

Kaden navigated the clogged shopping complex, dodging bulging bags, screaming strollers, and irate mothers. Large screens squealed their deals; this year almost everyone was working on a tight budget. Still, Thanksgiving was Thanksgiving, and cheap food and decorations were better than none.

He crossed Westwood Boulevard and strode down the littered sidewalk. Dozens of shaggy-haired, homeless people lined the street, waiting patiently in their worn-out hoodies for soft-hearted souls to share a slice of pizza, or some spare change. A rotund plastic robot navigated itself around parked cars, its mechanical arms screening license plates. Another arm pulled tickets from a slot in its body and clipped them to the windscreens of the offending vehicles.

He glanced across the road and spied a group of Asian businessmen standing before a construction site. Chinese investment had never been so conspicuous and no one noticed it more than Kaden, who wore his heritage like a mask he could never take off.

Ahead appeared his destination: the China Square. It was an iconic 180-foot white tower with an opulent façade of red and white swirls. Once upon a time, it had been called Eastwood Village, but a real estate conglomerate had purchased and re-branded it when Kaden was still a boy.

It took over an hour for him to find what he wanted in the small specialty shop. When he did, the counter girl wrapped the gift neatly and topped the box with a red ribbon. She made small talk and when Kaden answered that the present was for his dad she almost swooned. Kaden considered asking for her number, before realizing he could never date a girl with pigtails.

Walking down the street he felt the box in his pocket, and wondered if he should rip off the decoration. He wanted to show his dad he cared, but he didn't want to make it seem he'd been up all night curling ribbon. His finger circled the knot, but he stopped himself, deciding his father would probably find some use for it.

He was so engrossed in this internal debate that he almost failed to notice the small object his foot sent skittering across the pavement. Taking another step he paused, the elegant leather wallet lying just a few steps ahead.

It was a black calfskin piece with a silver 'H' on the clasp. Looking around, he bent and opened it to peer into its contents. At once he was met with a thick wad of notes and cash cards, as well as a set of black credit cards. Kaden whistled to himself—no one except the rich and famous owned a credit card these days, and a set of black ones at that—the ultimate passports to luxury nightclubs and private lounges. This guy must be a somebody.

Each of them bore the same name: Mr. Li Lei.

No wonder. Another Asian fat cat. Inside one of the pockets was a business card with Li's address.

Kaden flipped through the dollar notes, thinking of how good it would be to surprise his dad with a new air conditioner. Damn, there was enough to buy him a car and all the gadgets to make it wheelchair friendly. *No one would know any better.* Unfortunately, the word integrity had been drummed into him before he'd learned his ABCs. As Peter Sun said, to live without it was to sacrifice one's soul.

But there had to be at least ten grand...

He didn't even manage a step before he'd taken the wallet out again. He *tsk*ed at himself, disappointed by his unprofitable sense of righteousness. The owner's place wasn't far away, only a twenty-minute bus ride. It was a weekend and...what the heck, he might as well complete the whole Boy Scout routine.

In no time at all he found himself pressing the brass button at the gates of a palatial, sandstone mansion, his face tipped toward the glass monitor above. A robotic voice boasting a vague English accent demanded to know what he wanted.

"Uh, my name's Kaden Sun. I found a wallet belonging to a Mr. Li Lei and came to return it." Kaden held up the wallet awkwardly, certain he was being viewed, even though the screen before him remained blank.

A moment later the gates swung back and Kaden walked up the drive to two imposing mahogany doors. One was open, revealing an electronic servant that was cutting edge, moving with almost human fluidity. The machine even had a crop of dark brown hair and smooth, artificial skin. The thing paused a moment as it assessed him, Kaden guessing it was performing a wireless security check and informing Mr. Li of his arrival. He stood there, shifting from foot to foot, before the android finally moved to one side. "Please come in, sir."

The entry hall was the size of his father's two-bedroom cottage and lined with modern artworks that contrasted against baroque walls. Kaden followed his host, his tattered, unwashed jeans suddenly feeling too tight. Mailing the wallet would have been easier, instead of waltzing over there like some kind of hero.

Kaden was directed into a sitting room and invited to take a seat on a pristine white sofa. Longing to stand he reluctantly obeyed, at once launching into a detailed study of the woven beige cushions at his side. The android returned soon after, deftly placing a Bohemian China tray full of pastries and coffee on the table before him.

Kaden's stomach grumbled as he surveyed the puffy cupcakes topped with moist pink icing. Beside them, a row of cucumber sandwiches. The fragrant coffee wafted up and he was lost in the sumptuous fantasy of cramming one bite-sized treat into his mouth after another, when a short, quiet figure glided into the room.

"Mr. Kaden Sun." The foreign voice had him sitting bolt upright. "I am most grateful to you for finding my wallet." Mr. Li wore a dark black suit and round spectacles, his hands clasped politely before him. "Cancelling credit cards is such a disturbance."

His black hair was combed over to hide the thinning mop and when Kaden looked again he realized he was in fact in a tuxedo. Jumping to his feet he tried to straighten his pullover, without much success.

"Nice to meet you, Mr. Li."

"You too Mr. Sun…or may I call you Kaden?"

"Of course, sir."

He waved a small hand impatiently. "Please call me Li Lei. We Chinese don't use the—"

"I'm aware of the surname being placed in front," Kaden interrupted, feeling foolish. "And that it's custom to greet with the name in full."

Li Lei raised his thick eyebrows and nodded in approval. "Ah, someone who understands our culture, excellent," he beamed. Then his expression changed. He raised his fingers to the rim of his spectacles, inspecting Kaden as if he were an object of curio. Kaden shifted uneasily.

"Aren't you the chief strategist of the Bruins team?" he said, his expression clearing. "I saw you on TV."

Kaden shrugged and gave a weak smile. This foreigner was probably pleased he'd lost the final, given Hom's connections.

"Yes," Li added, chuckling. "You gave the umpire…how do you Americans say it? The smackdown?"

Not quite right, but whatever.

"You were brilliant that day."

Kaden blinked.

"You were ingenious," Li Lei continued. "Even though your team was at a disadvantage."

Kaden's shoulders relaxed. He'd expected the man to ridicule him like the rest of the world had, but he actually seemed sympathetic.

"Ingenious or not, we lost."

"As I see it, you won. But then again, you're not here to discuss the past." He removed some bills from his wallet. "You've spared me a great deal of trouble. Please accept this as a token of my appreciation."

Kaden held his hands up, tempted, but far too embarrassed to accept such a gesture. "Oh no, sir. I'm not here for the money. It was only a few bus stops away."

Li Lei seemed surprised at the refusal, which was understandable given Kaden's sloppy attire. He felt himself blushing and wondered what excuse he might make to exit as quickly as possible.

Just then, beyond Mr. Li, a young lady appeared in the hallway. Catching Kaden's eye, she put her dainty finger to her lips and crept toward the older gentleman. As Li Lei spoke about the virtues of honesty Kaden did his best to appear undistracted, but couldn't help flinching as the girl took a few light steps and tapped his shoulder.

Li Lei spun around, laughing. "Where have you been all day, Alexis? You know we have a dinner thing this evening."

"Oh, here, there, and everywhere, Father," she replied. Kaden dropped his eyes, but not before noting she was young, slim, and an intriguing combination of light and dark; her pearl-white skin framed by ebony hair that draped like silk over her fine shoulders.

"You're just like your mother. Always on the go, with no respect for dear old father," Li Lei said with a chuckle. "Kaden, let me introduce you to my only daughter and treasure, Alexis. Sweetheart, this young man recovered my wallet."

Kaden extended his hand, which easily enveloped hers. In an instant her pale cheeks had flushed pink, and she looked away as her father continued to tease her.

"Ah, my little girl has grown uncommonly shy. Usually, she waves boys away like fruit flies."

"Thanks, Father!" Her face was now scarlet, though more from anger than embarrassment.

Li Lei winked at his daughter. "Kaden, please allow me to recompense you somehow; our butler will take your contact information. In the meantime, you must excuse us. We have a dinner engagement with your Vice President Koch, and it wouldn't do to keep him waiting."

Kaden's smile was strained as he glanced at the untouched offerings on the table. Doing his best not to appear a complete fool, he tried to return Li Lei's bow only to simultaneously shake his hand, ending up with an impersonation of the Tin Man suffering a cardiac arrest.

Passing through the high, iron gates, he could only shake his head at his self-conscious behavior. As he reached the street corner he was surprised by the relief that lightened his shoulders. For the first time in an hour he felt free to breathe again.

Eight

FBI Headquarters, Washington, D.C.

Special Agent Jack Raven aimed his dart at one of the many 'wanted' pictures on the far end of the wall. He had just turned thirty, but with his unshaven face and a slew of recent stakeouts, he was depressed to know he passed for forty.

Married just after college graduation, Jack had fallen hard for a brunette arts student called Milla. Theirs was a whirlwind romance, but Jack had never regretted it—even after waking up one morning to find a goodbye letter propped against the handgun at his bedside. Maybe he'd been too engrossed in his work, or been an unromantic husband, or both.

Whatever it was, Milla wasn't one for second chances, though Jack would have readily given up all he had—work, energy, everything—to get her back. It would also have kept his four-star general of a father off his back with the constant *told you so's*.

With a loud thwack the dart imbedded itself in the forehead of America's public enemy numero uno, a silver-haired man who happened to look a lot like his father. Jack pumped his fist at the target.

"Get a load of this, Jack. An alert just came in." Senior Special Agent Rick Botelli waved him over from the other end of the room.

"Hmm?" Jack dropped the rest of the darts on the table and walked to Rick's desk, spying a video clip on his partner's holographic screen. Rick swiped his finger over a sensor and the voice of the newscaster grew louder.

"...the collapse of the Western banks has devastated the entire business community and, as a result, the man on the street. Authorities suspect key banking executives colluded in hiding highly leveraged assets, evading federal supervision for years. The president has ordered the arrests of several high-profile..."

Rick paused the broadcast. "They're scapegoats. Hidden bank subsidiaries and over-leveraging...it's as if these operatives didn't give a damn about the effect their actions would have on the market."

"Or someone wanted the crash to happen," Jack added, frowning.

Rick nodded. "Our friends in the CIA picked up a coordinated series of large shorts and dumping."

"They'd have to be very powerful, judging by the scale of the assets involved."

"Could be," Rick agreed. "Take a look at the rest of the clip," he said, swiping across the screen.

"...men, who face sentences of up to thirty years in prison. Bank runs have caused commodities to reach incredible new highs, with gold breaching the 3,000 mark, currently at 3,380 and rising. Silver is closing at 75. The Fed announced early this morning that QE 5 is now a strong possibility. The government has appointed Russian trillionaire Luka Lermontov, a recent recipient of the American Friendship Award, as part of its advisory team to help stem the economic fallout."

A bearded man with a pale, bony face appeared on the screen. Jack flicked his chin. "Our government must be really desperate if they're bringing in the head of the Red *Mafiya*."

Rick shook his head. "He's also the richest man in the world, with a net worth that commands one-sixth of the global financial market, directly or indirectly. Makes me think of the 1895 Morgan Bonds, when President Grover was forced to strike a deal with JP Morgan in order to save the Treasury. Morgan wasn't considered a saint then, either."

"They're miles apart, and JP was at least American. This is like inviting the devil to din—"

Rick waved at him to be quiet. "Wait, listen…"

The newsreader lifted her hand to her earpiece. "We've just received an official statement from the Chinese government in Beijing. A spokesman has announced that China will no longer continue its debt purchase from the United States of America."

The woman's face changed from confusion to shock. "They've put up a strongly worded statement, and I quote, '*The Chinese economy has large stakes in American debt; however, we believe the country is no longer in a position to service these obligations. We have made our concerns known to the world for many years now, but without a concerted effort to effectively remove itself from the current conundrum, China will have no choice but to stop the purchase of US treasuries…*'" The woman frowned into the teleprompter as if unable to believe what the producer was telling her. "The

CIA has confirmed a new Chinese leadership deposed the last of the old Communist Guard last night. The new government is Western-educated, aggressive, and ambitious."

Rick gave a scowl, enhancing the deep scar line etched on his forehead. If Raven remembered correctly, a Russian mafia thug had attacked him with a knife during a night raid. They were now the dominant ethnic powerbase in Washington's criminal underworld. "I'd rather the Communist regime any day to these guys. With this move, they've gutted us. The World Order's gonna change."

He closed the clip and pulled up another. "There's more. This time it's an announcement by OPEC from their HQ in Vienna. It happened precisely five minutes after the Chinese's press statement."

"Today, the members of OPEC made a decision that will take effect from December 25, 2030, zero hundred hours Greenwich Mean Time. That is, OPEC will no longer accept payments of oil in the United States, or Euro currencies." The tall, gray-faced man looked as if he'd just crawled through a battlefield and was yet to reach safety. "We stress that this was not an easy decision to make, given the ramifications. At the moment, there is just no other way..."

"Christ, December 25, is that some sort of sick joke?" Jack's jaw hung slack from his mouth. "This is going to bankrupt our country."

"It's already happening," answered Rick. "The US Dollar Index has sunk by half already. Our greenbacks are turning into toilet paper."

Nine

Political Science Class, UCLA

The lecture hall was full; the majority of undergraduates were American with a large contingent of foreign students crammed in for good measure. After a lecture on the history and differences of the East-West divide, Professor Goodlum paused for an intellectual exchange with his students. Scrawled on the projection behind him were the words: types of GOVERNMENT: The dragon Vs. the eagle.

Kaden sat in the front row listening to the students declare their Western-centric views. American democracy was touted as infinitely superior, but some made the argument that Uncle Sam had sold out to the elite, allowing them to dictate policies and influence politicians. Where capitalism ruled, the dollar became God; some ten billion dollars had been spent in the last election race alone.

"All right, everyone settle," the professor bellowed when the class booed a young woman who spoke about immigration and the fact borders had become increasingly meaningless.

Another girl wearing a gray bandanna stood up. "The governance of the US rests in the hands of the American people. A government that is of the people, by the people, and for the people."

"Very good," said Professor Goodlum as Kaden rolled his eyes. That morning Kaden had walked past the government's 'American people' lying homeless under neon signs that promoted an endless array of useless products.

"And how about some comments regarding the form of Chinese government?"

An Asian student with a heavy accent raised his hand, his gold Rolex shimmering under the ceiling lights. "The rule of Chinese government has stood the test of time—five thousand years of civilization."

This was met with an emphatic "boo," the spontaneous thumping of tabletops reverberating across the lecture room. "Last we heard, the Chinese still have no right to vote," someone hollered. The majority of the crowd issued a hum of agreement.

"The Chinese system is a variant of both communism and capitalism," the student continued, somewhat recklessly. "We have always been capitalists at heart, since the dawn of our history. But we are ambitious as a unified race, not as a series of individuals who compete against one another."

The students jeered and Kaden felt a prickle of anger course through his body. The guy was discussing interesting ideas and all they could do was taunt him. An hour later the very same students would be in the cafeteria, moaning about the government's ineptness and betrayal of the people.

Kaden lifted his hand and the professor nodded.

"I agree with what he's saying. China has historically been ruled by emperors, feudal warlords, and then socialist or communist leaders. But the unspoken rule of evolving governance has served the country well. No civilization in the world has managed to continue so long, so they must be doing something right."

Professor Goodlum furrowed his brows. "So you're prescribing a rule of government where the people have no right to democracy?"

Kaden glanced at the hostile faces, the foreign kids remaining carefully neutral. "Look, there is no universal model of a government that can solve all problems. Each country faces its own set of unique circumstances and the Chinese have just adopted a new leadership that appears to follow a Western approach, without the vote. But the Chinese are ruled by their values and culture, which have been refined over many years. That forms their contract with the people, social and political. Over here, we call it The Social Contract. It's a unique culture the West cannot understand, because it has no faith in leaders to do the right thing for more than four years at a time."

"The Chinks have grown and multiplied," said a tall, red-haired guy to his right. "They're taking our jobs and companies, but your dad's probably one of them!"

A few people in the crowd called for the guy to shut up, but the professor seemed happy to let his casual racism slide and most of the audience clapped in agreement.

"I'm American," he said, emphatically. "All I'm trying to say is that instead of viewing democracy as the only means to an end, we should include a strong value system to back it up. If not a religion, then a philosophy of some sort."

The jeering and whistles became louder and Kaden decided he'd had enough. He stepped onto his chair to allow his voice to travel, just as a half-eaten apple soared past his ear. But after years of being attacked for being different, he was used to it.

"The United States is decaying. It has lost its soul and sense of purpose. What happened to the American Dream? Our leaders are not hearing our voices anymore, even with our supposed right to vote. Crony capitalism is a sham." Kaden had to shout to be heard, most of the students banging their hands on the tabletops to drown him out. "I say it's time to review the system!"

"Now, now, students," Professor Goodlum thumped his fist upon the lectern. "This is a political debate, not a free-for-all. I want you to retain your intellectual disposition. As much as your ideas and thoughts are radical, Sun, they have some merit."

At the far side of the lecture hall students crowded the doors, waiting for the next class to begin. The professor raised his hands, as if surrendering to the fact the class had to end. "Okay, people, exams are next week. To all of you, and especially those who have no wish see me again in class next year, do well and"—he paused, seemingly scanning the crowd for his favorite students—"all the best." This helped lighten the mood, but that didn't alleviate the glares Kaden did his best to ignore.

He stuffed his books in his bag, threw it over his shoulder, and walked out, leaving a trail of muttered insults in his wake. Deep in thought, he almost bumped into the two suited men waiting in the corridor.

"Excuse me," he mumbled, trying to get past.

"Kaden Sun?"

Both Chinese, their features were uniformly stark, with high, chiseled cheekbones and expressionless eyes. They were possibly twins, creating a human wall that spanned almost two meters across.

"Who are you?"

His classmates moved around them, casting suspicious sideways glances and whispering among themselves. The first man retrieved a white envelope from his breast pocket and handed it to Kaden.

"From Mr. Li Lei, chief of the China Foreign and Economic Development Board. He would like to invite you to the Consulate Ball."

All too aware of the attention he was attracting, Kaden searched for a private place to talk. The men seemed to guess at his intentions, immediately leading him to a nearby fire escape.

"Look," he said, "I'm not interested. I was happy to return Mr. Li's wallet, but I don't want anything from him."

"Not our problem, sir," said one of the twins. "Our job is to hand you the invitation. But based on the debate you just had with your classmates, you might find it in your favor to go."

"Right." Kaden crossed his arms, scowling. *And what was that supposed to mean?*

"Like we said, our job is only to hand you the invitation. Good day, Mr. Sun."

Ten

WarGames Stadium, UCLA

Kaden was lost in thought at his sentry post when the field opponent ghosted right past him.

"Wake up, Sun! Your enemy moseyed through the checkpoint with his whole damn family in tow and you didn't even raise the alarm. Drop and give me fifty!" bellowed Manager Johnson.

It was only a practice session, and Kaden had opted to drill with the team when he could have spent the afternoon looking over strategies in the tower. But Johnson was right; he hadn't been paying attention and those kinds of slips could cost them a game. Or a championship.

As Kaden dropped to the ground he spotted Zac's boots pounding toward him. "What's with you, buddy? Johnson's gonna announce his selection for next season's captain and vice today."

Kaden groaned, pumping through the push-ups. "Seriously, today?"

"If you were listening you would have heard him say it."

It was one thing to be chief strategist, but the captain of the squad got all the glory. This year he was hoping to secure both roles. He might have cost them the championship, but his cunning plays had gotten them to the finals in the first place.

Ten minutes later Johnson strode across the field as Kaden finished up the last set. "Right, everyone, get over here." The squad huddled in a circle around the manager's hulking form. He was huge, and knew how to use his size to pull them into line.

He squinted at the young men and women assembled before him, face flushed and taut as a drill sergeant's. Kaden's heart skipped a beat when Johnson looked in his direction, but then his eyes swept past to settle on a senior standing at his side, Carl Lung. "Your new leader," he announced, confirming the decision with a meaty hand, placed on Lung's shoulder. The players clapped and whistled as Kaden stood silent beside them. He had fantasized about winning captain, but he was only in his second year on the team. And it wasn't over yet. He'd been chief strategist for their biggest game, and while it hadn't resulted in the victory he'd hoped for, no one was more qualified for the role of VC than him. Across the circle Zac gave an encouraging wink.

"Choosing Lung as your captain was a no-brainer," Johnson continued, once the group had fallen quiet. "He has excellent leadership skills and is well respected among you all." His hooded eyes moved across the players. "But at this moment, your vice captain is yet to be decided." A murmur of surprise rolled through the team. The manager raised his hands, silencing them. "Two stand out, Kaden Sun and Jeremy Gate."

Almost instantly, people began to voice their support for both names and Zac raised his hand immediately. "I vote for Kaden. He's our MVP and led us to the finals."

This stoked a rumble of disagreement from some of the players, which Johnson ended by barking an order for quiet. "We all know who you'd vote for, Zac. But this is a team, so let's make it democratic."

Kaden felt his face flush as the players glared at him through the dirt and sweat covering their faces. It was clear that most felt he'd cost them the championship, even though his strategies—risky, but effective—had been integral to getting them there. Anger prickled down his spine at their ingratitude.

Screw it, he didn't need to stand there while they walked all over him.

"Congrats, Jeremy," he said, locking eyes with his rival. "I wouldn't lead these losers if you paid me."

"Kaden, wait!" Zac took a step forward, blocking his exit.

"Forget it, Zac. For once just let it go."

Kaden stormed out of the arena as his teammates crowded their new captains, cheers and whoops of celebration taunting his every step.

He finally reached the solitude of the locker room and was annoyed to see that Zac had followed him.

"At least you were nominated," Zac said, slumping onto a bench.

"Why do I get the blame for losing the season, and not the umpire?"

"You tackled the guy, Kaden." Zac shook his head in disappointment. "Maybe we could have appealed his decision, but the moment you attacked him it was all over."

Kaden slammed his palms into the lockers, the concrete room vibrating from the impact. "You're right." Collapsing forward, he pressed his brow against the cool steel. "I'm not cut out for leadership. I'm too hotheaded."

"An Arizona chili pepper," added Zac.

"I have a temper."

"That's an understatement."

Kaden glared at his friend.

"Sorry," Zac said with a smirk, not looking sorry at all. He took his water bottle from his bag and offered it to Kaden, who declined.

"My dad's gonna have something to say about this. I've been telling him all the extra practice was to make VC. That will be a fun phone call."

Zac looked at him with an odd expression. "Well, at least he gives a damn."

"You can keep him," Kaden said with a sigh. "All that man's given me is a nervous disorder and enough Asian genes to make sure I'm hated everywhere I go." He knew the words were unfair as soon as he said them, but they were true.

"Still better than nothing."

"Trust me, dude, dads are not all they're cracked up to be."

Zac stood up, slamming his water bottle down so hard he sent water splashing everywhere. "How can you say that to me, Kaden? I have no one, and you sit there complaining because your dad cares *too much*. Seriously, dude, pull your head out of your ass!"

Shocked, Kaden put his hands on his best friend's shoulders only to have them shrugged away. "Dude, I'm sor—"

"They're not even dead!" Zac's chest moved up and down as he fought for breath. "They abandoned me, so they could spend all day getting high. That's how much I mattered." He stabbed his finger in Kaden's chest, eyes glistening. Kaden had never seen him act like that before. Zac always seemed so happy.

"I'm sorry, man. Really."

Zac waved it away and slumped back onto the bench, the air seeming to leave him. "Forget it. I don't want some pity party. I just think you could appreciate what you have a little more. At least you know you're worth a damn. If I died tomorrow, you're the only person who'd notice." As they stood there in silence, Zac's trademark smirk appeared at the corner of his mouth. "And God knows you only keep me around to get the girls."

Kaden punched him in the arm. "And you keep me to buy the beers, tight ass."

Zac laughed and punched him back, grabbing Kaden's palm and gripping it.

"Brothers?"

Kaden squeezed back, hard enough to hurt his fingers. "Brothers."

Eleven

The Tipsy Orb
Los Angeles, California

Kaden sat at the bar watching a skinny guy hammer away at a piano on the stage. Zac hadn't been able to come drown his sorrows, stuck working the night shift at Wendy's. And Chet... well Kaden couldn't remember the last time they'd successfully pried him away from his weekly geek club meeting.

He surveyed the faces around him. Young, nerdy executives were wobbling to the music—not the usual crowd. Probably some staff party, or another business shut down; the suits getting drunk on their severance checks. In a corner booth just behind him another set of businessmen, bankers probably, were checking out a large holo-screen with a serious-looking reporter. Kaden could have guessed what was being said, that the outbreak of the banking crisis was leading the country into a total financial ruin—it had been the same message for months, in different variations. A tipsy forty-something guy threw a glass through the projection, yelling obscenities. Kaden turned back in his seat and focused on his half-empty beer. And waited.

It didn't take very long, half an hour to be exact, for her to appear on stage. Kaden's pulse raced like he'd just done another round of Johnson's sit-ups. Katy Collins picked up the tiny microphone on her lapel and clicked her tongue, a sound check. She was a natural beauty, all cream skin and soft blushes, and pink lips that curled into the slightest smile. Stopping by the pianist she ran through the song sheets before laughing at something he said. She was untainted, unblemished by the ugliness that surrounded them, and Kaden longed to fall into her world.

It was then that she looked up, her light blue eyes locking right on his. Caught in his dreamy regard he almost fell off his stool in embarrassment, and the singer smiled before looking away.

Was that for me?

Kaden gazed downward, overwhelmed by the sensation of his chair rolling beneath him as his head grew light. She was halfway through her first song before he found the courage to glance up again.

Suddenly, the pianist stopped, Katy's voice also halting a few seconds later. The cheery mood was broken by the sudden silence and the partygoers around the dance floor looked around in confusion.

It was then Kaden noticed the Chinese thugs making their way onto the stage. The leader of the intruders, hair dyed platinum blond, pointed his finger at Katy and the pianist. Kaden tensed. *What did they want with her?*

The burly gangsters manhandled the pint-sized musician out of his seat and pushed him into the crowd. Another one grabbed

Katy. She screamed and the partygoers started shouting at them to let her go.

Without a second thought, Kaden had leapt off his chair and was lifting himself up onto the platform.

"Get off her," he growled, wrenching the guy's hand off her shoulder. Somewhere at the back of his mind a small voice warned him to keep his cool, but it was too late for that. With a few short, sharp commands, Blond Hair had ordered his men to ring-fence the couple, barring the crowd from offering assistance.

Kaden gulped. They'd wanted a spectacle and that was what he'd given them; now he'd be beaten to a pulp for sheer entertainment value. He edged closer to Katy, trying to shield her with his body. He could only hope they were men enough not to hurt a woman. As the assailants inched closer, he tried desperately to plan some kind of escape, but it was hopeless.

"Don't you dare touch us!" came her soft voice from beside him, but there was no time to react. The first strike came from nowhere, Kaden ducking as the knuckles glanced off his cheek. The next guy lunged from his side, and while Kaden managed to block the shot with his elbow, it was clear he stood no hope against six or more men. The punches rained in succession, Kaden doing his best to give as good as he got. They were better trained and they outnumbered him, but Kaden was fighting for his life. *And her*. It gave him an edge that seemed to take them all by surprise.

Blond Hair must have been irked by how long the slaughter was taking. Through the booing crowd and slamming body shots, Kaden could hear him snarling at his men in Mandarin.

The rumbling discontent grew louder as one of the thugs pulled out nunchucks, another sporting a club. Katy screamed at them to stop as they started thumping into him, a star-inducing crunch to the temple leaving his eyes blinded by blood. Through the red haze he could only try to curl up and defend himself; he had no chance at landing punches now.

The whole environment had turned surreal and the blows raining upon him dulled as his body started closing down. As he sunk to his knees and then his side, the punches turned to organ-shattering kicks.

"Stop! You're killing him!" Her voice seemed much further away now, but for all the pain he was suffering, he couldn't help but feel pleased she was screaming out in his defense.

And just like that, they stopped.

The crowd had fallen strangely silent and the crackle of a police radio announced salvation. Voices were blending as arguments started and blame was laid, and then his world went from red to black.

Twelve

The room was unfamiliar and uncomplicated. A mantelpiece was decorated with yellow trimmings and colorful paper lace. Inside the fireplace danced the warm orange glow of twenty or so candles stacked side by side. A small vase holding a pair of pink carnations reminded him of his mother—they had been her favorite flower. It felt cozy, and safe.

The room was small and even through a splitting headache Kaden could make out the photographs on the mantel: a little girl with long, golden hair standing proudly by her parents. There were pictures of her smiling into the eyes of her mother, her father lifting her up high with a school trophy—a loving family.

A twinge of envy wiggled through Kaden's chest.

He tried to turn over, only to stop and groan. Gripping the side of the sofa he made a second attempt, a cold cloth sliding from his head and onto the floor. He brought his fingertips up to his forehead and found it bandaged with muslin. A thick layer of congealed blood was sticky to the touch and his sides ached with every breath. Kaden tried to tilt his chin and assess the damage, but a surge of pain ricocheted down his spine, forcing him to remain still.

"Don't fuss, you're safe now," a voice cautioned. It was familiar, very familiar. With mortifying certainty, Kaden realized he was beaten, battered, and bleeding on *her* couch. He stared at the worn carpet, heart thumping, not knowing how to face her. "Can you raise your arm at all? If I don't apply some ointment to your side it'll be worse in the morning," she said, upcapping a tube of something. A strong cinnamon smell permeated the air.

Kaden tried to mumble his thanks and ended up choking on his swollen tongue. He could barely talk to her on a normal day; with a broken face he had no chance.

"You were very brave, but completely stupid." She made a small tsking sound. "You might have been killed. What's your name?"

"I, Ka...den." *Christ...*

"Right...Aren't you one of the regulars?"

"Nnngh," was all Kaden managed as she rubbed the ointment across an open wound.

"Sorry, but I guarantee this will make you much better in the morning. I got it from a Chinese medical *Sifu*. It's stinky but good. Some sort of secret herbal concoction that's a thousand years old."

Her soft, smooth hands felt painful and pleasurable at once— Kaden would have endured his beating over and over again to feel her touch.

"Not much of a talker, are you?"

"Ahm sorry," he stuttered, "I…can't find good…words." He groaned, wanting to chew his rebel tongue off.

"Don't worry, Kaden. No explanation needed."

She took his hand and Kaden shivered as her palm settled against his. "I haven't thanked you, and I should. I don't know what they wanted with me, but they've been watching me for weeks now." He felt her shudder. "I think the blond one has a crush on me or something."

Kaden's protective instinct overtook him as her voice caught on the last word. She was putting on a brave face, but he could see she was terrified. He brushed her hair across her forehead with his index finger.

"I…I'll protect you."

Katy wiped her eyes and gave a half smile. "You *can* speak."

"You make me speechless," he blurted.

Katy's pink cheeks turned rosy at his words. "Is that why you've been stealing glances at me?"

"You noticed?"

She laughed. "Well, the first few weeks I thought you were just some zonked-out drunk, or on a weird high. Tonight I wondered if you might be a little slow…"

Kaden's eyes widened. "I'm sorry if I scared you. I was just…"

"What?" she pressed.

"Forget it." Kaden's head pounded as more blood flushed to his already swollen cheeks. "It's embarrassing."

Katy rested her finger atop one of his bruised knuckles. "Say it, or I'll activate the pain button," she threatened playfully. "If I have a drug addict on my couch, I have a right to know."

He hoped she was joking, but decided there was no way out but the truth. Kaden huffed. "Fact is, from the first time I saw you sing, I haven't been able to take my eyes off you."

"Oh."

Katy leaned backed and surveyed Kaden, her smile so slight he couldn't quite read it. Did she think he was a nutcase? It seemed a hasty subject change was in order. "Your parents, are they coming back soon?"

"Hmm?"

"Your parents. Will they be home soon? It's late, so I'd better leave."

Katy glanced at the pictures on the opposite wall. "No, they won't be. I lost them when I was a little girl, in a traffic accident."

"I'm sorry."

"No, that's all right." She bit her lower lip. "It was a long time ago."

He saw the pain hiding behind her eyes, recognizing it as his own. "I know what it's like to lose someone you love. Ever since my mom died, nothing's been the same."

Katy nodded, drawing up her knees and settling into the couch. "I miss them so much. I used to dream that they'd returned, and everything was fine and happy again. Then I'd wake up and wish I'd never had the dream at all."

He watched her as she fiddled with the woolen blanket tossed over his legs, unsure of what he should say. Then, she broke the silence for him. "Hey, I've been meaning to ask. What's that scar on your cheek?" The tiny smile returned. "Some kind of trademark?"

Kaden touched the right side of his face. "It's nothing. A scratch from childhood."

"But it seems like it was carved out on purpose. I thought it looked cool."

"It actually marks the most humiliating moment in my life." Katy's frown left him scrambling to reassure her. "No, that's all right. It's ancient history now."

"Well, get on with it." She rolled her eyes and leaned forward.

"Um, it's just that I am, er…one of the last direct descendants of Sun Tzu, the guy who wrote—"

"*The Art of War*," Katy finished.

Kaden's brow lifted in surprise. "You're into Chinese literature?"

Katy laughed. "My dad loved that book. He applied it to all his business dealings and he'd read sections of it to me whenever I had a problem at school, or team tryouts." She smiled at the memory. "'*In the midst of chaos, there is also opportunity,*'" she quoted in a deep, serious tone.

"I was so proud of my heritage, I used to brag about it at every opportunity. Then a bunch of tough guys decided to put me in my place behind the football stands one afternoon." Kaden twitched at the memory, momentarily reliving the fear and confusion. "They pinned me down and carved an 'L' for 'Loser' in my cheek with a penknife." Katy gasped, and he smiled in turn. "It was fine. My friend Jose called the teachers over before they could spill too much blood. And I learned a valuable lesson about shooting my mouth off."

Katy's chin balanced on her knees, her eyes wide with concern. The look thrilled and flattened him at once. "That must have been awful." One delicate finger extended outward to trace the outline of the mark. "I think it looks more like a 'V,' for 'victory'," she whispered, and Kaden laughed, earning himself a serious frown.

"You say you learned a lesson," she said, "but you didn't keep your mouth shut in the bar earlier."

Kaden grimaced. "True, but that was different."

She tilted her head at him. "Why?"

"Because I thought they might hurt you."

They sat in silence for a moment, her finger dropping from his cheek. Finally, she said, "Who am I to you? No one."

"Perhaps," he answered softly. "But I'd rather get a beating than see them lay a finger on you."

She stared at him intently, lips parted, and for a moment he thought she might lean forward and kiss him. She didn't.

"I have a story of my own," she murmured. "Want to hear it?"

He nodded, entranced by her candlelit features. Katy twisted to her side and stretched out her right leg, pulling up her skirt and pointing to the smooth, white flesh at the back of her thigh. An angry, red welt in the mark of an 'X' marred the otherwise flawless skin.

"How did that happen?"

With her chin tilted down, her golden hair fell around her face, masking her from him. "I'm almost too ashamed to say. I've never shown it to anyone before."

"You have nothing to be ashamed of," he said, placing his hand softly atop hers. "We all have histories, good and bad."

He sensed her swallow, as she sought the words.

"I did it to myself, Kaden."

His fingers tightened atop hers at the words. It was such an awful injury that he almost couldn't believe it.

"When Mom and Dad died it hurt so much, I didn't think I could bear it." She sighed, letting out a slow, deep breath. "But when I hurt myself, for a tiny moment I felt in control. As if the world couldn't hurt me, I could only hurt myself." A small, nervous laugh escaped her. "Well, that's what some therapist said, anyway. I think it's true." Her blue eyes looked at him from under her lashes. "Do you think I'm crazy?"

Kaden blinked, transfixed by her. "I think you might just be the sanest person I know."

She smiled, moving her hand from beneath his as if suddenly uncomfortable. "Tell you what," she said, sounding cheery. "It's midnight, and I'll bet you're hungry. I'll make some pasta and treat you to some ridiculously overpriced Gruyere I picked up at the markets."

Kaden's head still throbbed with unbearable, pulsating pain, but the thought of lying back and watching her float around the kitchen was too intoxicating to say no to. Ignoring the twist of his queasy stomach, he smiled and said, "I'm starving."

Thirteen

Consulate General of the People's Republic of China
Los Angeles, California

Kaden climbed aboard the rusting bus and was met with the pungent odor of urine. He shuffled toward the open windows at the back, his limp still noticeable a fortnight after the attack at Orb's. In place of the bandage on his head, Katy had plastered a white medicated tape over the laceration. It made him smile every time he passed a mirror.

The evening was chilly, winter gusts buffeting the side of the vehicle. The streets of LA were littered with trash since municipal services had been restricted, and it wasn't unusual for the bus to veer suddenly in avoidance of debris. California's bankrupted budget had affected them all.

After his interaction with the Chinese gang, the last thing Kaden wanted was to attend the consulate ball, but Katy had said that was where he might meet some "movers and shakers." To which Kaden had replied he'd rather move and shake with her on the dance floor at The Tipsy Orb. "Just watch yourself," she'd pouted, ignoring his suggestion.

"That goes without saying."

"I meant with his daughter. She's annoyingly attractive; I googled her."

He'd felt a small thrill of pleasure at her jealousy. "I'll do my best," he said, "but I can't help it if women throw themselves at me." This had been met with a pretty painful punch to the arm, followed by a long, slow kiss that made it even harder to leave. A lot had happened since that fateful night in the club. Kaden felt like he'd known Katy forever, even if each new kiss was just as breathless as their first.

He arrived at the Chinese Consulate General, now housed in a recently constructed colonial villa in one of the city's wealthiest districts. Bold uplights gave a dramatic aspect to the Edwardian architecture and European classical music wafted through the frigid air. Apparently, sanitary budgets had not been cut in this part of town.

A fifty-foot 'snow-covered' Christmas tree dotted with cherry red baubles stood majestic in the middle of the manicured lawn, a golden star resting atop its highest point. Kaden sucked in a deep breath at the grandeur of it all and found himself stumbling closer to the dusted branches. To his surprise, the faux snow was something like crushed glass…or were they crystals? Probably ground-up diamonds, he thought with a snort, casting a critical eye at the sheer opulence of it all.

He adjusted the undersized dinner jacket he'd borrowed from Chet and joined the stream of guests heading for the entrance hall. Li Lei's android butler James stood at the entrance to the limestone foyer, dwarfed by a towering marble column wound with shimmering garlands of gold and green. A large baroque chandelier hung over the main landing, casting a warm glow upon the guests as James scanned them through. Other uniformed robots stood in a long line, bearing trays of champagne and collecting coats.

"Mr. Kaden Sun. Very pleased to meet you again, sir. Please come in," James said. Kaden entered, head tilted back as he inspected the majestic ballroom. It had the feel of some long-lost palace in Europe, lined with gilded fretwork and white paneling.

A blonde lady brushed past him in a cloud of gleaming silk and glittering jewels, her plunging neckline showing off a bronzed décolletage. She warmly greeted a Chinese woman in a cream gown and pearls, which seemed sedate by comparison.

"We're pleased to see you again." Li Lei appeared from the crowd with his daughter, Alexis, beaming at his side. "We were worried you might not come."

Kaden bowed. "Wouldn't miss it for the world, sir."

The short, stiff gentleman put a hand on his shoulder, pulling him down and whispering in his ear, "You saved me. Your possible attendance was the only way I could convince my stubborn daughter to come." He straightened, adding loudly, "I'm sure you must be famished. Why don't you and Alexis peruse the buffet? It's all by Louis Peroux, the best chef in town."

Kaden smiled and offered the young lady his arm. She was certainly a beauty, though she seemed unaware of the many looks cast her way. He could just picture Katy rolling her eyes, and the thought put a grin on her face.

"Are you hungry?" she asked.

"Just a little." He hadn't eaten since breakfast and was actually ready to devour the first thing he came across. They walked through the end of the cavernous hall and entered a warmly lit chamber. The buffet tables were lined along three sides of the room, with large Chinese paintings suspended above.

Kaden's eyes widened. It was an outstanding spread. Fresh oysters, legs of roast lamb, prime cuts of aged beef, caviar on eggs, lobster tails, foie gras, and an out-of-place but equally delicious tray of Chinese dim sum…and he hadn't even checked out the dessert section.

"Where do we start?" Kaden asked.

"How about we pile up the plates and go somewhere to gorge?" Alexis suggested, her eyes twinkling.

Her waist was small enough for him to circle with his hands and Kaden couldn't imagine she'd ever gorged anything in her life, but instead of arguing he shut up and followed.

"What is this stuff?" he asked, sniffing at a large sliver of something on his steak.

"That's truffle," she explained. "But not just any truffle, an Alba white. The specimen it came from cost a million dollars."

Kaden nearly choked, realizing he was about to eat his college fund. Alexis caught his expression, her own smile mischievous. "See that, there?"

"The slices of cantaloupe?"

"Yubari King melon," she corrected. "Twenty thousand dollars, each, flown direct from Japan."

The pair loaded as much as their plates could hold and stole away to the sanctuary of a sheltered garden. The shimmering grass looked like a blue sea under the moonlight, an oak bench at the center providing the perfect place to sit and stuff their faces, though Kaden remained convinced Alexis would be too polite to do more than pick at her food.

He cursed himself. They had forgotten to bring cutlery.

"Forget the formality. Let's use our hands," Alexis said. "Actually, I have an idea." She put her plate down and daintily walked over to a table by the door, stripping it of its linen cloth and returning to lay the fabric on the grass. "Let's have a picnic!"

They lounged on the ground, slowly working their way through the culinary extravaganza. Steak pinched between his fingers, Kaden ripped off a chunk and groaned in satisfaction. "I haven't eaten this well in years...if ever."

Alexis giggled. "You have the passion of a connoisseur, but you're just a regular old glutton."

They ate in companionable silence, until he caught Alexis watching him. She looked away, shy, before blurting out, "What happened to your head?"

"Nothing, just some gangsters at The Tipsy Orb."

"Chinese ones?"

Kaden paused to swallow a large chunk of meat. "You know them?"

"Not personally, but word of their behavior has reached my father." Alexis picked at the flesh from a lobster tail. "Daddy was posted here to establish relations between the American people and Chinese investors. These thugs aren't helping."

"All those corrupt officials China purged during the 2010s have brought their dirty money over here, and now we have to live with them."

Alexis lowered her head and nodded. "It's also unfair to the hardworking, honest Chinese who are now dangerously misunderstood."

"Even the good Chinese are costing us jobs," Kaden replied, surprised at how much he suddenly sounded like the classmates he was usually debating.

"But we've created countless more," Alexis countered. "When the early investors arrived, they sought the services of US consultants on mergers and acquisitions, and each time local advice was to downsize. Our government realized the problem, and since then my dad has been tasked to help ensure that any Chinese investments in the US must create a winning scenario for all."

Kaden took a deep breath. "I don't envy him that job."

Alexis shrugged, staring blankly at the unfinished plate before her. "Well, enough of all this political talk. How about dessert?"

"Sure," he said, halfheartedly wondering what a twenty-grand melon might taste like.

The pair made their way back inside to the buffet and headed to the dessert section, which stretched the full length of the great chamber. Kaden's eyes lit up at the dainty, colorful delicacies, his mouth watering. It didn't matter if his waistband was already straining, he was tempted to try everything: the deep red, chocolate-covered strawberries and, beside them, elegant crème brûlées overlaid with gold leaf. He smiled as he took it all in. Katy would love the famously expensive Chinese bird's nests, dusted in rock sugar with small, cream sparrows nestled in each center. That would—

"Kaden." There was a tug at his elbow.

"I'm sorry, did you say something?"

Alexis smiled. "I said, the melons are gone. Everyone went for them the moment a new tray appeared."

Kaden shrugged. "Guess we just don't have the luck."

"Not if I can help it," Alexis said. "Stay here, I know where the secret stash is kept."

Suits me fine, he thought to himself as he watched her trim figure sashay toward the service doors. Without Alexis beside him, all sense of formality melted away. Within minutes, Kaden had sampled almost everything the long table had to offer. It was only after he'd finished his second vanilla cream bird that he realized Alexis had failed to return.

He turned back to the doors she'd left through, feeling guilty for allowing her do the dirty work of stealing the costly melon and lugging it back to them. It was then that he heard a shrill cry of alarm, coming from the direction of the main ballroom. A moment later the classical music ground to a halt. Kaden jogged through the large doorway separating both spaces and found that everyone in the room had frozen, and all seemed to be staring in the same direction. Kaden pushed his way between the whispering spectators.

Ahead of him, near what looked like a second service entry, a pair of men were holding Alexis. They were dressed as catering staff, but the knives in their hands were directed at her throat. For a moment, he wondered if she'd been caught stealing the melon, but it quickly became clear this was some kind of hostage situation. She whimpered at their rough handling and his heart skipped a beat. Just steps away Li Lei was holding up his palms, pleading with the kidnappers to release his daughter and take him instead. Kaden glided behind Li Lei, eyeing the perpetrators. They were around his age: a black youth with close-cropped hair and a taller guy who seemed Hispanic, his longer locks falling in his eyes. Judging by their disposition and trembling voices, they were amateurs, though the Hispanic seemed oddly familiar. Kaden's eyes locked on Alexis', her teary eyes seeking deliverance from the nightmare.

"Stay back!" the Hispanic growled, waving a gun at the crowd. The onlookers ducked as the weapon pointed in their direction.

"Tell me what you want," Li Lei cried, gingerly advancing a step closer to the kidnappers. "I promise you a safe passage out of here if you'd let her go…please."

The Hispanic curled his lips and gave a sardonic laugh. "You think I'd trust a Chinese? What happened to the job security you promised us? After the takeover of OGE you threw a thousand plant workers out on the street like old rags!"

"Look, we can—"

"There's nothing you can do, man!" he screamed, his weapon-wielding arm flailing dangerously above him. "We're gonna die anyway."

A security officer appeared beside Li, whispering in Mandarin. Kaden's grasp of the language was rusty, but the message seemed clear enough: their men were in position and ready to end the mess at Li's call.

Kaden returned his gaze to the outlaws, disgusted by their actions but sympathetic to their cause. Few of the men in the room could relate to that kind of struggle. But then again, Alexis was innocent. She didn't deserve to be made the target of something she had little to do with.

He tried to assess the situation, haunted by the increasing sense he'd met the taller guy somewhere before. It was at that moment he turned and swept the hair out of his eyes. It was a gesture Kaden recognized immediately.

Jose 'Pudgy' Gustavo was the school friend who'd saved him from the knife-wielding bullies, all those years ago.

"No!" he cried, as Li Lei looked up at him sharply.

"Please, sir, let me talk to them," he whispered. "I went to school with the Latino guy."

Li pressed his lips into a thin line.

"Mr. Li, if your purpose is to improve Chinese relations with Americans, hurting these boys will not help your cause and, regardless, Alexis could be caught in the crossfire. Give me a chance."

Li glanced at the security officer, then Kaden. He gave a tacit nod, but it was clear Li's men would be ready to end the kidnappers' lives at a moment's notice.

Kaden moved to the front of the cordon, the security chief following close behind. Jose was no longer pudgy but gaunt, with a half-crazed glint to his eye. As Kaden took a tentative step forward Jose jerked Alexis back, making her scream.

Kaden lifted his hands. "Jose, it's me. Kaden Sun, from elementary school."

The flushed face tilted in suspicion. "Which elementary?"

"Fisher, dude. Don't you remember me?"

"Yeah, I remember a terrified Asian kid, who followed me around like a puppy for a few weeks. Is this what's happened to you, Kaden?" He jerked his chin at the crowd. "You've become one of them?"

Kaden shook his head, but before he could utter a word, Jose cut him off. "They took our jobs, Kaden. No termination benefits, no medical insurance, nothing!"

The black guy shifted nervously beside him, and Kaden sensed the security at his back switching the safeties off their guns. Alexis gasped out his name, and for a moment Kaden thought a shot would ring out. Somehow, silence prevailed.

"Our savings, the banks...They lost our money, took our deposits, and then closed up. We have nothing left, man, NOTHING, you hear?"

"Hurting innocent people won't help your family."

Jose made a bitter sound at the back of his throat. "What family? My wife is dead, caught pneumonia at twenty-one and we couldn't afford her medical bills. She died at home in a freezing room, with no electricity. That's what these pigs have given us!" He spat on the floor, tears streaming down his cheeks.

Kaden gave a quick glance at Alexis. Although he could see that she was afraid, she had calmed down as Kaden stepped closer.

"Jose, let us help you. Mr. Li here"—he pointed at Li—"is the head of American relations at the Chinese Consulate. It's his job to make sure American families benefit from Chinese investment. But I want you to put your guns down and release Alexis. Hurting her will do nothing but make your movement look heartless and irrational. Trust me."

Jose and his confused friend looked briefly at one another, and Kaden knew he'd at least given them pause for thought.

"You've made your point, now quit while you're ahead."

Jose lowered his head, his gun dropping to his side. His companion lowered the blade from Alexis' throat and she stumbled forward into Kaden's arms.

Li Lei strode to Kaden's side, his voice raised so that the entire crowd could hear. "I promise you, Mr. Jose, we will do whatever we can in our power to investigate and rectify what happened to you and your families."

Jose's partner stared him down with bloodshot eyes as security staff stepped forward and removed their weapons. "How do we know we can trust you?"

"Trust in my word," Li said solemnly, "and in your friend Kaden's judgment."

Their hands were quickly secured behind their backs, but before Kaden could ask if that was necessary the two men were pushed through the service doors, surrounded by a ring of black suits.

Father and daughter hugged, Li Lei's fingers trembling as they grasped her shoulders. After a moment, Li turned to him and gripped Kaden's hand, his touch steadier now. "Thank you. Alexis is safe because of you."

"It was just a coincidence that I happened to know one of them, Mr. Li. I'm glad everything turned out all right."

Li's expression turned serious. "Sun, you're quite unlike anyone I've met. A hybrid of Eastern strategy and Western courage."

Kaden felt his face grow hot. "Er, thank you, sir."

Li gripped his daughter tighter at his side. "You would be of great value to me in my work, so I want you to join my team." Alexis, still pale from her fright, smiled weakly at his words. "You've seen how important this issue is," Li continued, "and we need capable men like yourself who understand the plight of the people and the way of ours."

Kaden swallowed. Such an offer was flattering to say the least, but based on his initial interactions with the Chinese he wasn't sure he wanted to involve himself in such a tense environment.

"I'm not even out of college yet. I can't imagine I would be very helpful."

Li's smile was patient. "Well, it's been a dramatic evening. Let's discuss this another day. I see great potential in you, Sun." He paused, squinting. "Did you bring a car here? I can arrange for my driver to return you to your dorm."

"Dad, I'd like to go home now," Alexis said, peering at the concerned guests who continued to crowd around them. "Can he drop me off first?"

Five brief minutes later Kaden found himself in the back of Li's *Hongqi* limousine, Alexis sitting at his side. As they traversed Los Angeles they made several detours along the way, the driver informed by the escorting security detail that numerous riot outbreaks and lootings had occurred that evening. Alexis did her best to keep up an awkward conversation, but Kaden's attention was drawn to the looted shops and burning trash piles whizzing by. At one point, someone threw a bottle at the vehicle and Alexis cried out as it shattered against the windscreen.

The driver sped up, switching on the radio in an effort to calm her. Unfortunately, the song that started playing was cut short by a news update, the announcer stating that savage protests had been held across the US, with most of the violence directed at banks and government institutions. The White House had called for calm and a state of martial law had been declared.

Alexis shifted closer to Kaden, her small hand settling upon his arm as she rested her head against his shoulder. The position was too intimate for comfort, but she seemed genuinely afraid.

They passed through the cold night, safe in their leather cocoon as Kaden mused at the recent twists of fate he'd faced and somehow survived. All he could do now was roll with whatever came next and hope that happier days awaited them all.

Fourteen

Botanical Gardens, UCLA

Years of neglect had allowed the Mildred E. Mathias Botanical Gardens to regain its creative freedom. To Kaden and his friends—perched upon crumbling stone benches, gorging sandwiches—the reality of downtown LA's strikes and riots seemed a literal world away.

News reports claimed over three thousand had been killed or injured in the streets over the past week, with similar losses seen across the country. For the first time in modern history, hospitals were turning people away, and the National Guard had been deployed throughout urban hotspots. Even in the sanctuary of the gardens, faint siren blasts occasionally punctuated the rustling leaves and birdcalls.

"Hey, Chet, got another baloney and cheese for me?" Zac asked.

"You've just had three," Chet said. "We're supposed to have three each."

Zac tipped his head. "I've eaten two. Hey, wait a minute. You've had four."

"Cool it, you two." Kaden offered Zac his remaining sandwich. "We're lucky we've got something to eat. Inflation hit double digits yesterday." He shook his head in disbelief. "This country is doomed. I'm not sure why we even bother going to classes."

"Our man doesn't need nutrition, or an education," teased Chet. "He's full of love."

Zac laughed between chewing. "Yeah, snagged his dream girl with an epic beating. Commendable."

"Best beating I ever had," Kaden said, lightheaded as he recalled that first evening with Katy.

Chet placed his lunch on the bench, taking out a strange rectangular device from his green backpack. "I'll show you guys something that makes lover boy's obsession pale in comparison."

Zac jabbed Kaden in the ribs, forcing him to leave his thoughts behind to focus on his friend's show-and-tell.

Chet pressed a knob on the metallic casing. From a rudimentary glance, it appeared to have a lot of blinking lights and way too many controls. The computer scientist glanced over his shoulder suspiciously as the screen flickered, a soft purring sound revealing it had booted itself to life.

"Here it is, my friends. A pre-Christmas treat from master inventor CHET WAKANA!"

Kaden and Zac looked at each other, unsure whether to laugh out loud or try to maintain some semblance of politeness, at least in return for the sandwiches.

An image appeared on the screen of a beaten-up vehicle. It was red with a dozen or so knocks on its sides. The bumper was falling apart, and it looked a lot like…

"What is my car doing on your little screen?" Kaden asked, voice dangerously neutral.

Chet rubbed his plump hands together in glee. "Oh, *now* I have your interest, do I? Let's see what this baby can do." He clicked on one of his controllers and the vehicle started to shudder. Without sound, it took a moment for Kaden to realize the engine had been switched on.

"How did you just do that?" Zac's eyes were dinner plates, but Kaden remained silent.

"That's not the main act, dude." Chet pressed another button and began to manipulate the miniature joystick. "*Aia ho`i*, you're gonna go nuts over this one."

Kaden and Zac watched in amazement as the hazard lights flicked on, the vehicle jerking forward like some kind of demented rodeo bull.

"And it's honking, too. You just can't hear it," Chet said, chin lifted.

"Sweet Jesus—" Zac stopped mid-sentence, mouth wide open.

"Careful, Chet," Kaden said, finally breaking his silence. "That cost me two summer's worth of savings. Break it and I'll break you."

"Seriously, how did you manage to do this?" Zac asked.

"Well, the beauty is I can control anything with an electrical impulse. Your comms, TV, auto, whatever. Everything from pacemakers to web servers. Getting into your vehicle and its electronics was easy, even if you've installed the latest state-of-the-art telematic crypto-security software. Ghosting around systems without being detected is where it gets hard. I'm working on it."

Kaden smiled as Zac yawned, his limited attention span already stretched.

It seemed a good time to change the subject. Kaden congratulated Chet on his masterful invention, before slapping Zac on the back and asking what he was doing for Christmas. Every year he tried to convince him to joins the Suns, and every year Zac said no.

"I was going to work through the winter break, but I need to find another job. Wendy's let me go last week. They're closing the shop until things return to normal."

Kaden peered at Zac's worn-out shoes and duffel bag, splitting at the seams. "Gonna be tough finding a job when you look like a hobo," he teased, trying to sound cheerful.

"That's what the university degree is for, right bro?"

Kaden nodded, but couldn't hold his friend's eye.

"Hottie, nine o'clock," Chet said, staring off into the distance, eyes glazed. "She's out of my league, but that's not going to stop me trying."

Kaden turned to find Katy walking toward them and hastily swept the breadcrumbs from his shirt. A large stain had appeared near the worn hem and the stitching was coming undone. "Don't even think about it."

"Hey guys."

A shadow fell across his face, two long, slender legs meeting his gaze as he looked up to face her. She was wearing skinny blue Levi's with a dark trucker jacket. Kaden's voice caught in his throat.

"Thought I'd pay you a surprise visit before you leave for the holidays. Your comm unit said you were in the park."

"What a nice surprise," he gulped.

"Are these your friends?" Katy asked.

"Not really," he replied, ducking as Zac punched him in the arm. "I guess you could call them acquaintances. Zac and Chet."

She nodded and shook their hands, doing her best to discreetly wipe her palm on her jeans after doing so.

"Shouldn't you guys be at the forum now?" Kaden prompted, before it could get more awkward.

"Forum? Which one?" Chet was clearly horrified by the idea of missing any kind of opportunity to geek out.

Zac rolled his eyes, standing up and brushing his pants off. He was a good-looking guy, but Kaden was pleased to see that Katy wasn't ogling him like most girls liked to. Zac pulled Chet to his feet, laughing. "It's called, 'Taking a Hint: 101.' Nice to meet you, Katy. And Kaden, send my regards to your dad when you see him."

They watched the boys walk away, Chet casting furtive glances back at Katy, until Zac clipped him over the ear.

"I'll miss you during the holidays," Katy said, sitting beside Kaden. The smell of fresh lilac wafted around him as she flicked her hair over her shoulder.

"I'll miss you too. But I thought you said your aunt was arriving today to spend the week with you?"

Katy sighed. "She's been delayed. The strikes have affected the train schedules."

"You should have called me to come get you. I don't like you walking around the streets alone."

She squinted at him, a small wrinkle forming above her upturned nose. He loved the tiny quirk. "I wanted to surprise you…"

He smiled, unable to keep the stern expression on his face. "Come on, I'll show you around campus." He grabbed his sling bag and an envelope dropped out.

"What's this?" Katy picked it up.

"Oh, nothing. An invitation."

"To?"

"Li Lei—that consulate guy—has been trying to rope me into some community awareness project. I told him I didn't think I'd be much help."

"You mean the guy who invited you to that ball?"

"Mm hmm."

The small wrinkle above her nose returned. "It might be a great opportunity for you. I mean, you're studying political science."

"I know. But the Chinese aren't particularly popular right now."

"Which is why they need Chinese Americans like you to help get both sides to communicate. Foreign investors aren't going anywhere, but if they talk to the local people more, maybe the situation will improve."

Kaden pondered her words. "You really think so?"

"Yeah," she replied. "And there are, like, no jobs going around, so you'd be an idiot to turn it down."

"And you don't care if his daughter is involved in the project?" Kaden asked, meeting her provocation with his own.

"Should I?" she replied, blue eyes locked on his.

"Of course not."

"Great." She smiled at him sweetly. "I'd be horrified to think a young, beautiful girl, who's clearly obsessed with you, might be some kind of distraction."

Kaden chuckled, nervously. "She's beautiful? I hadn't noticed."

A small, fierce growl came from her slender throat as she lunged at him, the two of them tipping back off the bench and rolling across the grass, laughing like children.

Fifteen

Oklahoma City, Oklahoma

Kaden stared at one of the many pictures lining his father's wall. It showed a raven-haired boy kicking a soccer ball, his mother bending down and smiling behind him. Her eyes were hidden behind a large pair of sunglasses, her blond hair blown back by the breeze.

He remembered that moment, even though he'd only been five at the time. He could still feel the childish joy of pursuing the ball as it bounced away, his father shouting encouragements from behind the camera. Had it really happened that way, or had the memory been forged by all the times he'd stared at the picture, wishing to return to that moment?

The photo beside it was of his mom, just months before she died. He was in her lap, head tilted as he peered up at her. She had her hand crossed over his arm, and his over hers.

Kaden looked away, unwilling to allow the feelings of loss and anger to surface. What was the point in feeling them any longer? It had been over a decade, and he longed for the day he might look at her face without being overcome with emotion.

The next picture was one of his favorites. In it his dad proudly wore the fireman's regalia, surrounded by his colleagues. As a boy, Kaden had swelled with pride every time his dad picked him up from school in his deep blue squadron T-shirt and reflective pants. In the photo, Peter's best friend, Rob, stood with his arm loosely draped around his dad's shoulder, his face split into a broad grin.

Kaden had been six when the incident happened. On the radio they'd said that Peter and Rob had tried to save some students trapped in a forest fire when the wind turned without warning. Rob and the teenagers had been lost to the flames, Peter dragged from beneath a fallen tree with a broken spine and a pair of lungs that were barely working.

His father's voice broke his thoughts. "Dinner's ready. Prepare the table, *Zaizai*," Peter Sun shouted from the kitchen.

"It's done, Dad."

Though he was wheelchair-bound, Peter kept the house just as clean as when Kaden's mother had been alive. The living room looked homey, and a fresh-cut Christmas tree stood in the corner, decorated with glass balls and silver bells. He'd even managed to string tinsel and mistletoe above the doorways. Kaden felt a weight in his stomach, suddenly aware of how little he'd been around to help his dad out.

Three chairs had been set around the dining table and four sets of cutlery. As he wheeled himself in, Peter used one strong hand to hold the plate of roasted, brine-soaked turkey, charred and glazed in all the right places. The other navigated the control on his wheelchair from the kitchen door to the table. Kaden closed his eyes as he savored the scent. His mother's recipe had been lovingly replicated all these years, though several holiday dinners had passed in disaster before Peter started to perfect it.

Kaden's father slotted his chair into the empty spot at the table, and together they prayed. When Peter went to carve the bird, Kaden held his hand out for the knife.

"Dad, allow me."

He hesitated, then smiled, holding the handle outward.

The days of Kaden being cared for as a boy were over. In that simple gesture, both acknowledged Kaden had assumed the weight of responsibility.

He took the best slice of the meat and placed it on his father's plate, doing the same for the empty places beside them. Finally, he served himself a piece and sat down to eat.

They chewed in silence, enjoying the tender and moist cuts.

"Mom would have approved of your cooking, Dad. This roast turkey is better than hers."

"Watch your tongue, son." He raised his eyes to the ceiling. "She's listening." They chuckled, and the old man's head bowed in acknowledgment. "I must admit I've outdone myself this time. Though it would go down even better with a beer, eh?"

Kaden sprang up. "For sure. I'm on it."

He reappeared from the kitchen with two Carlsbergs in hand, Peter waving away his offer of a glass. They clinked bottles.

"Drink up, son."

Kaden grinned. It was seldom that he saw his dad in such good spirits. "Dad…"

"Yes, *Zaizai?*"

"We're not going to argue about my degree anymore, are we?"

Peter Sun frowned and closed his eyes, seeming to ponder the question. He took a long, slow gulp of his beer, before gently putting the bottle down. "You're old enough to think for yourself. If you're going to go ahead anyway, I want you to do it with passion and hard work. That's all a father can ask of his son."

The dark eyes were moist, and Kaden felt his own prickle in response. He grabbed his father's hand and wrapped it in his grip. This was the first time in years they had managed to settle an issue without an argument, and it filled him with hope for what their relationship might be in the future.

The buzzer rang.

They exchanged curious glances. It was a cold, moonless Christmas Eve, and the Suns were not accustomed to taking visitors. Kaden could only imagine it was someone in need of help, or trying to sell them something.

"I'll get it, Dad." He slid his chair back and walked to the door. It was too dark to see who was standing on the porch beyond the vaguest shadow. Through the frosted glass, Kaden sensed it was a man.

Sixteen

Li Lei was dressed in a heavy mink coat. The warm air of the Sun home had fogged his round glasses, making him appear like an older version of Alvin the chipmunk.

"Surprised?" Li Lei asked.

"Yes." Kaden peered down at him in wonder. What on earth was the man doing standing on his porch, on Christmas Eve? "How did you know I was here?"

Li Lei took his hat off, presenting Kaden with an excellent view of his bald head.

"That's the easy part," he said, brushing the snow off his coat. "But you wouldn't want to keep me out in this weather, would you?"

"Sorry," Kaden said, turning his focus away from the pate. "Please, come on in."

His father's gaze tracked Li Lei as he stepped into the house and approached the dining table.

"Dad, this is Mr. Li Lei of the Chinese Consulate in L.A." He turned and added, "Mr. Li, this is my father, Peter Sun."

Li Lei made a half bow. "A merry Christmas to you. Pleasure to make your acquaintance, Mr. Sun."

Peter nodded, then waved his hand toward a seat beside Kaden's. "Please, sit."

He started moving toward the chair Kaden's mother traditionally occupied, but Kaden knew his father wouldn't approve, and gently shifted Li further down the table.

Li Lei looked at the two plates, piled with untouched food. "You have more guests coming?"

Kaden shook his head, feeling stupid. "Just an old family tradition."

Li nodded, quickly dismissing the distraction. "Mr. Sun, I'm sorry to intrude upon your dinner. I've missed my own Christmas celebrations to come looking for your son. He is a wonderfully talented young man, but I'm sure you already know that."

Peter gave a small smile. "He is talented, as well as young and overconfident. Be careful not to inflate his ego."

Li Lei laughed, though it sounded slightly forced. "I'm interrupting your night, so I'll be brief." He leaned forward, shifting his gaze toward Kaden. "The consulate needs your son's help with an important project."

Peter peered at him with a curious frown on his face. "It's his life. You should address him about such things."

Li looked down, chastened. "Of course." Turning back to Kaden he said, "You are trustworthy, brave, and have a proficient mind. I would like to mentor you to greater heights."

As the black eyes locked upon his, Kaden felt goose bumps shiver across his skin. Peter narrowed his eyes at his son, the message clear.

"Thank you, Mr. Li, for your offer." Kaden looked down into his lap, as if the right words might be scrawled across his napkin. It seemed crazy to turn down any chance of work—good work—when families were going hungry on the streets. But he'd told his father he was committed to his degree, and he was. "As you know, I'm in college. I just don't think I'm ready for the opportunity."

Li sighed. "Kaden, do you know the story of Lord Liu Bei, who sought the help of master strategist Zhuge Liang, in the Three Kingdoms? It took the lord three humbling visits to Zhuge's home before he agreed to assist his superior."

Kaden smiled, at which point Li looked at him severely. "My boy, you are not the legendary Zhuge, but I can see your potential, and I am prepared to do the same. I have offered you the chance twice now. If there is a third occasion, you will say yes."

Kaden glanced at his father, who was studying Li intently. From the look on his face, his initial impression wasn't positive. "Mr. Li, I'm sure you have good intentions," started Peter, "but the sensitivity between the Chinese and locals is complicated, and dangerous. Kaden's aim has always been to serve his country, not a group of controversial foreign investors."

Li Lei nodded, his lower lip curled as if holding back the words he wanted to say. After a moment he murmured, "I'm offering your son a chance any enterprising young man would kill for." He glanced in Kaden's direction, without meeting his eye. "He will be well compensated, and we expect this project to wrap up before his new school term. If Kaden likes the work, he can support us on future assignments during weekends and leisure hours."

"Tell me," Peter said, glaring at the man. "Why all this trouble, for an undergrad?"

Li Lei chuckled. "Do you forget your roots so quickly, Mr. Sun? One belief governs us, a belief you Americans do not appreciate or understand." The black eyes twinkled with excitement, and something else. "Fate."

The small, stately man stood, gathered his coat, and briskly walked to the door. As it gently shut behind him, Peter and Kaden looked at one another as if trying to decide if the last fifteen minutes had been some strange figment of their imagination.

The sound of Li Lei's limousine leaving the driveway was soon replaced by heavy silence. Eventually, Peter Sun's smooth, calm voice broke through the night. "How did you meet such a man?"

Kaden sighed at his look of disapproval. Only a moment ago they'd been happy in one another's company, and instead of feeling proud that his son's skills were so highly desired the man was acting disappointed.

"I found his wallet and returned it to him. It contained a lot of money, and I guess he saw it as an honest thing to do."

Peter pressed his lips together. "I expect nothing less of you. But don't go there, *Zaizai*."

"Why?" Kaden took a swig of his beer, returning it to the table with a little more force than intended. "Do you know how hard it is to find work at the moment?"

"I don't trust him. He is manipulative and ruthless."

Kaden shook his head. "Dad, that's not fair. You only met him for a few minutes."

"I want you to focus on your political studies, as we agreed. That's final."

Kaden's heart pounded. It seemed Peter's speech about letting Kaden live his life had all been bullshit. He glanced at the picture of his mom on the wall and wished more than ever for her voice of reason. Instead, she watched them silently.

That night, Kaden couldn't sleep. It seemed the world around him was hurtling into a new age, with his life dragged along for the ride. As the country fell apart, he was being offered new, unthinkable opportunities. Thank God he had Katy at his side, encouraging him to progress in life. Why couldn't his dad trust him to make good choices too? It was almost as if he envied him his youth and success.

He tossed and turned, contemplating Li Lei's offer. How many political science students got the chance to work directly with the very people who built societies? It was a well-known fact that employment with a Chinese conglomerate—a luxury generally reserved for native-born Chinese—was like striking the jackpot. As Li Lei had said, many would kill for the job.

Kaden got up from his bed and sat at his old desk. He flicked the reading light on and pulled out a writing pad, still covered with scribblings from his senior year.

Dad,

I know we're at odds. I hate to argue with you, I really do. I also know that you love me, but it's time for me to make my own decisions. All I need is your support, even if my choices seem wrong.

I didn't get a chance to tell you, but I've met a girl. Her name is Katy Collins. I'd like to think that one day we might have a future together. The truth is, we are living in strange times and a man must take chances to survive in this world. Know that in everything I do, I'm guided by what you've taught me. To be honest, hardworking and ethical, always.

I have decided to take Mr. Li's offer. His job will allow me to help the current situation, and support the country that we call home.

Maybe it will turn out well, maybe it won't. Either way, I'll succeed, or dust myself off and learn along the way.

Goodbye, Dad, I'll see you at Easter.

Kaden put down the pen and was met by his reflection in the window. The face staring back at him looked like a younger version of his father, but there was no denying their expressions were different. While Peter Sun's face was usually set in cool self-assurance, Kaden wore a mask of grim determination.

Seventeen

The Li Estate
Los Angeles, California

If Kaden had been impressed by Li's sitting room, the man's study was even more ostentatious. It spanned a thousand square feet and was adorned with luxurious silk paintings of the Tang and Qing Dynasties, reminding Kaden of photos he'd once seen in a National Geographic article.

At the far end of the study room stood a large redwood desk, strategically positioned to resemble an emperor's throne. Two golden dragons crawled up the solid marble legs as if begging at their master's feet.

Li Lei sat in the oversized rosewood chair, looking every bit like the last Chinese emperor, Pu Yi. Though the chair made him appear smaller, there was no mistaking the quiet power behind his smile.

"Kaden, I am glad. Though I thought it was I who would come to you."

Kaden nodded. "I thought about your offer and decided I would be a fool to turn it down. But before I agree to join you, I must know one thing."

Li Lei tilted his head, inviting him to ask his question.

"Why?" He swallowed, his throat suddenly dry. "Why all this effort, to get me onboard?"

"As I told you and your father, I believe it's fated." He pulled out a small gold box. "Do you mind? It's a bad habit of mine. I'm the traditional type—those electronic things just aren't the same." Li Lei took out a roll of tobacco and lit it. "It seems I find the urge to smoke whenever I am forced to divulge my inner feelings," he added, smiling.

As a young boy, Kaden's father had taught him to listen more and speak less whenever he needed to assess someone. Then again, his father was overly cynical, and Kaden felt a pang of guilt as he wondered if this was why he was sitting in his house now, bitter and alone.

"I'll tell you a secret, Kaden Sun. I come from a humble background. My father was an illiterate farmer from the province of Henan. When I was a little boy, I aspired to be one of the great leaders of our nation: Mao, Deng, the lot of them. I studied hard, very hard, and somehow turned out to be one of the top students in the country." He puffed on his cigarette, then tapped it over the ashtray. "I joined the Party, and they groomed me." Li Lei's stare remained fixed on the ash before him. "When I was studying at Oxford, I met a most excellent man, an exceptional and brilliant thinker. He was an influential person then, but even more so today. At that time, I was a nobody, a naïve student like you." Li Lei pointed his cigarette at Kaden. "But I think he saw something in me, and he mentored me in the ways of the Western world. I learned to see things…differently. The hard, endless work of the farmer was not noble, but entirely avoidable. My father was a good man, but his mind was small. I could see there was a whole world waiting to be conquered."

"With all due respect," Kaden ventured, trying to mask the slight tremor in his voice, "you haven't answered my question. Why me?"

Li chuckled. "Ah, Sun, you only continue to prove why you're such a valuable asset to my team. As for answers…"—he shrugged lightheartedly—"that man was my mentor, and perhaps I can be yours. That's the only answer you'll get."

Kaden clasped his hands and stared at the dragon leering up at him. What harm was there in taking the job? After all, he had the option to leave whenever he chose to, right?

He glanced up at nodded at Li Lei. "Okay, let's do it."

"Excellent!" Li Lei gave a clap of his hands. "Do well, and you'll be handsomely rewarded. But if you fail me…" His face darkened, and for a moment Kaden expected him to say he'd be thrown to the sharks. "I'll be forced to fire you."

Kaden smiled. "Yes, sir."

That afternoon, Kaden was put to work straightaway. The consulate was funding a project for underprivileged kids, and they wanted Kaden to consult them regarding their community engagement. Li brought up a hologram with a brilliant display of the proposed facilities. Children's playgrounds and modern classroom settings flashed across in 3D, complete with impressive stats and upbeat music in the background.

"This is a sample of the free childcare our Chinese investors propose to build in one of the state's urban centers. The project has received an in-principle approval from the governor, and if it's successful we intend to roll out close to one hundred of them. However, a small but vocal group of parents oppose the plan."

"Why would they do that?"

Li Lei sighed. "We want to introduce Mandarin studies to the curriculum, over a quarter of the classes. They rejected the idea."

"And it's a deal breaker?"

Li Lei shrugged. "No, we're getting desperate enough to let it go in order to get their support. Half a year has passed since the provisional state approval. If this drags on any longer, I'm afraid even the governor will be forced to review it."

"I'm sure you have a public relations team working on it. What's the problem?"

Li Lei scratched his head. "I don't know. We've spent over two hundred thousand dollars on print and digital campaigns. We've tried to organize workshops, awareness programs, meetings with families, social media ads—the works. But people are always suspicious of getting something for nothing. They think we have an agenda."

Kaden sat back in his chair, trying to play devil's advocate.

"Mr. Li, have you ever thought about what foreign investments mean to the average American?"

Li Lei's eyes widened behind his dark-rimmed spectacles. He hesitated, seeming to ponder over what Kaden meant. "They're afraid?"

"Of course."

He nodded. "I get your point. We've been going through the motions, trying to justify our intentions without considering what the community really wants: support and reassurance."

Kaden was blunt. "Exactly. Your presentations are slick, but have no soul. The message is aimed at appeasement, rather than promoting what a difference these free services will make to a single mother, trying to hold down two jobs."

Li Lei folded his arms and leaned back. "What would you have me do?"

"No conditions, no rules. Bring the concerned parents on board. Let them be on the team that develops the curriculum. Use every chance to explain the benefits, from the perspective of solving their problems. I mean, who wouldn't want their child to speak Mandarin, if it drastically improved their job prospects?" Kaden straightened in his chair, hands clasped together. "Once the key ringleaders get it, they'll spread the message to the rest. If they are on the other side of the fence, they can't and won't hear you. Let them tell you what they want, not what you think they need."

Li Lei tapped the table in agreement. "That's a good idea! But we haven't had much luck in getting them to trust us, let alone join our team."

"Use champions, sir," Kaden replied.

"Champions?" Li Lei frowned. "You mean celebrities?"

"Anyone with a positive reputation, known in the community for good initiatives. Founders of charitable causes, lobbyists, media personalities. They'll be your voice, and influence the others."

"What about the magazine adverti—"

Kaden cut him off. "You need a grassroots movement, no more flashy campaigns."

Li Lei thumped his fist against the marble, his face flushed beet red. Clearly, he was upset. Had Kaden been too candid with his words? His new boss took off his spectacles and wiped them with quick, impatient strokes.

There was a solemn look in his eyes, and behind the glasses Kaden discovered a cool hardness he had never seen before. The older man got up from his seat and stood, shoulders hunched, his hands curled into fists.

Almost a minute passed before he spoke. "*Ta ma de,*" he finally whispered. Kaden tensed upon hearing the bitter expletive, raising his palms in apology and kicking himself for going overboard in his delivery.

"Young man, we've spent hundreds of thousands of dollars with worthless PR agencies, and in the process we've wasted time. That's the resource I treasure most of all." Li Lei pressed his lips into a thin line, shaking his head. "In less than twenty minutes, you've helped me grasp key issues that seem to have escaped my advisors all these months." Li Lei looked down and shook his head, and then lifted it, revealing an earnest expression. "Kaden, I want you to work with my team starting tomorrow morning. I know you have some weeks before your next term. Alexis will be back tomorrow. She'll support you with the project."

Kaden blinked at him, trying to mask his surprise. "Does this mean you accept my recommendations?"

Li Lei opened the gold box a second time and offered Kaden a cigarette. Though he didn't smoke, he thought it best to take one.

"I knew you had potential, Sun, but I think you might just prove to be absolutely invaluable."

Eighteen

Bank of America
Oakman Boulevard
Detroit, Michigan

Agent Jack Raven stood at the front steps of the Bank of America, gazing at the spectacle before him. An impressive lineup of anti-riot police had formed along the stretch of Oakman Boulevard, stoically guarding the BoA. They were dressed in all black, their expressions hidden behind reinforced reflective shields. Emblazoned across their bulletproof vests were printed white words: "State Police."

The falling snow had lasted through the night and the sky was gray with thick, billowing clouds. The snowflakes fell softly upon the uniforms, like so many snowmen waiting for their carrots and scarves. Of course, these wintry figures bore Taser shotguns instead.

Positioned alongside was a white Ford Alpine riot-control vehicle. The unit was a multipurpose armored car with a revolving water-and-dye turret on top. Parked beside it was a box-like military van with an octagonal disc on its top, and an angular black cross sculpted across its surface. This was a state-of-the-art Active Denial System, one of many new technologies to emerge from the Pentagon's Non-Lethal Weapons Program. Like the microwaves used to zap frozen dinners, the Raytheon-built weapon produced an acute, searing pain across the target's skin without causing serious harm.

The throng of demonstrators facing the police troopers numbered more than one thousand. Bunched around the parking lot of an abandoned building, they shouted slogans with banners that read *WHITE COLLAR ROBBERY* and *WALL STREET SCUM*. Some threw beer cans and stones at the bank, growing rowdier every minute.

Agent Jack Raven paced before the glass doors and peered into the building. Tailored executives were moving around, frantically trying to destroy documents and evacuate through the fire escapes. He blinked at the scene, conscious of the electronic contact lenses on his eyes; his pupils controlled the focus of the video feed to FBI HQ. "Rick, are you receiving the images?"

"Yeah, it's not looking good," Agent Rick Botelli replied. "Same as everywhere around the country. What d'you expect when the bank closures are shutting off all avenues for the people to take back the only money they have?"

Jack scrutinized the crowd once more, picking out two of the more vociferous characters. They held loudspeakers and gave instructions through their comm devices. "See those two over there? This one's more organized that the others have been."

"Copy that. We've received reports of mob's involvement. NSA's been intercepting lots of chatter."

Jack scanned the view from the doorsteps of the building in order to give his partner a better view of the situation. Gang members moved like serpents through the crowds, whipping up the hysteria. *Now, why are they keen to be so involved?*

Leading the three hundred-strong anti-riot battalion was Captain Brad Hedley, a local boy born and bred. His troop had to prepare for action, and Jack watched as they stood tall, waiting for his command.

Taking his place behind Hedley, Jack listened as the captain gave instructions to his lieutenants to break into two sections; one to deal with the advancing crowd, and the other as a reserve against the group throwing stones and projectiles. A few Molotov cocktails had also been added to the mix.

"Lieutenant Korres, use the water cannon on the advancing targets. Lieutenant Brown, hit the ADS on any who break through. The rest of you, hold your positions."

It was freezing cold, but the captain's forehead was beaded with perspiration. *A thousand against three hundred.*

The sound of the crazed civilians reached fever pitch. Like animals, they snarled at the police, gesturing their intent with clawed hands and teeth bared. Provoked into a frenzy, Jack watched as the horde broke ranks and started tearing toward the law enforcers. "They are starting their attack, Rick."

Within seconds the water cannon punched a hole into the center of the crowd. Jack watched with startled eyes as the impact of the jet hit one fellow, ripping his shirt off and flinging him into the gutter. Another man was pushed to his knees and trampled by those behind him.

"Masks on. Engage the tear gas."

Jack got his out and pulled it over his face. The grenades were lobbed into the melee and exploded in balls of large, yellow puffs. The thick, caustic fumes were like angels of torture, curling around their victims until they dropped to their knees, covering their eyes and coughing violently. The crowd began to scatter, torn tees wrapped around red faces as the worst affected tried to escape the searing bite of the gas.

"Activate the ADS," Captain Hedley commanded. Beside the grenadiers, the Octagon antenna emitted multiple streams of two-second 95 GHz wave bursts, heating up impacted skin to 130 degrees Fahrenheit. Red patches of burnt derma formed on the bodies of those struck. Jack observed a wild-eyed man running into the police line, skin seared black, as the officers lashed at him with their batons. Jack twisted his face away from the stench of burning flesh.

The mass faltered in their advance and Captain Hedley's men took the opportunity to neutralize the rioters, beginning to arrest and disarm. Setting his vision on the wider scene for his partner and colleagues back at headquarters, Jack breathed a sigh of relief. "Looking good, Rick, situation stabilizing. The bank should be safe, but it came close."

He met Captain Hedley's gaze, gave a salutary thumbs-up and got a wave in return. Turning back to the bank, he walked up the stairs to see if the staff had left. There were still plenty of people milling around inside, but they seemed slightly less frenetic.

The calm hadn't lasted more than a few minutes when his razor-sharp ears heard it.

The slow rumbling turned to a roar as they advanced. A new group had formed in the streets further up the block, and they were coming. Jack scanned beyond the immediate crowd; thousands of them. The second wave appeared better prepared, wearing portable masks and goggles. They were armed with knives, machetes, and guns, some he discerned as heavy assault rifles. One of the officers pointed upward, and Jack watched as masked vigilantes positioned themselves on the rooftop of a nearby auto-repair shop, rockets launchers hoisted upon their shoulders.

"Kill the RPGs!" he heard Captain Hedley scream out. His officers took aim with their guns, but before a shot was fired the rocket launchers had shot off their deadly payload against the water cannon and Octagon ADS. Jack counted four smoking missiles from the rooftops. They disappeared into the hulls of the police vehicles and exploded into fireballs, rolling up toward the afternoon sky. Windows shattered everywhere and acrid black smoke from the burnt tires made it impossible to see what was happening.

Crouching, Jack shouted into his comm. "Rick, this is far more than some gangsters. This is a like a damn war."

Like starter guns in an Olympic race, the blast sent the crowd berserk, Captain Hedley's men staggering backward as the wall of humanity crashed toward them. Without their superior defensive weaponry, there was nothing they could do but band together like three hundred Spartan soldiers, cornered by the two approaching armies.

With a jolt of shock, Jack realized just how intelligent the enemy—whoever that was—had proved to be. The first protest had been nothing more than a bluff to test their defenses.

"Jack, get out of there. Get the hell out of there, *right now!*" Agent Botelli's voice screeched in Jack's earpiece.

But all the agent could focus on were the roaring faces of the men running toward him. He shouted at Captain Hedley to use deadly force, but it was futile. Even as some of the leaders were shot down, the crowd continued, developing a mind of its own.

The riot control officers began to fall beneath a mountain of blows and kicks, Jack crying out as he watched the arm of an officer get hacked off, shortly before the attacker took the ax to his head. When the rioters reached the bank's steps, Jack retreated inside and instructed the doors to be bolted. His desperate gaze met the manager's. "We can't hold them, you've got to leave now!"

The man froze, his eyes staring off toward the doors. Jack turned, a cool prickle of terror flushing across his skin as trash cans and heavy objects thudded against the glass. Just as the first pane began to crack, a group of employees raced up with boxes in their arms.

"They're at the back doors!" a young woman cried, cheeks streaked with running mascara. "Where are we meant to go?"

The bank manager swore; there were too many people to fit into the safes. Jack tightened his grip on his automatic weapon and gritted his teeth. He could hold off a few, for a little while, but who knew how long it would take for reinforcements to arrive, assuming the city had any to spare.

New gunfire crackled and the doors exploded in a storm of glass. Jack dropped to his stomach, but not before an intense, searing pain informed him he'd taken several hits. Boots thudded toward him as he clutched at the bullet wounds, trying to stem the blood, but it was pointless. It was everywhere, and spreading beneath him in an ever-expanding pool. With equal parts horror and disbelief, he looked down and saw he'd been struck near the stomach. Part of his gut protruded from the flesh wound beneath his bulletproof vest, and his fingers prodded it back into his abdomen. There was no pain now, only an overwhelming sense that it had to be a bad nightmare he'd soon wake up from.

He tried to look for the fleeing staff, and knew it was too late for most of them. The place was filling with smoke and all around him people were screaming over the blast of gunfire, an older man collapsing beside him with blood streaming from his throat. Helpless calls from HQ rattled his ears and he pulled his earpiece out, unable to bear Rick's panicked voice any longer.

The pounding of heavy boots paused as one set came to a stop beside him. Jack glimpsed the silhouette of a large man with his gun raised above his head.

"Government scum!"

The butt of the weapon came down, hard, and through a fog of shock Jack felt the blunt object crunch against his skull. *This is it*, he thought, *murdered by some guy in a leather jacket and a blue bandanna.* As his eyes were flooded with tears and blood, Jack thought briefly of his ex-wife and happier times. When the moment came, he stepped willingly into the impending darkness, glad to be anywhere but there.

Nineteen

Matsuhisa Japanese Restaurant
Beverly Hills, California

"**W**hy did we come here? We can't afford this." Katy glanced around, adjusting the collar of her dress for the fourth time since they'd taken their seats.

The restaurant *was* impressive. Hanging chandeliers looked like giant inverted beehives, and the dining area was cozy but austere. Large vases of red roses added a romantic touch, and candles floated in golden bowls. Around them, richly dressed guests laughed over steaming plates of assorted delicacies. Kaden went to adjust his new tie, before stopping himself.

"I've got this, babe. Don't worry."

His girlfriend glanced at a striking brunette in a shimmering dress to her left, and sighed.

"What's wrong, Katy? You've been sneaking peeks at that woman since we came in. You know her?"

Katy shook her head and held her tongue, eyes down. She had a habit of going suddenly quiet whenever he subjected her to the finer things in life, or introduced her to a fancy new acquaintance.

"You look absolutely stunning tonight," he said softly, squeezing her hand. "Didn't you notice the men ogling you as you walked in? I had to stare every one of them down."

Katy gave a small, cynical laugh. "If they were staring, it's probably because I'm dressed like one of their maids." She bent toward Kaden and whispered, "When I took my seat, that girl smiled at me." She nodded toward the brunette. "Not like a friendly smile, but a sympathetic one. Like she felt sorry for me."

"She's just jealous you've stolen her limelight," he chuckled. "Those pearls are gorgeous on you, and her diamonds are probably fake anyway."

"You like them?" Katy's expression brightened. "They belonged to my mom."

"*Mei li,*" Kaden replied.

"What's that?"

"It means 'beautiful' in Chinese," he said with a grin. "We'll go dancing later and I'll show you off to everyone. Tonight, we're celebrating."

"Dinner, dancing…How can we afford it?" Katy said. "We haven't even paid our rent yet."

"Because the project worked out," Kaden said, nodding as the waiter delivered two flutes of champagne and smiling at the thought of the new two-bedroom flat they shared in one of the safer suburbs in town. "Li Lei compensated me well and I want to treat you to the kind of date you deserve."

"Project? You mean that kindergarten job you spent the last few weeks on?"

Kaden nodded. "Yeah. The folks who had opposed the investment are singing our praises now. Two hundred families will receive world-class childcare for free, in exchange for Li Lei's terms. It's a win-win."

"That's wonderful news! Mr. Li must be so pleased with you."

Kaden took her hands, soft and smooth, and lifted them to his lips. "Thanks to you. Remember, I wouldn't have accepted his invitation if you hadn't pushed me to do it."

"He must have compensated you well," she said, biting her lip. "This is one of Beverly Hills' most expensive restaurants. You'd have to wash a week's worth of dishes for the tip alone."

Kaden rolled back in his chair and tried not to look too smug. "I think fifty grand should cover it, and a tip."

"Fifty thousand dollars!" Katy gasped so loud that several heads around them turned. Lowering her voice, she added, "For just a few weeks of work?"

"*Successful* work," corrected Kaden. "The project would have been held up indefinitely if we failed to win over the protestors." Kaden released her hand and rubbed his eyes, tired just thinking about it. "The parents wouldn't budge. It took them quite a while to understand it was our offer, or nothing. Li Lei was so happy when they signed. You should have seen his face."

"That's incredible." Katy grabbed his hand once more and squeezed his long fingers with her tiny ones. "I'm proud of you, Kaden."

"It's nothing." He dipped his chin, feeling his face grow warm. It had been years since he'd heard those words spoken, at least by someone who meant them.

"Did you manage the project all on your own?"

"No, I had assistance. Some PR people and Li Lei's staff."

"And?" Katy asked, her eyes narrowing.

"And what?" Kaden murmured, sensing the question to come.

"And what about Alexis, wasn't she in the team too?"

"Oh yeah…" He fiddled with his napkin. "She was responsible for—" The waiter arrived and Kaden breathed a sigh of relief, smiling at the grandiose plate of charcoal-grilled Kobe beef laid before him. The guy launched into a long, foreign-sounding explanation of the produce, sauce, garnishes, and a million other things Kaden didn't understand or really care about. Still, he was smart enough to nod dumbly, off the hook from Katy's least favorite subject.

"Eat up, babe," he ventured, as the waiter finally walked away.

Katy kept silent, chewing on a slice of the meat as though it was a limp piece of rubber.

"You know, this restaurant was founded by a man named Nobu Matsuhisa," continued Kaden. "His dad passed away in a traffic accident when he was a boy. He managed to overcome all odds—"

"So was Alexis your personal assistant?" Katy asked in a low voice.

Kaden swallowed, his mind going blank. Katy looked so beautiful in the soft light, the pearls glowing against her flawless skin. She glanced up at him, as if shocked by his silence, and he knew he had to speak or risk looking as if he were guilty of something he wasn't.

All of a sudden, he found himself kneeling at her side. Kaden could feel the heat of curious onlookers surrounding them. With a flush, he realized it probably looked like a proposal.

"Katy, ever since I met you I've seen no other girl. Forget about Alexis, you're everything—"

He lowered his voice as his words attracted discreet laughter from the closest tables. "Mr. Li wanted his daughter to help out. But she's nothing to me. I swea—"

Kaden ground to a halt as Katy tipped her head back and laughed. Just like that, the room seemed suddenly brighter.

"Most girls would find you melodramatic. But I happen to know that's part of your charm."

"Charm?" Kaden swallowed, wondering what had happened in the last thirty seconds.

"I was teasing you, silly," she said. "Now get up. The whole restaurant is looking at us funny."

He felt his stomach unclench, then remembered the long, velvet box nestled in his breast pocket. "Uh, wait. There's one more thing."

Katy ran her fingers through his hair as he slipped a hand inside his new dinner jacket and pulled out the gift. Lifting the lid, she watched in shock as speckles of light bounced out in a thousand different directions.

"Kaden…"

He slipped the diamond bracelet on her wrist. "If I'd known, I would have bought you pearls."

Eyes moist, she swallowed and shook her head, her lower lip trembling slightly. "No, no…the diamonds will do just fine."

At first, she'd seemed happy, but as he looked up at her the silence began to gnaw at him.

"Too much?"

She sniffed and looked away, rubbing at her eyes.

"I can change it if…"

Katy's hand gripped his, willing him to be quiet. "No, I adore it." Her other hand wiped away the tears streaming down her cheeks. "It's just that no one has given me anything so lovely… ever."

He took Katy's hand and rotated the bracelet around her wrist. "Look at it, Katy. Can you guess the secret message?"

The two blue eyes peered closer, a watery smile upon her lips. The diamonds had been lined up in vertical strips, each separated by a silver band of varying thickness. Kaden kneeled by her side, watching in amusement as she tried to decipher the code.

"I won't stop until I get it," Katy muttered, a frown appearing on her forehead.

Kaden placed his palm over hers. "No, let me tell you…it's a message that should be spoken, anyway."

"Really?" She tilted her head, looking at him as if he were some odd object found on the side of the road.

"It's Morse Code," he said, taking a deep breath as he tried to swallow his nerves. "I…I love you, Katy."

After such an indulgent dinner, Katy declined the dancing and instead asked if they might go to a food distribution center she sometimes worked at. Together they prepared meals for homeless families, toiling over pots of spaghetti and vegetable soup late into the night. When the last bowl had been ladled out and the last pot scrubbed clean, Kaden took Katy by the hand and strolled toward his car.

Before he could unlock the vehicle, he felt the brush of soft fingers against his arm. He turned to her as she pulled him close. Their eyes met, Katy's body trembling in his arms as she raised her lips to his. Her mouth was warm, sweet and intoxicating, and for a moment he lost himself in the pleasure of her kiss. To stand together as one, in the deep quiet of the night, was the closest Kaden had come to feeling at peace in a very long time.

They broke apart as heavy clouds passed across the silvery moon, and flashes of lightning lit the landscape of abandoned buildings and crumbling houses.

It was time to go home.

Twenty

Detroit Medical Center
Detroit, Michigan

Special Agent Jack Raven opened his eyes, but the harsh sunlight streaming in from the windows was blinding. *Where am I?*

His hand touched his head, Jack grimacing as his fingers pressed against damp fabric—it felt as if a hammer had been knocking nonstop upon his brain.

A quick scan revealed he was in a white room, and he slowly twisted his head sideways to get a better view of the surroundings. A searing pain shot from his side to his chest and he jerked back to his original position, shocked at his body's severe reaction. He was in the midst of studying the intravenous tube running down his arm when the door opened.

"Ah, he lives!" A doctor appeared, followed by a middle-aged nurse carrying a plastic case and clipboard.

Jack made an effort to speak, but his throat was so parched it was impossible to do more than grunt.

"How are you feeling, Agent Raven? We weren't sure you'd ever wake up." The doctor leaned over, shining a torch in his eyes and nodding in satisfaction.

The nurse came over and inserted a plastic tube between his lips, Jack's weakened vision centering on the syringe as the plunger dropped. Cool water trickled over his tongue and into his throat.

"You're lucky your FBI pal got priority authorization to get you into this ward. We've got patients lining the corridors."

"How did I get here?" Jack croaked.

The physician slipped on his stethoscope and placed it over Jack's heart. He seemed to take forever as he listened to the instrument, the nurse busying herself with preparing medication and unwrapping an oversized needle from its packaging.

"You're in Detroit Medical Center. Brought here concussed and shot in your right shoulder, upper arm and lower abdomen. Your vest took another four shots, so you've got some nasty bruising. You've been in coma for a week now."

Jack's eyes fixated upon the white plaster of the ceiling as he struggled to remember. Broken images flashed through his mind, the pain of being struck by the bullets…blood on the floor…the sounds of bayonets entering flesh…and the cries for help.

He forced his eyes shut, as if that might suppress the horror of it all. It didn't; the mental videos kept playing in the dark recesses of his mind. A superheated metal rod was pressing hard along his ribs, and as the doctor prattled on the moment became unbearable. A deep, tortured sound broke from somewhere in his chest, and the only way out of this insanity was to scream.

Twenty-One

The Riviera Country Club
California

"**F**ore!" The small white ball veered toward a parade of golfers in their buggies. Before it could strike, it clipped the branches of a cherry tree and careened harmlessly to the side of the group, causing exaggerated headshaking from the would-be victims.

"Years pass, but I cannot master this stupid game!" Li Lei threw his driver at the caddy in disgust.

"I think you've got to reduce the paunch a bit, Dad. It's affecting your swing," Alexis laughed.

An assistant handed Li Lei his comm; a fine-leather wrist strap with a flexible layer of HoloGen film. Li Lei took his place in the four-seater buggy with Kaden and Alexis as it auto-piloted itself to the waiting golf balls.

"*Nihao! Zhe shi Lao Li,*" he said, as the device projected a vertical image of a Chinese man wearing a bow tie, checkered suit, and excited expression. He greeted Li Lei, then played a series of videos of rolling grass plains and urban maps.

"Shi ma? Tai hao le! Hao, jiu zhe yang, xie xie!" Li Lei returned the gadget to his assistant. "Hate wearing this on my body," he said. "Humans are becoming cyborgs, and I want no part of it."

"Good news?" Kaden asked.

Li Lei's brows arched upward. "So you do know a little of our language? You surprise me, as usual."

"My dad taught me. Even Mom, who was American, spoke some Mandarin."

"Ah, another secret of your past unraveled," Li Lei said with a smile.

The buggy reached Alexis' ball first, and the party alighted. The caddy handed her the appropriate club, but she shook her head and took one from her father's bag instead. With a smile, she turned and handed it to Kaden. "Here. You have a go."

Kaden held up his hands. "Nope. Not my game. If I tried I'd probably kill a bird or something."

"It's good for you," said Li Lei. "Especially useful when entertaining clients."

Kaden shook his head. "It's better if I start from the range, thank you."

"Come on, don't be a poor sport." Alexis dragged him to the golf ball at the fringe of the fairway and motioned for him to keep a distance. Gripping the iron, she lightly swung, demonstrating the proper motion.

Kaden studied her posture as the rays of afternoon sun burst through the cloud cover. Dressed in white and gray, she was almost glowing. Her body tucked itself into a golfing stance, her jet-black hair rolled into a glossy bun atop her head. The caddy was clearly drooling over her svelte figure, and the long pale legs that ended in her pleated skirt. But to Kaden, she was like something you might admire in a pretty shop; an object of marvel, but one he had no desire to possess. Everything he wanted was waiting for him at home.

When the fairway iron was handed over he took it with apprehension, grabbing the end like a hockey stick.

"Here." Alexis stood beside him and held his hands over the club. "That's the way to hold it." She shifted her body, demonstrating the swing. "When you raise it, use your left hand to swing down, not your right. And loosen your grip." A rush of anticipation thrummed through Kaden as the competitive nature in him began to take hold, and he found himself absorbing Alexis' instructions with great interest.

He made the prescribed motion. "Yes, that's right," Alexis encouraged. "Remember, your left arm maintains control. If you swing correctly, you don't even really need the right hand. It's only there for adjusting the flight and angle."

"Well, here goes." Kaden pictured the movement and swing of the golf pros he had seen on TV and Alexis' demonstration. He twisted his upper body ninety degrees, his left hand straightened high above his head. The motion reversed as his torso unwound in the downswing like a brand-new rubber band. The resulting force of the clubface meeting the sweet spot of the golf ball sent it rocketing almost two hundred yards toward the flag.

The group was silent for a moment, until Alexis exhaled the breath she'd been holding. "You hit that far with a six iron?"

"As I said, you continue to surprise me," Li Lei added with a pat on his back.

"Beginner's luck," Kaden offered.

"No, I knew you'd be a natural," said Alexis, slipping her arm through his.

"Let's see if you prove as capable on our next project." Li Lei clasped his hands as he motioned Kaden along his path. "I've just received good news regarding a vast tract of land in California that is currently open for bidding. The federal government expressed concern about losing control over such an expanse of land, and enacted a law to deny foreign investors the right to bid. We've been lobbying to regain those rights, in the hope of building public housing for low-income families.

"Today, we've heard that the White House has at last approved our participation in the bidding process. We will have a lot of projects coming our way, and need your help yet again."

Alexis walked alongside them, clutching Kaden's arm as she navigated the grassy path. He'd been dragged along to their golf game after dropping by their home to thank Li Lei for the generous funds that had appeared in his bank account. The thought of future work hadn't even occurred to him, as he was preparing to return to his studies.

Kaden rubbed the back of his head with his hand. "I don't know, sir. That seems like a pretty big project. More than a few weeks."

"Rest assured, this is not a one-man show," he answered. "And we are up against an influential group of congressmen, backed by illegal cartel money. Their leader is Senator Damon. They want the land to build resorts, and I don't think we have much of a chance against him, but we have to try."

Kaden stared at the man who had quickly become his mentor and boss, a question hovering upon his lips. With a quiver of nervousness, he decided to ask it.

"Sir, what is China's endgame in all this?"

Li Lei stopped in his tracks and turned toward him. "What do you mean?"

"I mean, some say China wants to slowly gain economic control so it can seize political power too. Buying up half of California supports that argument."

Li Lei chuckled, then laughed. "Over five thousand years of our history have you ever noted a fanatic, warmongering China making its way out to foreign territories and conquering them?" He shook his head to emphasize his point. "No, my son, China *detests* foreign intrusion, and it has never hungered for new domains. America, Europe, Russia, they are the imperialists. But that is not in our nature."

"That's why we built the Great Wall of China, to protect ourselves from outsiders," Alexis added.

"So why the huge buy up?"

"Chinese people like to make money," Li Lei said, rubbing his forefinger and thumb together. "Investment properties, good business, and a little gambling: that's in our blood. As I said, America is in financial distress, more than it has ever been in its short history. In truth, there are a lot of available assets on the cheap, but that's business. Without us, investment ends and the economy fails."

Li Lei was right. When China had been at its lowest political point, its enemies had come and plundered his ancestral homeland. Then, as the country learned to stand on its own feet once again, multinationals had come and invested. With new money, China had grown into the largest economy in the world.

Li Lei's expression turned dark. "Self-centered leadership and corrupt officials are driving this nation down. The term they use for this is *kleptocracy*, is it not? It's easier to blame evil foreigners for problems caused by their own administration."

Kaden dipped his head and mulled over Li Lei's words as the group walked to Li Lei's golf ball, resting precariously on the lip of a deep sand bunker. Taking a club from the caddy, Kaden turned to Li Lei. "May I?" The older man nodded.

He squinted at the target and measured the direction, swinging the iron in a single fluid motion. The *ping* resounded across the cool afternoon air and the ball thundered toward its destination like a tiny cannon ball. Hitting the fringe of the green, it rolled toward the flag.

Li Lei stood tall with his chest out and a wide smile splashed across his face. "I knew you wouldn't be a one-shot wonder!" He clapped his hand on Kaden's back. "You'll go far my boy, very far."

Twenty-Two

UCLA
Los Angeles, California

"We can do this, guys. What d'you say?" Kaden grabbed a large sheet of paper and placed it on the lawn, adding some small stones over the corners before resting back on his heels and looking at his friends expectantly.

"I don't know, bud." Zac laid down beside him, chin cupped in his hands. "We don't have much experience."

"I'm a techie," added Chet. "What do I know about getting the government to support a land project?" He tried to lie down like Zac, but rolled over and sat cross-legged instead.

"Okay, consider this. If corrupt congressmen win the bid, what happens?" Kaden asked.

"According to you, they'll build a bunch of luxury resorts," Chet said.

"And?"

"And, Li Lei wouldn't be able to develop the land for the lower-income folk?" Zac offered.

"Correct!" Kaden smoothed his hands across the paper. "And corrupt Senator Damon wins. That's why we have to stop him."

"But that's also why Li should be hiring professionals," Chet said.

Kaden stood, too impatient to remain crouching. "Li Lei has promised experts and resources, and I've been tasked to develop the concept and engagement strategy. It's all about public opinion. I know you can help me with this, guys."

"Sure, but it's all a bit sudden—"

"Do you need to earn some money?" Kaden asked.

Chet nodded, and he turned to Zac. "How about you?"

His best friend rolled his eyes. "What do you think?"

"So hear out my ideas." He clapped his hands together, and waited for his friends to nod their agreement. "Good. I've developed some plans, but first, we need to map out a few things."

He knelt and wrote the points down with a marker. "Like who are the decision makers, an analysis between the competition and Li Lei's group, the stakeholders involved, and what value propositions we need to bring on the table to get this over the line."

"So what help can we offer?" asked Chet.

"Before we even go there, I want you guys to know that we will share the proceeds equally if we win this project." Kaden glanced at Zac's worn-out shoes. Silver tape was bound around the front sections, as if the soles had started peeling back.

"What kind of proceeds are you talking about?" Chet asked.

"Would you believe me if I said *two-hundred thousand dollars*."

Zac shook his head nonstop while Chet stared at him, gaping.

Kaden laughed. "Good, because it's only one-hundred thousand, which still isn't bad for a few month's work."

Zac shook his head, a smile playing across his lips. "Seriously?"

"Thirty-three thousand, three hundred and thirty-three dollars and thirty-three cents for each of us, with a penny to spare. When can we start, boss?" Chet beamed.

"Now," Kaden said. "Fact is, I've drawn up tasks for both of you. But I'd like to know if you have any suggest—"

"I can help you understand the needs of low-income families," Zac said enthusiastically. "Like creating places that don't cost a lot to heat, and bedrooms that work for two or three kids. I've lived in enough dumps to know."

Kaden grinned at his friend. "Nice."

Chet was ready with his contribution. "We need to let the decision makers understand the consequences between choosing our option, versus that of the dirty congressmen. I'll build an interactive real-time opinion poll that will be available to all stakeholders. It will have a strong bearing on political circles and the media."

"Sounds great." Kaden rubbed his hands together. "If we can score with public opinion, which is ninety percent of the battle in politics, I think we can nail this."

Kaden looked at his friends, heart beating at the thought of helping them out of their own cycle of poverty. If they worked hard enough, and tried their best, maybe a brighter future awaited all of them. But first, they had to win the pitch.

Twenty-Three

Detroit City
Detroit, Michigan

Senior Special Agent Rick Botelli and his men took cautious steps along the empty street. The odd police siren or passing emergency vehicle was all that kept it from feeling like a ghost town.

To Rick, the sirens seemed superfluous. There were no other cars on the road, and each wail ripped through the late afternoon as if to prove that anything was better than silence. The streets were littered with burned-out cars, bent streetlights, smashed windows, and empty beer cans. It looked like the aftermath of a sporting match gone ugly, in one of those countries where people found any excuse to riot. It wasn't something he ever thought he'd see in America.

Rick's front men cleared the debris to the side of the path, rifles at the ready. Bloodstains were dark against the lighter layer of ash covering everything, and as Rick stepped on something soft and squishy he hopped back, expecting to see a dead rat beneath his boot. Instead, he found a decomposing hand, the broken fingers curled over a bloodied palm.

His unit passed by a Vietnamese café, its windows gone and insides looted. The small building had been firebombed, the furniture broken and charred. A row of deserted townhouses, their doors and window panels missing, looked like blackened skulls with hollowed-out eyes and gaping mouths.

Brightly painted red and orange X codes marked the front façade of every home. Rick noted one as he slowly passed. Above the top 'V' was the date rescuers had last passed through, and the left side of the X bared the code 'MA-TF1,' identifying the search unit. He grimaced at the large, scrawled 2-0 in the bottom quadrant. Two dead, zero alive found inside. There were too many bodies to remove in a single sweep, so the government had reverted to simply listing the places bodies could be found. But there was no natural disaster to blame now, like there had been in the days of Hurricane Katrina when X codes were first utilized. These people had died at the hands of their fellow citizens for the crime of living in an upper-middle class neighborhood. Rick shook his head at the next home, a large red '1' beneath the X and beside it, a hasty amendment: "+ 1 in basement."

Worst of all, there was no end in sight to the violence. How could they negotiate with opposition groups that had so much blood on their hands they'd made themselves outlaws? The media wasn't calling it a civil war, but only a battle could explain this kind of carnage.

They reached the entrance of the Detroit Medical Center to find the reception area empty, no nurses or attendants in sight. Rick signaled his unit to stand down and glanced around the room. He could hear footsteps in the hallways and knew the system was under strain, but the complete lack of staff made him nervous. Protestors wouldn't raid a hospital, would they?

After a few seconds he hollered out, "Is there anyone here?"

There was no reply.

He ordered his men to guard the exits and sat in the receptionist chair, rummaging through the files. It appeared most of the records and computers had been removed.

One terminal remained and Rick poked tentatively at the keys. The screen opened with a request for security identification.

"What are you doing?" a loud voice boomed across the hall. Rick could have sworn he saw the glass of water beside him jump as the sound waves hit.

"I was looking for the room number of my colleague, Special Agent Jack Raven," he said, scowling at the widely proportioned matron with whatever authority he still maintained.

She advanced toward him with a speed that defied her size. Taking over the computer, the woman scrolled the mouse with her large fingers. Then, without glancing up, she bellowed, "Level three. Use the stairway, turn right, ward two, second bed. Don't look at the signs, we've changed everything, so just remember the directions, okay?"

"Yes, ma'am. Thanks for your help."

Leaving the woman to her work, Rick told his men to stay back and glanced up the stairway. When he'd heard Jack was in a coma he'd wanted to come right away, but the fighting had been too intense to leave central command. Now his partner was awake again, but as Rick slowly trudged up the steps he felt more fear than excitement. He had no idea what kind of man was waiting for him in ward two.

Twenty-Four

Agent Jack Raven had just finished a lunch of cooked rice and some soggy green stuff they passed off as lettuce. He had to eat them to keep himself nourished but it seemed doubly unfair to be injured, and tortured too. He reminded himself of the many people on the streets scavenging through garbage cans for their next meal, and swallowed the last revolting mouthful.

Turning his head, he noticed a shadow hovering around the doorway. In just two days of consciousness he'd recovered most of his faculties, and aside from an intermittent ringing in his ears, he was feeling stronger.

Rick's head poked out from behind the open door.

"Hiya, partner." He reached the side of the bed and stood there awkwardly, his hands shoved into the back pockets of his integrated battle pants. "I'm off working my ass off, and you're lying in here having a holiday."

Jack grinned in return. "Any excuse to get away from you for a few weeks."

Rick laughed, pulling a chair over. "Sorry I couldn't come earlier. Chief has posted us all over the place. I thought it wasn't going to end."

"All good," said Jack, waving his hand. "So, how's the situation out there?" Noting Rick's frown, he added, "That good, huh?"

"I won't lie, it's a bitch. Intel suspects there's something more to the protests and riots. That it's all connected by some sort of central command."

Jack pushed his food tray away and pushed himself up. "I agree. The banking crisis and the riots felt coordinated to me. Could be that our old terrorist enemies are learning some new tricks."

"I'm onto your line of thinking. But why?"

Jack stroked his chin. "I don't know, but I've got to get back to look into it. The nurses here won't even give my comm back."

"You stay and recuperate. You've had enough fun for one week. We'll come for you when you're ready."

"I'm ready!" He thumped his hand on the bedsheet. "You gotta get me out of this place, Rick."

Rick closed his eyes. "Another inch and you would have had a bullet to the guts. And you were one blow away from permanent brain damage…"

Jack put his hand atop his partner's and gripped hard. "That's why I've gotta get out there, Rick. I've seen what these guys are doing, and…" His voice cracked. "Please."

Rick gave a loud sigh. "I'll talk with the doc, but no promises. If he says you're staying, you're staying, and I don't care how much you whine about it."

Jack squeezed Rick's hand 'til his fingers hurt. "If I'm not out there, I'm better off dead anyway."

"Sure," said Rick softly. "But let's not sign the death certificate faster than we have to. Okay?"

Twenty-Five

The Consulate General of the People's Republic of China
Los Angeles, California

With crinkled eyes and pink cheeks, Li Lei was either in a good mood, or drunk.

"Support for our bid on the land development is getting stronger by the day." He turned to Alexis with a hearty laugh. "To think I suggested mentoring this boy. Each day, he teaches *me* something new!"

Alexis hugged her dad. "But you spotted his potential, Father. Kudos to you for that."

"I believe your eyes spotted it first, my lovely girl." His chuckling turned to a cackle when her eyes flicked downward and away, her face flushing.

Kaden shifted in his seat, clearing his throat. He wasn't used to being celebrated, and he didn't want to encourage Alexis. Her crush was sweet, and more than a little flattering, but the closer they became the more he saw her as a younger sister. Li Lei's daughter was in many ways a girl, and he found their conversation easy when sticking to safe subjects like work and politics. The moment they strayed into personal topics, it grew awkward.

Kaden glanced up to see that Li Lei's smile had faded. "I've heard Senator Damon is rather upset about the situation. Apparently he's been asking a lot of questions about you. Be careful, my boy."

"Of course he has." Kaden almost added a curse to the statement, holding it back out of respect for his company. What hope did the United States have with every politician protecting his own corrupt interests? It was lucky he had a spotless record, or the senator would have no doubt found some excuse to haul him into jail.

Li Lei leaned forward, his face earnest. "Kaden, I'd like you to consider joining my organization full-time. We have countless projects that need you. You and your team would be well compensated."

That offer was not unexpected, but it still managed to catch Kaden by surprise. He'd agreed to consult on an ad hoc basis, but a full-time job was a different thing entirely. Opportunities and risks raced through Kaden's mind like a supercomputer, but beneath them all was a small, niggling voice that refused to be silenced. He sighed.

"Your faith in me is humbling," he said. "But I can't do it for one reason."

"What's that?" Alexis asked, looking more disappointed than her father.

"My dad. I promised him I'd focus on school before anything else. And I think he's right."

"Hmmm." Li Lei shrugged. "It is good to follow the wishes of your father. Still, I won't stop trying to convince you, for your own good and mine."

Kaden nodded. "I wouldn't expect less."

"On the topic of your father, I had my government contacts look into his situation." He waved away Kaden's look of surprise. "We are one big family here Kaden, we look after one another. And it appears Mr. Sun has not received his pension in some months. Were you aware of that?"

Kaden stiffened. "Yes, he mentioned it to me in passing last week, but he was confident it was a short-term delay."

Li Lei made a sharp sound of disgust and strode toward the window. Alexis glanced at Kaden. "What is it, Dad?"

He didn't answer, his eyes fixed on the gardens as if he'd spotted an enemy walking through the roses.

After a tense silence, the Chinese consul slowly turned to them. "The US government will never be able to pay off its fiscal obligations to your dad, or to any of its citizens for that matter, Kaden. America is bankrupt, as is the EU."

A small group of analysts in the newspapers had said the same, but it seemed impossible. The United States had been a powerhouse for too long. It was too big to crumble.

The telephone beeped and Li Lei walked to the intercom. Upon pressing a button, the secretary's voice announced that a Mr. Jeffrey Zhang had arrived.

"Okay, let him in," Li Lei answered gruffly, before lifting his finger off the panel. "Jeffrey Zhang is Alexis' second cousin. He has just returned from some time in China. I'd like you to meet with him, as he's assisting me on a few key tasks." He looked toward the door, and added softly. "He's a...brash young man, and could learn much from you."

The office door opened to reveal a figure in dark shades, and a two-button mohair gray jacket with scarlet silk handkerchief tucked jauntily into the breast pocket. His lapels were pulled up, and the word *dandy* popped into Kaden's head. He wasn't sure where he'd heard it before, but if the suede shoe fit...

Ignoring Kaden he walked to Alexis, embracing her tightly and kissing her on both cheeks, in the manner of the French. Kaden couldn't help but notice her pull away slightly, lips pursed.

"Jeffrey, meet the brilliant young man I've been talking to you about. Mr. Kaden Sun."

He offered his hand, and the guy grabbed it as if he'd walked in on Kaden cleaning a toilet. Up close, he had very pale skin, gold chains, and a dragon tattoo that peeped from behind his high, starched collar. Kaden couldn't see the eyes behind the sunglasses, but he seemed familiar. His eyes fixed upon his bleached blond hair, carefully shaped into a helmet of spikes.

"So, this is the prodigy," Jeffrey said.

"Mr. Li is too generous," Kaden replied. Then, tilting his head in speculation, he added, "Have we met before?"

Jeffrey flashed the white points of his teeth. "I believe we're both patrons of The Tipsy Orb. But the last time we met, we never really had the chance to talk, did we?"

Kaden leaned back. He remembered it now, the bleached hair, strutting around, groping Katy and watching in amusement as his thugs did the dirty work.

"You know each other?" Alexis asked.

Jeffrey nodded. "Yeah, sure. Mr. Sun is a local hero." He shifted his focus to Li Lei, who was watching them both with a quiet intensity. "Uncle, you remember the nightclub chain Dad bought? Mr. Sun broke up a fight there. He was good with his fists and left a lot of black eyes," he said with a laugh. "I agree that he'll be able to teach me much about The American Way." Looking back at Kaden he gave a light wink. "Isn't that right?"

Jaw clenched, Kaden bit out, "Of course. We could start with a study of the justice system."

"Wonderful!" Li beamed. "I can see you'll make great friends. I have a meeting to attend, but why don't you young ones go out for drinks, and get to know each other?"

Kaden shook his head. "Sorry sir, I've got to get back to class."

Alexis flew to Kaden's side. "Will I see you tomorrow?" As he nodded, he noticed Jeffrey's face turn sullen. He could only imagine the look concealed behind the dark glasses, and felt Jeffrey's hatred of him radiating from every pore of the young punk's body

"Nice to meet you, Jeffrey," he said, unable to stop himself from placing his hand at Alexis' back as he led her to the door. "Mr. Li."

The older man smiled at them before looking into his comm in apparent dismissal of the nephew hovering at his shoulder. Head held high, Kaden closed the door.

The punk would have murdered him that night if the cops hadn't shown up, and God only knew what he'd planned for Katy.

Kaden's body clenched with resentment. It seemed he had a new arch nemesis, in the form of a tall, blond party-boy. Nothing he couldn't handle.

Twenty-Six

UCLA Bus Terminal
Los Angeles, California

The bright orange bus sported the Chinese *Dami*, or 'Big Rice' brand, now the world's largest mobile communications company. It was irritating to see the garish *DM* logo bandied all over the country, in shops, cinemas, and even within the confines of the public vehicle he was riding. Twenty screens recycled the trademarked jingle on a continuous loop.

During the ride his thoughts wandered back to his dad. What if Li Lei was right, and the government was no longer able to support its pensioners? Peter Sun was a proud man. He sure as hell wouldn't be caught in one of those food lines, or accept help from his son. Kaden did some quick research on his comm.

The American banking system had twenty trillion dollars in assets, with six of the largest banks owning more than two-thirds of the total. Kaden scrolled through the reports and came across a key point: in all, they faced 250 trillion dollars of leveraged exposure. It was unthinkable. The government wasn't just on the brink of bankruptcy, but complete annihilation.

The past fifty years had witnessed the total US debt balloon from three to thirty trillion dollars, which meant over seven-hundred billion dollars every year just in repayments alone, at nominal interest rates. The government's annual budget wouldn't even come close. Especially not with an annual budget deficit of over five-hundred billion dollars.

It appeared that Li Lei was well informed, after all.

The bus heaved along Hilgard Avenue, screeching to a stop at the terminal. A darkening sky hovered over Kaden as he stepped out and trudged toward his apartment. Drops of rain started to fall. He looked around, but the place was quiet as death, spare a handful of crows searching discarded food wrappers.

He'd started to cross the street when a black limousine ground to a stop directly before him. Two burly men stepped out, the taller saying, "Kaden Sun?"

Kaden glanced up the street, wondering if they'd been waiting for him the whole time. He smelled trouble; seemed to attract it of late.

"You're working for the Chinese on the Nimrod Land bid, right?" The thug was colossal, his fists like balls of iron as he crossed his arms and grimaced at the rain falling upon his face. Kaden could try to make a run for it inside, but if these guys worked for the government there was only so long he might hide.

Before he could answer, the two men rushed at him. He raised his fists in defense, but was restrained after a few quick jabs to his abdomen. Looking around and seeing no one, they dragged him inside the waiting limousine.

Wheezing like a geriatric, he looked up to find a middle-aged gentleman in a deep-blue suit seated beside him. The man had white hair in two puffs on the sides of his head, and a distinct, jutted jaw. He'd seen him in the paper only that morning.

"Senator Damon," he coughed.

"Mr. Kaden Sun, nice to have made your acquaintance," he said with a Southern drawl, his hands clasped together in front of him.

Kaden swallowed the fury prickling through his body, and smiled instead. "You must be losing a lot of ground, to have to resort to this."

A twitch betrayed the senator's irritation. "I don't lose, Sun. And I'm certainly not afraid of a few rice-eaters." His chin inched forward even further. "What I'd like to know is how a born and bred American like yourself can so quickly turn his back on his country?"

Kaden sneered at the words. "I'm helping my country by helping my people. Your American Dream is to rob everyone blind."

At this the man snorted. "What do you think Li Lei and his thugs are doing? Are they international philanthropists?"

"Whatever," Kaden said, straightening as the pain began to recede. "I don't think you brought me here to discuss ethics."

The senator sighed, taking a crystal decanter from the side cabinet and pouring a generous splash of something brown into his glass. It smelled like whiskey. "A drink, young man?"

Kaden shook his head.

"You see," the senator continued. "I don't care about the battle, my eye is on the war." He took a sip and closed his eyes in enjoyment. "If Li Lei and his consortium win this round, things would, shall we say, get a little more complicated in the future for me and my investors. Thankfully, I don't allow luck to dictate my destiny."

Kaden blinked at him. "Are you trying to bribe me, or threaten me?"

He smiled. "I was going to bribe you, but your misguided loyalties make it clear that would be a waste of breath. Thankfully, that also works to my advantage," he added, taking another sip.

"Hmm?" Kaden tried to act nonchalant, but his pulse was racing.

"Loyalty makes you vulnerable. Emotional. Irrational."

"So you are threatening me?"

"Of course not!" he said with a laugh. "I'm simply persuading you, according to your own set of values. What means more to Kaden Sun? A political agenda, or the young lady waiting for him upstairs?"

Kaden fought the urge to grab the glass out of the bastard's hand and smash it in his face.

"Careful, Sun," he said softly, "that temper of yours might land you in trouble one day. I'm not sure your father would appreciate putting you in the ground, having already lost his wife."

"Go to hell," Kaden growled, lunging across the seat. He landed a solid blow to the senator's heavy jaw, before being wrenched out of the car by his bodyguards.

As he kicked and screamed they tore his comm from his wrist and pushed him to the ground, silencing his shouts with some heavy kicks to his back and sides. Winded once more, he lay there gasping as the rain fell upon his face.

"You've had your warning, Sun. Stay *out* of our business, and we'll stay out of yours."

As a parting gift, one of the large black boots suddenly swung toward his head, snapping his neck back as the toe connected with his cheek. As the pain radiated through his body, he heard rather than saw the limousine pull away. Head pounding, he couldn't help but grin. The senator was clearly desperate. He didn't know that Kaden already planned to leave their dirty little wrestling match. But even if he thought he'd scared him off, Kaden had given him a shiner to remember him by.

The thought made him chuckle, until he dropped his head and let the darkness catch him.

Twenty-Seven

The Li Estate
Los Angeles, California

"**H**e's coming around, thank heaven," Li Lei murmured.

"It's lucky he's young and fit," came a voice that sounded like Doctor Ren, the embassy physician who Kaden often heard reminding Li Lei to take his heart pills. "He should have suffered more than just a broken rib, judging by these bruises."

"Kaden, can you hear me?" Alexis' voice was unusually high, and he wondered how many people were crammed inside the room.

Cracking open an eye, he saw that he was in fact in Li Lei's house, surrounded by red silk walls and expensive artwork. But his vision was cloudy, his second eye opening only slightly, and completely blurred. It shocked him momentarily to think he might have gone blind.

"You're fine, son," the doctor said, as if guessing his fears. "It was a nasty hit, but your cornea is still attached. You'll be seeing spots for a while, though."

His tunneled vision shifted to Alexis' reddened eyes. *Where was Katy?* The girl held his palm, adjusting the blanket higher over his chest with her free hand.

"You're in my guestroom, Kaden," Li Lei confirmed. "I became concerned after hearing of Damon's recent interest in you, and sent a man to watch you. Unfortunately, he got there too late." He paused, face taut with concern. "Did you get a good look at the men who did this?"

Kaden felt slightly surprised by the news Li had ordered to have him followed, but his brain was too hazy to question the news. "Yes. The senator was there in person." The three faces above him wore equal expressions of shock. "They threatened Katy, and my father."

"That is unbelievable!" Alexis hissed, gripping his hand. She swiveled toward her father. "Dad, how can he get away with this?"

Li Lei didn't respond. He ushered Dr. Ren out of the room, whispering as they went. Kaden was still adjusting his vision using his one good eye. He gingerly ran his fingers over the lump where his other eye should have been. The thin membrane of his eyelid pulsed with pain. He imagined how he must look.

Alexis was fussing over him, scooping small chunks of vinegary fish and herbal soup out of a large porcelain bowl and into his mouth. Kaden felt a pang of regret at her worried frown. His right hand crossed over to her arm and gripped it as a gesture of thanks, and apology.

"I called your friend," she said, glancing at him from beneath her lashes. "The name was in your comm. Dad's men found it in the gutter."

Kaden frowned, tilting his face away from the spoon. "You shouldn't have. I don't want people worried over nothing."

"You've been sleeping for a day," Alexis said. "They could be anxious…there are riots everywhere."

"A full day?" Kaden gasped. "Who did you call?"

"I looked in your 'favorites' list. There was one name with a heart next to it." Alexis stared downward. "She must be your… girlfriend?"

"Yes," he answered carefully, knowing what that would mean to Alexis. "I'm glad you didn't call my dad, he would have had a heart attack."

Alexis nodded, her face muted. The atmosphere felt pensive and awkward, their silence broken by the arrival of Butler James. "Miss Li, you have a guest. A friend of Mr. Sun."

She nodded, without looking up. "Send her in, James. Thank you."

A moment later he heard a softly spoken, "Hey you." As the lovely voice floated into the room, Kaden's pain dimmed to a low ache.

"*Hey, you.*" He smiled as Katy knelt at his side, placing a trembling kiss upon his temple. In the corner of his eye he sensed Alexis drop his hand and fold her arms. Kaden swallowed uncomfortably, knowing she was suffering an injury all of her own. He hadn't encouraged her affections at all, but in wanting to spare her feelings he'd avoided talking about Katy. In hindsight, that was a big mistake. Their intimacy shouldn't have come as such a surprise.

"God, you frightened me," Katy whispered. "When I couldn't reach you, I pictured you in a gutter somewhere…" Her voice caught on the words. "Seems my worst fears were correct." She pressed her lips against his cheek, so fiercely he guessed she'd forgotten he was hurt. "I'm never letting you go," she said. "Never ever." Her eyes were swimming, her face caught in the same look of fear and longing she'd worn that first night she spoke about her parents.

"Thank you for taking care of Kaden." Katy tilted her face up. "You must be Alexis."

Alexis' smile was set rigidly on her face. "Please don't thank me. My father and I have failed in our responsibility to protect him."

Kaden lifted his right hand. "Don't say that, Alexis. Those people are bullies, and cowards. That's not your father's fault."

"Still, I think we should stop this project and call it quits. It's not worth it."

"Well, it had better be," came Li Lei's voice as he sailed back into the room. Reaching the bedside, he smiled broadly. "Kaden. We won the bid!"

Twenty-Eight

The Tipsy Orb
Los Angeles, California

"So this is the flagship in the chain?" Li Lei glanced over his shoulder at the crowded joint. "Not bad; at least it's busy."

"Yes, Mr. Li," Kaden shouted over the din. "The Tipsy Orb's a popular club, it's where I met Katy. Your relative has good business sense."

"I'm not much of a businessman myself." Li Lei half smiled, gesturing at his ineptness. "Just a government official trying to make the big boys play nice."

"You're head of International Economic Development for all of China. I'd say you know more about business than most CEOs."

"Bah! All Chinese titles sound big." He waved his hand as if to dismiss the silly words. "Look, Kaden, I have something important to talk to you about, you must know that—"

"Let me guess. The full-time job?" He put his drink down. "As I said, I'm happy to offer some advice now and then, but—"

Now Li Lei cut him off. "You've been key to our success, Kaden. Success that even our leaders in Beijing are taking an interest in."

"And?"

Li snorted. "And you fill the gap, where our Chinese advisors can't. You understand our culture *and* the American way. Our leadership expects big results from me, and it's only now that I'm starting to deliver them."

Kaden took a deep breath and fixed his gaze on the stage. The malnourished pianist was bent over the keys again. It was Katy's day off, and he was looking forward to relaxing with her at his side. He looked at the entrance once more. She was already half an hour late.

"I'm glad to have helped you, Mr. Li." He gave a resigned shrug, "But I promised my dad I'd keep my focus on my studies. He's already given in to me studying the subjects of my choice, and I want to finish my degree."

"That is, if UCLA can survive the disaster befalling your country," Li Lei scoffed. "The world is changing, and the banking crisis is only the beginning. China is a rising dragon; you'll learn a lot more working with us."

"I'm sorry."

Li Lei pulled his jacket lapels and sighed. "Very well. I know you have a deep regard for your father's wishes, like any good son." He retrieved his hat from the table and placed it on his head. "I've got to get back to the consulate. By the way, Alexis asked if you could drop by tomorrow. She's preparing a surprise of some sort, I believe."

Kaden wondered if he should ask Li to make it clear to his daughter that he wasn't interested, then decided against it. If she was going to get the message, it had to come from his lips alone. "I'll go and see her," he said.

He watched the back of Li Lei's head as he wove his way through the pulsing crowd. He looked like someone's old uncle at a wedding, bobbing along to the music and giving the thumbs-up to a young couple grinding to the beat.

Just as Li Lei disappeared out of sight, there was a soft tap on his shoulder.

"Did I miss Mr. Li?"

Kaden turned and took an appreciative glance at Katy's tight blue dress and tussled blond hair.

"I think Mr. Li missed *you*, babe."

She laughed, kissing him on the cheek. He was now almost completely healed, and no longer winced each time she touched him.

"Is he still trying to get you to work for him?" she asked, adjusting his collar. "Make Alexis' dreams come true?"

Kaden rolled his eyes. "What happened to thanking her for nursing me?"

"I guess I'm being unfair," Katy pouted. "After all, I can't blame her for loving you, when I do too."

He flushed at the words. The L word had been used between them already, but it hadn't lost its novelty yet. "You love me so much, you'd try to steal me away from another woman?" he teased.

"Of course," she said. "I'd steal you, right after tearing her eyes out."

Katy made a playful gesture of performing the act, and accidentally struck his left arm. It had taken the brunt of Damon's attack, and he recoiled from the pain. The stitches had recently been removed from a small cut on his forearm, but the skin was still darkened by bruising.

Katy reached out. "I'm sorry. I didn't—"

"No, it's nothing," Kaden said, rubbing the bumped surface.

"Should you see the doctor again?"

"I have, twice now. Dr. Ren had to open up the gash to clean it out, but it's healing."

Katy bent her lips to the small, raised ridge and kissed softly. "All better?"

Pointing to his mouth, Kaden smiled cheekily. "Uh, I think I bit my tongue, too."

The blue, seductive eyes gazed deep into his, and for a moment he forgot to breathe.

"Are you trying to tell me that you need me to kiss your mouth?"

"Hmm," he murmured in vague agreement, staring at her lips.

"And I guess you should get what you want, since it's your birthday tomorrow." Katy leaned closer and Kaden's lips parted in anticipation. Her breath was warm and sweet, the sounds of the nightclub muted against the soft whisper of her words. He must have been breathing somehow; she smelled of lavender and bergamot.

"I have a present for you." Her lips brushed his, only to draw away again.

"What is it?" he groaned, hungry for them to return. The blue eyes flicked up at him, teasing and challenging at once.

"Me."

Twenty-Nine

General Pershing Boulevard
Oklahoma City, Oklahoma

Peter squinted into the last rays of the fading sun. He needed a drink, a strong one. Headed south along the boulevard over the smooth tarmac, a slight incline made the sweat bead at his brow. Alongside the road sat dilapidated houses, painted in a dozen shades of beige. No one was in sight, with the evening curfew about to begin.

Peter's hands gripped the wheels of his chair tightly. The previous night Kaden had revealed that while he wouldn't be working with Li Lei full-time, he planned on continuing to assist the man. Peter had his reservations. Anyone who openly declared their hunger to succeed via all means necessary had to be viewed as a liability. His son was naïve if he thought he could dance with the devil and step off the floor the moment it suited him.

Peter sighed, glancing up at the clouds and wondering if his wife was shaking her head. Maybe he needed to let Kaden decide his own path, even if that meant learning the hard way. And perhaps he needed to admit to himself that the idea of Kaden earning in one week what he had once earned in a month was slightly humiliating. Especially now that the government had cut his pension dues and left him feeling like a penniless old man.

Peter powered his wheelchair toward his gate only a few houses away. In the distance, two beaten-up vehicles motored toward him.

He steered his wheelchair onto to the road shoulder, leaving ample room to pass. As the lead car drew nearer, Peter could see a scarred man with an empty eye socket in the front passenger seat. The man's ratty hair fell from the top of his head like a dirty old mop, and Peter watched in increasing alarm as he leaned out of his window waving a machete around, like some kind of madman.

Peter pushed his chair further off the road, the wheels bumping as they hit rocks and broken glass. He glared at the hooligan, now only a stone's throw away, as he swerved even closer.

The man leaned out his window, a heavy sawblade knife held tightly in his fist, and Peter's annoyance crystallized into fear. It wasn't a bluff, but an attack.

The last thing Peter saw was a thick silver bracelet hanging from the meaty wrist. The blade flashed, and the world crashed around him. Through the blinding pain and then eerie darkness that followed two lone figures stood, waiting to catch him as he fell: his wife and his son.

To have them together.

At last.

Thirty

Blue River, Oklahoma

Kaden stood at the river pier, shoulders drooping. Flanked by Katy and his best friends, he'd never felt so alone. This was the place his dad had brought him to learn to fly-fish, and where he'd grumbled about the cold, the boredom, and the fact that his warm couch and Xbox were waiting at home.

At the intersection a few feet away, the smooth, calm waters cascaded down a small rapid. The resultant foams floated aimlessly near the small party of mourners. It was drizzling, the droplets of rain creating small rings on the surface of the river. The dark, distant sky lit with flashes of lightning.

Kaden gazed at the clearing behind a clump of trees and remembered his father singing a mix of Cantonese and Western country songs. The combination seemed bizarre to him now. A bright blue dragonfly landed on his shoulder, as if to welcome an old friend who had returned.

When Fire Chief Sutton had called him a few days earlier, he'd rushed home in a state of confused disbelief. A hero's funeral had been packed to the rafters by firefighters and friends.

Eulogies were given, and the hurtful words from their last phone call swirled around Kaden's head as better men expounded Peter's virtues.

He took the urn from Katy and uncapped the cover. The reassuring squeeze of Zac's hand upon his shoulder helped him find the words he wished he'd said that night.

"I love you, Dad." Tears mingled with the rain on his cheeks as white ash slipped through the open vessel and disappeared into the running current.

"You're with Mom now, where you belong." Kaden's voice cracked, his hands threatening to drop the urn. "And you'll see. I'll be the man you dreamt I'd be. I promise."

To his shame, Kaden dropped to his knees, unable to mask the full weight of his grief. Katy wrapped her arms around him, absorbing his sobs into her chest.

When the emotion had abated enough for him to release her, he bowed toward the ground three times, as was the Chinese custom.

"You will be avenged, Dad, or I'll die trying. I promise you that."

Thirty-One

The Consulate General of the People's Republic of China
Los Angeles, California

"I'm deeply sorry for your loss, Kaden."

He nodded. "I appreciate that, Mr. Li. Thank you for seeing me without an appointment."

"Whatever I can do, let me know," Li said, hands outstretched. "All my resources are yours."

"I'm glad to hear it," Kaden answered, glancing down. "Because I need your help."

He sensed him pause and looked up to see the man staring at him intently. "Of course. What do you need?"

Kaden stood unflinching before his mentor. "What do you think? Revenge."

The room fell silent. Eventually, Li put his hands in his pockets and stood up, pacing behind his table as he contemplated. Kaden's eyes followed him, waiting for his answer.

"This is a grave matter. Do you know how powerful the senator is?"

"That's why I came to you." Kaden leaned in. "I've tried talking to the state police, but they won't listen to me. They almost locked me up for perjury."

Li Lei nodded. "I empathize. We've got officials in China not unlike your corrupt congressmen. Senator Damon has strong links throughout the police and legal system. It would be difficult to incriminate him."

Kaden glanced down at his white knuckles, slowly relaxing them. "I'll do anything. He was only an old man..." His voice caught and he blinked quickly. "He was in a goddamn *wheelchair*. I mean, who could hurt someone so..." The words became choked and he was forced to stop.

Li Lei sighed and shook his head. "I'm only a foreigner in this land. I do feel for your loss, but..."

"Please." Kaden would have fallen to his knees if he had to. "You're the only one I know who can help."

Li Lei slumped into his cavernous chair, hands clasped under his chin. After what seemed an eternity, he said, "I may be able to help, but I have one request."

"What?"

"That you do what I have been urging you to all along. Join us."

Kaden shook his head, looking down at his hands.

"The senator may be sending hitmen after you, too. You need my protection."

"Let them come. I'll deal with every one of them."

"Don't be a fool, Kaden."

He glanced up at the sharp tone, and found two black eyes boring into him.

"I won't rest until I find justice," Kaden muttered, pulling a thick silver bracelet from his pocket and tossing it on the table.

"And this is?" He looked down at the trinket distastefully.

"This is what was found beside my dad. They gave it to me thinking it was his, but it wasn't."

Li Lei inspected the bracelet before returning it to Kaden. "Look, if I help you there will be political consequences. Can you handle the fallout?"

Kaden needed no second thought. "Yes."

Li Lei smiled. "And your studies?"

"Retribution is my focus now."

"Very well." Li Lei bowed his head in agreement. "I will make some calls, and in the meantime I want you to expand your mind with new things. In fact, there's a confidential undertaking that requires immediate attention. It will serve both our agendas."

"What is it?"

Li Lei stood from his great chair and, like an old Chinese schoolmaster, placed his hands behind his back. "We have been collecting data about your corrupt congressmen and federal officials," he said, walking to the windows. "Senator Damon and his clique included."

"What for?"

Li Lei gave a disarming shake of his index finger. "Not the way you might think. You see, your country is bankrupt, but of course your government will deny this for as long as possible.

In fact, they've hidden information from the public to protect themselves from the blame game that must come."

"And?"

Li Lei moved to an ancient redwood table at the far end of the room and gestured for Kaden to join him. There was an array of small, Chinese teapots formed of unglazed terracotta.

"Let's have some tea," Li Lei suggested, gesturing to a set of jade cups.

With deft hands, he took a large kettle of boiling tea and poured into the cups.

The water was a very pale green. Kaden clamped his fingers around the moss-colored cup and prepared to drink.

"No, no. It's not ready yet," Li Lei advised. "That was the first pour, to season the cups." He cast off the initial tea into a bowl, and then refilled. This time, he invited Kaden to drink. It was light, and bitter.

"It's in our interest to destroy corrupt officials like Damon, to protect our investments. If their powers aren't legal and democratic, it won't be long before our assets start being unfairly affected."

Kaden took in his solemn face, the thin mouth set in its grim line. "So what's your plan?"

"We need your help to prepare a groundswell of public opinion against Senator Damon and his lackeys, so that they can be removed from their positions of power and brought to justice." He removed his glasses, cleaning them quickly. "We have the evidence to support our case. We only need a strong voice to lead the charge."

Kaden took another sip from the jade piece. The flavor, the bitterness, was starting to suit him. "If you help me bring the senator to justice for what he did to my father, I won't just give you a groundswell, but a witch hunt."

Thirty-Two

The Tipsy Orb
Los Angeles, California

"You guys in with me on this?" Kaden yelled over the music.

Chet scratched his head, taking another bite of the cream doughnut he'd smuggled inside. "I don't know, man. Seems highly political."

Kaden turned his attention on Zac, drumming his fingers on the tabletop as he awaited his response.

"Er, is it against the law, or anything?"

Kaden puffed his cheeks out in exasperation. He had just spent the last half hour detailing his new project, and this was the best response they could muster?

"I know how you feel about the senator," Zac added quickly, "and I'd be the first to support you…"

"But?"

"Slandering these guys sounds pretty hardcore, man, and for the Chinese to sponsor it all…" Zac shook his head, Chet nodding in reluctant agreement.

Kaden wasn't in the mood to listen to their objections. The senator had killed his father, and the debt would be repaid.

"Listen guys," he said, snatching Chet's doughnut from him and holding it hostage.

"Hey!"

"The Chinese may be funding us, but Li Lei didn't seek me out on this. I asked *him* for help. We're rooting out crooks here, and the bastards need to pay for their crimes."

"We get the message, dude." Chet put his hands up. "But I had to line up twenty minutes for that doughnut."

"Are you guys with me, or not?"

Chet nodded, and was soon back to devouring his treat. Zac didn't look so sure, but he gulped the rest of his beer and patted Kaden's shoulder. "I'm with you brother, always. But for your sake, keep your wits about you. Ever since you've known Li, trouble's come sniffing." He got up and slung on his jacket. "And where there's a stink, there's usually something rotten."

Chet brushed the sugar from his fingers. "Thank God for foreign funding, it's the only reason UCLA's lab is still open. Though Zac's right, something feels off about all this." He smiled at Kaden's frown. "Just let me know what you need, when you need it."

As Kaden watched his friends head for the exit he gripped his beer, finishing it in a long gulp. Li was the one person who gave him hope for the future of their country. *How could Zac and Chet get it so wrong?*

People were always pointing the finger at anything foreign and unknown, and they could never accept that someone wealthy might have achieved what they had through fair means. It was envy, nothing more.

"Hello, boyfriend."

Katy had walked right up to him, without him even noticing. "Girlfriend."

She smiled and pulled him toward her, her warm, soft body pressed snugly against his. Raising her hand, she brushed his hair back with her fingers. "You look so troubled, you'd miss the sky falling. What's wrong?"

Kaden shrugged. "Nothing. Just disappointed, is all."

"Disappointed?"

He rubbed at his eyes. "Zac and Chet just don't get it."

"Is this about the senator thing Li Lei wants you guys to work on?"

"No," he said, a little roughly. "The senator was my idea, not his. We just happen to be drawn to the same target. I am the one in control, using him to help me avenge my father."

Katy gave a pained smile. "I know you're itching for justice, but you really have to think this through. I'm sure your dad would want you to be happy, not anxious all the time."

"Don't tell me what my dad would have wanted," he said. "You barely knew the man." She looked away, and Kaden knew he'd spoken too quickly. "I failed him," he added, chest tightening. "And it's chewing me up inside."

"Oh, honey. Please don't let it consume you."

Kaden glared at her. "How can I not? Your father died, but he wasn't murdered. He wasn't decapitated in a goddamn wheelchair." He pulled away from her, seething. "Don't try to pretend you have any idea what I'm going through."

Judging from her expression he'd crossed a line, and the fear of losing her suddenly overwhelmed him. He brought his hand to her elbow and tried to pull her trembling body back. "I'm sorry, Katy…please."

It was easy to forget that the past weeks had been hard on her, too. But the guilt that had formed in the deepest parts of his heart had developed into something far more powerful, a demon that toyed with his emotions at will. Every night he'd been plagued with nightmares, each bad dream leading to another, and each seeming longer than the last…

"Oooh, the man of the hour!" a grating voice rang out behind him. Kaden turned to see Jeffrey Zhang and his group of followers, their eyes locked upon Katy.

Wonderful.

"What do you want, Jeffrey?"

"Nothing more than to say hi to my new colleague."

Suddenly, Katy was nestled back at his side. "Isn't that the douche that beat you up?" she hissed.

Jeffrey walked up to them, too close for Kaden to respond.

"Alexis, and a sweet little blonde on the side, too? Some men have all the luck." His friends chuckled obediently. "We Chinese have a saying for that. 'Two pretty flowers growing in cow dung.' Poetic, right?"

"I think you'd better leave." Kaden's fists were clenched, but he had no intention of getting into a fight with Katy standing there.

Jeffrey's mouth dropped open in mock surprise. "Are you asking me to vacate my own property?" The two thugs on either side of him edged forward, but he stilled them with a lift of his hand. "Few men insult me like that and walk away."

Kaden swallowed as the creep's eyes slipped up Katy's body. "Though I can think of one way you could make it up to me."

Jeffrey leaned forward, brushing a lock of hair behind her ear. She flinched away. "Touch me again and you're the one who won't be walking away," she whispered.

Kaden looked at her, shocked by the edge in her voice. As the thugs started laughing, Jeffrey's face grew murderous.

"I'll touch what I like, when I like," he spat, grabbing her.

Without thinking, Kaden jabbed him in the stomach, pushing him into the arms of his bodyguards. As Jeffrey gasped for breath the bodyguards cornered Kaden, who raised his fists in defense.

The retaliation was sure to be fast and brutal, but before the first blow could fall a shout was heard in Mandarin. The brutes paused just long enough for two Chinese men in suits to move between Kaden and his attackers. Kaden blinked, recognition starting to dawn.

"What are you doing here?" he asked the pair, having not seen them since they'd stopped him in the hall at college.

They ignored him, wrenching Jeffrey to his feet as the bodyguards stepped back, heads bowed.

The suited men spoke to Jeffrey in hushed tones. He listened to them, panting and expressionless, but as they finally pulled away Kaden caught a look of hatred so vicious it made him instinctively reach for Katy.

Without a word, Jeffrey stalked away, his pack of dogs following. The two suited men disappeared into the crowd without so much as a backward glance.

"You all right, babe?"

Katy was standing there staring ahead, her eyes glazed over. She slowly nodded. "Where did you learn to punch like that?" she asked, her voice as soft as a child's.

Kaden sighed. "Li's got me training under a martial arts grandmaster. For my own protection."

She shook her head. "Can't you see, Kaden? Before you met the man, you didn't need protection." Her voice rose. "Is this the life you want? Thugs and criminals and strange men in suits who appear and—"

"Katy, please." He grabbed her arms, trying to quiet her, but she pulled away from him.

"Don't shush me! What kind of people are you working with? That weasel called you his colleague!"

Kaden ran a frustrated hand through his hair. "I'm working for a man who supports me and what I care about, which is a damn sight more than you or my friends manage."

As the music pounded around them, she slowly shook her head. "I love you, Kaden Sun," she said. "But I'm not sure I love the man you're becoming."

"Yeah?" he said with a laugh. "Maybe that's who I was all along and you just didn't want to see it."

She shook her head and started to say something, but he brushed past her and kept walking, the heavy base thumping through his bones.

Thirty-Three

IMF (International Monetary Fund)
Washington, D.C.

Christian Begnaud waited patiently as the chairwoman of the US Federal Reserve completed her holo-message. He was aware of the implications of the conversation and had expected the call, thanks to an early tip-off from his longtime associate and friend, Luka Lermontov. He could barely keep himself from laughing in her face.

The chairwoman's dialogue was polite, which in itself was unusual. Most correspondence with the US Fed tended to be instructive, rather than solicitous.

"…and a substantial loan needs to be provided, or guaranteed by the IMF, to help tide over the United States' cash-flow deficit. Without a short-term loan, we can't service our debts. I don't need to outline the global chaos that would result in."

As CEO of the International Monetary Fund, Begnaud expressed his eagerness to help. After all, he was a politician as much as diplomat and knew his role only too well.

"How much are you suggesting, Chairwoman Gale?"

She seemed to take a deep breath before stating, "Initially, five hundred billion cash, supported with two trillion in guarantees."

Begnaud hid his smirk. For years, he had seen the United States using the IMF to further its strategic causes. Financing desperate governments to control political outcomes was one of their preferred methodologies. But this time, the US of A. found itself on the wrong end of the stick.

"Chairwoman, you *do* understand that the IMF's resources are limited." She nodded at him solemnly. "Even with the combination of the SDR, NAB, and the GAB, your request exceeds our ability to commit. Given the unprecedented scale of the current situation, and Europe also seeking assistance...I'll do my best. But"—he lifted his hands helplessly—"it all comes down to the Board."

Begnaud glanced at the giant Labyrinth Aquarium, recently presented to him by the head of China's International Economic Development. He had a dinner appointment with Mr. Li Lei that very night. The man was always meticulous in his selection of restaurants and, of course, excellent wines, Begnaud thought with relish.

"Thank you, Christian. We do appreciate your cooperation. I'll be in touch again tomorrow."

Begnaud smiled as he pushed the 'off' button, musing at Lermontov's spot-on prediction. Of course, the Russian trillionaire's forecasts had grown more accurate since joining the US Administration's Committee for Economic Restoration. No Western leader had the foresight and genius of the man who, he knew, was already controlling a sixth of the world's financial system. The politicians were always one step behind.

It was easy to spot the ultimate victor. It wouldn't be the Chinese or the Russians. Siding with the big players would only reap rewards in public office, but the smart money was on Lermontov Corporation. The coming war for supremacy would make a lot of men rich, and few of them would be in government.

One thing was sure, the Western states were nearing their final days. They no longer had influence, much less control, over the IMF and the UN. Begnaud had no intention of falling with them.

He would go through the motions and submit a report to the US Fed chairwoman as promised—it was impossible for the IMF to provide the full financial backing Gale had requested, as the report would conclude. Gale would be disappointed, but hardly surprised. However, the chairwoman would get a shock to learn that, without board consensus, the US would only receive a pittance of the support needed. A lifeline might be extended should Washington agreed to a host of austerity demands, as Lermontov had intimated to him. This included the significant reduction in military funding, at a time when the country was descending into civil war.

Wars are expensive, Begnaud mused. America's coffers had officially run dry.

Thirty-Four

Kaden Sun & Associates
Los Angeles, California

Kaden sat in his office chair and rubbed his eyes. Four months had passed since he'd left school to join Li Lei and front a PR firm that operated outside the Chinese Consulate.

He looked out of his glass-flanked room into the large, open-spaced office filled with workstations. Each was occupied by a member of his staff, busy with tasks that were both legitimate and created. The money from Li Lei's projects sponsored some of them to do little more than sit and compile research on key political figures. It beat being out on the streets begging. He surveyed his domain and, for a moment, it reminded him of sitting in the WarGames' crystal tower, though these soldiers were waging an entirely different kind of battle.

His assistant, Cindy Goodman, knocked lightly on his door with his afternoon coffee in hand.

"You look worn out." She glanced at the black leather sofa in the corner of his office. "Did you sleep here again last night?"

He did his best to stifle a yawn. "Was up 'til dawn on the Richter Project." He met her look of concern with a wry smile. "Doesn't matter. These days I don't sleep well, anyway."

"I heard there was another successful revision of the Foreign Ownership Act." She placed the mug on his desk. "Surely Mr. Li couldn't ask for more."

Kaden picked up the beverage and breathed in the heady brew. He needed a pick-me-up, and was glad she'd made it strong. "Someone's got to pay the bills."

"The staff are grateful to you, boss. We all know you only need a fraction of us here." Cindy gave him a tight smile. "Well now, I'd better get moving before the curfew starts."

Kaden sat up. Had the whole day passed so quickly? "Uh, before you leave, could you let Zac and Chet know I won't be able to meet them after all? And also Katy. Tell her I'll be home late. I've got a meeting with an important associate of Mr. Li's."

Cindy nodded, and he watched the staff file out as the sun dipped behind the buildings. The last to leave was an accountant named Mary Linden. Just a fortnight ago he'd met her while strolling back from yet another grueling meeting.

It had been late and he'd been looking out for gangs when he walked upon dozens of corrugated boxes piled outside a decrepit building. More were being hurled through the open door as Mary pleaded to a short, angry woman not to evict her. A crying baby was gripped in her arms and a toddler tugged at the hem of her dress.

Before he'd known what he was doing, Kaden had walked up to the women and demanded to know what was wrong. From that moment on, Mary's problems had become his own.

Kaden returned to his file and scanned through Li Lei's assignments. These involved lobbying for policies and regulations, supporting select politicians, and his favorite, exposing and destroying corrupt officials.

He swiped his index finger across the 3D image on his desktop, glancing at a photo of Li Lei shaking his hand and grinning after the dismissal of a law that prohibited the foreign purchase of local telecommunications networks. Before Kaden had become focused on expanding his staff, he'd gone and blown the windfall on a swanky new house and two-door Mercedes. With prices in the current market at an all-time low, even drug dealers and pimps were suddenly able to afford Maseratis and three-level penthouses.

A message blipped in his virtual pop-up box from Zac. *We're at Orb's. Ditch the meeting and come on over.*

The missive hit him with a twinge of guilt as he rested his chin on his knuckles. He hadn't seen his best friend in weeks, and today would be no different. Another last-minute arrangement, another business commitment too important to miss.

Kaden sighed and flipped through images of recently jailed congressmen in an effort to improve his mood. Draken, Hayes, Walker…all of them Senator Damon's corrupt associates. He hadn't landed the big fish yet, but he would.

The judicial process was quick. As America slid into its worst social and economic depression of all time, the media and courts had grown eager to throw stones. Kaden was only too happy to help, providing evidence and testimonials that were unofficially sponsored by Li Lei. Some of the crims had been sentenced in under two weeks—a new record for the American judicial system.

Kaden frowned at the picture of his father beside his desk. His pulse quickened at the sight of the fireman's uniform and Peter's face alight with a cheery smile. Katy had been right, though he hated to admit it. His fixation with loss and revenge had engulfed him, haunted him, and at times twisted his words and decisions. The nightmares were getting worse every day.

Kaden started at the sound of his calendar alarm. *6.30 p.m., time to get moving.* As he waved his wrist over the desk, the comm system authenticated the electrical impulse of his heartbeat and logged out. Kaden gulped the still-hot remains of his coffee and grabbed his jacket.

He couldn't help feeling nervous. Tonight he was meeting Li Lei's anonymous mentor. The man had to be quite something; Li Lei himself was no small fry. Everyone, including the chief of the Chinese Consulate, bowed with respect when encountering Kaden's boss.

He locked the office doors and activated his wireless key. The sleek, mercurial Mercedes F029 started its engine and auto-drove from the car park to the pavement, its gullwing open on the pavement side. He climbed in. "Destination, Diamond Nightclub." The door closed.

A small knot had formed in his stomach, perhaps from the suspense of it all, or the questionable egg sandwich he'd had for lunch. It didn't matter. Kaden felt sick, tired, and restless to get home. He could only hope that meeting Li Lei's mentor would leave him feeling better, not worse.

Thirty-Five

Diamond Nightclub
Los Angeles, California

The F029 purred to a stop outside the door to the club. The curfew was in place for all but those bearing a special red pass, and late-night reveries were more popular than ever. If there was one thing the rich and powerful loved, it was the liberties they held over the average Joe. A young valet came up, an involuntary wrinkle of the nose seeming to question how a twenty-something-year-old might afford such a nice ride.

It didn't bother Kaden, who flicked him the keys and strode into familiar territory. He took the first steps before noticing Li Lei's limousine pulling to a stop, and decided to wait for him. As he paused, his comm flashed up an image of two naked butts with a text that read: *Get your Tipsy Orb down here!* Smirking, he clicked the image closed as Li Lei appeared before him.

"Kaden, my boy…" The smaller man patted him on the arm. "I heard the good news. Another discriminatory law overturned."

Kaden shrugged off his congratulations. "America needs funding, desperately," he said.

"And that's the very reason you're here tonight."

"Ah, the mysterious mentor," Kaden said with a smile.

"Mysterious perhaps...brilliant, certainly." He peered up at Kaden earnestly. "I trust you, young man. Which is why I think you're ready to enter the inner circle."

Kaden felt he was already pretty deeply embedded, and wondered what new revelations might be made. Catching the confusion on his face, Li Lei added, "I admire your loyalty and patriotism, Sun. But sometimes the best way to save something is to let it go." Confounded, Kaden tried to clarify his meaning, but Li Lei silenced him with a hand on his shoulder. "An open mind Kaden, that's all I ask."

The pair passed through the heavy security at the entrance and walked toward the back of the club, where the private rooms were found.

A young lady with long pink eyelashes opened a Moroccan studded door to reveal a space filled with plush cushions, thick carpets and so much gold Kaden was left squinting. A gentleman was sitting alone with champagne and cigar in hand, looking at one of the most sophisticated comm devices Kaden had ever seen. With a full head of salt-and-pepper hair and carefully trimmed beard, he had a grandfatherly vibe that reminded Kaden of Li Lei, though there was a coldness to his eye that Kaden's mentor did not have. The corners of the man's mouth ticked up when he caught sight of them.

"Welcome to L.A., Mr. Lermontov. How was your flight from New York?"

Lermontov. Kaden's brain struggled to place the name.

The man shook his head with a sigh. "Not so smooth. I think it's time I changed pilots. But enough of that. Who is this tall, proud man standing before me?"

"Let me introduce you to my American prodigy, Kaden Sun. He's been instrumental to much of our recent success."

Lermontov inspected Kaden with a steely stare, wrapping his bony hand around Kaden's with a light grip. Pointing his cigar at him he said, "We treasure people with talent, Kaden, and loyalty. I'm told you have an abundance of both."

Kaden remained tight-lipped, overcome with a sudden sense of discomfit. He wanted to honor Li Lei by respecting his mentor, but he couldn't help feeling the man before him was hiding something.

"A man of few words," Lermontov laughed. "Perhaps some Glenfiddich will warm you up." He gestured to the bottle of Janet Sheed Roberts Reserve 1955, sitting beside his champagne. "This beauty used to cost an easy fifty thousand pounds, back when the British currency was worth something. These days, that wouldn't even cover a shot of the stuff."

Kaden watched the man pick up the bottle and pour them each a generous glass, recognition slowly dawning. Could it possibly be the elusive Luka Lermontov, owner of the Lermontov Corporation the richest men on earth? Li Lei's mentor was a heavy hitter, after all. Kaden swallowed.

"So, the boy's ready to join the discussion?" he said in his deep accent, flicking his head in Kaden's direction.

"I think of him as my own son," Li Lei announced solemnly. "And I can only hope he thinks of me as a loving father."

Kaden grimaced. The man was a mentor, certainly, but he would only ever have one father. Still, he was certain the words had been said with good intentions.

Lermontov nodded, watching Kaden as he passed him his glass. The gray eyes were always shifting, like a reptile emerging from a cave.

"So, how was the meeting with the governors this morning?" Li Lei asked as they took their seats. "My apologies for not being able to attend. Conference call with the Politbur... ah...the Council." He laughed at his fumbling words. "A force of habit. A change in government requires an overhaul in everything, it seems."

Luka nodded. "Congratulations are due to you, my friend. You have finally purged the old Communist leadership, which took what, seven years?"

"Seven and a half." Li Lei lifted his index finger. "They were naïve to think they could remain a benevolent superpower. Things had to change. To create a New World Order, we needed more flexible ideologies."

New World Order? Kaden glanced at the men before him. *What did that even mean?*

"So, the meeting...?" Li Lei repeated his question.

Luka took a long puff on his cigar and Kaden held his breath as the pungent smoke filled his nostrils. He'd never enjoyed the stench of tobacco and stopped himself from waving at the air before his face. He didn't want to offend, or attract those deadened eyes back to himself.

"The federal government's penniless. The White House wants to force the states to cough up their fiscal reserves and bail out the poorest parts of the nation. They even demanded that the state governors turn over all their gold holdings. It's an age old smash and steal."

"The United *Socialist* States of America," said Li Lei with a smirk. He clasped his hands together and leaned toward Lermontov. "And the governors?"

Lermontov looked at Kaden with a wary glance. "You're impatient today, Li Lei." He took another puff of his cigar, drawing out Li Lei's suspense. "The situation is…promising. Our friends are against Washington's demands and Governor Henderson is publicly stating that most of the states in the West Coast and Northeast have been paying an unfair share of the national tax."

"And what did you tell them?"

Kaden had never seen Li Lei as he was now, hovering on the edge of his seat. It was unsettling, as if a different man had joined them. Why would Li Lei take such pleasure in hearing about the government's cash problems? Even if a crisis led to greater investment opportunities, it seemed uncharacteristically heartless.

"I seized the opportunity and said, 'Friends, who do you owe your allegiance to? Your constituents, or the White House?'" Lermontov paused, staring at them both. Kaden had to glance away, concerned his eyes might betray the fear and anger coursing through him. Then he remembered—hadn't this man been a recent recipient of the United States *Friendship* Award? And here he was sounding as if he wanted to start a civil war!

"I told them, I sit in the Federal Economic Restoration Committee, and the numbers I see..." Lermontov closed his eyes and shook his head. "They understood what I meant," Lermontov continued. "It was uneasy at first, but staying in the union and sacrificing state reserves for the rest of the country is throwing good money after bad, objectively speaking of course."

He puffed on the cigar, leaving his words to settle upon them. "Politicians are stupid," he sighed. "I had to explain to them the basics of corporate restructuring and bankruptcy. You can't allow emotion to dictate such things, you must keep anything that's valuable and cut the dead weight."

A heavy feeling was building in Kaden's stomach. Lermontov's ideas made some sense economically, but socially and ethically? They could only result in the destruction of the nation as they knew it.

"So," Li Lei prompted. "Are they open to declaring independence from Washington?"

Kaden looked at his mentor in surprise. What madness was this?

"I told them that with the coalition of newly formed states, they'd be in a position to form their own military and economic bloc. Their combined entity would make them the fourth-largest economy in the world, gaining them acceptance from the global community. As we agreed, China, Russia, and our many allies would recognize them, and our banks would provide immediate credit facilities. A phoenix rising from the ashes of the United States."

As the two men continued their excited conversation, Kaden tried to find his breath and calm himself. Clearly, Lermontov was mad, or power-crazed, or both. They were chatting about dismantling one of the greatest countries on earth in the same way two buddies might discuss a weekend poker game. Kaden refused to believe Li Lei could ever truly support such an idea; he had clearly been swayed by his mentor. Alone together, Kaden would make Li Lei recognize the Russian's insanity for what it was. In the meantime, all he could so was maintain an impassive expression and listen closely.

"So they're in?" Li Lei ventured.

Lermontov waved his hand in dismissal. "Of course. I plucked each of them from political obscurity years ago and groomed them for this moment; they have no choice but to heed my advice. I even suggested a title for them: The Confederate States of America, or CSA for short." He winked at his friend. "Cute, yes?"

Li Lei laughed. "So we have the whole West and Northeast coasts?" He turned to Kaden, as if suddenly remembering he was in the room. "Those are key to our success."

"Why?" Kaden heard himself croak.

"I'll explain later," Li Lei said, watching him carefully. "Go on, Luka."

"California, New York, New Jersey, Washington, Massachusetts, Connecticut..." he briefly closed his eyes in concentration, "and Oregon, Delaware, Maryland, and Hawaii are all on board. The rest are mulling. And Texas, of course. They'd secede even without our prompting."

"Excellent, excellent." Li Lei rubbed his hands. "Time for phase three of the operation."

Kaden's mind reeled as he sat in dumb silence. What the hell had the first two phases been? With creeping dread he began to wonder just how much of his own efforts and time had gone toward furthering this terrible plot.

"Yes." Lermontov stroked his index finger below his lower lip. "The governors' support is not enough. The states will have to go through referendums. It's imperative we secure public opinion through the media, isn't that correct, Kaden?"

Public opinion. Kaden stared at the two men eyeballing him. The most powerful tool in a democracy, and they were using it to their advantage.

Li Lei filled the silence. "Legitimacy, that's what we seek. With it, the states that seek to secede will have the support of the international community. China and Russia will back them to the hilt."

Li Lei placed his hand on Kaden's, still resting beside his untouched drink. "With this guy on the case, 'a true blue American,' the people will be screaming for secession in weeks."

Bowing under the pressure of their attention, Kaden smiled. *Jesus Christ.*

Thirty-Six

The Li Estate
Los Angeles, California

Li Lei was perched on his embroidered sofa, wearing a charcoal single-breasted jacket and cream waistcoat. He adjusted the napkin on his lap as the android served them tea.

"Thank you, James," he said, fingers pinching the dainty handle of the china. Kaden sat beside him, waiting for his answer. "I wasn't expecting you for another hour."

"I couldn't sleep, and we have a lot to discuss." Kaden's suit felt too tight, and the room too warm.

Li Lei shook his head and chuckled. "That's the trouble with youth; everything must be dealt with yesterday."

"Mr. Li, what is your relationship to Lermontov, and is he seriously supporting a separatist movement?"

"Hold on, Kaden," Li chuckled. "One question at a time for my old, tired brain."

Kaden rankled at the lighthearted tone, but kept his face impassive.

"Luka is my mentor," Li continued. "As I have said before. He found me when I was still at Oxford, a young, wide-eyed innocent abroad. He taught me everything about world economics and politics, and I don't mean the textbook stuff. He opened my eyes to great things."

He groomed you, Kaden thought bitterly. Weren't those the words Lermontov had used the previous evening?

"Why is he pushing for the states to secede? It would be the end of...everything."

Li Lei adjusted his glasses. "Perhaps the system needs to come to its end. Look around you, my boy, it's chaos. And frankly... secession is an American tradition, isn't it?"

Kaden shook his head in disbelief. "And what are your political motivations in all of this?" As Li's face grew taut, he knew he'd crossed a line. The Chinese were very sensitive to subordinates questioning their authority; the conversation was probably over before it had even begun.

Li Lei took a sip of the steaming tea as if the liquid were lukewarm. After an awkward pause, he returned the cup to its saucer. "Kaden, I wasn't lying when I told Mr. Lermontov that I considered you my son."

Kaden lowered his eyes, suddenly struck by the memory of his own father. Peter had questioned Li's motivations from the start, and Kaden had dismissed his warning with the arrogance of a young, brash idiot.

"Ever since the day you walked in here with my wallet, wearing threadbare clothes and dirty shoes...well, your honesty and courage is all I ever hoped for in a son. Though I am fortunate to also find those qualities in my daughter."

Li's face softened as he thought of her and Kaden sat silent, at a loss for words. Since boyhood he'd had to fight tooth and nail to feel that he belonged. *That he was wanted.* Perhaps it was down to poor social skills, or speaking his mind too quickly, but he always seemed to attract the mean kids like flies, or the weak kids, looking for a scapegoat. There had been an overwhelming influx of Chinese into the States, and Kaden couldn't blame young minds for fearing the unknown. But for all his tan skin and dark hair, no one seemed to care that, at heart, he was American.

Kaden took a deep breath. This man offered him a home, support, success. A man of his own ancestry, from a place where his family name was infamous, rather than ridiculed. Could he turn his back on that, for a flag that had taunted him almost his entire life?

"You haven't answered the question," Kaden said softly.

Li Lei sighed. "We have to protect our investments. Trillions of dollars are based in the states we wish to secede. We can't lose everything just because your government made a huge mistake mismanaging the economy."

"But Mr. Li—"

"Kaden, let's focus on what's important. I cancelled my schedule to see you today because I have news about Senator Damon." The name struck Kaden silent, and though he wanted to continue discussing the secession, he found himself leaning forward.

"Luka and I spoke about him last night, after you left. I want you to know that he said to me he would deal with it."

"Deal with it?" Kaden frowned. "How?"

"Young man, we Chinese do not question our seniors. Senator Damon has been a growing thorn in our side, and we haven't been able to stop him via conventional methods. Mr. Lermontov is going to personally see that he's plucked out."

"This is my fight," Kaden said, louder than he'd intended.

Li Lei gave him a long, cool look, before pushing his breakfast tray away and removing the silk napkin from his lap. "I think our discussion is done for the day. I've got to prepare for a function."

Kaden sat fuming as Li Lei walked to the door, James whirring behind him with hat and briefcase in hand.

Vengeance was his to have; Kaden had been working too hard to simply hand his satisfaction to Lermontov on a platter. He leaned back into the couch, head tipped back on to the thickly worked fabric.

"Kaden?"

"Oh, hi, Alexis." He gave a half wave as she walked into the living room dressed in her tennis attire.

"What's wrong?"

"Nothing, it's just that—" He paused as an idea came to mind. "Tell me, what do you know about Lermontov?"

"Uncle Luka?" She looked at him in surprise. "Where do you want me to start? He's been a close friend of Father's my whole life."

Kaden nodded. "You need to help me."

"How?"

As she sat beside him he took hold of her hands and looked into her eyes. She was staring at him intently, thrilled to finally be given an opportunity to please him. He felt a pang of guilt; it was wrong of him to exploit her feelings and pull her into the mess. But he needed to know. "I have a research project for you."

Thirty-Seven

Grand Hope Park
Los Angeles, California

The park was dark and silent, only the soft shuffle of the resident homeless to keep him company. Kaden had been sitting there since midnight and so far, there had been no activity near the meeting point. They must have known the place well—few spots remained that offered any privacy now that the destitute had overtaken the parklands in the hundreds.

Alexis had gone way beyond the call of friendship to give him the information he needed, just as he knew she would. Not only had he learned that a meeting had been arranged between Luka and the senator, but she had helped him discover the time and venue as well. She must have hacked into her father's comm somehow, a last resort Alexis would have hated. He ran his fingers over the data stick in his pocket. It contained the entire communications log from Li Lei's phone messages and email. Li would blow his top if he ever found out.

She had handed him the drive less than an hour ago, when Li had finally retired to his bedroom. There had barely been enough time for Kaden to locate the information and scramble over in his Merc. Then again, Luka's voice message was days old and could have become outdated. The suggested meeting time had come and gone, and there was still no sign of them.

Then he heard it, softly, slowly, the light sound of shoes stepping through wet grass. Kaden squatted behind the bushes, hoping they'd choose to sit on the bench directly before him. The observation area was within a small clearing, and his hiding place was perfect.

As he waited, listening, another set of footsteps became apparent, followed by the soft creak of timber as the two men took their seats. Through the leaves, Kaden could see another two men standing at a polite distance.

"I thought Lermontov—or at the very least Borovsky—would be here," the heavyset man in the dark suit grumbled. The voice was familiar. The same self-entitled, Southern drawl he'd heard in the limousine that day.

The second man was almost bald on one side, with a shocking bunch of hair erupting from the other. Even in the weak light of a half moon and heavy clouds, Kaden could see the deep scar running down the length of his profile.

The man took out a pack of cigarettes and lit one, seeming to ignore the senator's complaint. As he blew a puff of smoke in his face, Kaden sensed the senator's anger.

"Lermontov doesn't need to be here to tell you that you're becoming an obstacle. One he doesn't appreciate."

"Political opponents are usually obstacles," the senator spat. "It's called a democracy." The man stood, stamping his feet against the cold. "You can tell Lermontov I'll be glad to kick his ass out of the country if he ever wastes my time like this again. And if he wants me out of the senate, he can—"

Kaden peered through the foliage, confused by the dull thump that was quickly followed by gurgling. His skin crawled as he watched the senator slump down onto the bench, then another sound become apparent: the slow slide of wet steel entering flesh, quiet but unmistakable. Kaden ducked lower, listening to the heavy thud of footsteps of the senator's bodyguards racing across the grass, shouting for the murderer to stop.

Unable to bear not knowing, Kaden risked lifting his face once more. Before him stood the senator's men, guns drawn and faces stretched into grimaces of horror.

"Get away from him!" one screamed, as Scarface bent over the body.

The man held his blade to the senator's throat. "Drop the guns. Now!"

They glanced at each other in indecision, before reluctantly tossing their weapons at his feet. What came next would continue to haunt Kaden for months.

The guy could have picked up one of their guns, but instead he went after them with his knife, but not before opening up the senator's throat with a flick of his wrist. Kaden winced as the first bodyguard went to strike, the man's pointed, sawblade knife flashing from his side. It looked like a tactical ops machete Kaden had seen once in an Army magazine, but this one was blackened by blood.

The clouds that had hidden the moon cleared suddenly, and the grisly scene grew brighter by the second. Again came the wet, slick sound of a blade cutting flesh, followed by groans of agony as the bodyguards fell in quick succession. Kaden's jaw dropped; they hadn't even landed a punch.

Caught in indecision, part of him leapt at the chance to run to their aid even though they were the same muscle men who'd attacked him so unjustly. The other, louder, voice in his head screamed at him to run. He backed away from the scene as one of the men stumbled to his knees before him, his hands grasping at the intestines that spilled from his half-split belly.

Crack.

Kaden froze, his heel half lowered upon the only dead branch in the whole damn place.

Shit.

He watched as the killer paused and turned in his direction. He had to get out there, fast, or be executed on the spot.

Scarface moved in rapid steps toward him, silently stepping over a body with the cool, calm focus of a professional.

Kaden turned and ran.

As his feet pounded across the grass, he knew he stood no chance fighting the guy one-on-one. A race on foot was his only hope. Branches whipped his face as he leaped past trees and bushes, his ragged breath and thumping heart too loud to hear the footsteps behind him.

Not far now, he thought, as he sighted the gleam of his blood red F029 in the distance. *Come on Kaden.*

The car was parked under a steep slope and Kaden slipped his trembling fingers into the pocket of his hoodie, feeling for the key. Finding it, he wrenched it out and pointed it at the car, the data stick leaving his pocket at the same time. He sensed it fall somewhere behind him and swore at the loss, but he wasn't ready to die for it. Instead, he focused on pressing the car button, and screamed as the whistle-shaped control shot straight out of his sweaty fingers.

He slid to a halt and dropped to his knees, searching for the key and lamenting the fact he'd been too busy to set up the vehicle's voice-activation locks. As his eyes swept the gravel, the crunch of footsteps stopped him cold.

He looked up to see the silhouette of the scarfaced killer, sprinting toward him with his knife raised high, just as his fingers brushed atop the smooth surface of the key.

Kaden picked himself up and ran.

Thirty-Eight

Kaden had made it less than ten steps down the slope when he found that he'd left the earth altogether and was now flying toward his car. Landing awkwardly at the foot of the hill, his mouth became filled with grit and his lips felt slick with the salty tang of blood. He spit out the dirt and grunted at the effort as he heaved himself up. The car was only yards away, but even as he scrambled over the sharp, loose rocks, he knew it was too late.

A hand grabbed Kaden's belt and yanked him backward with gorilla-like force. Before he could get to his feet a fist slammed into his side, and he twisted away from the pain, but to no avail. Raw heat throbbed through his body, his lungs frantic for oxygen. Then another sharp blow in the same spot. He crumpled.

Fight or flight? As Kaden crawled on his hands and knees he knew there wasn't a chance of striving for the latter. He would fight for his life, or die. Adrenaline surged through his system, the screams of the two murdered agents still loose inside his head.

He scrambled to his feet and the killer whipped his fist at Kaden's chin, making a small huff of annoyance as Kaden ducked out of the shot. Taking advantage of the pause, Kaden straightened, landing a combination of short jabs his fighting master had taught him. Scarface stepped back and blinked, as if rapidly reassessing his opponent. Kaden was able to right himself and, for the first time, meet his attacker face-to-face.

It wasn't a pretty sight.

The assassin's black eye patch had come undone, revealing the empty socket beneath. The deep shadows from the bright moon made his appearance all the more chilling—angry scars bleeding across his cheek and forehead, tight and raw like badly healed burns. Only a small patch of hair grew on the right side of his head. He wore army fatigues, and in his belt jutted the handle of a long machete. The vision was depraved...like some undead soldier who'd crawled from the trenches of a zombie movie.

"That wasn't too bad." His voice was that of a smoker's, deep and gravelly. "Fast, accurate, and furious. A little raw, though. Where'd a kid like you learn to fight like that?"

Kaden swallowed, fists raised before him. "Why did you kill the senator?"

"Just doing my job," he answered slowly, grinning. "I'm just a disgruntled ex-Ranger, eking out a living from my new masters. What more do you need to know?"

He pulled his machete from his belt in a fluid motion, and Kaden knew in that moment he was about to die. He was tired and outmatched. The man before him was too strong, too experienced, and armed. Kaden didn't stand a chance.

Almost without thinking, he ran his fingers across the thick silver bracelet on his wrist. The bump of the jewel-studded skull was little comfort. He would never avenge his father's killer, but he would die knowing he'd done his best.

The killer's gaze darted to his hand, as if expecting Kaden to pull a weapon of his own. But instead of raising his machete, he cocked his head and took a step closer. "You found it."

Kaden stared at him in confusion. "Found what?"

The ugly head gave a small toss of disbelief. "You know what I'm talking about. Why else would you be here?"

Kaden struggled to understand, following his gaze down to the bracelet. "This thing?" He thrust his wrist up, the silver links bright in the moonlight.

The assassin was probably trying to play some kind of mind game. Distract him before he landed the killing blow. When the killer stepped forward Kaden took a step back.

"They call me 'Skull'," came the gravelly voice. "And that there is mine."

Kaden shook his head, trying to deny the truth that was spreading through his mind like a dark virus. *It was impossible.*

His mind went blank, cool shock wrestling against a hot, rising fury.

"You murdered my father," he said, almost refusing to believe the words. "Why?"

The assassin looked at his machete, still mottled from its earlier work. Kaden watched in shock, still refusing to accept that the man standing before him had killed his dad, a defenseless senior in a wheelchair. The last thing Peter Sun had seen was the demented head, and long blade that now flashed before him.

With a war cry, Skull swung the blade down and Kaden somehow dodged it, but there was no contest. Within a few moves, his foe had him on his back and in the dirt. A meaty hand twisted in a vise-like grip over his throat, Skull's foul breath floating across his face as he straddled him.

"I thought you looked familiar, though all you slanty bastards look the same to me."

He squeezed his hand tighter, obviously expecting some kind of struggle. Kaden only stared up at him, tears pooling in his eyes.

"Why…" Kaden coughed, the words catching in his throat. "Why did you…kill him?"

"Because I could," he snarled. "I would have done it, even if there wasn't a price on the old parasite's head."

Kaden felt his body convulse with a sob, Skull lifting the machete blade to his lips as he glided his tongue along the steel. The smell of blood and sweat hung heavy around them, and Kaden wrenched his face away in disgust.

"You should have seen his face." Skull's eye grew wide and white in the darkness. "When that blade came for him, he looked like a turtle who'd lost its shell." Skull's heavy body gyrated as he mimicked the motion of Peter frantically trying to wheel himself away. "I wouldn't be surprised if they found a big, hot pile of shit on that chair when they carted him off."

"Liar!"

Skull continued rocking his hips, lost in his blood lust.

"Oh, I don't lie, boy. I'm the angel of truth."

His body tensed as he lifted the machete high above his head. Refusing to turn away, Kaden kept his eyes on his murderer. Then, as the final blow was about to land, the grotesque silhouette was lit by a bright beam of torchlight.

"Skull!"

The blade twitched, and Skull turned to squint into the glow. "Switch that damn thing off!"

"Yes, boss." The world grew dark once more. "But you can't kill him. He's one of Mr. Li's."

To Kaden's surprise, Skull looked genuinely shocked. "Li?" He shook his head and sheathed his machete with a sigh. "That man is more twisted than a bag of snakes." Kaden felt his body shift as the pig leaned down, bringing their faces together. "Don't worry, boy, we'll have our day."

Before he could open his mouth, Kaden watched the face loom forward in a sudden, brutal collision. The faint sound of laughter was the last thing he heard.

Thirty-Nine

Li Lei's Study
Los Angeles, California

Kaden's chair was positioned alongside Li Lei's desk, his body sprawled in exhaustion. It was just after four in the morning.

"You're lucky my men came in time," Li Lei said sternly. Kaden twitched as Alexis dabbed a damp, stinging piece of cloth against his cheek. Beside them stood the punk, Jeffrey Zhang. Kaden's skin crawled as his shadow hung over him. He'd been silent since Kaden had woken up, but watching Alexis nurse him had made the creep's jaw begin to twitch.

"My father will not allow this problem to fester," he finally hissed. "MSS must take over this case."

Alexis paused in her work. "What? Why would you involve the Secret Service?"

Kaden's interest piqued at mention of the organization, but he kept silent, watching Li Lei as he took out his glasses and wiped the lenses. It was a gesture the man often made in the midst of a crisis, as if cleaning the lenses might somehow clear his mind as well.

Kaden needed answers.

Clearly, Skull knew who Li Lei was, which meant Li Lei had probably heard of Skull. Had his mentor known the identity of his father's murderer all along?

Kaden brushed off Alexis' hands and sat up. "How do you know Skull?"

"Skull?" Li Lei glanced at him and laughed. "Sounds like a pirate."

"He knows you."

Li Lei shrugged. "Many people know me. I am a powerful man."

Kaden tried to breathe deep, frustration threatening to smash through his calm resolve.

"He works for your mentor, and he killed my father."

Li Lei continued cleaning his spectacles in silence.

"Answer me!"

Alexis jumped at the outburst, and Kaden felt a momentary pang of regret that she was involved in the mess. She didn't deserve any of this. Thankfully, Li was yet to discover her role in the night's events, for now.

"Was that a question, or a demand?" Li asked evenly.

"If the senator killed my father, I don't think he would have been killed by his own assassin. Do you?" The next words seemed to leap from his lips with a will of their own. "Was Lermontov behind it?"

Li Lei put his glasses back on. "Look, Sun, you're tired and emotional. Why don't you go and rest? We have an important public referendum on the secession tomorrow. I'll need your help."

"I want answers, now!"

Jeffrey's face flushed a deep red. "This is ridiculous, Uncle. You're letting an outsider talk to you as if you're dirt. And he's threatening our plans."

"No, Jeff. He's not an outsider or a threat. We need him."

This seemed to only infuriate Jeffrey more. "Nations are on the brink of war, and you let your attachment to this American *peasant* overwhelm you?"

Li glared at his nephew, removing a napkin from his breast pocket and dabbing at the spittle flung from Jeffrey's mouth.

"What are you two talking about?" Alexis' voice was soft, childlike.

"The conquest of America," Kaden said softly, the reality of it almost too awful to say aloud. "Your father has been working with Lermontov to wrest control of the US states. Not so much investment, as invasion." He looked up. "Am I right?"

Li Lei doled out a restrained smile. "We are not 'wresting control,' only helping—"

"Bullshit."

"It's not a bullshit, Kaden. It's a reality that's going to happen. You have Chinese blood coursing through your veins. You know what I'm talking about."

"I'm an American," Kaden snarled. "And more than that, I'm a man. One that doesn't appreciate being tricked into some twisted plot—"

He paused as he felt Alexis grip his arm, tears streaming down her cheeks. "It's not true, Kaden, it can't be! You have to believe him; he would never want to hurt you, or any other Americans." She turned her eyes upon her father. "Right, Dad?"

Li Lei nodded, but looked away. "These issues are greater than us, Alexis. Greater than the lives of men."

Her eyes widened in confusion. "What do you mean?"

He sighed. "For thousands of years, Chinese leadership has shielded us from the outside world, hoping that barbaric foreign powers would simply leave us alone. But even the Great Wall could not protect us from the Mongols and Manchus, the Western and Japanese imperialists. It's time China changed its defensive ideology into an offensive one. The dragon must rise, if we are to secure our future in this world."

"And you used your investments to buy your way into our system and people, like a Chinese Trojan," Kaden snapped. "Childcare…low-income housing…what a goddamn joke. You offered an apple then robbed the orchard."

Jeffrey sniggered. "Spoken like a peasant."

"Quiet, Jeffrey." Li's look was murderous, but the damage was done. It was true, the whole thing had been a giant sham. Which meant…Kaden felt sick to his stomach.

Kaden stood up so quickly his chair toppled behind him. "You knew, didn't you? You probably ordered my father's death yourself."

Li tried to put his hand on Kaden's arm, but he was slapped away.

In a flash, Jeffrey pulled a small, black pistol from the belt of his pants. Alexis shrieked, and Li Lei turned to his nephew in horror. "Put the weapon down!"

"I'll kill you," Kaden hissed, staring him down.

The young man sneered. "I highly doubt it. You're little better than your headless father."

His words fell like an explosion that sucked the air from the room, leaving in its wake an eerie silence.

"Jeffrey! Enough of your nonsense!"

Jeffrey glanced at his uncle and back at Kaden, a soft smile stealing across his face. "Nonsense, Uncle? Your ridiculous faith in this *American* is what's nonsense. Where do you think his loyalties lie? You want him to be your son, but even murdering his father could not make it so."

"No!" Alexis' outburst drew the men's attention to her and they watched as she collapsed at Kaden's side, bereft. Kaden could do nothing but take in the scene around him as if it were some terrible nightmare, one he couldn't quite wake up from.

He looked at Li for some kind of sign it was a huge mistake. A smile, a gentle word, or even the anger of staunch denial. What he found was far worse. Fear.

Li Lei was looking at him as if a monster had been unleashed in his study, and Kaden glanced down to find that his hands had curled into white fists, his entire body trembling.

"Kaden…"

The plea was not enough to stop Kaden from leaping forward, ready to claw his mentor's throat out. A gunshot exploded in the room and Kaden staggered back as pain seared across his shoulder. The bullet had only grazed him, a red stain spreading across his already bloodied shirt. Despite the hit, Li Lie's throat remained gripped in his hands, the vile creature wriggling at the end of his arm like a fish on a hook.

"No!" Alexis screamed, lunging toward them.

A second gunshot reverberated through the room, the shock of the sound making them freeze. Kaden tensed, waiting for the bloom of pain that must surely erupt from his chest or torso, but there was none.

"Alexis!" Li gasped, wrenching Kaden's hand from his throat. He dropped to his knees, picking his daughter up from the ground. She was curled into a ball, her hands clutched around her abdomen. With a sickening finality, Kaden watched the white cotton of her nightgown turn scarlet.

Jeffrey's gun thumped to the ground, clattering to Kaden's feet. Jeffrey was staring at Alexis, his face twisted into a terrible mask. Part of Kaden wanted to pick up the gun, but the thought of touching it revolted him.

"I'm sorry…so sorry, Kaden," she gasped from inside her father's arms. Li shushed her, demanding she be quiet as he triggered the emergency signal on his comm.

When Alexis tried to speak again Kaden fell to his knees, stroking the strands of black silk from her eyes.

"He's not a bad man—"

Kaden placed his finger to her lips, imploring her to spare her energy. Fury was still coursing through his veins and the thought of her trying to protect her father, even as she lay dying, disgusted him. Li Lei had never been worthy of such a girl, of either of them.

She jerked her face from his fingers and stared at him.

"Go to the control panel and key 'Alexis' into the code box. A panel in the wall will reveal a passage behind the bookshelf. Do it, now!"

"*Shan Shan*, stop this immediately," Li Lei cried.

Alexis ignored him. "Do it!"

Kaden was caught, wanting to help her and knowing he couldn't. "Please!" she whimpered. Li Lei pressed his daughter's cheek against his own, the blood on her lips smeared bright against the old man's jowls.

"Alexis…" He reached for her once more, but she pushed him away. "There is a letter opener on the desk," she said, each word seeming harder than the last. "Take it with you. You have a tracking device somewhere under your skin." She cast a tortured look at her father. "Something I was told was for your protection."

Kaden grabbed her by her arm. "Come with me."

Alexis smiled. "You know I can't."

Jeffrey seemed to come to life at the words, staggering over to them. "Do you think I'll just watch him leave?"

"Yes." Alexis' voice was weak, but determined. With a trembling hand she grappled for the handgun at her feet and lifted it to her temple. Her eyes locked with Kaden's. "I loved you from the moment I met you, Kaden Sun. I only ever wanted you to be happy, even if that could never be with me." A large tear rolled down her alabaster cheek, Li Lei's shoulders heaving up and down as he sobbed, silently. "Save yourself, for Katy. For both of us."

He nodded, struck dumb by her words. As he turned to leave he was stopped at the whisper of her voice.

"And Kaden?" Her eyes were bright, fiercely so. "Forgive him." She looked at her father as he continued to hold her in his shaking arms, sadness and longing etched across her face. "Forgive us both."

Forty

The panel slid shut behind him, a long row of fluro lights blinking to life. Behind the steel barrier Kaden could hear muffled shouts for help. He staggered forward as if drugged, body and mind overwhelmed by the lies and loss that warred inside him. His friends and family had warned him about Li Lei, but he had ignored their words. Now his father was dead, and Alexis lay dying. This must be some sort of a dream, a nightmare.

He staggered through the tunnel in the only direction it offered. It took some time before he composed himself and remembered the small, silver letter opener clasped in his hand.

Li had tricked and manipulated him, but inserting a tracker into his body? It was too surreal. His hands trailed across the back of his neck, expecting a bump, scar, or something. The skin seemed smooth, untouched. Where was it?

He kept walking. His heart thumped so loud he thought he could hear it echo against the cold, damp walls. Fighting through the fog of shock, he reminded himself he was in mortal danger and quickened his walk to a jog. The tunnel led to a dim platform and below it, he made out the lines of a mini railway track. Alexis must have led him to an emergency escape route. A metallic panel was the only indication of how the system worked, at its center two buttons. One was red, the other green. He hit the green.

A bullet train—more of a streamlined cart really—glided to a stop before him. It was small, only enough to fit six people. Kaden stepped inside and took a seat, running his fingers across his neck once more. They were probably tracking his location at that very moment, and once they caught him, he could only imagine what they might do. If there was one thing he knew about Lermontov and Li, it was that neither man would tolerate any complication to their plans, and he now knew too much.

The train lurched forward, the cart increasing speed as the tracks turned a corner and began to run straight.

Kaden's fingertips swept behind his ears and across his throat. There were a hundred different places they could have placed it. Just as he was wondering how he might break into a clinic with an x-ray scanner, he remembered the day he'd been almost beaten to death by the senator's men and awoken at the estate. Li Lei's doctor had made a few, small stitches in his arm, explaining that the flesh had been torn. Days later he'd returned to have the wound checked and cleaned by Dr. Ren, but what if something had been added?

Kaden prodded the still-tender tissue, too bruised to feel anything other than a continuous, dull ache. As the train sped onward, he knew his trip would soon be over. Who knew what was waiting on the other side?

The letter opener was polished to a thin edge, but it was far from sharp. He pressed it to the flesh of his forearm, atop the small, pale line left over from the stitches. What if the tracker wasn't there, but somewhere else? He swallowed, mouth parched.

The blade was too blunt, bruising the skin rather than cutting it. With a grimace he realized that using the tip was his only option. That, and blunt force.

This is gonna hurt.

He lifted the opener and stabbed it into his arm. "Urngh!" The silver jabbed into his flesh, bright blood oozing out. With a small cry he worked the point deeper, a long list of expletives exploding from his chest. He couldn't feel any object beneath the blade and started to grow desperate. The pain was searing, but in some ways it also felt good. He'd been attacked, lied to, his heart battered just as much as his body. This pain, at least, he was in control of. For a moment it dulled the thoughts of his father, and of Alexis lying in a pool of blood.

He made a final push, the blade hitting bone.

The sensation was intense and he screamed at the force of it. Taking a series of deep breaths, he wriggled the point around and finally detected the faintest resistance of something floating in the muscle. Without a pincer his only option was to dig the damn thing out. His arm was on fire, but the thought of leaving any part of Li Lei inside him was worse. Using the tip of the blade, his trembling fingers managed to coax the item upward, until one end was tilted to the surface of his flesh. It looked like a white capsule, with transistor-like legs attached to one end.

The bullet train stopped smoothly and the doors unlatched.

With a final groan, Kaden pressed his fingers to the cut and pulled the parasite capsule free. Disgusted, he went to toss the thing away but stopped himself, pocketing it instead. Then, with a hand pressed to the wound, he staggered toward a wall panel, pressing the exit button and half expecting the system to lock down. It didn't. Instead, the door slid open just as the wakeup alarm on his comm unit beeped, announcing it was five a.m.

The exit was cleverly hidden behind a screen of vegetation, veiled by what appeared to be some fake construction works. A few steps later he was standing by the roadside and staring into the first dull glow of the morning sky.

It was a busy road, cars sweeping by in a flash of headlights. He put his thumb out and one car slowed, its window rolled down. An older woman poked her head out only to catch sight of him and shriek. Before he could stop her, she was speeding past.

"Wait!" he cried, jogging beside the car, but it was already pulling away. With a final spurt of energy, he pulled the capsule from his pocket and launched it through her window, watching it bounce off her headrest to land somewhere inside the cabin.

He was panting, doubled over as his hands rested on his knees. Looking up, he saw an empty cab rolling down the street. Kaden raised his hand. The simple gesture felt foreign to him, as if he hadn't performed it a thousand times. With a dull jolt, he realized he might be in shock. The vehicle came to a stop and he wondered if it might be a trap. Exhausted, he climbed inside anyway. Trapped now or later, it no longer mattered. Kaden was a dead man.

"Where to?" the driver asked, apparently unaware of his battered appearance.

"Anywhere but here," Kaden muttered. Exhaustion threatened to overtake him and, as he collapsed back against his seat, he had to fight the impulse to sleep. It seemed Li Lei had not been able to get his men to the tunnel exit fast enough, and he could only hope that meant they now had no idea where he was. But what would their next move be? With a jolt, his entire body went rigid. From being half asleep, he was suddenly more awake than he'd ever been.

Katy!

Forty-One

Kaden tapped his comm and redialed, but again there was nothing. *Come on!*

Beads of sweat rolled down his forehead. Had they taken her already? Or worse, was she...The thought ground to a halt inside his head, too painful to be considered.

His hands had turned clammy. He kept trying the phone as the cab sped to his house, his fingers shaking nonstop. Maybe she was out.

At dawn?

He needed a plan, some masterful scheme for whisking her away without falling into their snare. But he could think of nothing. Holding Katy in his arms and killing anyone who dared come near them was all his tired brain could manage.

"Please, please, please..." Kaden chanted. "Pick up the phone, honey."

The cabbie shot him a suspicious glance from the rear mirror and Kaden tried to smile in reassurance, twitching at the small voice that crackled in his earpiece.

"Kaden?"

The comm screen revealed her concerned expression, partly concealed by the tussled blond hair falling across her face. He let out a huge breath and tilted his face heavenward in a small prayer of thanks.

"My God, I tried so many times to reach you."

"I was so worried when you didn't come home," she replied. "I took a sleeping pill—"

"Don't worry," Kaden cut in. "Grab a jacket and leave the house. Now."

"What?"

"I don't have time to explain," he started, lowering his voice as the cabbie glowered at him in the mirror. "Your life is in danger. You need to get out now."

Instead of an argument, his words were met with an eerie silence.

"Katy?"

"Kaden," she whispered, "I hear sounds at the door. That's not you, is it?"

"Get under the bed," he hissed. He closed his eyes and shook his head. *Shit!* He heard Katy breathing hard and the rustle of moving blankets.

"I'm almost home. Stay hidden, no matter what happens," he said, trying not to sound panicked, and failing.

The cabbie was fidgeting in the front seat, probably wondering what sort of lowlife scum was currently occupying his backseat. On the back of his headrest was a sticker saying "Locked and Loaded."

"How much for your piece?" Kaden asked.

The driver's eyes shot up. He was a young man, no older than himself, and sporting a handlebar mustache. He looked as if he could hold his own; few drivers dared to work the midnight shift these days.

"I want no trouble, buddy."

"Neither do I. So, how much would it cost to buy your gun?" Kaden repeated.

"It's not for sale."

With equal parts fear and relief, Kaden saw that they were pulling into his street. He took a wad of notes from his wallet and pushed the money through the security mesh separating them. "I think that's five thousand dollars, give or take."

The driver's eyes widened as the money fell at his side.

Under Kaden's instruction, they came to a stop a short jog from his house. The driver paused, glancing around as if expecting an assassin to appear at his window. Picking up the notes, his shoulders slumped, and he leaned across to the glove compartment. A moment later, a black Beretta was being pushed through the flap. It was the most beautiful sight Kaden had seen. A tiny offering of hope, in a situation that seemed hopeless.

"It's loaded."

Kaden pulled the Beretta from his grasp with a nod. As he gripped the door handle, he paused to see another object appear beneath the flap. "You can have this, too."

Kaden took the electric shaver in confusion, before realizing it was an old-fashioned Taser.

"Good luck, man. Sounds like you could use it."

Kaden stuffed it into his jacket pocket, muttered his thanks, and slipped out of the vehicle.

Taking long, quiet strides down the street, he glanced from side to side. There were no cars lurking at the curbside, but he passed three motorbikes and felt a shudder run through his body. Three men at a minimum, up to six.

Coming to his gate he crept up the front steps. The door had been forced open and the lights were off; the small circuit breaker box in the entryway had been smashed by a large, blunt object and the circuit boards were still sparking. Kaden moved deeper into the living area.

Beyond the kitchen were the bedrooms, his blood draining from his heart and tingling at his fingertips as he heard the dull thump of heavy footsteps. There were no sounds of struggle, but it wouldn't take long for them to see the rumpled sheets and start searching the room.

Kaden gripped his handgun and stalked along the narrow passageway. He was outnumbered and probably out-armed, but he knew his way around the house and held the element of surprise. He could only hope that might be enough to give him a fighting chance, or at least allow him to take down a few of them while Katy made an escape.

Ahead he detected the dark outline of a masked intruder and another one turned against the first rays of sunlight. Kaden froze, unsure of whether to fire at them or wait and ascertain what he was up against. In the end, the decision was made for him; the first man turned in his direction.

Kaden pulled the trigger and watched the guy collapse against the wall. Before the second man could raise his gun, Kaden fired again—the man's head jolting back as a bloom of red and black appeared on the wall behind him. Kaden muttered a silent 'thank you' to his dad for the summer weekends they'd spent at the gun range.

Even if the whole lot of them descended on him, at least he'd momentarily drawn them from Katy. And if their main target was dead, they might just leave her alone.

He changed position as footsteps thundered toward him. The men would quickly determine where he was standing from the position of the bodies, so he backed into the living room.

This space was darker, which he hoped would work to his advantage. As he ducked behind a bookcase, plaster exploded next to his face. Jesus, it was a lucky shot. Then he saw the vague outline of a man moving down the hall. Night-vision goggles. *Damn it.* There were two men and both pumped bullets around him as he fell to his knees and scrambled backward, into the kitchen.

Kaden crouched low, his breath short and hands slippery. This was bad. Really bad. Once they reached the kitchen there was nowhere for him to go; the front door was only feet away, but required passing right before them. He'd never make it.

Think, Kaden.

An idea flashed by, a memory that seemed snatched from another world, another lifetime. *"Fry the fish..."* It had all been a game then, a fight for prestige, rather than life and death. But if it had worked at the WarGames, it might just work again.

Kaden crawled to the end of the room toward a storage box. Stacked high on top of cases of beer and soft drinks was a small, red box. A bit of fun left over from his Chinese New Year celebrations with Katy.

He glanced up and saw a head dart around the living room entrance. They only needed to take a step forward and start firing, and he'd be dead.

Kaden pulled a lighter from the utility drawer and held a flame to two of the larger firecrackers. With a light toss, he sent the box past the doorway, and seconds later the living room was exploding with a shower of squealing sparks. As a barrage of shouts and curses erupted, Kaden launched himself forward, the two men appearing before him with their hands at their heads, ripping off their goggles. The first dropped with a single shot, the second managing to fire off a round that skimmed past Kaden's already injured shoulder. He flinched, firing and hitting the guy in the arm. The thug dropped his gun and stood before Kaden with his hands raised.

"Are there more?" he shouted.

The guy shook his head. "No man—"

The bullet passed between his thick, black brows before he could finish his sentence. These men would have killed them both in cold blood and Kaden had no problem returning the favor.

He passed the corpses and ran into the bedroom.

"Katy?"

The curtains were drawn and he struggled to see, his eyes automatically darting to the black space under the bed. Before he could drop to his knees, he noticed the shadow in the corner, denser than the light around it. It moved forward to reveal Katy and, behind her, a large man with his arm clamped across her neck and shoulders. A gun was pressed to her head.

"Easy now."

Kaden stopped in his tracks, slowly raising his hands.

"You've done well," came the voice, "but the game ends now." Kaden thought he recognized him as one of Jeffrey's more senior thugs, but he couldn't be sure. It wasn't one of Li Lei's security detail.

"You don't need her," Kaden said. "She knows nothing."

"Kaden…" Katy gave a smothered cry. He lifted his palms, trying to calm her.

"Put down your gun and kick it over here."

Kaden swallowed. Losing the gun was pretty much giving up their last chance at survival. Odds were that both he and Katy were about to die. Was it better to go down in a shootout and hope he might drop the guy first? He imagined the thug's finger contracting as he fell, and Katy curled on the floor in her own blood just as Alexis had been.

Kaden dropped the weapon and shoved it over with his foot.

"Kneel."

Kaden remained standing, unmoved.

"Kneel!" The masked man pressed the muzzle hard against Katy's temple, making her whimper.

Kaden's knees hit the ground, his palms placed behind his head. The sun was glowing under the curtains, slowly lighting the room. As he looked up he saw the gunman release Katy to grab a small object from his pocket, which he tossed into his lap. Slowly, he lowered his hand and picked it up. A switchblade.

"Open it," the man instructed.

It felt cold and heavy in his palm, panic radiating up his arm to settle in his stomach. Was this some kind of sick game? Why on earth would the guy give him a weapon?

"You will die today, Kaden Sun. But if you want your woman to live, you'd better listen carefully."

Kaden pulled the blade free, looking at the sharp edge in confusion.

"You're to take the fist that punched Jeffrey Zhang, and remove every finger that dared to touch him."

"What?" Katy shrieked. "That pig! Don't listen to him Kade—" Her words turned into a strangled gasp as the man's meaty hand wrapped around her throat and squeezed her into silence.

"Don't touch her!" Kaden shouted. "I'll do it, but harm her and I won't stop until I've killed you."

The guy released her, but kept the gun pressed to her head.

Kaden looked down at the blade, oddly grateful that it was sharper than the letter opener. He'd be dead soon, anyway.

Beyond him he sensed Katy imploring him to stop, but as he began to focus on the task at hand it was as if a glass wall had been lowered between them. There was only the knife and the soft pink flesh of his fingers, slightly curled over before him.

There was every chance the bastard would watch him maim himself, then kill them both. It didn't matter; this was the only chance Katy had.

Just as he went to lower the blade a shot exploded in the room, plaster raining down from the ceiling.

"Do it!" the man said. "Or the next one goes through her brain."

"No…" Katy moaned.

Kaden clenched his jaw and placed the keen edge over his pinkie and ring fingers. The knife bit into his flesh.

"Now!" the man ordered.

He shut his eyes and rammed the blade down. With his chin lifted to the ceiling and neck stretched taut, he swallowed the scream that tried to escape him, gasping as the blade made its messy way through the two fingers.

"Ugh!"

"No!" Katy wailed, turning on the man like a woman possessed, her hands clawing at his eyes. The thug pushed her away with a rough shove, one hand clamped over the side of his face as a stream of profanities spewed from his lips.

Even through the pain Kaden glimpsed his opportunity, grabbing the switchblade and charging at the assassin. His uninjured hand plunged downward, steel penetrating the meaty chest. At once the giant body grew taut and the gun dropped from his hand. Somehow though, he remained upright. Kaden wrenched the knife out and stabbed it into his abdomen, and again. Katy's screams sounded as if they were a million miles away, and he looked up to see the thug's face contorted into a smile. *Damn you,* his mind screamed, *just die!*

His heart was pounding in his ears as he backed off, stunned to see the assassin bend down and pick up his gun. Kaden staggered backward, waiting for the flash and earsplitting crack that would finally end all the madness.

The man raised the firearm and rocked forward, before keeling over like a freshly felled cedar. The house shook as he crashed into the carpet and stayed there.

Seconds later he found himself wrapped in Katy's arms.

"Honey…" she cried, ripping her old cotton T-shirt off and twisting it around his hand. Through the pain and relief he noted the warmth of her body in the fabric. She sobbed, holding him tightly.

"We've got to get away from here, Katy. They won't stop till they find us."

Her tear-stained face looked up at him in terror. He didn't feel anger, or fear, only the sickening realization that his arrogance had brought this evil into their lives. Peter, Alexis, and now Katy…It was all his fault.

Forty-Two

Trimly Hotel
Los Angeles, California

The bedsheets felt coarse against Kaden's skin. How quickly he had become accustomed to Egyptian cotton. The hotel room was dark and dank, its every corner imbued with the smell of burned cigarettes and rotting wood. It was the best they could find under the circumstance, the only place that hadn't required an identity check and bio authentication.

He raised his right hand and inspected it. Katy had bound the bloody stumps of his ring and pinkie fingers across his palm. Congealed blood surrounded the wound, turning the white cotton the color of kidney beans. He lowered his gaze toward his arm and saw another bandage draped around the incision he had made that morning.

Ever since Kaden had known Li Lei, he'd been running for his life. If only he'd realized it sooner.

Kaden rolled to his side and observed Katy in her slumber. She was tucked into a fetal posture facing him, and making small snoring noises. Kaden caressed her cheek. Exhausted from the ordeal, it was only in the last hour or so that she'd managed to sleep.

How arrogant he'd been, driving his fancy car around and buying their huge house. Now they laid under a moldy ceiling, with darkness closing in on every side.

Because of my stupidity.

His thoughts wandered to Alexis and if she was alive. He had no doubt she'd been treated to the best medical attention money could buy and stem cell therapy could heal even the worst injuries. It was the only comforting thought he could think of at that moment. He'd never forgive himself if she…He shook his head, wiping at the wetness under his eyes.

Careful not to wake Katy, he stood up, stripped off his clothes, and walked into the shower. The small spray of water was freezing cold and tinted brown. Kaden took the tiny square of soap and tried to lather himself up with one hand.

Washed and clothed, he walked to the window and drew the blinds open a notch. The streets were empty, spare a few characters loitering along the curb and the usual homeless people propped up against the buildings. Most of the shops in the area had been stripped bare or burned out. The state had reduced public spending to the bare minimum, so security and enforcement personnel were few and far between.

His stomach growled and he checked his comm to see it was dinnertime. The battery was running low. He had called Zac and Chet from a public access point earlier in the day, and Chet had sent a software download link through the Darknet that allowed him temporary access to the grid even the NSA couldn't track. Kaden patted the device. *Thanks, Chet.*

Katy would be hungry when she woke up. He flipped open his wallet and checked its contents. Not much left—he'd given most of it to the cabbie. His many credit cards made his wallet look fat, but under the circumstances, they were virtually useless.

He returned to the bed and grabbed a notepad and pencil from the side table. Thankfully, he still retained enough fingers on his right hand to grip a pen, though the effort pained him. *"Out for food, back soon. Love, K."* He placed the note beside Katy and passed through the door, locking it behind him.

The air was calm, the dusk light gloomy. Kaden dropped his head and buried his hands in his pockets as he trudged past the beggars and hoodlums.

At the far end of the road the stark white light of a café beckoned. It was hardly inviting, but looked cheap enough to suit his budget. He entered the shop. Behind the gruff owner two shotguns lined the wall. God knew what else the man had under his counter. Kaden bought some sandwiches and drinks, leaving again before the guy could strike up a conversation.

As he walked his comm flashed with the latest bulletins, the holograms brightening as he entered the darkened street.

AMERICAN STATES VOTE FOR SECESSION!

It appeared Lermontov and Li Lei had influenced the governors to file their official intent to the White House. Would they succeed in getting the referendums through? There would be demonstrations, riots, and jailings. And then what would the federal government do? He wondered what might happen if he tried to warn them. Would they even listen? And if they did, wasn't the final outcome inevitable? Lermontov had been plotting his conquest for years, and the strategy was already in its final stages.

No, it wasn't his concern now; Katy's life mattered more than anything. He had failed his dad and left Alexis dying in her father's arms. The only way he might ever look in the mirror again was if he somehow managed to save the one person who was most innocent in all of this. Kaden crossed the street and walked toward the hotel, the bag of food and drinks in hand.

He was about close the comm screen off when he spied a smiling portrait of Alexis in the latest updates section. Frantically, he scrolled to the story.

The package of cold sandwiches fell to the ground with a muted thud, the soda cans tumbling out of the bag. He watched them slowly roll down the road, too stricken to do anything more than gaze after them, knowing he should pick them up, but unable to move a muscle. From nowhere, a deep sob broke inside his chest. He coughed and sobbed again, unable to stop his body as it started to convulse. Knees buckling, he sunk into the gutter.

The comm battery gave a final beep before the screen switched off, but the headline may as well have been etched in stone. *IN COLD BLOOD: DAUGHTER OF CHINESE CONSUL MURDERED IN HER HOME.*

Forty-Three

USS Springfield SSN-761
Submarine Squadron 4 (SUBRON 4)
Somewhere in the Atlantic Ocean

Commander Paul Keitel scanned his control room. Long gone were the dimly lit quarters of his father's time, when seamen were packed like sardines, perspiring in the intense heat and humidity. The USS Springfield resembled something closer to a space shuttle.

Before him, the sonar technicians stared at their screens as complex signatures of the underwater landscape evolved second by second.

The drill had ended and he relaxed in his chair, a celebratory e-cigarette clamped between his teeth. They'd banned all forms of smoking on board, but Keitel wasn't ready to sacrifice his one last vice.

The nicotine vapor curled down his throat, but even as his body relaxed a troubling memory plagued him. It had started when he met with the state adjutant general of the Governor's Office, shortly prior to setting sail.

"Commander Keitel." The general had sat back in his chair, head cocked in appraisal. "I won't beat around the bush. Connecticut is planning to secede from the federal government. Initial polls have indicated the public's support." He'd paused, as if waiting to gauge Keitel's reaction. "You know the Fed's bankrupt. It won't be long before they're unable to pay your wages, never mind your pension and entitlements." The man smirked, oozing confidence. Still, Keitel didn't believe the part about the public poll—that must have been rigged.

As he sat there silent, trying to think of what to say, the general added, "We'd like you to join the ranks of the Confederate Armed Forces. Most of the coastal ports will be within the hands of the Confederacy, once we secede, of course. We need men like you to help secure our shipping lanes." His bristling brows came together. "I won't lie. Should White House use force, we won't hesitate to fight back. Our responsibility to our constituents demands it."

"You mean a civil war?" Keitel replied, waiting to be corrected by the older man. He wasn't.

"The Chinese leadership has recently undergone a covert coup themselves. The new generation of Western-styled leaders have usurped the final vestiges of power from the Communist regime."

"And?"

The general smiled. "They, our friends, are willing to sponsor our breakaway and bankroll the economies of the seceding states. We'll survive this yet."

Keitel frowned, remembering the day he'd been sworn in as graduate officer. With a chest full of pride he'd declared his loyalty to the country, ready to defend its honor, even unto death. Now he was being asked to fight the flag? A searing headache was starting to build behind his eyes. He was a born and bred Connecticut boy…by swearing his allegiance, hadn't he been wanting to protect the land he'd grown up in, and the people he loved? Did they deserve his support, more than some administration that existed on paper only?

In the weeks since meeting the general, the initial shock of his disclosure had sharpened into a deep foreboding that pickled Keitel's stomach. He took a final vape of the e-cig and switched it off.

"XO, you have the conn." Paul indicated to his second-in-command to take over, but before the man could reply, the signalman was hovering in front of him with a message from HQ. Keitel rolled his eyes and sighed. No rest for the wicked.

He unfolded the message.

TOP SECRET
EMERGENCY ACTION MESSAGE
UIC 21020
FROM: COMMANDER, US FLEET
        FORCES (COMUSFF)
TO: USS SPRINGFIELD (SSN 761)
SUBJECT: END ALL EXERCISES WITH
        IMMEDIATE EFFECT
REMARKS: 1) HEAD FOR NS MAYPORT
           WITHOUT DELAY.
          2) DO NOT STOP FOR ANY
           REASON.

The commander did a double take and read the message again. *Mayport Naval Station?* His base was in Groton, Connecticut, a deepwater submarine installation. Mayport, Florida, was not designed to house his boat.

What the hell is happening here?

"Commander, another message." This time it was brought in by the XO. Keitel's forehead creased as he took the slip and unfolded it.

FROM: COMMANDER-IN-CHIEF,
    CONNECTICUT
TO: USS SPRINGFIELD (SSN 761)
SUBJECT: RETURN TO BASE
REMARKS: 1) FEDERAL COMMAND
      RECALLING ALL NAVAL UNITS.
    2) DO NOT COMPLY.
    3) RETURN TO GROTON
      IMMEDIATELY.

Jesus. The government really was bankrupt, to have its hand forced in this way. And now the state wanted to take over his ship.

Damn those useless bureaucrats. It was all one big greedy power struggle, and they were happy to destroy the world's greatest country in the process. He dropped his head, trying to think through his options. They were doomed either way.

"XO," he barked. "Set course for base."

"Which one, sir? Groton or Mayport?"

"Home," he replied, "Dammit, I just want to go home."

Forty-Four

Phoenix, Arizona

After two weeks, the money in Kaden's pockets had run out, and it was only intermittent support from Zac and Chet that had kept them eating, for now.

Kaden was careful not to rely on his friends too much—they could be tracked and monitored at any time. The use of cryptocurrency helped avoid detection. The US dollar was practically worthless, so trade with barter or virtual Bitcoins was rife.

Finding even the most basic lodging was increasingly difficult. The parks made for good resting places, but with the growing proliferation of violent gangs and criminals, it was hard to sleep with one eye open.

Only a week earlier they'd been sleeping under the shelter of some old play equipment when a hand had groped Katy's leg. Kaden had awoken to her shrieking as a group of hooligans pinned down his arms. It was utter confusion, and Kaden was sure the commotion could have been heard miles away in the dead of the night. But no one came to help. Their escape into the darkness was thanks to the Taser, and Katy kept the unit on her constantly now, unwilling to let it out of her sight.

Food was scarce, and their clothing hung from their bodies. Katy had even begun rolling her waistband over to keep her skirt from slipping off altogether. She sometimes joked she'd be able to join a modeling agency soon, but Kaden's smile barely hid the fact he was horrified by her physical deterioration. The sight of her lining up at the food banks—and trying to convince him to take half her serving—made his chest squeeze in a way he'd never experienced before.

He hadn't known what extreme hunger actually felt like until now. It was nothing like the typical hunger pangs from missing a meal, or two. No, true starvation came slowly, and mercilessly. His body grew weaker by the day, with shaking hands that refused to stop at times. Often he felt cold, and his body started moving more slowly. The thought of food haunted him constantly, until the burn of his stomach acid was so bad he considered eating anything: dirt, grass, an old cardboard pizza box, still greasy from the food it once contained.

Often Katy would appear like some sort of a guardian angel, carrying a miracle in her hands.

"Here, honey, try this." She'd press a tin of something unrecognizable in his hands.

"How?" Kaden asked, leveling a questionable look at her. "I already had my allocation. I'm not eating yours."

"A lot of people were sent to FEMA camps this morning," she'd say with a shrug. "They had extra."

"So where's your portion?" he'd persist.

"Right here." She'd pat her belly, but Kaden knew better. He was so hungry, he ate it anyway, his basic urge overriding his shame.

Katy's physical decline was as bad as his, but her emotional state was even more worrying. Each night he lay curled around her, listening as she turned and cried out in her dreams. Unconscious, she would grab at him like a drowning child. She'd already lost so much in her young life. They both had. She wasn't about to let him go, and that was exactly how he felt about her, too. But how long could he let her go through this, just so he could selfishly keep her to himself?

He harbored secret thoughts of surrendering himself to Li Lei. The man might let Katy off, or not. It was hard to know. At one time he'd thought of Li as kind and fair, but now he knew he was capable of just about anything, including using Katy as a pawn in his twisted games.

That morning Kaden's simmering concern has risen to a low boil. Katy had come down with fever and was resting. They had just arrived in Phoenix, Arizona, after making a trade with an old man for a beaten-up Chevy—Kaden's heavy gold watch was useless to him now. They didn't need to know the time; their movements were dictated by how hungry they were. Running around the country was unsustainable and they both knew they were living on borrowed hours, but that was a sentiment they kept deep within themselves.

Close to dawn they had checked into an old motel. It was a risk, a big one, as he had no cash except for his multitude of VISA cards. But Katy was too sick to sleep in the car, or hunched on a park bench—he just had to hope Li Lei wouldn't be alerted when his card was activated.

"Here, take some water," Kaden said as he handed Katy a glass. He took two tablets and placed them upon her tongue. "And some Paracetamol for the fever."

The hair was damp on her brow and her face was flushed. She grimaced as she tried to swallow.

"That's it."

She mumbled something incoherent, her hand grasping his with a strength that seemed impossible for someone so tired.

"Hush, honey, we're safe. I've got this under control."

Katy nodded weakly, eyes half closed, and tucked herself around his hand as if it were a small pillow. He had to smile, even as he ached from leaning over her in such an awkward position. There wasn't much else he could, so he fiddled around with his comm and read developments from around the country.

The standoff between the federal government and the seceding states had worsened. To his surprise, the public referendums had succeeded with all the filed states except one, and final legislative work had begun.

Many were crying foul and accusing the Confederates of poll fraud. A growing number of those most vocal in their objections had disappeared. The very idea of democratic process was laughable.

From what he had gathered from the news Li Lei's lobbyists had done sloppy work, the spinmasters too obvious in their manipulations.

The president had issued a final warning that the government would retaliate against what she termed a "treachery of historic proportions." Imploring American citizens to view the White House position as parallel to the Civil War, she argued that the betrayal could only be resolved with armed conflict.

Battalions of US battle tanks rolled across the streets of the District of Columbia, and forces massed across the borders of Maryland and Delaware. Swarms of attack helicopters dotted the skies like locusts, and the roar of the American fighter-bombers were all part of the government's "deterrent tactics."

In turn, the Confederate States had announced the signing of a Status of Forces Agreement (SOFA) with China and Russia, allowing 'friendly' military forces to be deployed in their territories. Already, the media had reported thousands of Chinese and Russian peacekeepers had landed on the shores of California and New York.

Kaden had to shake his head at the irony of it all. The USA had signed a SOFA agreement with South Korea and Japan years before, allowing them to deploy armed forces in these 'allied' countries, which had then acted as springboards for covering the entire Asia Pacific region. Now the Chinese and Russians had used the same tactics against them on their own soil!

The next article reported that the Russian Northern Fleet had reached the Eastern Coast of the US. Its flagship led a formidable taskforce, including the Admiral Kuznetsov aircraft carrier, Kirov class nuclear-powered cruisers, destroyers, and submarines. Their destination: Groton Naval Base, Connecticut, now controlled by the East Coast Confederacy.

Kaden sighed in resignation, shifting his attention away from his comm to place his hand on Katy's forehead.

The fever was clearing, but she was still murmuring in her sleep. Holding her small hand in his own, he suddenly found himself wondering how his dad had met his mom. They'd never revealed the story, smiling at each other whenever he'd asked for details. He supposed they had meant to divulge the truth one day, but then it had been too late.

Kaden jolted awake, unaware that he had drifted off at all. Beside him, Katy was stirring. She looked sweet until she snorted, making Kaden grin. That ski slope nose was capable of making all sorts of weird noises.

"Better now?"

Katy nodded, blinking at him. "You've been here all along?"

He didn't answer, only placed his lips to her cheek, her ear, the small dimple beside her mouth...

She turned her face and yawned.

Kaden sighed, his wrist comm vibrating as he sat up. He lifted it and glanced at the video streaming in, his heart grinding to a stop in his chest.

"Katy, we've got to leave, now!"

Forty-Five

The small, wireless camera he'd placed outside their room had done its job, alerting him to two shadowy figures lurking outside their door. Unfortunately, there was nowhere for Katy and Kaden to escape to. He kicked himself for not placing the monitor at the base of the stairs, or somewhere that offered them some opportunity for evasion.

There was a slight scratching at the door, as if they were trying to gently work the lock. It was an old-fashioned mechanism: the push-button kind that required a physical key to enter from the outside.

"Li Lei," Kaden whispered as Katy tugged on her clothes. "Though I can't imagine he'd only send two men."

He looked up to find her fiddling with her buttons, her hands shaking so much she couldn't get her fingers to work. He stilled her hands and tilted her chin up.

"There's no way out…" she hissed. "No windows, only the door!"

He pressed his lips to her forehead and spoke softly against her skin. "I'm going to open the door."

"No!"

He pulled the car keys from his pocket and slipped them in her hand. "While I distract them, you run and—"

"No!" She wrenched herself away from him, her voice loud enough to pause the scratching. Kaden gripped her, hard, but she wouldn't listen.

"We leave together, or I'll give myself to them."

"Katy, you don't know what you're saying!"

"I mean it, Kaden."

She squirmed out of his grasp and grabbed the Taser, handing it to him. Turning on her heel, she crept over to the door.

With a quick gesture she indicated that she would open the door and that he should prepare himself to fire. Kaden nodded, feeling like a team player back in the WarGames. This, however, was real, and he had a lot more to lose than some stupid trophy.

They had been fiddling with the lock for almost a minute, and Kaden was sure they'd burst into the room at any moment. He positioned himself beside the door and waited for Katy to act. With her eyes locked upon his, she gripped the knob and twisted. The door swung inward, but instead of running out or ducking, she abruptly stepped forward and started singing "The Star-Spangled Banner." The two men looked at her as if she were a deep-sea monster, not some blond-haired, blue-eyed college girl. It gave Kaden the extra milliseconds he needed to aim his Taser and fire a spray of darts into both of them. They dropped like electrocuted flies, shaking violently as the volts coursed through their bodies.

"Go!" Katy and Kaden shouted in unison.

Rushing through the front door, they headed for the stairs leading to the open-air carpark. Suddenly, Katy's scream rang through the early evening air. He whirled around to see one of the twitching attackers holding on to her ankle, in spite of his condition. Kaden kicked the man's arm, but his manic grip refused to loosen. The fat, tattooed fingers had hardened into a vise that no amount of stomping could overcome. Kaden was desperate—there wasn't any time left with the rest of Li Lei's crew certain to arrive at any moment.

Kaden threw himself at the attacker and tried to pry his hand open, as the man continued to quiver from the aftereffects of the Taser. Finally, with a sickening crack his fingers came away, the man screaming in agony as his breath returned.

Katy and Kaden looked at one another in shock.

"Hope he wasn't a pianist," she deadpanned, pulling Kaden to his feet.

As they ran down the steps he looked at the glossy blond head bobbing in front of him, more teenage cheerleader than fugitive.

Sometimes it was hard to tell if he was saving Katy, or if she was saving him.

Forty-Six

"**O**h, come on, Kaden, it's three in the morning. Can't it wait 'til tomorrow?" Chet yawned into the comm. Even in the dark of his room, Kaden and Zac could spot the familiar ruffled hair and heavy-lidded eyes. "And why are we on a three-way call? Don't you have class tomorrow, Zac?"

"Nope. I'm participating in a demonstration against the secession," Zac said. "But that's not important, Chet. Kaden's got something to tell us."

"Sorry," Kaden whispered. "I couldn't call you guys earlier… Katy can't hear this."

"Where are you now?" Zac asked.

"Some wild, God-forsaken desert."

"And Katy?"

"Back seat of the car sleeping, I hope," he answered. "She's been sick lately. I don't know how much longer she can keep up all this running."

"Sorry to hear that, bro."

"What can we do?" Chet asked, always practical.

Kaden took a deep breath, almost unable to believe what he was saying.

"I'm going to surrender."

The outburst from both his friends was loud enough to wake up half of Arizona. "Quiet, guys—"

"You can't do that," hissed Chet. "Li Lei will kill you."

"And Katy," Zac added.

As they began to bombard him with the many reasons he had lost his mind, Kaden almost had to shout at them to give him a moment to explain himself.

"I'm not surrendering to Li, I'm surrendering to the government. The FBI, CIA, police—whoever's willing to listen to me."

Instead of startled outrage or a burst of disbelief, this new announcement was met with silence.

"Guys?"

Zac looked tight-lipped. "What do you think is going to happen to you, Kaden? You think they'll welcome you with open arms? They hang people for treason."

"Or if Li Lei's insiders get to know about this, they'll murder you before you even step inside a police station," Chet added.

"That's why I'm calling," Kaden replied. "We can't keep running, and I need your ideas."

To prolong their game of hide-and-seek was impossible. Li Lei had too much reach, and Kaden had nothing but a rusty old car. He had hoped to keep going for another month, perhaps make it over to Mexico, but Katy's poor health had radically reduced that time frame. Whatever happened, he couldn't sit back and watch her wilt before him.

"There's no perfect solution," Chet conceded finally. "But if we can find some government people—uncorrupted ones—maybe they'll make you a deal of some sort."

Zac didn't look convinced. "That's best-case scenario, but either way it's game over for you two. They'll break you both up; you'll probably never see any of us again."

Kaden ran his hands through his hair. Nothing they were saying came as a surprise to him; he'd been mulling the possibilities over for hours.

"So be it," he said finally. "If she's safe and alone, that's better than being with me, and dead." This was met with another lonely silence, and he steeled himself for his next move. "Chet, how's your special project going?"

His friend blinked at him in confusion. "Very well, but it's hardly the time to discuss my school hobbies—"

"You said you could hack anything with an electrical impulse. Can you hijack a national media network?" Kaden cut in. "Say, CNN?"

"I could probably take over all the networks, for a few minutes," he said proudly, before turning suspicious. "Why do you ask?"

"I've worked out a plan, but I need your help to make it work. If Li Lei thinks he can corner me like a rat, he's gonna get more than he bargained for, and maybe, the government might thank me for it."

Forty-Seven

MD-295 - Route to Baltimore, MD

Agent Jack Raven sat in the moving jeep as his partner, Rick Botelli, kept their SUV rolling at a comfortable distance behind the column of US Army M1A3 Abrams and Ground Combat Vehicles, or GCVs.

Over fifty military vehicles were rumbling toward Baltimore, steamrolling state army and police checkpoints they encountered along their way.

"Watchdog leader to Watchdog 5, we're proceeding smoothly to Annapolis. What's your SIT over there?" His supervisor's was crystal-clear in his earpiece.

"No resistance so far, sir. We'll probably be able to make it home for dinner," he joked.

"Keep your eyes peeled. The White House wants this wrapped up ASAP, and with limited bloodshed. Watchdog leader out."

Jack's acknowledgment was drowned out by the sound of a US Apache helicopter gunship hovering above them, its air-to-ground Hydra rockets and powerful 30mm Chain Gun etching an ominous silhouette against the late-afternoon sky. Out of sight, F-22 Raptors from the Air Force 27th Fighter Wing and 94th Fighter Wing patrolled the skies.

"This is going to be a cinch," Jack hollered above the din.

"Probably so," Rick nodded. "The Maryland National Guard is too small to provide any real resistance. The president's right to sanction the attack here; hopefully the rest of the Confederacy will come to their senses."

The armored column rode through an array of stunned Maryland checkpoint soldiers. Jack peered through the high-powered binoculars and adjusted the magnification knob. The shocked expressions of the state guards was understandable.

Could they fire upon their own people? Could we fire upon them—our brothers?

Rick's voice interrupted his train of thought. "Problem is, Jack, we have limited fuel inventory and no money for a protracted war. Once our supplies ran out, we'd be forced to fight low-tech."

Jack nodded in agreement. "If the Chinese and Russians enter the fray under the SOFA, we're in trouble."

"It's a gamble. But when you have zero options anyway, perhaps *gamble* isn't the right word."

It had taken an hour to pass the checkpoints and reach the gateway into Baltimore. The sun was creeping lower on the horizon, and Jack leaned forward to watch a hawk dip across the road.

Without warning, a stray bullet struck the windscreen, splintering the glass.

"What the hell!" Jack exclaimed, rocking back into his chair. Some small-arms fire was lighting up in the distance, rounds ricocheting off the lead armor column.

"Who knew?" Rick said, sounding amused. "The bastards have some backbone, after all."

Anti-armor rockets were fired, one missile striking the lead tank. But it was not enough to stop the federal forces. US attack helicopters swooped, sending wave after wave of lethal munitions at the defenders.

Even from the relative distance and safety of their jeep, Jack felt the power of the immense destruction unraveling before them. The explosions rocked like thunderclaps across the landscape, and huge plumes of black smoke obscured the horizon.

"Two o'clock high, Jack," Rick shouted, squinting at the skies above. "Confederate F-16s!"

Lightning fast, the enemy fighters were still faced with a superior armada as the American Air Force F-22 Raptors moved in.

The battle was short and, as the president had hoped, resulted in minimal collateral damage. An hour after the federal attack—though it was unclear who'd fired the first shot—Governor Donovan gave an order for his staff and administration to retreat to the allied state of Delaware. Sporadic urban battles delayed the entry of the occupying forces, but the outcome was inevitable.

The Confederate state of Maryland had fallen.

Forty-Eight

The Li Estate
Los Angeles, California

Li Lei was slumped in his chair as he watched the news, a cup of cold tea heavy in his hand. News of the federal attack on Maryland that morning dominated the media. Throughout the country Americans would be transfixed by the gory images, anticipating a Civil War. Li Lei smiled. Luka's plan had entered its final phase.

Just as the reporter was describing the Maryland attack, the holographic screen blanked out for a few seconds, turned fuzzy, and was replaced by the image of a somber young man.

His eyes widened at the determined expression floating before him, a ghost returned from the grave.

"No…"

An odd camera angle made the V-shaped scar on Kaden's cheek even more prominent. Through the paralysis of confusion, Li's body began to tremble with rage.

Kaden was staring straight at the camera, delivering a message from a corner of a dilapidated room somewhere. He looked gaunt and ragged around the edges. That, at least, was some comfort. Li had hoped the arrogant young fool was suffering somewhere, and clearly he was.

"People of the United States of America, my name is Kaden Sun," he said, face taut. "I am the son of a firefighter, Peter Sun, and schoolteacher Julie Ness. Like you, I am a citizen of this country. I come to you today with information that must be heard, at a time when our country is rotting from the inside out." He paused, chest expanding as he took a deep breath. "I come to you as a traitor. A man who has worked with the Chinese Consular Office for one of the masterminds of the impending civil war, a man named Li Lei, and his master—the trillionaire Luka Lermontov."

The small ceramic cup dropped from Li's hand and bounced against the carpet, the cold tea splashing against his ankle.

"It was a mistake, one that cost me the life of my father, a proud American. It's cost me my honor and self-respect, too." Kaden looked pained, but then his features cleared. "As many of you know, the Chinese have used their significant investments to control corrupt government officials and America's financial system. Together with the Russians, they have orchestrated the financial collapse and subsequent secession over many years, and I have all the documents to prove it."

"*Da ma de!*" Li Lei muttered through his teeth. He tapped his comm and began issuing instructions to his team regarding damage control. They had to deny everything and discredit the bastard, though the fools in his communications team would probably only make things worse.

"You may hate me for helping the enemy, and I don't blame you. I supported these criminals throughout several pivotal projects, though I was not fully aware of what I was doing at the time. I'm here today because I believe our country is worth saving, and have arranged for a package of email transmissions and phone logs to be sent to every major media outlet, proving my claims. To the government I offer myself. Do with me what you will."

Li rolled his eyes. *Martyr.* Sun had always had such a high opinion of himself, the true blue American hero. He'd realize what a joke that was once he and his girlfriend were cowering in a shallow grave somewhere.

"Signing out." Kaden raised his bandaged hand, his remaining fingers forming an odd kind of 'v' symbol. "And God bless America." The video blacked out and a flustered reporter appeared on the screen, apologizing for the interruption.

Li Lei picked the priceless china cup from the ground and hurled it at the video projection. In all his years of political manipulations, he had never been caught wrong-footed, or been exposed so publicly. To lose Alexis, and now this…

After the white rage had cleared enough for him to regain some small control of his mental state, Li Lei closed his eyes and took a deep breath. Tomorrow, the Confederate governors would face a public inquiry, he was sure of that. God only knew what kind of files Kaden had in his media package. He had been careful not to share everything with his protégée, but he had trusted him implicitly, too. The media would flock around them like vultures on rotting corpses; the cause was hungry for scapegoats, and now they would feast on the co-conspirators themselves. He could only imagine what Lermontov was thinking. Li had presented Kaden to his mentor as the answer to many of their problems. Now, the traitor threatened everything.

The US government had made a successful attack on Maryland and was gaining ground on Delaware. But this was a scenario that he and Luka had expected and planned for. They had influenced the UN council—over which the Western powers no longer held much sway—to declare that the invasion was unlawful, since the secession was founded on public consensus.

The SOFA had given China and Russia the chance to assist the Confederacy with direct military support, or 'peacekeeping.' With the European allies in disarray after their own economic collapse, and Russia acting as a constant menace to the east, no noteworthy power was in a position to intervene.

Everything had been falling into place, the perfect Zugzwang strategy, until...

Li Lei cursed. For all his political aspirations, the worst truth of all was that if it weren't for that two-faced bastard, Alexis would still be alive. To think that he had once regarded Kaden as the son he never had, only to lose the daughter he'd lived his life for. He wouldn't be stupid enough to allow emotion to cloud his judgment again.

The phone rang, and Li Lei's attention turned to the gold-encrusted device beside the sofa set. He waved his wrist over it, and the 3D image of Luka Lermontov appeared.

"Have you seen it?" Lermontov's voice was controlled, but Li Lei knew from experience that his mentor was in a dangerous frame of mind. Someone would pay with their blood, but who, Li wasn't sure.

"Yes."

"You should have let Skull kill him that night. Now the final phase will have to wait until we've discredited him."

Li remained silent, watching Lermontov's face for any indication of just how angry he might be. Mild annoyance and maniacal rage looked much the same on his stony features.

"What files does he have?"

Li winced. "I'm not sure."

A small twitch in Lermontov's jaw indicated that the man was worryingly close to homicidal. "He's a strategist, as you said. He knows too much and he clearly has impressive technical support, though I doubt it's from the government. We need to eliminate him immediately."

Li bowed his head. "It will be done."

"And how do you propose we achieve that, without incriminating ourselves?"

"He'll disappear," Li said. "Just like felons on the run are prone to."

"See to it, then. You've made a mess, Li. I don't need to tell you how necessary it is that you clean it up." Li nodded.

Alexis was dead; there weren't many ways left for Lermontov to hurt him. But that didn't mean he wanted to test his mentor's capacity for punishment.

"We'll activate the attack phase for Operation World War A in two weeks. You have until then."

"Yes, Luka."

Forty-Nine

Santa Fe, New Mexico

Kaden stared at the crawly thing emerging from beneath its rock. It was ten feet away, but he remained ready to sprint back to the safety of the car. In the shade of the passenger door he could see Katy pouring the last sachet of cereal into a pot.

He raised his comm closer. "Okay, guys. I'm supposed to be collecting firewood. Shoot."

"I've made contact," Chet said. "And they want to take you in."

"Don't do this," Zac urged. "You'll lose all control. And you know how corrupt those bastards are."

"Did they promise Katy's safety?" Kaden asked.

"Yes."

"Have you got any idea if they're trustworthy?"

Chet's smile was best described as grim. "I've ghosted into some of their communications, but they're not stupid. They wouldn't incriminate themselves on any of the central networks. Which means we're going into this blind."

"I'll go with you," Zac offered.

"No. You stay there. I've got too many people in trouble already." Silence ensued momentarily as all three tried to ignore the choked-up emotion in Kaden's voice. "You sure the Feds haven't tracked your communications, Chet?"

"They went ballistic when they saw my message and couldn't pin down my location," he chuckled, chest puffed up. "I think I'm in the clear. No one's come knocking."

"Thanks for all the trouble you've gone to. And you too, Zac."

"You're my brother," his oldest friend replied. "And hey, you're a celebrity now, dude. Being friends with you makes me look badass to the girls."

"Yeah, some of our classmates are lodging a petition for you," Chet added. "Many refused to believe the majority of citizens would vote for secession. You've helped confirm their suspicions, especially with the media releasing all those documents."

"Good, that'll keep Li and Lermontov busy for a while," Kaden mused. "They'll be pissed, though, which is all the more reason to make Katy safe as soon as possible. When's the meet-up taking place?"

"Tomorrow, noon, at Loretto Chapel. Two klicks from your current position," Chet answered.

"Jeez, you know my exact whereabouts?"

"I'm a future Nobel laureate, dude. I know which brand you floss with."

Kaden laughed, but it sounded hollow. "Let's just hope I've still got all my teeth this time tomorrow. If the Feds don't beat the shit out of me, Katy will."

Fifty

It wasn't the punishment Kaden feared; he had already made peace with himself and was prepared for whatever might come. Losing Katy, however, was a different matter entirely.

As he watched her swallowing a spoonful of water and oats— *gruel*, she called it, he wondered how he had the gall to sit with her, to laugh and joke, when he alone knew what was coming. If she had even the slightest sense of what he'd planned, there would be tears of disbelief, pleading, and threats. But instead of facing that reality like a man, he sat there grinning like the coward he was.

Thousands of citizens had been herded into FEMA population centers, where American security forces were better able to manage food and medical resources. Katy would most likely end up in one of those camps. Would she be better there, really? *Yes*, he told himself. At the very least she'd have the basics for survival. All he could give her was his love and protection, and neither of those things had led to any good.

The weeks they'd been together had, in spite of all the suffering, been some of the best days of his life. Once upon a time he'd have scoffed at the idea of soul mates, but she had opened his eyes to possibilities he'd never imagined. They shared a connection that was unbreakable, something chemistry and psychology simply couldn't explain.

Katy was fiercely protective of him, and this worried Kaden most of all. There was nothing she wouldn't do to keep them together, and in time it would result in her getting herself killed. He knew it, just as surely as he knew that leaving her was the hardest thing he'd ever do.

She put down her bowl and settled back onto the old blanket.

"What would you do if Li Lei caught me?" he asked, settling beside her.

"Hmm?" she said, stroking his hair under a canopy of twinkling stars. "You mean …if we got caught?"

Kaden nodded. "Yeah, like I got captured and you managed to get free," he said, rolling over to check her reaction.

"That's not going to happen," she whispered.

"I wouldn't get caught?" he asked, propping his head up with one hand, "or you wouldn't get away?"

Katy kept her gaze focused upon the clear desert sky. "It won't happen, because I won't leave you."

She glanced up at him and smiled, humming one of her songs from The Tipsy Orb. He remembered the lyrics; it was an old country ballad about a cowboy who refused to leave his horse behind, and died under the midday sun. *The world is cold, but my body feels warm…*

It almost undid him. He was a fool to let himself be parted from her, but circumstances had forced his hand. Tomorrow their world would tip upside down, and while she would probably never forgive him, he would at least be able to live with himself.

The time he had with her dwindled into hours and like a death row prisoner waiting for the end, Kaden felt the minutes fly away like sand in the wind.

Fifty-One

Loretto Chapel
Sante Fe, New Mexico

If the faded brochures where anything to go by, Loretto Chapel had once been a tourist stop and wedding venue. Katy trailed her fingertips along the top of the dusty altar, and Kaden imagined leaning down to lift a white veil off her sweet, upturned face. He would take her hand and vow before their friends to love and cherish her forever. She'd make a beautiful bride, for someone a lot luckier than him.

"It's a good spot," Katy said, her dirty shawl wrapped tight around her. "It looks deserted, so we should be able to rest a while. Harder to jump us, as they'd have to come through one of the doors." She began to pile some dust sheets in a corner as a makeshift bed. "Though I still say we should have continued further east, away from that monster."

Kaden shifted his feet. "I think I have a plan to keep us safe."

"A new one?"

"I, er, worked out a solution with Zac and Chet," he ventured, knowing that she could read deceit upon his face in an instant.

She frowned. "And?"

"It's all about negotiation." He shrugged, trying to look nonchalant.

"You're fidgeting." Katy took his hands and looked into his eyes. "What negotiations? What aren't you telling me?"

"Everything's fine," Kaden stuttered. "It's just that…"

"Kaden?" She squeezed his hands and his heart tightened in response.

"Right on schedule, sonny," a deep voice boomed from the entrance of the church. Katy swung around, eyes widened with fear. The man wore a dark blue suit and shades; he couldn't have looked more like a Fed agent if he'd tried. Behind him, a second man appeared.

"Run!" Katy cried, grabbing Kaden's arm and wrenching him toward the side door. Beyond it was their car, but instead of following Kaden pulled her to a stop. She tugged at him again and again, and then paused in confusion. As the men approached with their hands lifted in a gesture of peace she turned and looked at him, the truth registering on her face in a look of disbelief and betrayal that made him ill.

"What have you done?"

Kaden didn't know what to say. All he could do was to try to hold her and tell her that everything would be all right, but she squirmed out of his grasp.

"You goddamn idiot!" she hissed.

She was right. He was an idiot, the very one who'd led them into this mess in the first place. But if there was one thing he could do to redeem himself, it was to make sure that no matter what happened in the future, Katy lived.

With a shriek, Katy rushed at the first agent and kicked him in the shins. A moment later his partner had restrained her, though she continued to thrash and wail like a woman possessed. As her cries echoed through the high-beamed ceiling, Kaden realized he couldn't take it any longer.

He was between them in an instant, prying their hands off her. He'd succeeded in pulling her into his arms when the sudden crack of a gunshot split the air. The impact reverberated against his body, but there was no pain. Then Katy went limp in his arms.

"No!"

He searched her body for blood and found it welling along the left side of her underarm. It didn't make any sense. He'd been watching the agents, and they hadn't drawn their guns. Had it been an accident?

"Take cover!" one of the men shouted, as his partner trained his gun toward the front of the building. Seconds later the timber pew beside Kaden exploded in splinters; he didn't need to be told twice. He pulled Katy behind the altar, forgetting all about the gunmen as he searched her pale face for signs of life, and touched the fine brown lashes resting against her cheek. She was too still, and for the first time ever he knew what it felt like to be truly frightened.

"C'mon, baby," he cried. "Stay with me."

Another set of air-splitting shots rang out, followed by the sound of falling glass as the church's stained glass windows smashed upon the timber floors. Peeking around the edge of the stone block protecting them, Kaden watched in shock as one of the agents was suddenly wrenched backward. A cloud of blood sprayed across the old cream walls, the chest impact so great it sent the guy crashing into the back pews.

Kaden pulled Katy tighter, her breath weak and sporadic against his cheek as her blood ran hot between his fingers. Yet again, he had brought her directly into harm's way, had taken her trust and abused it.

He couldn't bear to lose her. If Katy died in his arms, he would not be walking out of the church alive.

Fifty-Two

The surviving FBI agent scrambled past them, machine-gun fire nipping at his heels. The dark sunglasses had fallen away and his eyes were white with disbelief, or perhaps despair. Either way, it wasn't looking good.

Collapsing in the doorway opposite, he lifted his comm unit to his mouth and spoke into it urgently. Kaden watched as he paused, then tried again. There was no response. He could see blood running down his face, and guessed it belonged to his partner. "The bastards greased our back up," he muttered. "There must be ten guys out there, armed to their teeth."

Kaden expected to hear the sound of boots crunching across glass, but for the moment the church was eerily quiet. He leaned out from behind the altar and at once spied numerous shadowy figures crisscrossing behind the back windows. Sunlight flashed off their steel weapons and he knew that they were trapped.

The agent pushed himself to his knees, taking careful shots at the front door as it swung open. He was trying to conserve his ammunition, but what was the use? Bullets ripped dangerously past, the attackers shooting wildly. The ceiling and surrounding walls became peppered with bullets, as if they followed little strategy at all. A large, ornate stained glass window above their heads was the next to go, and jagged shards fell upon them like the broken pieces of a rainbow.

For a full minute they did not stop, nor did they shout for a demand to surrender. It was not an attempted abduction. *They want us dead*, Kaden thought with a grim kind of acceptance.

The firing stopped, followed by a small, metallic thump that sent his eyes darting to the floor. On the timber floor separating him from the agent rolled a grenade, too close to run from, but too far to grab and throw. Kaden had the semi-protection of the altar, the agent did not. Their eyes made contact, and in that split second he could see their thoughts were mutual—there was no escape.

Kaden turned in one swift motion and engulfed Katy in a fetal position. A flash of white light was followed by a force that seemed to pull them apart and push them together at once, the sound so loud it invoked a strange kind of silence. As they were swallowed in a storm of flames Kaden could only hold his breath and pray for a quick death, barely aware of the lacerations across his back or the splinters of wood embedded in his scalp.

All at once the oxygen returned, and Kaden looked up to see two masked troopers stepping into the chapel. They stopped before the dying agent. The man was on his side, eyes opened wide and body twitching with short, intermittent gasps. The blood seemed endless, painting the walls and door around him.

One of the men lifted his weapon and shot the agent in the head, twice. Two empty shell casings hit the floor, their metallic *clinks* dulled by the sticky wet mess. The assassins turned their attention toward the front of the church, inching closer to Kaden and Katy with every step. He could do nothing but lie there like a coward, Katy gripped tight in his arms.

Every fiber in Kaden's being cried out for him to close his eyes and pray that they shot him first, but he wouldn't allow himself that indulgence. He would bear witness to both their deaths, and stare their murderers straight in the eye.

As if conjured by his thoughts a masked face appeared above him, his gun muzzle still smoking. Kaden looked up, chin thrust forward and eyes unblinking.

The gunman smirked. "Mr. Li Lei sends you his parting gift: *jiàn yán wáng*, an interview with the devil himself."

He was trembling, but he kept his face impassive. He wouldn't give Li the satisfaction of learning he had begged for his life. The man pressed the gun to Kaden's temple, the metal searing hot against his skin.

In a single breath he would be gone, his brain splattered against the furniture, and everything would be over. In that instant Kaden was swamped with a surprising sense of relief. How hard he had fought for life, and for love, but it seemed destined that both were to be ripped away from him regardless. The time to fight had ended.

And it did. Shots could be heard outside the building, and the distraction was enough to make the assassin pause and face the red laser dot hovering between his eyes. There was a popping sound as his head exploded like a watermelon. Another bullet followed, then another, staccato bursts of ringing around the building in a brutal death hymn. A handgun dropped beside Kaden, the body of his would-be executioner slumping atop the altar. The second attacker raised his hands and dropped to his knees, only to be sent sprawling backward with enough rounds to kill ten men.

Shouts of "all clear" and "secure" were accompanied by the heavy fall of boots, and Kaden called out for help. Katy was still unconscious, but a light pulse continued to flutter in her throat. The leading men had bullet vests with the words 'FBI' emblazoned across their chests. Presumably the leader of the rescue team, a tall man yelling into his comm pointed his machine gun at Kaden and demanded that he identify himself.

"Kaden…Kaden Sun."

"We got him," he said, returning the unit to his lips.

"My girlfriend has been shot," Kaden pleaded. "She needs to get to a hospital, now!"

Instead of helping Katy, the agents moved in and pressed him face down into the shrapnel and broken glass, securing his hands behind his back. A hood was thrown over his head and the world went black.

"My girlfriend!" he yelled. "Help her, she's dying, you morons!"

The agents manhandled him through the wreckage and toward the entrance of the chapel, Katy's blood cool upon his jeans in the open air.

Screaming and fighting with each step, he threatened hellfire upon them all, but no one said a word.

This wasn't the deal. "Bastards!" he screamed.

Still there was no response, only the dull thud of helicopter blades chopping up the air above them. For all he knew, Katy had been left lying in the dirt and gore, slowly bleeding to death. In a final, desperate bid to make them do something, he twisted to the side and sunk his teeth into one of the arm's restraining him.

A string of expletives burst against his ear, and in the surprise of the moment he was able to pull himself free of their hold. Kaden tipped forward, trying to shake the hood off his head, but there were too many of them and he soon found himself restrained by a dozen hands. A heavy object struck the back of his legs followed by a punch to the jaw that sent his head snapping backward.

Kaden fell to his knees, sobbing like a broken man.

Fifty-Three

Kaden blinked at the white bedsheet spread over his body. It seemed like he was in a hospital ward, although there was nothing in the room except for the bed he was lying in. Other than a few superficial wounds, he appeared to be all right, and to his surprise there were no manacles on his wrists.

On the far wall was a door, also painted white. It was slightly ajar. He got up and pulled the sheet away from him. The place was quiet, empty, devoid of all life except his own. It felt eerie.

With great caution, he placed his hand over the handle and pulled it open further to reveal a long, empty corridor. Where was everyone? Opposite him, another door bid him to enter. Feeling as if he was floating, he stepped forward and pushed. What he saw in the room beyond made him gasp.

Lying on a white-sheeted dais was Katy, but she wasn't covered in cuts and bruises as he had feared. She seemed healed.

Kaden raced to her side and pressed his lips to her temple. When he pulled back she gave him a faint smile, and the tiny gesture sent a surge right through him. His cheeks were soon wet with tears, and his body trembled as he held her hand, wanting to pour out his apologies. She shook her head as she gazed at him, urging him to hush.

There was so much to say and so little time to say it. Kaden continued to babble, jumping as a warning alarm started to sound. Above him the ceiling seemed to be flashing, and he could hear a dozen footsteps but no one appeared. Katy clutched at his hospital gown, struggling to speak, but her voice was too weak to hear. He looked around for medical staff, yelling as Katy's fingers left his gown to grab at her throat. She was choking.

"Help…please!" Kaden screamed.

He ran out into the hall but it was still empty. The alarm was getting more urgent and louder by the second. The intensity increased until Kaden fell to his knees, crippled, with his head gripped in his hands.

"Get up, Number 4!" The sound of metal bashing against metal wrenched Kaden out the deserted hallway and dumped him back into his small, concrete cell. He groaned, turning his head toward the officer.

Another hopeless dream. Another hour spent slowly going mad.

"It's your lucky day, boy!" he sneered. "Seems someone knows you're alive after all."

Kaden rubbed at his face and found it covered in several days' worth of stubble. He'd undergone three interrogations, but he could only guess at how long he'd been inside. This section of the facility was lit by soft hallway lights; no sunlight was allowed to reach them.

Every day he pleaded with the guards for information regarding Katy and they responded by throwing his food in his face, or muttering sneers like "chink-licker." When his pleading requests had turned to threats, it had only made them laugh harder. For the last three meals he's refused to eat or drink, but the guards had simply removed his trays without comment.

The officer lifted a torch and shone it in his face. Behind him stood another man he did not recognize. Through the glare it appeared he might be wearing a suit rather than a uniform, and his hair seemed neatly combed. His face however, was cast in shadow.

The man opened the door to Kaden's cell, and gave a final warning *thunk* on the steel bars. "Don't let me meet you in the streets, chink." His wicked grin exposed canine teeth bound with steel wires. "If you think I'm a bastard in here, wait 'til you meet me out there."

The gentleman with the briefcase stepped up and introduced himself. "Mr. Sun, I'm Lieutenant Brad Cooper. I'm here to escort you to a meeting."

"With?" Kaden asked.

"I'm not obliged to answer at this point," he said, barely smiling. "But this way please."

Kaden refused to leave and when the guard stepped into his cell and wrenched him up he allowed himself to fall back upon the concrete, as if paralyzed.

"Tell me about my girlfriend, or you'll have to carry me out."

"I don't have access to information about your girlfriend," the lieutenant said. "But I can promise you one thing, Mr. Sun. You won't get the answers you seek rotting inside this cell."

Kaden rubbed his eyes, knowing the guy was right. These people needed the information he had, but if they wanted to access it they were going to have to divulge a few things in return.

They reached a vehicle with government plates and the lieutenant apologized before slipping a hood over his head. "Protocol."

The journey was about an hour. Initially, the car lurched along uneven roads, but as they neared their destination the surface grew smoother. They seemed to pass a checkpoint of some sort where their identification papers were reviewed, before pausing at another inspection point.

It was soon after this that the car stopped. A low, earth-rattling roar vibrated through his body. When the car door opened the sound intensified and hot wind blew through the dense, black cotton shrouding his face. Kaden could only guess he was feet away from a pair of very powerful jet engines. Rough hands pulled him from the soft leather and boosted him across the tarmac. He cracked his shins against something hard and a moment later was stumbling up a set of stairs.

"No!" he cried, dragging his feet. "I won't go until you tell me where Katy is."

Lieutenant Cooper's voice was almost sympathetic. "Trust me, Mr. Sun. It's in both your interests to take the next ten or so steps."

Kaden grunted as he was both pulled and pushed up to the door of the plane. As he entered the roar grew quiet and the soft murmur of voices suddenly came to a stop. The hood was lifted from his head and he blinked in the muted light. It was indeed a plane, and a very expensive one at that. Cream leather, plush carpet, and polished walnut lined every surface, the various holographic displays blinking off one by one, until the setting almost seemed old-fashioned.

The people on board refused to meet his eye. Those who did viewed him with expressions of suspicion.

Kaden was pushed through the central space and into a meeting room. The door opened, and the vision awaiting almost made him stumble. The official décor was immediately recognizable, having appeared frequently in the pages and broadcasts of media everywhere. Above the head of the table hung an eagle clutching an olive branch in one claw, and arrows in the other. The famous presidential seal.

Lieutenant Cooper appeared at his side. "Welcome to Air Force One."

Fifty-Four

"**S**o, this is our antihero," came a firm, feminine voice. Kaden turned and watched, awestruck, as President Elizabeth H. Cowen stepped past him and into the meeting room.

"Yes, Madam President," answered Lieutenant Cooper. "The terrorists were about to execute him when our reinforcements arrived."

She took her seat at the head of the table, flanked by her staff and a senior general with dozens of stars resting upon his shoulders.

"Do you know why you have been invited here, Mr. Sun?" President Cowen continued. She looked absolutely sharp in a navy suit, her blond hair styled back into a golden helmet.

"You want to know about my dealings with the Chinese."

She smiled. "Yes, there's that, and another matter. But we'll cover that issue later."

"I'll be happy to tell you all I know," he said, trying to keep his voice and gaze steady, "but first I need confirmation that my girlfriend, Katy Collins, is alive and being treated well."

The meeting room was quiet for a brief second, until someone bellowed, "You little bastard!" from the end of the room.

Kaden's attention was drawn to a 3D image of a man who looked like he was about to have a fit. "You're a traitor and a terrorist, and you dare to make demands?"

Every eye turned toward the president, eager to see her reaction.

"Let's give Mr. Sun an opportunity to defend himself," she said, shooting the screen a glance. "And I don't believe that hijacking the media airwaves was an act of terrorism, but patriotism."

Kaden blinked in surprise, but before he could answer the room was filled once more with outrage and indignation.

"With respect, Madam President," the man sneered, "Kaden Sun has been charged with murder and treason. He might be a media darling, but we both know he should be shot."

"As always, I appreciate your advice, Vice President Koch..." President Cowen tapped her bright red nails on her comm, clearly maintaining two conversations at once. "But I'd like to hear what the man has to say for himself."

The media portrayed the president and VP's relationship as one grounded in history, trust, and respect, but it certainly didn't seem that way.

Cowen turned to address Kaden. "Mr. Sun, if you are honest with me I will help you in turn. Do you agree?"

Kaden nodded. There was no secret he would keep if it meant knowing Katy was okay.

"Our people found it impossible to trace your movement and communications this past month. How did you do it?"

He flinched. Of all the questions for her to start with! He could only imagine the trouble he might get Chet into if he were to reveal the kind of technology his old friend had created. "I'm sorry, I can't answer that."

She took a deep breath and leaned forward. "That's not the start I was hoping for."

"I can ask my source to provide information on the technology used," Kaden said, "and I can guarantee that they are not a threat to you or national security. But I won't give away their identity."

The president leaned back in her seat. "I'm told the transmission signal bounced around the world within a closed loop. Only a top expert could cloak it so well, and you don't possess that sort of skill set." She pressed her fingers together and raised them to her chin, her eyes narrowed. "Was it the Chinese?"

"No," Kaden said intently. "The Chinese were the ones I was hiding from. And," he swallowed, "you guys, of course."

She nodded, looking suddenly weary. It was fascinating seeing her up close, real flesh and bones, when he'd only ever witnessed the powerful, brightly lit version on his comm. In the intimacy of a small room she was softer, warmer, than the presence she commanded on screen. He noted the fine lines radiating from her eyes and mouth, the tiny flashes of silver in her golden hair. Much of her usual makeup was stripped back, and while she still imbued the authority and power expected of the leader of the Free World, her smiling, open expression caught him off guard.

"As I said, Madam President, I'll tell you all I know about the Chinese—"

"Yes," she said, cutting him off. "We'll get to that, but there's something the United States needs your help with more."

Kaden kept silent, waiting. What could they possibly want from him, other than information?

"Citizens of this country have responded in an interesting manner to your pirate broadcast." Kaden nodded, guessing they wanted to make an example of him in some way. "And your public relations work for Li Lei was treasonous, but effective," she added.

Finally, it dawned on him. "You want me to work with you? With your propaganda team?"

The president's expression darkened. "We don't call it propaganda," she said, "rather, spreading the truth. Something robbed from them by people like yourself."

"Exactly," Kaden said, feeling sick with shame. "Most Americans would love nothing more than to see me swing. If I speak on the government's behalf, I'll probably make things worse for the administration."

The president arched her brows. "When was the last time you watched the news, Kaden?"

He shook his head. "A week maybe? I don't know how long I've been imprisoned."

She turned to her aide, a small smile playing at the corner of her mouth. "Henry, play the clip."

The young man pressed a button on his comm and a hologram video materialized on the tabletop. At once the screen was filled with pictures of looted shops and violent demonstrations. There were thousands of protestors, perhaps even tens of thousands.

The police vehicles had 'LAPD' printed on their sides and Kaden leaned in, trying to identify the location. The neon signs and shop displays revealed it was a busy street from the neighbor-hood near his school. This was the home of his people, being de-stroyed by his people, and the vision stirred something deep inside his soul. Closer to the camera a group of citizens was chanting something with raised fists, their expressions fixed in courage and determination despite the chaos reigning around them.

Kaden cringed as a group of soldiers—or foreign peacekeepers—began beating men and women alike with their batons. A young boy went down; his jaw smashed by the butt of a rifle, and as his mother leapt to help her teenage son she too was beaten to her knees. Around them people kept up with their chanting. He had no doubt his friends and ex-em-ployees would be part of the writhing mass of humanity. Zac, Chet...even his secretary Cindy. All of them were desperate, fighting for their lives and whatever was left of their liberty.

"Why are you showing me this?" Kaden heard himself say. "Do you want me to say sorry?" There was a hard edge to his voice, but he was beyond caring about the consequences now. "Fine! I'm sorry. I'll never forgive myself for causing part of that," he spat, jabbing his finger at the hologram. "But whether you believe me or not won't change a thing."

The president nodded, but kept her eyes on the report. "Look closer, Kaden."

At first, he could see nothing but a struggle between those with weapons and those without. Then, he began to notice a pat-tern. Members of the crowd had started to raise their fingers in a victory sign. Closer to the camera, a woman was carrying a plac-ard with a drawing of the same symbol. Above it was scrawled,

"Let Sun shine upon the truth!" Another read, "Free Sun. Free America!"

He swallowed, chest feeling tight. "What is that about?"

"Mr. Sun, these references are not just appearing in your hometown, though that's certainly where they started. You signed off your video with your bandaged hand lifted in a V-sign, and you created a symbol for the movement."

Kaden glimpsed at the remaining twin fingers on his right hand, the bandage now gone and a line of ugly stitches in its place. His head was spinning.

"I don't..." he started, unable to believe it. "The video was a confession. I should be getting persecuted, not applauded."

The president smiled wryly. "Oh, I'm sure there are plenty out there who are not so forgiving, but you have a following that's growing every day. Right or wrong, people trust you."

Henry—who now introduced himself as the president's security advisor—added, "The population at large don't believe in the secession. They want to fight it but..." He glanced uneasily at the president. "They've lost faith in the government, so they don't know where to turn."

Kaden waved his hand at the screen. "What you're seeing there is an accident. Those people don't know who or what they're following." He gave a bitter little laugh. "Trust me, I poison everything I touch. The last thing you need on your side is an ex-traitor with a lot of history."

"With all due respect, Mr. Sun," said the president, her piercing gray eyes fixed upon him, "I'm not asking for your opinion on what this country needs. I'm asking for help."

"Then you're asking the wrong guy."

Apparently, it was unusual for the president to be told 'no,' as this announcement attracted uniform looks of disbelief, including from the president herself. But Kaden had seen enough of politics to know it was one big game of smoke and mirrors, corruption and deceit. His days of public manipulation were over.

Cowen's lips thinned into a grimace. "And what about Katy?"

"What about her?" Kaden swallowed, not wanting to give away his desperation, and knowing that he already had.

"Doesn't she deserve your help?"

He clenched his hands, sensing he was trapped. They would use her as a pawn against him, and he would have to let them.

When he finally spoke, his voice was strained. "Can I ask you a question, Madam President?"

She nodded.

"I want an honest answer."

Again, the staff looked at him incredulously. One or two coughed into their hands.

President Cowen remained impassive. "Ask."

Kaden breathed deep. "How badly has the White House failed America?"

Before Cowen could blink, VP Koch was bellowing at them through the screen again. "Get this scum out of the president's chamber! How dare he even start to que—"

With a subtle tap of her hand, the president muted the VP's channel and the room fell into a stunned silence.

Kaden raised his hands. "No offense intended."

"None taken," she replied, glancing at the hologram of her red-faced colleague, his mouth still frantically moving on the screen. "My VP is...protective," she said, "but a brilliant politician. Please excuse him." Kaden nodded, wondering if the man was aware he was yelling at a deaf audience, or yelling more for that reason.

"I've actually thought long and hard about this question," she continued. "To the reporters and constituents I always answer that we haven't failed anyone, because I have to, you see. We don't ever say it aloud, but of course we all know the truth. We failed the nation to a degree that many would say was unforgivable. And no one can truly deny it."

Henry stretched his hand in her direction. "President Cowen, I don't feel that's entirely accur—"

"Henry, please. The economy, the political infighting...we should have seen it coming sooner. Once we realized what was happening it was too late." She stared back at her team, daring someone to challenge her. "The mighty eagle could never fall, right?" She made a sound of derision. "We've been arrogant for so long, we couldn't see the danger right before us."

The most powerful woman in the world pulled a packet of cigarettes from her pocket and lit one up. Apparently, you could still smoke on planes, after all. "When you apologized in the video, your words could have been my own," she said, blowing a plume of smoke up toward the ventilation screen. "I'm a patriot, but I still failed this country for no greater crime than being blind to the truth. And the saddest thing is, we're all that the American people have left. It's us, or nothing." She smiled, though it was bittersweet. "Is that honest enough for you, Mr. Sun?"

Kaden was so shocked by her sincerity that he found himself gaping at her like an idiot. As he fought to find words, a tap at the door announced the arrival of a government aide. The young woman rushed in and handed the president a typed message. She placed her cigarette in a tray and opened the crisp white paper. Her face turned grave. The hum of the Boeing 747-8 jet engine was all that kept them from a deathly silence, and they waited, breathless, for her to break her news.

"The renegade states have launched their offensive." She lifted her eyes to Kaden's. "We are at war."

Fifty-Five

Delaware Bay

The Kilo Class Russian submarines laid quietly off the coast of Delaware, their presence undetected even though they were within striking range of US shores—or Confederate shores, depending on where one stood.

The dawn cast a pale orange pall upon the small, independent fishing boats and their haul of yellow fin tuna and sea bass. Hundreds of seagulls swooped upon the writhing lines as they were slowly pulled in.

Without warning, the waters surrounding the boats roiled and gushed with foam, as if some terrible sea monster were about to surface. Instead, the spew of bubbles revealed sleek, white cylindrical projectiles, their gray cones pointed skyward.

Eight land-attack missiles broke free of the surface and made an angled turn westward, at a pre-programmed height of sixty-five feet above sea level. The onboard altimeter barometer kicked into gear, with the aid of a receiver and positioning data from the GLONAS satellite navigation system.

The two-ton warheads were initially powered by solid-pro-pellant rocket boosters. Once an optimal air speed had been at-tained, the boosters disengaged and toppled back into the water, dangerously close to the fishing trawlers. The seagulls flapped away, shrieking in protest at the disturbance to their morning meal. As the turbojet engines took over, the missiles reached a speed of Mach 0.7.

In approximately ten minutes, the explosive projectiles would near the end of their trajectories.

At Ocean View Elementary School, Norfolk, janitor Bob Smith trudged through the gates with slow, languid steps. He yawned, checked his watch, and went to the utility shed in search of his rake. As he swept up the dry leaves that had fall-en during the night, an ear-piercing wail screamed across the heavens.

Bob tipped his head and found it hard to believe his eyes. Long, white demons were painting trails across the sky. It wasn't unusual to see American jets on their way to and from the Norfolk Naval Base two miles away, but just as Bob was dismissing the sight a supersonic boom ripped through the morning that almost stopped his heart.

"What the hell?" he yelled, picking his rake up off the ground. "Dang these flyboys!"

He continued to gaze upward, cursing the arrogant military men, but his anger turned to confusion when he realized they weren't fighter jets after all. The cruise missiles, at least eight or so, were suddenly making downward adjustments.

An instant later, black puffs emerged in the sky around the projectiles and streams of orange tracers arced from the ground toward the warheads. Bob's eyes widened as he watched the spectacular scene, shoulders hunched and mouth agape. Now multiple small rockets shot up from the direction of the Naval Base toward the incoming objects. One hit its target, but the rest of the warheads pierced through, undeterred on their course of destruction.

The ground shuddered and the sky bloomed in a mushroom of oranges and reds, too bright to look at. If the earth weren't shaking so, Bob might have imagined it was a beautiful vision of some sort. Perhaps a holographic marketing ploy for the next big blockbuster movie. Secondary explosions erupted as the armories burned to the ground.

"Hell's bells," he cried out to the empty sports field. "We're under attack!"

Even as Bob cowered behind his raised arms, another thunderclap sounded to his right. Swarms of cruise missiles were falling in a simultaneous wave and slamming into Langley Air Force Base. A blinding flash followed as the entire area was vaporized. Bob found himself inside a ring of fire.

Thick black smoke soon covered the sky, hell rising to claim the earth. Sirens rang, and more explosions continued to roar around him.

His rake discarded, Bob knelt down and pressed his trembling hands together. He could still remember his father's words, when asked about surviving World War II.

"You'll never understand, son, the horror of those days. And I pray to God you never have to."

Bob lifted his hands to the dark sky, to his father, God, or whoever might be listening. "Please, oh please...save us all!"

Fifty-Six

Russell Street, Baltimore
East Coast Confederacy

"It's no use, Jack, we've got to evacuate!" Agent Rick Botteli swung the FBI vehicle across the snow-covered terrain toward the Baltimore-Washington Highway. High up, swarms of Confederate helicopter gunships swept the ground in search of US tanks and armored vehicles. "Damn it! Military bases and fuel installations have been destroyed all over the country. The bastards were just waiting for us to make the first move."

"We can't retreat, Rick." Jack punched the dashboard in frustration. "We can't just hand back the territories we've gained! General Perkins' orders were clear." He grabbed hold of the side bar as the vehicle lurched over the bomb-pitted streets.

"The Chinese and Russians had all this planned out, don't you see? If we stay, we'll just fall deeper into their trap." Rick glanced sideways at Jack. "They're destroying our oil tanks, refineries, supply lines, and power infrastructures. Our telecommunication lines, water supply, and heating systems...hacked. Everything's disrupted across Utah, Kansas, Tennessee, all the way to Virginia. Goddamn Homeland Security left us wide open!"

Rick was right. Russia and China could technically attack them on their own soil—in the name of defending their allies.

Within weeks of the government occupation of Maryland, Russia had deployed over 90,000 military and service troops, 2,500 battle tanks and armored vehicles, and 300 aircraft as 'aid' for their hosts, the Eastern Confederacy.

The Chinese had done one better: the transport ships lining the West Coast ports of Los Angeles, Long Beach, Portland, Seattle, and Oakland were offloading hundreds of thousands of troops and double Russia's weapons contribution.

Jack watched as a Confederate Apache gunship followed above a US Abram tank, scuttling for cover along W Ostend Street. The enemy attack helicopter hovered like a patient hawk, riding the thermals above a rabbit hole. He grimaced as the Apache turned, trying to line the craft up in its sights. It was helpless, and he could almost feel the desperation of the Abram tank crew inside as the gunship positioned itself for the kill shot.

Even through the screen of falling snow, Jack could make out the dark, reflective tint of the pilot's helmet. He turned to Rick, whose eyes darted from the road to the scene unfolding above them. It took a brief second for the enemy helicopter's machine gun spool to turn against its torque before the firing mechanism was set in motion. Three hundred rounds-per-minute of 30mm bullets cannoned off its M230E Chain Gun, peppering the retreating tank with high impact explosives.

Simultaneously, two anti-tank Hellfire missiles flashed out from the belly of the craft, and the Abram's final moments were spectacular, in a tragic way. The armored top was ripped open in a rain of fire, its interior releasing a fireworks show of unspent ammunition that popped and zinged as the flames engulfed it.

It was little relief that those trapped inside were killed instantly.

"We're like sitting ducks!" Rick shouted against the roar of the engine. "We've got to warn the top brass, tell them to consolidate our forces."

"But we can't just let our initial victory go to waste. The president's gamble has to go on, or we'll lose half of America," Jack cried. To retreat on home soil seemed unthinkable.

"There won't be an America at all if we don't get back and reorganize now."

Jack pressed his lips, but he held his peace. His senior partner was right, as usual. There was no point in continuing the fight when they were only falling deeper into the enemy's trap. If only they had known that behind the Confederacy had waited an armada of Russian and Chinese military forces, of a magnitude America had never seen before.

As Rick turned the vehicle toward Washington, Jack had to admit their enemies had played a smart game. For a hundred years the Department of Defense had focused on external threats, and by bringing the war to American soil, the enemy had effectively subdued the most powerful military arsenal they had; the US Navy. Brother against brother, they'd taken their forces and cleaved them, eradicating half their military might in the process.

A sudden jolt of the vehicle shifted Jack's attention back to the present. The snow had turned to sleet. He stared at the scene beyond their dirty windscreen and thought it looked a lot like a tableau of Christmas nightmares. The falling snow and heavy trees did little to mask the blood, fire, and chaos. Amid it all in the soft white, a vision formed that seemed almost surreal and inexplicable. The snow had come to life. It was jumping and dancing in little bursts, headed directly toward them. His spine tingled as the rounds punched their way closer with increasing speed. He couldn't see the gunship but, clearly, it could see them.

"Rick, get off the road!"

He began to turn but the cannon rounds slammed into the side of the vehicle, tossing it over like a toy. They flipped once and careened sideways for a few yards, before shuddering to a sickening halt halfway down an embankment. Smoke and fire appeared from beneath the bonnet and Jack knew bullets would start ripping through the cabin any second. Right on cue, aerial gunfire began to pepper them relentlessly, and as the car was struck it continued down the incline, rolling right side up once more. Jack protected his head in his arms and screamed as the world continued to destruct around him, and then, after an eternity, came the silence. Trembling, he glanced out and saw the Russian Mi-24 attack helicopter turn away in search of larger prey.

The windscreen had been blasted clean through and his face was both chilled by the arctic wind and scorched by the fire at once. A spasmodic sting shot across his upper body and his ears wouldn't stop ringing. As he turned to his right he discovered raw, burnt flesh and a barely connected arm—his own. It may as well have belonged to some unfortunate stranger. Despite his injuries, his training prevailed and Jack mused that he must be in shock. If he was smart, he'd move himself and Rick away from the large tank of gas waiting to explode at their backs.

Rick...

He shifted agonizingly toward his partner. His face was bloody, his arms bent like a ragdoll's. He smiled at the black eye already forming; Rick thought of himself as a lady-killer, and hated it when his face was marked. Even now, some of their pre-marriage antics made him grin...

Jack blinked once, and blinked again. A metal shard had carved a peculiar looking hole out of Rick's stomach. But that wasn't possible. Panic began to pierce through the impenetrable fog that had cloaked Jack's mind. It was a fatal shot, or as Rick would say, "a widow maker."

His partner was awake, and Jack stared into his eyes, wondering if he knew his life was melting away with each second.

"You okay, buddy?" he asked, his voice breaking.

Rick smiled at Jack with a resigned look. "What do...do you think?"

"I think that's gotta hurt like a mother."

He nodded slowly and blinked his eyes in slow agreement. The arm wearing his comm lifted and dropped again. "My wife...message..."

A cough wracked his body. Jack stretched out his hand and gripped Rick's palm. He was half talking, half crying, the words themselves unintelligible.

"I'll tell her..." Jack fought for control of his vocal chords. A sob broke from his lips as he watched Rick's body struggle through its final convulsions. Destroyed as he was, his heart continued to pump, his lungs continued to breathe, his body desperate to go on.

Blood foamed at his mouth. "Go..." Rick whispered.

On the road above them, vehicles rumbled past as US troops fled back to defend D.C.

A shadow appeared at Jack's side, shouting some gibberish and pulling at his arm.

"Get off!" he shouted.

A moment later he was forcibly extricated from the jeep, the men shouting something about the engine being on fire. It took three US soldiers to restrain him, and after a great deal of wrestling they managed to explain that there was nothing to be done for Rick.

It was none too soon for Jack.

The flames had reached the fuel tank and erupted into a burning wreck, entombing his friend forever.

Fifty-Seven

"**I**s it really you?"

A tear rolled down Katy's cheek. Kaden bent down and brought his forehead to rest gently against hers, their lips meeting with tentative uncertainty. Only a moment passed before he pulled away. Seeing her there—thick white muslin covering her chest—was too much to bear.

"I'm sorry." He closed his eyes. "I never wanted this, Katy."

"Shh," she chided, "we're together now."

Her smile was small, but it strengthened him.

"You just collapsed without a sound." His fingers traced across her bandages. "I was scared shitless."

"President Reagan was shot here." She tried to lift her arm and winced, pointing at her underarm. "Same spot. Punctured my lung." Katy pursed her lips, her voice catching. "The doc said I wouldn't be able to sing like I used to."

Kaden's eyes became fixed upon a section of plain, white sheet. He couldn't look at her. A wave of sorrow hit, followed by a flash of anger. First his father, then Alexis and now this…

"I'm sorry, Katy, I'm so sorry."

She wiped her eyes. "Don't say that." Her small hand found his and gripped it. "It's not your fault the world is falling to pieces, or that there are bad people out there." Breathless, she fell silent for a moment before continuing. "It went badly, but it was the right call."

"Right call?" Kaden snorted. "Like how I trusted Li Lei against everyone's advice, or how I got Alexis—"

"Kaden, do you remember the Chinese lotus?"

He paused, struck by the solemnity of Katy's voice. Hidden beneath her soft curves was a steely resilience he'd seen before; it reminded him of his father.

"Yeah," he whispered. "The water rolls cleanly off its leaf, without leaving the slightest trace."

A twinkle appeared in Katy's eyes. "So?"

"So, I'm more of a cabbage leaf," he said with a smirk. "But you're right, we're together again and nothing else matters."

Katy smiled, but a shadow crossed her features. Kaden wondered at what she was thinking.

If she was smart, she'd let him go...ask him to leave her in peace and perhaps rekindle things when the mess around them had settled. He was still a hunted man, and she deserved the kind of love that wouldn't get her killed.

"Kaden, there's something I need to tell you."

"Yes?"

He swallowed, waiting for the words, but instead she lifted her fingers and caressed his hair. Kaden laughed, his nervousness making it an awkward sound. "I thought I was the only one who kept secrets."

She sighed and dropped her hand. "It's nothing. I'll let you know when the time is right."

"That doesn't sound good. If it's important you should—"

"Hush now." Her hand pulled lightly on his tie. "You got a ball to go to, Mr. Sun?" The charcoal suit was met with an approving eye. "You look like a sexy, dangerous CEO or something."

"This old thing?" He glanced down at the borrowed Armani with a sheepish smile. "I guess you could say I have a new boss."

Katy's expression darkened in an instant, and Kaden felt a pang of guilt. After everything they had been through, he couldn't blame her for assuming his new occupation might be questionable.

"I'm working for President Cowen," he clarified. "We struck a deal: I help her propaganda unit, and we get to stay together. No jail time."

"The president!"

Katy's eyes were so wide, Kaden couldn't help but smile at her surprise. For once, it was a good kind of shock, and he was glad.

"What's she like?"

He shrugged. "Smart, honest, direct. What you'd want from a president."

"You've only just met her and you're already singing her praises?" Katy teased.

"Compared to Vice President Koch, she's an angel."

"Koch? The fat man who's always barking at reporters?"

Kaden smiled. "The very one. He would have sent me to the firing squad days ago if Cowen hadn't held him off. Now he wants me to work under him in the propaganda unit so that he can keep watch over me. I've just finished some basic training."

"Training?" Katy smiled as a nurse came in, glanced at the machine beeping beside her, and walked back out. "Like military training?"

"Like being slammed every day, in the balls, by big men with a lot of emotional problems." He laughed. "That's the military for you."

"But why military training? Won't you be working in an office?"

"Yes, as well as grassroots campaigns in hostile areas. We're divided into tactical units, each with a team leader, a strategist-cum-communications guy, a videographer, a Fed agent and two soldier escorts. And would you believe it, my videographer is this crazy chick who—"

"Chick?" Of everything he'd said, this seemed to surprise her most. "Is she horrible?" Katy asked, rather hopefully.

"Uh huh." Though he had to admit Zuri was an attractive brand of horrible, even with a Mohawk and biceps wider than his thighs.

"Zuri Harper is her name, but she hates my guts for some reason. Seems my lineup of adversaries never ends."

"You'll show them," Katy said with a smile. "You're so much more than they could ever know."

Kaden wanted to believe her, even as part of him felt like a giant fake. But Katy was right; he had to start seeing the world with a new perspective. He'd made mistakes, but he was an honorable person with a good head on his shoulders. People like Koch might try to tear him down, but the world would have to recognize him for what he was, some day.

Hopefully, he'd live to see it.

Fifty-Eight

Harrisburg Hospital
Harrisburg, Pennsylvania

"The patient has refused his therapy yet again, Dr. Gomez," the nurse complained. "He's on his fifth tantrum of the day."

The doctor removed his glasses and sent a long, withering stare toward the sulking figure down at the end of the ward. The patient had just thrown his cup, tray, and anything he could find onto the floor. Thankfully, his left hand was bandaged to his side, restricting his movement into an awkward kind of writhing. Two nurses stood back, watching nervously.

Dr. Gomez shook his head. "What's he so angry about? His arm?"

"Some military men came to make a report," the nurse murmured, "but he wouldn't talk about the incident. Must have been pretty bad."

"Hmm. Still rejecting our offer of the prosthetic limb?"

She nodded. "Hundreds are queuing for one, and he spurned it just like that."

Dr. Gomez tapped his comm, checking the patient's record. "We've got a deadline to meet. General Raven will be sending men to pick him up within a week." A loud squawk rolled down the hall as the man threw a half-eaten apple at one of the staff. "The general is expecting to us to return his son to him—one of the country's finest agents."

The patient groaned as he lunged out of his wheelchair and landed on his hands and knees, the IV bag toppling over behind him.

The nurse sighed. "It's going to take a miracle."

Fifty-Nine

Military Base # 4
Deep beneath the Cheyenne Mountain

Katy sat, beaming at the stage. The Officer-Candidate graduation was held in one of ten secret underground bases, constructed to house top-level government and military personnel in times of war or national calamity.

During an orientation of the facilities Katy had been shocked to learn that each of these bases, a few hundred feet in depth, was part of a vast underground network connected by bullet trains that moved at speeds of up to Mach 1. These massive infrastructures housed an array of communication systems and national and regional command centers. They also allowed for mass transportation of supplies, military troops, armor, and weapons, invisible to enemy satellite tracking.

The audience of family and loved ones sat watching the line-up of sharp-looking officers as they readied themselves for their new commissions and awards.

Kaden Sun was positioned near the end of the line and looked magnificent in his dark suit and tie, brass buttons, and two gold bands across the sleeves. With his thick black hair and sharp Chinese American looks, he was attracting plenty of stares, especially from the teenage girls at Katy's left, who'd whispered disturbing comments about "finding the hot one" at the banquet afterward. *He's mine*, she thought smugly, wishing she could waltz up onto the stage and slip her hand through the crook of his arm.

When he looked at her suddenly and smiled, a rash of goose bumps prickled her skin. She had taken her new allowance and bought a dress for the occasion: a pale blue silk shift with flowers embroidered along the hem and collar. After weeks of living in filthy rags and hospital gowns it had felt ludicrously over the top, especially after she then spent a week sewing cream beads into the center of each tiny flower. Now, looking at the women around her—diamonds studding their ears and gold bangles heavy on their wrists—she felt underdressed.

When the announcer read Kaden's name and said something along the lines of, "highest-performing Officer-Candidate," he gave her a wink that sent her straight to her feet, cheering wildly. When she finally sat down she couldn't help grinning at the little misses beside her and their matching frowns.

After the presentation of the awards the graduates mingled with the guests. Kaden hopped down the steps and within a few long strides had swept her off her feet. A gush of elation and warmth engulfed her, and she laughed unabashedly. It was a delightful feeling, one that she hoped would last forever.

"Surprised, babe? Never thought I would top the class," Kaden said with a smile, kissing her.

"Not surprised, only in awe of how good you look."

"Me?" Kaden spun her around, his dark eyes traveling the length of her body. "You're a goddess."

Katy lowered her head, a flush spread over her cheeks. Never had she felt so adored as in that moment, as if anything might be possible. Katy knew the time had come to tell him her secret. Even if he took it badly, they would make it through.

"Katy, I have something to tell you—"

"Me first," she interrupted. "I've got news too."

"Sorry, Mr. Sun, ma'am." A presidential aide in civilian attire cut between them. "You're wanted by the president, Mr. Sun."

"Of course," Kaden nodded. "I only need a minute."

"Sorry, sir, I'm ordered to bring you now."

"This instant?"

The man responded with a silent grimace.

Shrugging in resignation, Kaden bent toward Katy and gave her a chaste brush of his lips. "I'll see you soon, babe. I know we have so much to talk about, and we will..." The aide coughed politely into his hand and Kaden rolled his eyes. "We will finish this conversation when we don't have an audience," he muttered. "I love you."

Katy softly repeated the endearment, then watched her lover stride off into the crowd. She glanced down at her belly in apology.

"Next time," she whispered, "you'll finally meet your father."

Sixty

The Situation Room

The aide led Kaden through a maze of underground tunnels and into a large, brightly lit room. Inside, civilian and military staff hunched over workstations and communications equipment, some talking excitedly into their earpieces. Opposite, a smaller space beckoned, the sign at its entrance stating: "Situation Room."

The aide motioned him to go in, but not before imparting some advice. "Remember, there are very important people in there." His mouth twisted, "And you're not one of them."

What Kaden saw before him made him shift his feet. Around the conference table sat a full house of senior White House officials and military officers. President Cowen presided at the head in a deep red suit, flanked by the vice president and the rest of her cabinet members.

All eyes were fixed on Kaden as he entered the room.

"Who are you, young man? You're not cleared to join this meeting," a man barked, his uniform covered in medals and braid.

"He's here under my personal invitation," President Cowen said. "Lieutenant Kaden Sun is our highest-testing new graduate."

The man glowered at him, apparently deciding it was best not to directly challenge his commander-in-chief.

Kaden stood to attention, subtly scoping the various officials in the room. A lump formed in his throat. *What was the president thinking, inviting me into this?*

"Have a seat, Lieutenant," President Cowen said and smiled. Kaden nodded in appreciation and chose a chair in the far corner of the room. As he passed Koch, the older man gave him a cold smile.

"It's clear that the situation is desperate," the president began. "We are trapped in a perfect storm of national security break-downs, import restrictions, and a highly depreciated currency. Organized terror groups and the mafia have taken over large swathes of population centers in Nevada, Utah, and Arizona. Crime is up a hundredfold, social services are collapsing and there are more citizens living in poverty than ever before. I want ideas and solutions, not the quick fixes and band-aids we resorted to in our last meeting."

"The secessionists have territorial jurisdiction over our naval bases in the west and east coasts and have confiscated our ships. We need our harbors and ports back. That's the first priority," said an older man who Kaden guessed was an admiral. He pounded his pencil on the table, snapping it as he spoke. "Without them, the Navy will lose seventy percent of its operational strength. We'll have no recourse to international trade—we'll be completely landlocked and those foreign bastards will have a free pass to enter as they wish!"

"Admiral Wallace is right," nodded the general sitting beside him. "The Chinese and Russians are piling on their weapons and troops through the separatists' shores to help liberate their 'democratic ally.' It's outrageous!"

This attracted a murmur of humphs and racist comments that sent Kaden's eyes dropping to the floor.

"They've destroyed many of our fuel and ammunition installations, our refineries and crude oil storage tanks. Half of our power and communications systems are down," said another man, who looked more government than military. Kaden thought he recognized him from various news reports, but couldn't quite remember his name. "Most of all, they've hacked into our water control systems and cut off supply into our cities. We won't last an all-out confrontation with them."

In a sudden moment of clarity, Kaden remembered him as the government's secretary for Homeland Security. Only weeks before he'd been assuring the population that the country's defense was ironclad.

"Our people are turning into refugees in our own land, searching for water, housing, medicine, and food. The enemy will keep on destroying our facilities if we continue to hold back," said Koch, adding his bellowing indignation to the growing furor. "Half our oil reserves are in Texas and the secessionist states, so I say we go all-out on the offensive!"

"How are our European allies doing on their front, Vincent?" asked the president, nodding her head at the secretary of state.

"Not great, ma'am," he answered. "Spain is breaking up, as is France. The EU is about to collapse. The whole region is dealing with widespread unemployment, uprisings, and civil wars—"

"Which means we're on our own," she finished drily.

The more vocal members of the meeting had begun talking among themselves in hissed debates, the council seeming split between offensive and defensive strategies. As the arguments heated up one view would make it to the surface of the rabble only to be countered by another.

Kaden frowned. *Is this how a presidential council functions? The meeting of the country's top minds?* It sounded more like his neighborhood fish market.

Finally, VP Koch stood up and bullied them into silence. "There is no other option. We must summon all we have and attack! Send the scum back to the third-world slums they came from!" Again, dissenting voices arose up, cautioning the dangers of an impulsive reaction. Kaden glanced toward the president. She had been observing them, noting their points of views, and apparently thinking them through. But where was the ruckus going to lead them? Couldn't they see how futile this was?

Kaden couldn't stand it any longer. *They've got their priorities all wrong.* He cleared his throat and raised his voice. "Madam President," he began, only to be drowned out. He spoke a second time, louder, and her eyes settled upon his. She nodded her head and as he began to speak the rest of the room grew quiet.

"'He who wishes to fight must first count the cost...'"

"What?" VP Koch looked as if Kaden had just suggested swapping the military's guns for bananas. "What the hell did you say, boy?"

"A wise leader knows when to attack, and when to consolidate." He struggled to maintain eye contact with Koch, who looked apoplectic. "Trust me. I know after all the beatings I've taken over the years."

"You're reciting drivel to us from your schoolbooks?" Koch sneered. "If I want a Lincoln quote, I'll look it up myself!"

"It wasn't Lincoln." The voice was cool, calm, and cut through the room like a samurai sword. "It was Sun Tzu," the president added, "a Chinese general."

This announcement was met with a wall of stony silence.

"Perhaps we should listen to old Tzu," Koch eventually scoffed. "Clearly, the Chinese understand how to pillage and destroy as they wish, the goddamned—"

"Enough." The president's tone had an edge Kaden hadn't heard before. "I find your comment interesting, Lieutenant, but I'd appreciate an explanation."

Kaden's mouth went dry. "Thank you, Madam President. I only wanted to say that—"

"Louder, we can't hear you from the front!" a man called out.

"WHAT," he cleared his throat again, "what I mean is, your proposals are reactionary. 'The enemy has our ports, so we've got to get them back.'" Kaden paused. He knew he'd crossed a line by criticizing them, but they had to hear it— screwed-up faces and snide whispers be damned. For a moment, it felt like he was back in the lecture hall at university, and he almost shook his head at the thought.

"Go on, Lieutenant." The president joined her hands together and leaned forward.

Kaden took a deep breath. "The Chinese and their Russian allies had years of preparation to make this takeover happen. They've watched us and followed our weaknesses, biding their time as they bought up our people." He looked at the faces around him, some nodding softly, others cast in mottled shades of pink and red. "When working with Li Lei I was privileged to information, and trust me, the corruption goes right to the top. There are probably people in this room on a foreign payroll."

His words were met with the expected explosion of outrage, but Kaden had little trouble finding his voice this time.

"Listen!" he shouted, and was surprised when they obeyed. "If we commit all our resources to fighting back, we're giving them what they want. They're ready to finish us off."

The grumbling continued, but Kaden sensed few would dispute the claim. From day one, the enemy had maneuvered the US from one trap into another.

"If your enemy is superior in strength, evade him. Now is not the time to retaliate, but consolidate, and strengthen our core. If you think that the only resolution is war, then I say, avoid an all-out confrontation. There are political, social, and economic solutions that need to come into play as well, all implemented at different time frames."

Koch glared at the president. "You can entertain this if you wish, but I haven't served this country for thirty years to sit here and be lectured by a whelp!"

"If you must leave, then do so." Cowen's piercing eyes scanned the room. "If anyone else is unable to contribute to the meeting, they should withdraw also."

Koch looked at the woman with a mixture of shock and disgust. As he opened his mouth to spew more vitriol, she lifted her hand and indicated the door. Instead of leaving, Koch slumped back into his seat, his mouth snapped shut.

Following a curt nod from the president, Kaden went on to propose a rough plan to the council. It involved implementing a phase strategy, where the government would first engage the civilians and start to win back their—badly corroded—trust in the administration. Those in separatist states needed to understand the depth of the secessionists' deception, forcing them to revoke the referendum.

"The enemy has used the referendums to gain international legitimacy, bringing Chinese and Russians invaders onto our shores. Convince the people, break the enemy's legal position, and they will have no right to remain involved."

As Kaden spoke, he watched the faces around him. The range of expressions provided an indication of who was open to the message, versus those aggressively opposed. It seemed he was outnumbered, by a landslide.

With a deep breath, he launched into the final phase: consolidating forces to probe and strike at the enemy's weak

points. From there, the US would help form militia cell resistance groups and start a new fight from within the enemy
strongholds.

"Lastly, and most importantly," Kaden finished, "we have to
rid our administration of enemy agents. They're poisoning us
from the inside out."

When the room erupted into argument yet again, President
Cowen wisely broke the meeting up for an intermission.

"Lieutenant, please stay a moment," she said.

Kaden hovered awkwardly by her seat, and she pointed to
the chair just vacated by the vice president. As he settled into it,
acutely uncomfortable, he looked up and saw they were the last
two people in the room.

"I apologize, Madam President. I spoke too quickly, and
should have considered—"

"If I ever wish for you to apologize, you'll know it." She
smirked at his nervousness. "I don't punish people for speaking
their minds," she went on, "which might explain why trying to
run this council meeting is like herding cats. A little rowdy, passionate perhaps, but that's just my style." Her eyes dropped to
check her comm, speaking as her fingers scrolled through a long
list of special messages and updates. "You're a fan of Sun Tzu, or
are you his descendant?"

"A fan, only a fan."

"And yet you share the same name?"

Kaden gave a wan smile. He held a deep, private pride in his
ancestry, and didn't feel the need to share it right now. It seemed

in his best interest to ask a question to divert her interest away from this subject.

"Why is America alone in this war? We used to have so many allies."

President Cowen swung her glance from her comm and gave him a penetrating stare. "Wealth and power begets friends. Money has legitimized the Confederacy as the new America, which is much more appealing than supporting an old giant that's drowning in debt." She paused. "You worked for the Chinese. They were willing to sacrifice the trillions of dollars we owed them to fight this war?"

"What's a few trillion dollars compared to owning prime US property?" he pondered. "If they play this right, China will be the only superpower in the world."

President Cowen looked up from the screen and frowned. "Our analysts had derided that theory, thinking they wouldn't risk a global collapse."

"To be honest, President Cowen, I don't think the Chinese are territorially ambitious."

"What do you mean?"

"Historically, they have proven protective of their domain, but they are not dominion hungry," Kaden explained. "The Chinese have existed for over five thousand years, but have rarely ventured out to conquer other countries, or empires, for that matter. In fact, they built the Great Wall to keep out 'barbaric foreigners,' and in modern times utilized the air defense identification zone as a contemporary 'Great Wall.' So their focus has always been about the Middle Kingdom."

"So why now?" President Cowen asked.

Kaden thought back to the various Chinese he had met in his time with Li Lei. "There is a new breed of Western-educated revolutionaries who have adopted the capitalist approach and forcefully replaced the Communist old guard. But I think this is where our next action plan lies."

President Cowen leaned forward. "How so?"

"We can't fight them and the Russians all at once, not for a protracted period—"

"But our strategists believe this war will be a short one..."

"Just as we thought the conflicts in Iraq and Afghanistan would last only a year or two?" Kaden smiled wryly. "This Chinese leadership will stake everything they have on this success, because there is no road back from this."

President Cowen blinked.

"But this Western-styled leadership isn't part of the Chinese DNA, and will be rejected by their people if we create enough resistance. It's only a matter of time. Working behind the enemy lines with their citizens, I know we can overthrow their leadership. In China, the people are the real power."

President Cowen leaned back and watched as people began to filter back into the room. "No wonder Li Lei went to such lengths to rope you into his fold."

A bitter taste filled Kaden's mouth. "I was never in his fold. I was duped into serving him like the college idiot I was." He shrugged and added, "I haven't had much luck with people. Except for my best friends and girlfriend, everyone I know is either antagonistic, or just plain ready to kill me. Guess I lack the LQ."

"LQ?"

"Likability Quotient," Kaden explained.

President Cowen smiled. "Those who stand up will always attract the most attention."

"Perhaps," Kaden agreed.

"Sometimes they hate you because they're envious, and dislike being inferior in ability, or integrity. Often they detest you for no better reason than perceiving you as a threat."

Kaden understood the words in theory, but had never really applied them to his own life. It occurred to him that over the years he'd somehow started believing he was fundamentally unlikeable; that people like Katy, Zac, and Chet were the exception to the rule.

It was no secret the president had suffered her own critics; being the commander-in-chief of a failed administration—and a woman to boot—couldn't be easy.

"I have something for you," she said, lifting an item from her folder and handing it to him. The intricately carved pen was covered in a fine glaze of Chinese painting. It was exquisite. She fingered the item like a cherished memento before handing it to Kaden. "Please, take it," she said.

"Thank you, but I can't—"

"My mentor gave me this before he died." She pressed the pen into his palm. "He said he saw something in me, a potential that would transcend all men. I didn't understand it then."

She blinked and looked away, gazing at the faces of the many men she had transcended, now taking their seats around her.

"Keep it," she urged. "One day, you will hand this to some-one else."

Kaden pursed his lips, thrilled by the gift and oppressed at the same time. "Thank you." He would do his best to be worthy of the gesture, but felt destined to fail.

President Cowen nodded. "Gear up for tomorrow. We're leaving first thing in the morning."

"To where, ma'am?"

"Didn't you recommend we engage our citizens? I want to meet them personally, and your unit will support our efforts. Meanwhile, I will order a consolidation of all our forces and supplies."

Kaden glanced at the officials and aides milling around them; so many people, any one of them potentially on the enemy's payroll.

"Are you sure it's safe for you to fly at the moment?"

She shrugged. "I've got a job to do, even if that entails risks. I only need you to promise me that you'll do yours."

"I will, President Cowen, you have my word."

Sixty-One

One World Trade Center
Manhattan, New York

Luka Lermontov stood tall in his ninetieth-story office, surveying the Hudson River in all its majesty and history. He lifted his head and scanned the broad horizon of distant buildings and monuments. The setting sun was illuminating the office with broad, gold beams of light, and he felt bathed in God's approval.

Lermontov smiled to himself, a glass of Russo-Baltique Vodka in hand. Developments in the United States and Europe had worked out as planned. In fact, the interim results were even better than he'd anticipated.

The international community had begun to develop direct diplomatic and commercial ties with the Secessionist Confederacy. International trade and investments was flowing into the states, giving worldwide credibility to the secession story. As one media article had stated, "the American Confederacy has emerged like a phoenix, bursting from the smoldering ashes of Cowen's war."

For now, his allied forces were laying siege to the rest of the United States, closing out all options and forcing them into economic starvation. If things went according to his plan, the White House would get desperate and commit their all for one final battle, or *Armageddon*, as he labeled it. It was a simple as taunting a red rag before a bull. And when Cowen led the final charge, there would be ample excuse for his allied forces to drive inland and secure the rest of the country's vast resources. Agricultural land, shale oil, minerals, and infrastructure, all ripe for the taking.

Of course, it was not his alone; he had to share it with the Chinese, seventy-thirty, in their favor. They were the muscle of the operation, with superior resources and manpower. But that didn't matter now. He'd deal with the Chinese once America had been divided up.

He popped a couple of vitamin tablets and chased them with a swig of vodka, surveying the frescoed ceiling with his head tipped back. It depicted the breakup of the Roman Empire, and he couldn't stop the smirk that curved his lips. *Luka the Great*, it had a certain ring to it.

Luka's father had been a Great Man, universally admired. His funeral had taken place shortly after Luka turned twelve. There must have been thousands of people at the Red Square, but instead of pride he only felt an immense loss, and fear. He'd witnessed his father gunned down in the middle of Petrovka Street, the family walking to their limousine after a performance at the Bolshoi. A political act—someone had wanted to rid Russia of the honorable Minister Lermontov, whom many believed would be the next president.

Even at that early age, he'd known Russian politics was based on dynasties, and it stood to reason the rest of the family, his mother and he, would be murdered as well. A solitary bell had struck outside the Novodevichy Convent, somewhere. Despite the throng crowding around him, it had been the loneliest moment he had ever felt in his life.

But Alina Lermontov was a strong woman, a survivor—she had to be, for the sake of her only son. Prime Minister Bazhanov had had eyes for her since she was a girl and was their only hope for protection against the fangs of the enemy; a man who probably knew her husband's killer, if he hadn't ordered the hit himself.

She was forced to marry him, and with that, the threat to Luka's life was temporarily removed.

Then came her next priority: to destroy those who had plotted against her beloved Alexander.

Luka had played a large part in it too. By befriending the children of their enemies in school and during government functions, he was privy to information about their families' travel schedules and domestic affairs. Reports were sent to Alina, who had by then started to cultivate strong connections with the leadership of the Russian Mob, who in turn passed them on to the small army of hitmen who revered her as The Black Widow. Over three years the pair destroyed the eleven families who had either contributed to Alexander's death, or stood by and watched it happen.

In hindsight, Luka had to admit the murders he'd plotted with his mother were amateurish. Still, Alina was a good teacher, and Luka, her willing pupil. When most teenage boys were chasing girls or learning to drive, Luka Lermontov was bent over a code of conduct manifesto that he would use for years to come, founded on ruthlessness, efficiency, watchfulness, distrust, and, most important of all, planning.

That was where his father had failed, he reasoned.

At twenty-five, Luka found himself the head of his mother's mob, but asked himself, why live off prostitutes and drug addicts when the click of a mouse could translate into a ten-million-dollar windfall? Global finance was where the powerful made their money, and this required an entrenched network of influential partners, who allowed him to enter the game and eventually dominate it. Each successful exploitation brought him new wealth and influence, his expanded resources in turn extending his reach. In many ways, Luka had avenged his father, and become more than his stepfather in the process. Now fifty-five, and with his dear mother long dead, he controlled the fiscal universe like the Rothmans once had.

When a new opportunity had crystallized in Luka's brilliant mind, it was so grand it almost made him afraid of his own ambition. Over the past decade, Luka and his strategists had identified the US as an ideal asset, with its impressive infrastructure and plentiful resources. With the Russian mafia entrenched in all levels of American business and society, the base had been set for a takeover that would leave the world reeling, but would start so softly that few would notice the blade until it had already delivered the death blow.

No one considered the invasion of the world's second-largest nation a simple objective— no one that is, except Luka.

He took out a cigar from his treasured bone chest and appraised the red-and-gold label. "Gurkha His Majesty's Reserve," he read softly. Peeling off the plastic wrap, he took a long whiff of the Louis XIII Cognac-soaked stick, and proceeded to cut a portion off the rounded end. With a deft flick of the wrist, his rhodium-plated cigar lighter was torching its end, the heady scent of Dominican-fermented tobacco leaves slowly enveloping the room.

Lermontov creased his eyebrows. His brain had been churning away like a supercomputer for days, weeks…months even. There were outstanding matters unresolved as yet—two recent directives had been issued by him, but not yet executed.

"Get me Bishop, Linda," he said into a red comm device. "Scrambled secure line."

"Yes, Mr. Lermontov, right away."

It took Bishop a full five minutes to return the call.

"What took you so long?" Lermontov demanded.

"I was in a meeting," came the deep voice. "Not so easy these days to escape attention."

"You haven't delivered on both jobs. What's the delay?"

"Everyone's being watched. I can't take action at the moment…" Bishop's responses became increasingly frantic, and Lermontov pictured him huddled in a corridor somewhere, glancing over his shoulder.

"Act normal and you'll escape notice," he snapped impatiently. "More importantly, get the job done at all costs." He wasn't about to accept any further delays, even if it meant sacrificing the man. "You have one week to take out both marks."

There was a pause at the other end of the line, before a short, poorly hidden exhalation. "Consider it done. Out."

The secured line went dead.

Sixty-Two

Confederate California

"**T**his is crazy, Captain." Kaden wiped the monsoon rain from his face. "We're behind enemy lines, and the cell group we're meeting hasn't been cleared…"

"Your job is to obey orders, not analyze them, Lieutenant Sun," Hastings hissed. "Stay down and keep silent!"

Zuri Harper stood beside their team leader, fiddling with her waterproof camera equipment. "Thank God for the rain," she muttered. Kaden raised his brows at the statement. "No one can see you pissing yourself, Sun."

Repressed chuckling crackled through the group, and Kaden felt his cheeks burn. A year ago he would have reacted, but now he'd seen enough to recognize which battles were worth fighting. He had just been pulled off the presidential tour by VP Koch, and reassigned to what felt like a suicide mission. There was no time for squabbling.

Kaden pulled his poncho over his head and crouched in the mud beside the captain. It was a winter night and bone cold. Ahead, their two military escorts were striding toward the jeeps after doing a perimeter check. One of them, Sergeant Taylor, was middle-aged and heavyset, with a rocket launcher cradled in his arms like a baby. His pockmarked face brightened as he brought the barreled weapon up to bear on an imaginary target.

As if feeling his stare, Taylor turned and their eyes locked. He flashed Kaden a wide grin. "Best MANPAD ever invented, sir. Just point and shoot, and them enemy birds fall from the sky like flies. Rebel bastards better appreciate these babies."

Kaden nodded. He squinted up at the heavens only to see a moonless patchwork of darkened clouds and raindrops, each as large as a ball bearing. Why they would send a propaganda team out to perform a weapons drop was a mystery to him.

The past week had been eventful, with a successful media trip to Chicago. It had been a close call. They had accompanied the president in the first of her state visits, with ten thousand impoverished citizens gathering in one of the FEMA centers. It wasn't easy facing them, but President Cowen did so bravely and honestly.

Blunt and angry questions had been raised by the public, as well as the military forces guarding the garrison. Cowen had answered with openness and patience. She was smooth in her delivery like any professional politician, but it was her earnestness to rectify the wrong that struck him. Just as she said she identified with him in his video, he now identified with her, trying to make things work again. She had spied him in the distance and made his now-familiar 'V' sign, followed by a thumbs-up.

Kaden was jolted back to the present when Captain Hastings muttered a loud curse under his breath. "Damn these guys." He peered at his positioning equipment. "We're in the right location, so where the hell are they?"

"Maybe they changed their minds…" Kaden offered. "Or got compromised somehow."

"They confirmed just three minutes ago. In any case…no, wait." Captain Hastings waved Harper over. "There's something there. Hand me the night binoculars."

He made a visual sweep across the trees opposite. The wind was howling, and above, arcs of lightning lit the sky. "Damn the flash," he grimaced, lips creased upward. "There they are, one o'clock." Kaden squinted in that direction and saw a lone light emerging from between the trees. It moved left and right in a zigzag manner, then blinked three times.

"Acknowledge the signal, Harper," Captain Hastings ordered.

She did so, and a moment later the light began to come closer.

"You ready for your messages, Lieutenant?"

Kaden nodded. His role as communications officer was simple: train the trainers. That meant tutoring the cell group leaders, who would in turn coach their subordinates, then their members, and so on.

They also had limited time to exchange important updates, brief the rebel cell group on military matters, and provide the necessary support weapons. Once done, both teams would go their separate ways. Within months, they hoped to form sizable pockets of partisan forces within enemy territories—an intricate system all directed by central control.

The light in front of them flickered closer, Kaden's unit waiting with bated breath. About a hundred yards away the torch suddenly switched off.

"That's weird," the captain said under his breath. "They're not supposed to…" Hastings paused, muttering to himself. Just as Kaden was about to turn and ask what was wrong the commander screamed, "Get down!"

A wall of flashing muzzles opened up before them, the bullets ripping past his team and exploding into the trees behind.

"Return fire and retreat!" Hastings bellowed, but as he began to run toward the jeeps he was cut down by a new wave of bullets. He fell face down into the mud, his binoculars still clutched in one hand. Kaden scrambled over, tugging at the body, but there was no use.

"Get in the jeep!" Sergeant Taylor screamed.

Kaden crawled around to the door of one of the vehicles, his brain trying desperately to keep up with his body. A tremendous explosion sent him stumbling back, but he quickly regained his feet and pulled himself into the cabin. Only Harper, the Fed agent, and one of the military escorts had made it. With a sickening wrench, Kaden glimpsed the remains of the other soldier in the rocket-blasted crater beside them.

"Let's break into two groups, take both jeeps and head for the border," Kaden cried. "At least some of us may be able to get out alive."

He took the wheel and found Harper sitting beside him, blood trickling from a gash at her forehead. Bullets were thumping into the car, and as he sped past the open window of the other vehicle he screamed at them to keep their headlights off. Both vehicles careened desperately in an easterly direction, and he tried to think of who was now the commanding officer. To his dismay, he realized the mantle of responsibility had fallen upon his shoulders.

"Keep an eye on the GPS, Harper," Kaden ordered. "We can't afford to get lost."

A rocket exploded at the side of the car, and he swerved through the mud and increased speed. Everything grew quiet, and Kaden waited for headlights to appear in his rear mirror, or the hair-raising pop of tires being blown out. But only the roar of the engine could be heard, and as the two jeeps continued their journey, everyone heaved a cautious sigh of relief.

"Contact HQ, Harper. Tell them we've been ambushed and report the casualties. See if they can have someone meet us at the border."

If Harper had a snarky comeback, she kept it to herself.

Kaden kept his foot on the gas. They had another ninety miles to go, and he wasn't planning on cruising down an enemy highway under the morning sun.

He still couldn't believe it. They had been betrayed.

But was it an inside job, or had their rebel contacts double-crossed them?

Either way, it had been clear from the start that the mission was poorly planned and coordinated. A wild-goose chase.

He was about to ask Harper's opinion on the matter when, without warning, a glaring spotlight appeared in front of their path. It was cast from above, like the probing light of a spaceship in an eerie UFO movie. Kaden and Harper glanced up, the sound of a million locusts hovering above them.

"There's a red star on its side, must be Chinese!" Harper shouted. The jeep in front of him twisted and turned as the spotlight followed relentlessly.

He caught a glimpse of Sergeant Taylor trying to retrieve the MANPAD from the back compartment. The vehicle lunged left and right, and it made Taylor's job of slotting the rocket into the launcher and aiming almost impossible. Any second now and the helicopter would open fire, obliterating both cars instantly.

C'mon, Taylor, load and shoot!

The enemy gunship did a twist and then veered behind them, spouting deadly cannon fire and rockets. Taylor's jeep shot sideways into Kaden's path and the 23-mm cannon rounds from the attack helicopter ripped the cabin in half. It burst into flames and screeched to a smoldering halt.

Kaden's jeep fared no better. A missile whizzed past his shoulder as he opened his door, slamming into the back of his ATV. The next instant he felt a blinding explosion, then everything went silent. A wave of searing heat sent him flying from his seat and he landed with a heavy splash in an inch of muddy water.

Stunned, Kaden lay still on the ground. Above him the bright light continued to hover, the sound of the chopper replaced by a distant ringing sound that was slowly growing louder. His mouth and nose were open, taking in rain and soil as he tried to decide if he was dying. When the sound returned to his ears in a wave of chopper blades and popping flames, he concluded he might just live after all.

"Harper," he moaned, "where are you?"

To his immense surprise, a gruff voice came from the dark. "I'm hit, can't get up."

He rolled onto his shoulder. "Then play dead!"

But it was too late. He watched Harper lift her rifle up to the beam of light and fire with the last energy she had. When the gun was emptied it dropped to her side, and she turned her face away from the glare of her executioner. But instead of finishing them off quickly, it arced over and prepared its approach from the far end of the road. They may as well have been two mice entertaining a very bored cat.

Kaden crawled to Harper with all the speed he could muster. His body ached with a dozen unseen injuries, dragging roughly over a bed of gravel and stones. Grabbing her arm, he tried to pull her under the car.

"No, arghh!" she screamed. "I think my hip's broken."

Kaden couldn't see clearly in the dark but he could feel her waist; it was warm and slimy, slick with blood. At her side lay her rifle and camera.

"It's okay, Harper. I'll get you out of here."

"No, leave me." She grunted at the effort of pushing him away. "None of this hero bullshit, Lieutenant. A woman's got a right to a good death, just like any man."

"You've got a right to live, too," he grunted, tugging at her as the helicopter powered toward them.

"Piss off, you bastard!" she cried, as he began to wiggle her along.

He stopped and withdrew his army-issued pistol, aiming it at the gunship. They both knew it was a futile gesture, the bullets bouncing off the armored plates like flies hitting a wall, if he was even able to hit the target at all. Still, it was better than lying there and waiting for the ax to fall.

"Get out, Kaden!"

He pushed himself to his feet, waiting to be shot down as he limped over to the wreck of Sergeant Taylor's jeep. Taylor lay dead, his body pulverized by the merciless canon rounds. Beside him was the rocket launcher, his hand still firmly clutching the tube. The weapon looked undamaged, but he couldn't know until he tried. Kaden raised it to his shoulder and aimed.

The gunship had been focused on Harper, but it hovered uncertainly, sensing a new threat. Its chain gun made automatic adjustments, the spotlight centering on Kaden as if lighting an actor on the stage.

Was the damn thing even loaded? It didn't matter; they would live or die in the next three seconds. Kaden's index finger depressed the metallic activator, anticipating the kick and rush of the rocket exhaust...

But nothing happened.

Sixty-Three

"It's jammed!" Kaden yelled.

Spying the weapon, the enemy pilot wrenched the helicopter back as the chain gun sprouted bright red lead toward him. The cannon rounds thumped the wet ground just meters from Kaden's feet, lacerating the tarmac.

"The safety!" Harper cried.

Kaden fiddled along the side of the firing mechanism, found the small safety catch, and flipped it down.

He squeezed the trigger and, like an amateur, closed his eyes. As the rocket exploded from his shoulder, he opened them once more and watched a streak of orange propulsion blaze toward the front of the chopper. The very fabric of time and space seemed to rip apart as a massive detonation struck his still-tender ears, the snarling face of the gunship erupting in a fireball so large it sent him sprawling backward. Frozen in dumb awe, he bore witness as the rotor broke from its top and the craft pitched sideways, as if drunk. It crashed before him, the heat so intense he lifted his hands to his face and was surprised to find the skin unblistered, his lungs wracking and coughing as he fought for air.

With great effort, he picked himself up and tried to move away from the burning wreck. Harper was propped against the first jeep, alive, but only barely.

"Can you move?"

The beaten expression on her face was cast in sharp relief by the glow of the fire behind them. She shook her head. Kaden ran his hands through his hair and groaned. He had no transport, no support, and knew that the place would be swarming with enemy forces in no time at all.

He had to prepare a makeshift stretcher. Searching the vehicles he found a poncho and two twisted steel bars, and began to rope them together into something semi-functional. There was a medi-pack under the passenger seat, and he gave Harper a shot of morphine to ease the difficult task ahead. Loading her on, he dragged her along the muddy ground, further from the secondary explosions that continued to rock the wreckages behind them. It was tough on him physically, but Harper's agonizing moans made each exertion gut wrenching. At least the heavy rain had stopped, and for that he was grateful.

After half an hour of heavy hauling, he found a small gully between some rocky embankments. Harper was unconscious.

For the third time, Kaden punched the dials of his military-issued radio. "OneAm Five to Mother, can you read me, over?" The radio buzzed in static silence. "OneAm Five to Mother?" he repeated. The same silence.

Come on, talk to me.

As if finally deciding to follow orders, the radio crackled into life. "Mother to OneAm, we read you. What's your status, over?"

"This is Lieutenant Kaden Sun, with Zuri Harper, who is badly wounded. Our squad is..." He tried to remember the code words that signified total devastation, but couldn't. "We're all that's left. We need immediate EVAC."

There was a slight pause at the other end before the voice returned. "This is Mother. We note your location is within a red zone. You need to get to the agreed EVAC point, over."

"Damn it!" Kaden screamed, breaking further communication protocols. "I have one seriously wounded and no transport. The EVAC point is miles away!" Then, as an afterthought, he added, "Over!"

Another pause. Kaden waited. The operator was probably discussing the situation with his supervisor, and if the supervisor had no authority to make the decision he would then send the request to higher authority for approval, until someone gave a yes or an emphatic, no.

"This is Mother. Sorry, Lieutenant, this is no go, repeat, no go. Please proceed to preset coordinates. Out."

"Shit!" Kaden sunk down, squatting beside Harper and noting dully that blood stained the grass at his feet. The cold rain started to fall once more.

Five hours to dawn.

Sixty-Four

"Leave me, Kaden."

"What?" He turned from his radio set toward Harper, who was grimacing as she readjusted herself against the uneven ground.

"You'll have a better chance making it alone to the EVAC point."

Kaden glowered. "You think I dragged you for an hour through the mud just to leave you here?"

She gave a weak snort of amusement. "I'm leaking faster than a refugee boat. You're wasting your time."

Kaden checked the map on his comm—they had an eighty-mile hike ahead of them.

No chance without transport.

His mind whirled for an answer, a magical solution to an insurmountable problem.

"Tell you a secret?" Harper said suddenly, interrupting his thoughts. "Unless you got somewhere else to be?"

"Hmm?"

"I had reservations about you."

"That's no secret," Kaden said with a laugh, "and you're not the first." He squatted beside her. "Half the people at the base think I'm some kind of terrorist vigilante."

"Well, if it's true then the American army is screwed. You've got more balls than half that base put together."

Kaden looked away, suddenly uncomfortable. He'd never enjoyed receiving praise, and coming from someone like Harper it felt doubly embarrassing.

"Thanks," he mumbled.

"Just sayin' it how it is." Grunting, she shifted herself once more, and Kaden could only imagine the pain she was in. He caught himself wishing she'd let it all go and drift away into the night, then flushed, ashamed by the thought.

"Want to know why I joined the corps?" Her reticence seemed to have evaporated away, for now at least.

"Sure," Kaden encouraged. "I'd like to know why any person would pick this hellhole, over Hollywood."

"I've got my reasons. I'm a second-generation immigrant," she said. "Baltic."

"But your last name…"

Harper gave a curt laugh. "My father had it changed from Jagielończyk. But that was the easy part. You know, people like us know we have more to prove. We've got to earn our place here."

Kaden lowered his head. "I know the feeling."

"But I also think it's bullshit."

He looked at her in surprise.

"Our families weren't born on some hick farm with an American flag and a whole lot of entitlements. They risked every-thing to come here, and become citizens." She coughed slightly, brushing Kaden away when he went to help her. "And that's what I'm fighting for. That dream they had, a dream that's turned out to be nothing more than a mirage."

"We can still make it happen," Kaden whispered. "The dream isn't over yet."

Harper's white teeth glowed in the moonlight. "And that's why I like you, Kaden. You're still living the dream."

He felt his comm vibrate on his wrist, the caller ID dull upon the screen. He still had it set to combat mode.

"Zac?" He almost couldn't believe it. "Are you there?"

"Just finished work at the Chinese restaurant," his friend drawled. "Thought I'd call and see if those thugs have killed you yet."

Kaden thought about sending the call to his earpiece, but Harper seemed amused by Zac's words so he left the speaker on. "They haven't got me yet," he muttered, taking in the desolate expanse of mud, rock, and shrubs surrounding them. "But I'm stuck behind the Californian border, so Li Lei's men are the least of my worries."

Zac gave a long, low hiss. "Damn."

"Yep. Long story short: we were betrayed. Seems to be a bit of a pattern for me."

Zac laughed, though it sounded bittersweet. "So what now? You got a squad coming to pick you up?"

"Nope."

"But you have transport out?"

"Nada."

"Then what have you got?"

Kaden groaned and rubbed his hand across his eyes. "An empty gun, an eighty-mile hike, and a badly wounded comrade."

This was met with a string of curses so long and varied, there were a few Kaden had never even heard before. "Those assholes are leaving you to die out there, after everything you've done for them?"

Harper chuckled, speaking up. "This isn't Disneyland. No free airport transfers."

"You got a *girl* there?" Zac sounded genuinely shocked.

"We've been in the army for about fifty years now, sunshine. And I'm a woman, not a girl."

"A woman left injured behind enemy lines…" Every molecule of Zac's Southern gallantry was offended.

"A *soldier*," Harper snapped.

"Shut up, Zac." Kaden grimaced as Harper began coughing. "You're working her up and she needs to take it easy."

"I'm coming to get you," his best friend replied.

"What?"

"I'm a Texan," Zac said proudly. "We don't leave brothers in need, or ladies in danger."

"Well, that's chivalrous," Kaden rolled his eyes, knowing neither of them could see him, "but I'm not going to let you kill yourself for no reason."

"I know where you are," he replied. "Chet has your location. Don't move, now."

Kaden hissed at him to stop being an idiot, but the Southerner replied with characteristic nonchalance.

"I'm coming for you, brother."

Sixty-Five

The refrigerated truck appeared as dawn was about to break, the head of an enormous fabricated Peking duck fixed upon its roof. As it bumped across the rocky terrain, the giant yellow beak threatened to jolt forward and smash through the windshield. It was so bizarre, Kaden had to laugh.

Zac puttered to a stop beside the rocky outcrop, looking around as if he expected an army to rise from beneath the mud.

"That is the ugliest thing I've ever seen," Kaden said.

His best friend flashed a grin from under his Dong's Duck cap. "The limo's in the shop."

Getting Harper into the back of the truck wasn't easy. Her body was fractured in a dozen different places, and she cried out at the slightest movement. Once they'd laid her upon the cool stainless floor, they then had to shift her behind packages of blood-spattered duck carcasses. By then, dawn had broken.

Kaden scrambled into his hiding spot and covered himself beside Harper. It was freezing cold, and she clasped her hands over her chest, her body curled into itself. Kaden found a heavy sackcloth and laid it on her along with Zac's jacket, though there was little else he could do. She was in too much pain for them to share their body heat.

"Hey, Zac." Kaden caught his friend's eye as the door began to close. "Thanks, man." Zac gave a wink and a thumbs-up before darkness enveloped them.

It was not a pleasant ride. The truck was old and the roads pitted, a far cry from gliding down avenues in his state-of-the-art Mercedes. Each jerk or jolt brought a low moan from Harper, and he was constantly holding back the boxes and carcasses that threatened to topple over her. It was impossible to know how long she would bear the pain, and when her moans turned to whimpers, and finally a heavy silence, the thick black nothingness was more frightening than her loudest complaints.

In the dark, Kaden tried to picture the person who had betrayed them, the rage inside him lifting from a simmer to something much more volcanic. He would find out who it was, and when he did…

The truck shuddered to a halt and his body grew tense. They hadn't driven long enough to reach the EVAC point.

There was a dull thump as the front door of the truck slammed shut, followed by muted voices outside. The conversation was indistinguishable but they were men, and their tone was demanding.

Border guards.

The compartment door opened and the endless black was suddenly a dazzling gray. A gust of warmer air gushed inside, the relief quickly lost to panic as heavy boots began thumping toward them.

"Just dead ducks?" came a gravelly baritone. "No refugees hiding back here?"

Kaden's heart thumped in anticipation, his hand shooting out to smother Harper's mouth as her eyes fluttered open. There was a brief gasp of her breath against his palm, but he brought his index finger to his lips, and she nodded.

"Nothing back there but a whole lotta poultry," Zac called, sounding almost bored. "Duck for breakfast, duck for lunch, duck for damn dinner. Them Chinese love their Pekings."

Kaden flinched as a heavy metallic object dropped beside him about a foot away. It sounded like the butt of a machine gun.

"You mind if I take some? My commander's a Chinaman. He might like one, since they're too expensive for a soldier's wages."

The box immediately above Kaden's head began to shift about.

"Sure!" Zac called, his sneakers sounding softer inside the vehicle. "But you'll want one of these babies." The box stopped moving, and Kaden could hear his friend rustling around against the far left wall.

"Why's that?" the soldier asked. "You hiding something back here?"

There was a scrape as the gun lifted up off the floor, but Zac's voice stayed light and carefree.

"No need to point that thing, brother. I just thought you'd want a fresh one, so that your commander isn't cursing your name from the toilet. See? Killed yesterday. The bad boys over there are a week old."

The truck jolted as both men exited the compartment. Kaden took a deep breath and exhaled, eying Harper as she stared up at the metallic ceiling above them, tears streaming down her cheeks. The door slammed shut and it was dark once more.

"It's okay," Kaden whispered. "Almost there."

For once, Harper remained silent.

Sixty-Six

Kaden leaned against the back of the truck, Zac standing at his side. Lifting his comm to his lips, he scanned the horizon for signs of trouble. Day had broken, leaving them completely exposed.

"OneAm Five to Mother, this is Lieutenant Kaden Sun, do you read?"

"This is Mother, OneAm Five, go ahead, over."

"We're at the EVAC point. Two survivors, one badly wounded. We require immediate transportation."

There was an extended pause, Kaden and Zac exchanging glances as the sun beat down upon their heads.

"Mother to OneAm Five. All our transport has been deployed elsewhere. Request you wait until we have availability. ETA is six hours. Acknowledge, over."

"What?" Kaden shook his head, unable to believe the voice squeaking up from his arm could be serious. "We're out of time. Private Harper is in a critical condition, and we're endangering a civilian life by being here. I want you to send the drone, right now!"

"OneAm Five. Please maintain communications protocol. We're sorry, but there's nothing we can do."

"Then call VP Koch. I need to talk to him."

"No can do, Lieutenant. That's against protocol and regardless, he is directing operations at this time. We request you to wait, Lieutenant. Out."

Kaden slammed his fist against the truck door. "Damn your protocol! How could he pull every available aircraft for his operations? What about us?" Silence. "Talk to me, you bastards!"

Zac was staring at the comm as if Kaden had a rattlesnake wrapped around his wrist.

"Are they for real?"

"Oh yeah," Kaden said, "believe it or not."

"Where's your nearest base, bro?"

"Arizona, beneath Sedona. Why?"

"Beneath Sedona, like, underground?" Zac ran his hand through his hair. "Heck, how many secrets does the White House have?"

"Too many," Kaden snarled.

"It's four hours' drive away, in this wreck. Come on, buddy, load up."

"No," Kaden said, lowering his voice. "Harper won't make it that far, and I won't have you risk your life for me alone." He clamped his hand on his friend's shoulder and squeezed. "Get out of here, man."

"I'm not leaving the two of you out here for the crows." Zac's blue eyes searched his intensely. "We go now, together, or we stay here and wait."

Kaden took a long breath stared out into the distance. "Don't do this Zac." His voice broke on his friend's name, but he pushed on. "Too many people have died trying to help me. And if I lose you too…"

"You, won't," Zac whispered. "But if we're going to make it out of here we have to go, now."

Sixty-Seven

Kaden stayed in the fridge with Harper as the truck roared its way back to base. Flitting in and out of consciousness, her condition had deteriorated rapidly. His comm confirmed they had another hour to go.

Kaden flashed a torch across her face, now a worrying shade of gray. Blood had congealed around the makeshift bandage at her side, and the tissues surrounding the injury had swelled into a small hump. Her eyes remained closed. Kaden squeezed her hand.

"Come on, soldier, wake up."

Harper stirred, her eyes squinting against the glare of the torch. He switched it off.

"Thought you were Dad," she murmured. "He used to wake me up with those words—an army man, through and through. Always wanted a son, but he got me." She sighed. "Where are we now?"

"A few miles from base. But you got to stay awake, okay?"

When she didn't respond, he flashed the torch on her once more.

Harper licked her lips. "I'm thirsty."

Kaden took the aluminum bottle from his hip and removed the cap, holding it above her mouth and trickling the water between her lips. When she started to cough, he stopped.

"My video…" she spluttered, groaning as they jolted through something major, like a grenade crater. "I filmed the helicopter go down and transmitted it back to base when you guys were talking outside the truck."

"That's good, Harper." Kaden edged closer, cupping her jaw as she drank once more. She turned her head from the bottle and swallowed.

"You look pretty heroic, with all those explosions going on behind you."

Kaden laughed. "Maybe I'll get a movie deal."

Harper started to smile, then her eyes narrowed. "Why are we still on the road? What happened to the drone?" Before he could answer, she began to shiver. "It's freezing, Kaden. This fridge is going to kill me, if my wounds don't."

Kaden brushed the hair from her face. "We switched the fridge off a couple of hours ago. You'll be fine."

When her eyes rolled back, Kaden's chest tightened in panic.

"Stay with me, Harper. I'm not going to lose you this close to home."

Her lashes fluttered, her eyes wide and frightened in torchlight. "Hold me, please. I don't want to die here, like this…"

Kaden squeezed himself in beside her, putting his arm across her chest and holding her to him. He must have been hurting her, but she didn't seem to feel it. "Don't be afraid, we're almost there."

The torchlight bounced across the defrosting carcasses, like some kind of carnival house of horrors.

For a moment, there was only the roar of the engine.

"Don't get any ideas, Lieutenant," Harper chuckled weakly.

Kaden felt the truck speed up, bouncing over yet another series of potholes. Harper didn't flinch.

"Open your eyes, soldier."

He squeezed her tighter and felt her body start to convulse.

"No," he cried, trying to shake her awake. "Don't you dare give up this close!"

But it was no use. Harper's body was limp in his arms and her blood warm on his hands.

There was nothing he could do to bring her back. And so he held her tight and hoped that wherever she was she knew she hadn't died in vain, and would one day be avenged with the rest of them.

Sixty-Eight

Underground Military Base #2

Kaden strode into the command center with a single purpose. Some of the staff noted his arrival and stood in admiration, others applauded. The majority gave him scant attention or whispered among themselves. Kaden ignored his fans and critics alike. Stomach twisting with bitterness and anger, he set his eyes upon the office of VP Koch.

"Sir, you are not allowed within the vice president's premises without permission," said the secretary, standing in protest at Kaden's sudden intrusion.

"Where's Koch?"

"Do I need to call the guards, sir?"

"Go ahead." Kaden pushed past her into the interior room. Behind a large desk, VP Koch held a handpiece to his ear. He looked up and grimaced, before barking a few words into the device and hanging up with a sharp prod of his meaty finger.

"I'm sorry, Mr. Koch. He just barged in—" the secretary said, hanging at Kaden's elbow.

"It's fine, Allison. Close the door as you go."

Koch left his enameled table and walked toward Kaden, his annoyed expression slowly replaced with a smug one.

"Our hero is back. Everyone's talking about your exploits."

"Exploits? We were set up, and my team was murdered."

Koch's lip twitched, his emotions held in check. "Really? I was told Captain Hastings made an error of judgment with his meeting point." He shrugged. "The man dumped you into the middle of a viper's nest."

It would have been easy to believe him; the words were delivered with calm assurance, as if Kaden would be a fool to question army intelligence. But he'd been there, he knew better.

"He was checking and double-checking the GPS coordinates. I saw it myself."

"And he lured you straight into a trap, my boy."

"He was as surprised as the rest of us. He was the first to fall, for God's sake."

"Our enemy is ruthless. They will sacrifice their own, as you know only too well."

"Are you any different?" Kaden spat. "We traveled eighty miles to the EVAC point and got zero assistance. Harper might have lived if—"

"Look, Lieutenant. I can't expend valuable resources on two people when hundreds are at risk in active combat." Koch turned his back and sauntered toward the door. "Are you done with your questioning?"

Taking a deep breath, Kaden reminded himself to play it cool; too much was at stake. "Lives were lost, sir, as a result of poor planning and sabotage. I will be demanding an investigation."

Koch laughed. "On whose authority? We're at war, if you haven't noticed. Men are dying every day."

Kaden shook his head. "You know what? That's the reason America failed. No accountability, no responsibility. Just fat men in big offices, laughing at the rest of us."

Koch's flushed face signaled he was on the edge of losing control. "Excuse me?" He stepped toward Kaden, chest puffed to make up for what he lacked in stature. "I can have you deactivated and placed under twenty-four-hour surveillance with a single call." His canines peeked from beneath his fleshy lip. "You could be a double agent, for all we know."

Koch could do it, and worse. But Kaden had been threatened so many times he'd grown immune to bullying. "I was requested by the president to be part of the team and I will answer to her. I won't allow Captain Hastings' reputation be sullied, or Harper and Taylor's lives to be sacrificed for nothing. They died with honor and they deserve justice."

Koch walked to his desk in a deathly silence and pressed a small red button beside his comm. A moment later three large men walked in and restrained Kaden. He didn't bother to struggle, knowing the president would be outraged to hear of Koch's actions. As they began to walk out the secretary appeared at the door once more, her eyes wide and face drawn.

"What is it?" Koch demanded.

"I've just received a priority message."

"And?" he hollered.

With a trembling voice, she said, "Air Force One, sir. Enemy fighters have shot the president down."

Sixty-Nine

Solitary Confinement
Deep Underground Military Base #2

Kaden sat in a small cell, his back to the cold concrete wall. He wasn't sure how long he'd been there, but guessed it was more than a couple of days. Even within the confines of the prison he could sense the dark mood that had befallen what was left of the nation.

The story was told everywhere, from the whispers of the wardens to the TV that played in their watch station: The president had insisted on meeting all her constituents, but as she neared the end of her journey in West Virginia, Air Force One and its escorts had been ambushed by a horde of enemy fighters.

Rumormongers speculated it was an inside job, as all her flight plans had been kept secret. Moreover, the considerable fleet of enemy planes couldn't just appear within an American territory at a specific time to coordinate.

And yet they had.

Vice President Koch had been quickly installed as the 47th president of the United States. The thought of the country's hope being placed solely in his hands left Kaden's head hanging in despair.

Surprisingly, they had allowed Zac to visit. His friend had come and announced he didn't want to go back to the confederate states. It was clear they were now run by foreign powers, and those who resisted tended to disappear without a trace. It wasn't the kind of place he wanted to live.

Kaden sat alone in his cell. He took out the pen President Cowen had given him and fingered it thoughtfully. Her mentor had given this to her just before he died, and now she had done the same for him. He had no right to such a treasure and had done nothing to earn her regard, and she had believed in him anyway.

Now she was dead, killed by those she had trusted and a system that continued to fail all of them.

A flash of brown caught his attention at the end of the cell. A moment later the rat was beside his foot, sniffing tentatively.

"I fed you an hour ago, dude."

"Brewster" had appeared the night he was arrested, refusing to come closer than a yard. Over the time Kaden had been incarcerated, he'd slowly convinced the tiny creature to take food from his fingers. Now Brewster even tolerated a short scratch behind the ear. The rat was the one small pleasure Kaden allowed himself, when he wasn't thinking about Katy or struggling to work out the many unanswered questions plaguing his mind. It was that, or stare at the wall and go slowly insane.

A few days later, Kaden had a visitor. The man wore a single-breasted gray twill blazer, with one of the sleeves pinned where his right arm had been amputated at the shoulder. His chin was dusted with stubble, but it wasn't entirely unkempt. There were scars on his face and neck. Kaden thought he had a sad countenance, as if he'd gone through some kind of hell.

"Special Agent Jack Raven, FBI," he said, offering his hand in introduction. "It's in your interest to cooperate and answer the questions I need to ask, Mr. Sun." Apparently, his intention was to ascertain if Kaden had been responsible for the sabotage of his last mission. As the sole survivor—who also had a history of working with the enemy—even Kaden had to admit it didn't look good. He thanked the heavens he hadn't been privy to the president's flight plans; otherwise, he'd likely be under suspicion for her assassination also.

Agent Raven stayed in his quarters for hours, asking the same repeated questions about the failed operation, over and over again.

"This interview's wearing you down more than me," Kaden said, after the second day. They were seated in an interrogation room at a long steel table. The institution seemed to be crumbling at the edges, the surfaces unclean and the lightbulbs overhead flickering continuously. Kaden eyed a cockroach scurrying between his feet and went to stamp on it, before setting his heel back on the linoleum. These days he could empathize with even the lowest of God's creatures.

He looked up to see Agent Raven staring at his tablet, before shrugging in resignation.

"You're right. I can't do this."

When Kaden didn't respond, the investigator drew a deep breath and sighed. "I was a field agent, got injured, refused to retire, worked out a deal and got sent here on a desk job."

"Your dad's work, I imagine?"

He tensed. "How did you know that?"

"Besides sharing the same surname, I heard you arguing with the general last night outside my cell."

"The man's a tyrant," said Raven, visibly relaxing.

Kaden smiled. "I felt the same way about my dad too, once."

"You don't know General Raven."

"Maybe not." Kaden leaned forward and said, "But I need to ask, what does Koch want with me? Is this whole thing an effort to find out the truth, or just an excuse to destroy me?"

Raven averted the gaze. "I can't say. But the truth has been obvious to me for the past twenty-four hours."

Kaden sat back in his chair, fingers thrumming atop the steel. Would Koch ever give up his vendetta, or was he destined to be persecuted forever?

"How can you tell? I haven't told you much."

"That's my expertise, isn't it, Mr. Sun?" Raven gave a rare grin. "Until recently, my partner and I had been working on hauling up corrupt members of the congress. We had a dossier on you the moment you started working with Li Lei."

The name instantly conjured months of sleepless nights, tediously going through ream after ream of evidence that Li had somehow managed to assemble. Kaden had felt so righteous at the time.

"Thinking of what could have been?" Raven asked.

"Oh, perhaps."

"Well," Raven said and glanced at his comm, "I think we're done for the day." He slipped his tablet back into its case, then stood, offering his hand. "I won't waste anymore of your time."

Kaden couldn't help but laugh. "Time? That's all I have left."

The agent nodded, walking toward the door.

"Wait," Kaden said. "Can I ask you something?"

The room seemed suddenly quiet as Raven turned, squinting at the request. "Guess it's fair, given all the questions I've asked you."

"And you trust me enough to answer?"

Raven shrugged. "That depends on what you ask. But given the mandate, I would have released you with immediate effect. As I said, you're no traitor."

Kaden focused on the man's face, trying to read his solemn expression. "Are you guys going to get the moles, or is it too little, too late?"

He paused, head cocked to one side. "The new president has decided to focus on offensive maneuvers. He's disbanded your propaganda units as well."

"*What?*"

"New engagement policy," the agent replied. "He wants to frustrate the secessionists and gather them together for an Armageddon of sorts. Says they need to pay for the murder of President Cowen."

"He's playing right into their hands," Kaden said, shocked by the new president's lack of foresight. "They know their best chance to defeat us is with a short, brutal war." He scrubbed his hands over his eyes, exhaustion and defeat finally overwhelming him. "Does General Raven agree with his strategy?"

Jack shook his head. "He was a close confidant of President Cowen's and was the first to disagree." Glancing back to the door he lowered his voice and added, "Koch seems to have widespread support. I think General Raven has been sidelined, but he's too proud to say so."

"What is the point of an offensive plan if we have spooks in our midst? How can we fight without the element of surprise?"

Agent Raven straightened up. The interrogator-turned-interviewee was lost in thought, before saying, "You've managed to raise more questions than answers."

"Please, just let the General know."

"I'll talk to him," Raven said, "but there's only so much he can do. One thing I can promise is that President Koch won't stop until he has a case against you. And if he can't find one, he'll make one."

Kaden smirked. "That's the least of my worries."

Seventy

New York State Capitol
Albany, NY

N ew York Governor Phil Cardena's eyes narrowed to slits. He wasn't a blue blood; he'd grown up on the mean streets of Brooklyn and knew how to use the two fists hidden beneath his desk. Had it been any other occasion, he might have. Sitting opposite was his longtime associate, Luka Lermontov, joined by several of their Russian military commanders.

During the past few months, Cardena and his fellow separatist governors had gone from fidgeting in their seats over the federal invasion of Maryland and Delaware, to regaining their territories and toasting all things Russian-Chinese. Now, with their boundaries secured, his foreign friends continued to flood his harbors and ports with more military hardware and 'peacekeepers.'

But his partners had become uncompromising of late. On many occasions, they were controlling confederate military maneuvers without even consulting him or his fellow leaders.

Like all the secessionist states, New York had prospered despite being at war. They had direct recourse to international investors via the newly formed confederacy, and most of all, the economic backing of their global allies. It was also true that Cardena's personal wealth had exploded into figures he could have only dreamed of a year ago.

Could he complain? Hadn't he arrived, and helped his people in the process? The international media were already hailing them as 'liberators of the free world.' And, what's more, his peers had nominated him for the presidency of the Confederate States of America. It was what every politician secretly desired, whether they admitted it or not.

So why the niggling doubt and simmering resentment?

Lermontov might have been the most powerful businessman in the world, but how did he *dare* order around Cardena's state military, as if he were the chief of the Armed Forces? He wasn't even an American citizen.

Dissatisfaction weighted his brows as he studied the cool, calm face before him. The war with the federal government was just beginning, and there was a lot of work to be done. All their necks were on the line. They needed to work as one. Cardena realized that it wasn't the time to deal with petty insecurities and personal skirmishes.

With a deal of effort he relaxed his fists and stretched out his fingers, the throbbing sensation in his hands returning to normal. Silent, he continued to watch Lermontov direct instructions to a Russian general, who then briefed the confederate air force general Robert Young. General Young turned to Governor Cardena for his decree, a slight hesitation hidden in the action.

The governor smiled, and nodded.

Seventy-One

"**C**het got back to me on your request," Zac whispered, body pressed to the steel bars of Kaden's cell.

"Let's hear it."

Zac frowned in concentration, struggling to regurgitate the words. "He said it was tough, even with his 'quantum access system.' Apparently, he used some sort of 'ghost process'…"

"Ghost protocol?"

"That's it. The ghost protocol allowed him to access your base's communications and radio network."

"And?"

"And…not much really. Something about the moles adopting codes and ciphers. He managed to get some names. Not sure what they mean, though."

"Spill them."

"Uh, the main guy is called 'Bishop.' Lots of chatter with his friends outside. He's been running a network of insiders and double agents all around the country. Chet thinks he is currently residing at your base."

Kaden stiffened. It was one thing to know these people existed, but the name made it real. *Bishop, puppeteering his brood of traitors…They'd undoubtedly had a hand in President Cowen's death. And Harper's.*

He turned slightly, not wanting Zac to see his expression. "Anything else?"

His best friend's voice became low and terse. He glanced back at the sentry patrolling a short distance away. "Someone's watching you. Your name comes up in messages quite a lot. They're reporting your movements and visitors back to the central contact." He flipped sideways to check again. "Katy's name was mentioned too."

Kaden's mouth went dry, an odd chill tingling up the back of his arms. It was one thing to know they were watching him; he'd expected that. But to hear they were still tracking Katy…

"Look, Kaden. We've got to get you both out of here. This place isn't safe for you. And Katy needs to know the truth."

Kaden pressed his face to the bars. "No, trust me on this. Let Katy continue to think I'm on active duty. Don't get her worried, but make sure she stays inside the government compound. She can't be allowed to leave."

Zac nodded, though his lips were pursed in a way that made it clear he was uncomfortable with the situation.

A baton began to clang loudly against the metal door at the end of the hallway. "Time's up," the guard called.

"Take this," Kaden urged, handing Zac a small note. "It's for her."

"This better not be a goodbye letter," his friend murmured.

"I can't run, or hide, Zac. They won't let Katy and I off, no matter what I do. But I have a plan."

Light flooded the concrete floor as the hallway door opened, and Zac made cursory steps from the cell to appease the guard. "What, then?"

Kaden swallowed. "I'm going to flush the Bishop out."

Seventy-Two

Kaden was surprised by the return of Agent Raven. He made a silent observation of the man as he walked in, his maimed body seeming tired and lopsided. Why had the agent refused to install a bionic arm? With the advancements made in robotic technology it would have made him physically superior, instead of handicapped. Kaden guessed he had his reasons.

Raven placed his tablet on the desk. "I've got updates."

"Me too," Kaden replied. "But you first."

He nodded, the bags beneath his eyes darkened by the harsh light overhead. "Which one first? The bad news, or terrible news?"

"Why not start with bad."

Raven gave a rueful twist of his lips. "Okay, I'll start with you. I recommended your immediate release. The request was rejected."

It was no surprise, but Kaden's spirit slumped nonetheless. "What right do they have to keep me here?"

"Koch has the authority to detain anyone accused of colluding with the enemy, indefinitely. It's under the NDAA."

Kaden seethed with injustice. Clearly, he was destined to be beaten down by one enemy after another.

Sometimes they hate you for envy, or because you're a threat... President Cowen's words were so vivid he almost expected to turn and see her standing behind him.

"And the terrible news?"

"President Koch has confirmed the plan of attack. The offensive launches from dawn the day after tomorrow."

"That soon?"

Raven lowered himself into the chair opposite, wincing slightly. "Yep, too soon."

"Have you discussed the spy threat with General Raven?"

"Without evidence or material suspects, we're firing blanks." he said. "Everyone's focused on Armageddon, instead of the devil lurking inside the house."

Kaden pursed his lips. "We're going down."

"Not necessarily—" Jack began, their conversation broken by the sound of the hallway door being unlocked. Moments later a warden appeared holding a food tray. It wasn't his regular guy; Kaden hadn't seen this one's face before. His hair was long and unkempt, covering his pale forehead, and clumps of it jutted out of the back of the ill-fitting jailer's cap.

"JailFood express," the man grunted, sliding the plastic platter through a slot in the door. Kaden stood and took it before he dropped it to the ground.

"You're in luck. Some spam to add your rice, Chink."

The guard walked back to the door whistling an off-key tune, and Kaden sat at the edge of his bed, the tray balanced across his knees. Agent Raven eyed the contents.

"Appetizing. They treat you better than us." He waved at the tray. "Don't let me stop you."

"No. I'm not hungry anyway...not just yet."

He put the tray to one side and laughed as Raven gave a startled shout at the small brown missile dashing over his shoes. "Goddamn, is that a rat?"

"His name's Brewster," Kaden said, breaking off a corner of the spam and offering it to his upstretched paws.

"This place really is falling apart."

"He's proven to be a loyal friend," Kaden smiled, watching as Brewster sat back and sniffed at the clump of meat in his tiny paw. Apparently, spam was a questionable choice, even for vermin. "Beggars can't be choosers."

Jack leaned forward. "I feel your pain," he said with a wry half smile. "My father's been sidelined by Koch. He's like the least popular kid at school right now. Still, he's subscribing to some of Cowen's strategies, which I've heard had your input."

Kaden sat up. "Which means that he might be willing to work with us?"

Jack nodded. "That is, if we have anything to develop. And if my father and I can join forces, instead of fighting all the time." He sounded strained. "Anyway, I've done some snooping around. There are over two thousand service staff in each of our ten underground bases. We know the bases are fortified against unauthorized transmission signals, which means that our insiders should find it hard to communicate."

Kaden frowned as he thought about Chet and how easily his friend had managed to circumvent their systems. "Can we trace anything?"

"I've got an old contact, excommunicated from the NSA but one of the best in the game. He's discovered anomalous transmissions from Base Camp 2, our base, cleverly hidden within standard radio waves. Unfortunately, he wasn't able to decipher anything out of it, or pinpoint the source."

Kaden narrowed his eyes and said softly, "I have a friend, too. And he's told me about someone by the code name 'Bishop.' Seems like he is controlling a crawling network of spooks within the system."

"Seriously? How does he know?"

"He has his ways." Kaden was willing to trust Raven with his own life, but not that of his friend's. "What if Bishop is already sending details of our offensive plans? The enemy could simply position themselves in ambush and wipe out our entire force. We lose this round big time, and the whole of the USA will be rich pickings to the invaders."

"We need evidence, Sun. Something concrete."

"And if I can get it for you…"

Raven's head shot up, his face taut with so much anticipation it was clear he'd been about to declare the whole thing hopeless.

"I need to meet with Li Lei."

"That's Field Marshal Li Lei," Agent Raven corrected.

"No, I mean the chief of the China Econom—"

"That's a cover-up for his real role. Our intel indicates Li Lei is leading the Chinese military."

Kaden swallowed, astounded by the revelation. The quiet, tea-sipping bureaucrat, a military commander? Li had been a serpent from day one, sliding through the grass unseen. What else was he capable of?

"All the more reason to meet him then." Kaden's hands began to tremble, so he grasped the steel frame of his bed. "He's shrewd, but we have a history. If I can make him angry enough, he'll spill something."

Jack folded his arms. "And how do you propose this meeting? It's not like we can call Li's people and set up a lunch date."

"I'm the bait, so we just need a venue." When Jack frowned in confusion, Kaden continued with, "If Li Lei knows that I'm out of the protection of my base, headed somewhere like my old office space, he'll likely be there to shoot me himself."

Jack grimaced. "I know of your history together, and Alexis."

"It wasn't like that," Kaden replied. "We were friends, nothing more. And I didn't kill her, but he blames me anyway."

"He'll murder you, or his men will." Jack leaned forward on the rickety fold-up chair. "And you might get nothing from him."

The agent was right, but what option did they have? Could he sit back in his cell, alone with Brewster, and wait for Katy to fall prey to some kind of revenge plot? Or watch his country fall into the biggest trap laid in the history of human warfare? Each week another chess piece fell, with a regularity and insight that indicated the deception ran right to the top. They weren't fighting an enemy, so much as themselves.

Deception that ran right to the top… Kaden froze, a new thought occurring to him that seemed unthinkable and yet entirely logical. One man had gained from President Cowen's destruction. One man seemed happy to play right into the enemy's game plan.

Staring at Raven, Kaden was almost unable to say the words.

"What if the Bishop is…Koch?"

Seventy-Three

"**Y**ou must be kidding, kid." Raven's forefinger oscillated, reinforcing his disbelief. "President Cowen trusted him like a brother."

"And look how he's honored her game plan," Kaden replied. "It wouldn't take much to look into Koch's history and see that he's probably received a huge amount of financial support from foreign sources over the years. Lermontov and Li Lei are masters in the art of recruitment and promotion."

He had a grudging respect for their strategy. While it wasn't necessarily his way of doing things, it was infallible. Control the leader and their dominion would fall as surely as a house of cards.

Jack Raven was slowly shaking his head, unable to conceive even the remotest possibility it could be true.

"Bishop is capable of transmitting information out of the base at will, and at all hours. Not many personnel have that sort of flexibility."

"He's a decorated war hero. No one would ever believe you," Jack argued. "I'm not sure I even do."

"So let me prove it."

"How? Koch would have to let you go, first."

Kaden's mind cleared as the pieces started to fall together. "He will, if he's Bishop. Give him the excuse to approve it." Kaden stood up, pacing the tiny cell as his body flushed with excitement. "Tell him I know about Bishop, and that I have information stolen from Li Lei. You can say I hid it in my old office before running for my life. If he's the mole, Li Lei will be waiting for me when I get there."

"What information would be so valuable that you haven't told us already?"

"Information that resided in Li Lei's comm," Kaden said. "I made Alexis download everything onto a data stick so I could find out about a meeting that was taking place between Lermontov and an enemy of mine." He paused, looking away as a tinge of regret shot through his chest. "Well, I thought he was an enemy. In fact, he was just another one of Lermontov's victims. Anyway, I would bet my right arm..." he stopped pacing and glanced at Raven, flushing.

"Don't worry about it."

"I'd bet that Li knows his comm was compromised that night. Alexis wasn't a professional hacker by any means. What Li doesn't know is that I lost the stick while running for my life through the park. He probably thinks I'm sitting on a whole lot of incriminating evidence, biding my time."

Raven leaned back and drew a deep breath. "As wild as it sounds, it could work...if the whole thing's true," he added, compressing his lips.

Kaden's short, fast steps ground to a halt. At his feet lay a small, furry body, blood at its mouth and a chunk of spam still grasped in one paw. He knelt over Brewster in disbelief.

Raven, watching, leaned over to see what had made him stop so abruptly.

"Looks like the little rat just saved your life, Sun."

Seventy-Four

Kaden stood at the gated mouth of the cavernous hangar. Behind him, the engineers were making final preflight tests on the aircraft. The engine of the small stealth X-wing drone purred as the security officer pressed a switch to open the entrance of the cave opening, exposing the empty black of the valley below. The wind gushing in was strong and bitingly cold, and Kaden wrapped his flight jacket tight around himself.

Below stretched the arched, concave mountain corridor of the base's west wing. Small, twinkling lights indicated a hive of activity within. He lifted his disfigured hand to his lips, before lowering it in a silent goodbye to Katy.

Agent Raven had said that she'd recently been assigned to the presidential detail as a catering assistant. With the offensive due to launch in a few hours, the key leadership was probably sweating in the War Room, Katy running about with coffee and sandwich trays balanced in her arms. At least she would be safe, Kaden hoped. Li would find it almost impossible to target her in the heart of operations.

She had been distracted the last few times they'd spoken, and Kaden wondered at the thoughts she was harboring. He hated the idea of them keeping secrets and pulled a jewelry box from his pocket, looking at it wistfully. It contained a ring with a small heart-shaped diamond. He had been meaning to surprise her with a proposal on the day of his graduation, but then everything had gone to hell.

He put it back in his pocket and zipped it up. Could he ask her to spend her life with him, if there was a good chance he wouldn't even live to see another year? He hoped with time Katy might forgive his choices. Everything he'd ever done had been for her, even if she never knew it.

Agent Raven stood to the side of the tarmac, perhaps the last friendly face he would see.

"You know, Koch twitched when I said you knew about Bishop," Raven smiled. "Or maybe I was reading too much into it." His shoulders were slightly drooped, his eyes locked upon Kaden as if staring at a mirage. "In any case, make it count, Sun."

"If I make it there at all. The enemy has been known to shoot down planes," Kaden said, glancing at the aircraft.

"There's a chance," Raven agreed. "But this plane's built to avoid radar detection. It's state-of-the-art technology, and will only fail if its profile is broken."

"Profile?"

"The drone flies in stealth thanks to a specially designed outline. Break it—like allowing a door or hatch to come open—and your plane will light up like a Christmas tree on the enemy's radar." Raven clapped his hand over Kaden's shoulder. "But you're not planning on dropping any bombs, are you Sun?"

"Not if I can help it." He grimaced. "If I fail to deliver the goods, you'll be hung out to dry."

"I've lived through worse."

The purring of the engine had turned into a roar. It was time to leave.

"Remember," Jack shouted, "scramble the hell back the moment you get your admission. We don't need a dead hero."

"Keep Katy safe for me," Kaden countered as he walked up the steps, "and we have a deal."

Jack nodded and gave a thumbs-up.

Kaden climbed into the pilotless plane and took his seat at a padded bench. Through the small, round window beside him, he could see steam start to curl up the side of the aircraft. A short takeoff announcement was made, followed by a loud *whoosh* as the catapult system released. The plane shot forward in a huge gush of white vapor.

Kaden gripped his harness through intense shuddering as the runway was cleared, then the craft started to veer west, heading for Los Angeles. The low-lit environment grew silent, spare the hum of the turbine. He looked around, alone in the small, dark space. It felt like a crypt.

So this is it, Kaden thought, *a one-way trip to nowhere.*

In another few hours, President Koch would launch his pointless attack. Kaden tapped on the black metal disk hanging from his neck, smiling as he thought of the near scandal he'd encountered with the WarGames cheerleader who'd been wearing something similar.

Booby traps, he thought, pleased with the pun and glad Katy wasn't privy to his lewd thoughts. This time he was walking into a trap of his own making, and while he'd invested a lot of thought in planning his entrance, he hadn't even considered his escape. If he could get any incriminating evidence, it would be captured on his pendant recorder and transmitted back to Agent Raven instantly.

Then he'd make a desperate dash for home. Otherwise…

Checking his weapons, he ran his hands over the pouch of grenades Raven had sourced for him. If it came down to it, he'd say goodbye to this world and bring Li Lei and his men along for the ride.

Seventy-Five

Wiltshire Building
Los Angeles, California

A jackal in the shadows, Li Lei waited behind the overturned tables and broken chairs littering the decrepit office. Bishop had delivered.

Hunched and unshaven in his Chinese military uniform, he waited and watched, his right hand keeping a firm grip on the pistol at his side. It had already been an hour of antagonizing impatience, every muscle coiled, hardly daring to breathe.

More than six months had passed since he last saw his *protégé*, six months and twenty-two days of disrupted nights and bleary mornings, the traitor slipping through his fingers at every turn. This time, however, he was ready. He had entrusted Kaden's assassination to others in the past; today he would end it himself.

He had no taste for theatrics. Watch the target walk into the room, point his gun, and fire. At least, that had been the plan until Luka had *insisted*—in his quiet, dangerous way—that Li first reclaim Kaden's data stick.

They were winning the war against the administration, but international relations depended on the world continuing to believe it was a liberation, rather than invasion. They couldn't afford the release of embarrassing documents at such a crucial time.

Some days after Alexis' death Li's security personnel had informed him there'd been a breach with his comm. At first, he'd refused to believe the digital signature was Alexis', but security footage had shown her hunched beside his bed in the middle of the night. He'd wondered why she would do such a thing, until he realized only one person could tempt her into such a betrayal. It disgusted him. The girl had fallen for the fool in her youthful naivety; Kaden using her love against her own father. Without any concern for her welfare, he had pulled her into his schemes and killed her. Li's hand gripped his pistol so tightly it began to go numb, and he was forced to relax his fingers for fear he wouldn't be able to fire when the precious moment arrived.

Alexis' deceit had come as a terrible shock, but it explained a lot. Like how Kaden had learned about the meeting between Lermontov's assassin and Senator Damon. Who knew what other intel he now had access to. Most of the files were encrypted, but they contained critical material about his informants and NOC list.

At first, Li had suspected the Feds had the files, but with Bishop and other key agents remaining unexposed, it seemed Kaden had been keeping the information up his sleeve as some sort of insurance policy.

Until now, when Koch had revealed the data stick had been hidden in California all along.

Li's men had searched the office high and low for the drive and turned up empty-handed. But Bishop's intel had always been solid in the past; Li trusted it implicitly.

When Lermontov had guessed Li's murderous intentions, he'd insisted on sending a kill squad to "support him." "That boy is too astute, and shrewd," was Luka's curt explanation. "Hasn't he escaped your attempts countless times before?"

He had. In fact, after all he'd suffered, Li knew that it would take the blood of a million Americans—and Kaden's head rotting on a spike—to give him any sense of satisfaction. He hoped to have both, soon.

In five hours the United States of America would launch an all-out offensive against the Confederate states. Bishop had provided the complete details of their assault: air, sea, land, even cyberattacks and media releases. The fools were playing right into their hands and instead of a long, protracted battle, they would destroy them in one fell swoop.

Lermontov had planned it to perfection.

The Chinese North Sea Fleet was positioning itself off the West Coast, with carriers *Liaoning* and *Kunlun* already fueling up their bombers and strike fighters, ready to thrust inland. Li had recruited every man, woman, tank, truck, bullet, and bomb they had to blast the Yanks out of existence. This went against the advice of his Council leaders, who tended to be overly precautious. Li no longer cared.

He would lead the 380,000 troops, massing off Arizona. The combined forces of Chinese and Western Confederate armored units, air force, and infantry divisions would first ambush the American offensive, then push inland to link up with Texas, and drive into the great Midwestern plains of the United States as the Russians and the secessionist states moved in from the East.

Li should have been in the command center going over the plans and directing his generals. Instead, he was sitting in the dark in an abandoned building, his thirst for revenge so strong he could no longer deny it. With Kaden's blood on his hands, he would wage a battle from which America would never recover. Then he would breathe deep, stand tall, and walk as an upright man once more.

The sound of light footsteps interrupted his musings.

A flicker of light grazed the debris filling the hallway, before beaming through the door. The tall, slim shadow paused before moving with nimble agility into the room.

Li Lei's gaze followed Kaden as he headed toward the main office. Lermontov's kill squad were in the room behind him, ordered to stay back unless required. He had agreed to their presence on the sole condition that he retain the right to slay Kaden himself.

The traitor had his back to him now and was softly releasing the latch on the office door.

"Kaden Sun," Li said, his voice cracking on the name. He coughed. "The serpent returns to his nest."

The figure froze, slowly turning to meet the voice that called him. Surprisingly, he didn't lift his torch, but left it pointing at the ground.

"Hello." His voice was light, unafraid. It made Li Lei's blood boil.

"What I would give to kill you," Li said through gritted teeth. "But if you give me the files, I will let you live," he lied. "You don't deserve to walk this earth, but those are my orders."

The smooth, cold steel of his Chinese QSZ-92 pistol tempted his hand. Damn the intel, it made more sense to kill him now. But Luka had forbidden it.

Li Lei relaxed his grip.

"You must be keeping some terrible secrets in those files," Sun said, as if amused by the whole thing. "Like Bishop, perhaps? I guess it might be awkward for the Free US to discover President Koch is a spy."

Li flinched. There had always been a possibility that Kaden knew the truth, but hearing it from his lips was still disturbing. "You're the fool who sided with him," Li stuttered, "knowing he was a traitor. Koch has been on Lermontov's payroll since you were crawling around in diapers. Your *United States of America* is nothing more than a mirage."

Kaden laughed. "Is that so? Thank you for the confirmation, Mr. Li."

"The data," he hissed. "Where is it?"

"There is no data." Kaden shrugged, crossing his arms. "I had a copy of your comm at one time, but only found a few appointments on it. The trip here was just a ploy to expose Koch."

Li Lei felt a slightly tingling of dread curl down his spine. Had he been played, yet again? Luka would have his head, and rightfully so.

Hands trembling, he raised the pistol and pointed it at Kaden's heart. He was standing only ten feet away, and couldn't miss. As his finger tightened on the trigger, an odd sound crept through the abandoned space.

He froze.

It came on soft, haunting and melancholy at once. The lilting strains may as well have been the blast from a nuclear explosion; Li felt his soul break apart into a billion tiny, disintegrating atoms. Whatever was left of him drifted back to that night, when Alexis had sung him a birthday dedication. It seemed so long ago. How much could change in an instant.

Li Lei cringed; his palm gripped the left side of his chest. He tried to take a step forward, but his knee faltered.

"Hurts, doesn't it?" Kaden said, tapping off his comm. His voice sounded hollow in the darkness. "I felt the same ache when you killed my father, just to get your way. I'm only sorry that Alexis had to bear your shame before she died."

The pistol in Li's hand wavered before him. Now was the time. The double-crossing viper had spoken the last of his lies.

A familiar metallic click cracked through the night, Li's mouth falling open in surprise. When a deep thud—like a rolling billiard ball—rattled through the room, every cell in his body screamed at him to get out of there.

Li's reflexes took over, his body exploding into action as he dove for cover with an agility and speed that belied his age. The blast that chased him made the entire building tremble, sucking out the oxygen to leave only smoke and flames.

"Coward!" he screamed, scrambling to his feet. Fresh air gusted in through the shattered windows, reams of paper swirling around like feathers after a pillow fight.

His ears rang with a piercing screech, and his eyes refused to focus. He could only just make out the blurred image of a man dashing for the door.

Raising his gun, he fired a few shots at the shadow and heard the bullets ricochet off the steel filing cabinets opposite. "Come back and face me!" he cried, stumbling into a smoldering table.

Shots began to fire from behind him, the kill team rushing into the room and sprinting after Sun. One of the men, older than the rest, stopped and turned to Li with a look of disgust. His face was caught in the glow of the fire, and Li felt his heart stutter as his features cleared through the smoke. He was terribly disfigured and missing his right eye. The man spat on the ground and raised his automatic rifle. For a moment, Li thought he was going to shoot him on the spot—so malevolent was his expression. Instead, he turned and stalked out the door, leaving Li alone in the rubble.

Seventy-Six

"They're right behind me!" Kaden shouted into his headset, mounting the military bike and kick-starting the engine. "Did you record it all?"

"Yes, though part of me wishes I hadn't," Agent Raven muttered. "Now get your ass out of there, Sun."

He hit the accelerator and the bike wrenched forward, Kaden almost flying off the back. "Go to the general now," he cried, "we don't have much time." As Kaden sped up and took the first corner he almost came off once more. What was in this thing—rocket fuel? He'd driven it to the office from the drone parked two miles away, without any idea of its capabilities. It made his old, rusty bike of the past look like a tricycle. "Koch is coordinating the attacks with Lermontov." He gunned down the street, overtaking an old sedan and catching a flash of shock on the driver's face. "If the offensive goes ahead, we're all doomed."

"I'm on it. Get back to the drone—that face is too pretty to waste."

"Doing my best," Kaden said, eying the rearview mirror. A pair of headlights passed the sedan. "Jesus, they're right behind me."

Two off-road military motorcycles were on his tail, each carrying a pillion rider. The passengers had machine guns at their sides, small bursts of light erupting with each jerk of their hands.

"Not good, Jack," he screamed, ramming the accelerator as fast as he dared to go. Blasting through the open desert was one thing, weaving through concrete streets another. The *thump-thump-clomp* of the enemy's hot lead were closing in, shattering the glass windows of cars parked on either side of him.

"Kaden, give me a status. Are you—"

"Jack, don't worry about me, I've got this. Go alert the general." Kaden zigged and zagged, the machine gunners crisscrossing their bursts of fire. He slipped into a series of alleyways and backstreets, providing a little more cover but slowing his speed considerably. The LED display on his comm glared up at him.

Distance to drone: 1 mile…0.9…0.8… Beside the countdown, a small skull-and-crossbones symbol appeared, informing him he was about to pass one of the checkpoints. The road had opened up into an industrial area, the bullets starting to spray closer.

When the comm beeped, he pressed the symbol and waited for the preplanted grenades to explode. Instead, he felt a bullet hit the engine between his legs, grazing the inside of his calf. "Shit!"

Kaden fought to stay upright, but the tires slid across the gravel as the bike came out from under him. He hit the road hard, tumbling a few feet before coming to a stop against a parked car.

The bikes had stopped behind him, guns still firing. A trace of bullets chewed up the road toward his legs and—

BOOM!

Multiple grenades erupted in unison, consuming bodies and bikes from both sides of the road. Flames lapped the uniforms of the riders as they rolled on the ground screaming. A cloud of black smoke enveloped the scene.

Better late than never, Kaden thought.

He dropped his head in relief. He'd expected a chase of some sort and the plan had worked. Now he only had to make it to the drone, ditch the bike, and—

His thoughts ground to a halt at the sight of a lone figure staggering to its feet, gun in hand. It was like something from a hellish nightmare, a demon raised from the dead. Kaden pushed himself up and stumbled to his bike, still idling on its side a few feet away. He righted it just as bullets nicked the taillight, sending plastic flying. Without a backward glance, he kicked into gear and started careening down the road, the sound of a second engine soon joining him.

The giant backlot soon appeared before him, surrounded by an old wire fence and overgrown weeds. In its center was the smooth outline of the stealth plane, quietly waiting to lift him to safety.

But it was hopeless. Kaden would be riddled with bullets as soon as he tried to board, the plane itself incapacitated by gunfire if he was somehow lucky enough to make it in.

He had to end it, now.

The bike lurched a third time, a bullet hitting somewhere near the exhaust. The next impact clipped his thigh.

"Aargh!"

There was nowhere to go, no way out. Why hadn't he brought a team? he wondered in despair. *Because there have been enough deaths in your name,* came a dark voice. *Just give up,* it hissed, *be grateful it's a quick death.*

He swerved to a sliding stop, his wheels spinning a hundred and eighty degrees before the body of the plane. A few hundred yards away the freak on the bike had also braked, probably wary of more explosions. The thug paused, gun aloft, waiting to see if it was some kind of trap. Kaden snapped his visor shut and revved his engine.

There was only one way out: the ultimate game of chicken.

This time when the bike jerked forward Kaden was sitting low and forward, his body melded to the machine. A bullet slammed into his headlight, extinguishing it in a shower of sparks. Still Kaden drove.

When the roar of the thug's bike met his own, he glanced up to see the distance between them quickly disappearing. His opponent had given up his firing. Somehow they both knew there was only one way this would end. The two projectiles hurtled closer, the calamitous collision quickly becoming unavoidable as both refused to change course.

What kind of paid gun would waste his life so recklessly?

As the bikes chewed up the final few yards, Kaden's heart constricted. He knew that head anywhere.

He was about to smash into The Skull.

Seventy-Seven

Kaden lay face down on the rocky soil. It took several minutes to raise himself enough to see the burning backdrop of his mangled bike, meshed with the freak's.

He'd woken up expecting to find a large, gleaming machete floating above his head. Instead, the man ordered to kill him was lying on his back ten yards away. Kaden ignored his instinct to run and tottered toward the body, feeling at his side for where his pistol hung. His fingers met with ripped leather and empty air.

The body lay still, eyes open but unseeing, mouth ajar. His hand still clutched his broken machine gun. Kaden winced as he noticed an unusual bulge in the man's neck—a shard of metal had pierced it, his blood pooling in the dancing glow of the fire.

Kaden turned and hobbled along the road, unsure he would even make it to the plane let alone be in any condition to launch it. His vision flickered like a defective television and his hearing was muffled.

He finally reached the door, pressed the access code, and clambered in. The indoor sensor recognized his presence and an activated voice asked him to "Authenticate."

Kaden took his seat and tried to utter the code, but all that left his lips was a weak, guttural mumbling. "Authenticate," the machine repeated.

Sweet Jesus.

Kaden punched a button beside him and a panel slid back, exposing the plane controls. He keyed in the numbers and was gratified when the voice continued with, "Target destination?"

"Return...to base," he coughed.

The inflight computer seemed to recognize the words this time, and the engines purred to life. Outside, the flaming bikes lit the empty road.

Empty?

The door began to close behind him as Kaden scanned the wreckage for Skull's body. It was gone.

Behind him came the sound of the door sliding closed, only to stop and strain suddenly. He turned in his seat and watched in horror as a badly grazed arm lay lodged between the seal and closing mechanism. In its hand, a gleaming machete.

"No!" Kaden cried, tapping the 'close' activator like his life depended on it. When that didn't work, he tried to override take-off protocols and make the craft lift off with the main door open. An alarm blared and the craft refused to budge. The actuator system whirred painfully as the gears strained under the load, but the intruder was stronger. As Kaden rushed forward to try and beat him back, the door clicked in protest and began to open.

Seventy-Eight

Kaden stared at the reality before him in disbelief, the on-board computer calmly announcing that takeoff procedures had begun. The soft rumbling of the plane's engine turned to a roar as it taxied for a short distance then took off at a twenty-degree flight angle.

Skull stood there, shrapnel still lodged in the side of his neck as his ragged gray T-shirt slowly turned red. He smiled, removed the automatic pistol from the holster at his side, and dropped it on the ground. His machete followed.

"No weapons," he said, chin lifted and arms open. "You and me, fists and teeth." His canines leered in the dimmed cabin lights.

"I'd rather bite into roadkill," Kaden said, leaning against the controls. Skull grunted in apparent amusement, before stepping forward to kick him brutally in the side. Fissures of pain radiated from his hip to his torso as he doubled over. A blow from Skull's elbow followed, sending him to his knees.

"C'mon now," the man drawled. "Don't make it too easy."

His steel-capped boot connected with Kaden's ribs and sent him sprawling to his side. The force of the impact made Kaden bite his tongue and he started to choke as his mouth filled with blood. There was no use fighting back. He'd fought enough.

"Little cripple," Skull spat. "Just like your daddy."

To Kaden's shame, he started crying. A deep sob wracked his body as Skull laughed at the pathetic mess before him. "Dammit," he said, "I'll put you out of your misery."

As he turned to pick up his knife, Kaden seized the opportunity in a last, desperate lunge, tackling Skull around his knees. The momentum sent them crashing toward the flashing instruments at the left side of the cockpit, Skull's face slamming into shards of glass and plastic.

He roared, raising his arms and smashing his palms on the sides of Kaden's head. Stunned, Kaden staggered backward as vague shapes and spots swayed before his eyes. Through his terror and confusion he forced himself to speak. "That's all you got?"

"Boy, that was just the foreplay." Kaden fell backward into the pilot's seat. "You wanna lap dance?" Skull said, jerking his hips suggestively.

Kaden blinked, trying to clear his senses. If he was going to die, there was no way he was going down alone. His hand drifted to the control panel and tapped lazily across the keys. The bomb bay swung open, though no artillery was loaded.

"You think I'm just gonna jump out?" Skull leered.

"I can only hope," Kaden smiled, blood trickling down his chin.

Skull lurched to the side, pushed about by the freezing air that swirled through the small space. "For a slanty-eyed dog, you didn't do too bad," he said, bending down to pick up his machete. "You ain't no ninja, but I've fought worse."

He lifted the blade and rested it on Kaden's heaving shoulder, as if preparing to knight him. "First the father, now the son," he said, speaking to the blade.

It lifted in a high arc just as warning lights began to flash overhead. The missile-evasion system kicked in and the drone made a sudden, violent flip to one side. Kaden gripped his seat as Skull stumbled backward. The plane continued to beep and screech, swerving to the left and right. A missile passed only meters from the nose of the craft, an eerie orange flare in the darkness.

"What did you do, boy?" Skull shouted, gripping wildly at the control panel. "You did this!"

A spray of tiny fireworks fell from the belly of the plane, trying to divert the heat-seeking missiles.

Skull gripped on for dear life, Kaden barely able to stay in his seat. His ears popped as the plane suddenly hurtled upward, then fell into a nosedive. Suddenly it was a freefall inside, Kaden and Skull thrown to the ceiling of the cockpit. When the plane leveled, they fell back to the ground and Kaden saw the machete sliding along the aisle toward him. He extended his arm, making a grab for the weapon.

With the cleaver in one hand, Kaden allowed gravity to push him toward Skull, sprawled against the side of the plane and pinned down by the accelerated descent. His single, gray eye followed Kaden.

"What happened to a fair fight, Sun?"

Kaden shrugged. "At least you're not in a wheelchair."

With a strength that seemed delivered from the heavens, Kaden drove the knife down and felt the steel pierce Skull's flesh, grind past his breastbone, and slide through his heart. Even as he died, Skull squirmed with all his might, but it was useless. Kaden fought the urge to laugh, cry, and scream into the man's face, watching in elation and grief as the killer gasped his last breath, mouth full of scarlet froth.

"This time, stay dead, you bastard," he panted, wrenching the knife out and drawing it across Skull's throat.

Seventy-Nine

Skull's head fell forward, his neck spurting red like a macabre drinking fountain. Behind them, the incessant alarms continued beeping. Kaden threw the machete aside and stared at his hands, stained with the lifeblood of his father's killer.

He should have been overwhelmed with satisfaction. For months he'd used this moment as a balm for the rage that welled within. Now that it had come, all he saw was that one desperate eye, glaring at him in silent fury. Nothing had changed. His dad was still dead, and now he had more blood on his hands.

A blinding flash filled the cockpit, and the plane wobbled on its downward spiral. A missile had erupted beside them, the drone pursued relentlessly. Suddenly, Kaden no longer wanted to die.

He kicked at the body, watching it slide toward the hatch and fall through like a rag doll into a giant garbage disposal.

"Close...bomb doors!" he cried, throat ravaged. The computer system did not acknowledge. The blaring alarm system wasn't helping.

Groaning, he pulled himself up to the controls. The plane continued to twist and dive, throwing him up one moment and sending him crashing to his knees the next. "Please," he cried, on the verge of blacking out. "Close the damn doors."

The plane coasted downward once more, giving him the reprieve he needed to stagger to the control panel. His finger was slippery, but only God Himself would stop him. He jabbed the buttons and watched as the bomb bay closed. A trio of dots blipped across the radar, slowly dropping off, one at a time. When the last had fallen off the screen he sunk onto the deck with arms spread and vomited until there was nothing left inside him.

"Geez, d'you host the Texas chainsaw massacre in there?" Jack's eyes narrowed as they scanned the blood and gore throughout the cockpit. He looked so tidy, the sleeve for his missing arm neatly pinned up.

Kaden flashed a bitter smile. "More like a meeting with Jack the Ripper."

Jack took in his ravaged appearance as the medical team came forward, but Kaden brushed them away.

"Katy?"

He nodded. "She's fine."

"Has Koch been arrested?"

Jack didn't answer, supporting Kaden with one arm as he ambled out of the plane.

"Well?" Kaden pressed.

"Come on, there's a lot to discuss. But not here."

The agent led him out of the hangar and through a series of tunnels, Kaden realizing he hadn't been to this side of the base before. Just when he grew convinced his legs would give out they reached the end of a musty passageway and a small, dimly lit room. Jack helped him limp inside and he collapsed into a flimsy metal chair. Before him sat two military men, the older one looking slightly familiar.

"General, this is Kaden Sun," Jack said, with a hint of awe. "He's the one who brought in the video evidence of Koch. Kaden, this is General Raven and his assistant, Lieutenant Byant."

The two men looked at Kaden as if he were a zombie, risen from the dead. He guessed he looked the part.

"So has Koch been arrested, or not?"

General Raven's smile turned cool. "Lieutenant Sun, still as feisty as the day I saw you address the war council." He sat back in his chair, arms crossed. "Unfortunately, bringing down a president isn't as simple as pointing a finger and screaming spy. This isn't some Hollywood movie."

Kaden winced. Clearly, they considered him a clueless amateur.

"You've done a good job," he added, and Kaden glimpsed the father behind the soldier. "But I need time to build the case and ensure key members of the secretary of defense and chiefs of staff are convinced. If we get this wrong, Koch and his faction will destroy us and then the nation will be well and truly lost."

"Then what are we waiting for, sir?" Kaden protested, his bloodied palms open in frustration.

"Koch has called an emergency meeting," said Jack, speaking in a soothing tone. "All the top brass are there. Our people are also inside, secretly talking to the various leaders and gauging support." He nodded at the general's comm. "As soon as our insiders feel the foundation is there to stage a coup, we'll be notified. Until then, we could come out with guns blazing and walk straight into a trap."

Kaden glared at them both, barely able to contain the frustration simmering through him. By now, Koch would have learned of his escape from Li, so all their lives were in danger, Katy's included. The man wasn't going to sit around and wait for a set of handcuffs. But Kaden was in the military's hands now, and he had to follow their rules.

"What's Koch's overall offensive plan?" Kaden asked. "Where is he sending our troops?"

The general nodded approval for his assistant to divulge this information. "A direct thrust into California and up the West Coast," the young man said, "combined with an eastward drive into Maryland and then the Northeast secessionist states."

"Okay. So let's say we focus on the West," Kaden proposed, staring at each of them in turn. If you were an enemy strategist, how would you lead the combined forces of the Chinese and Confederate states against such a frontal attack?"

The general nodded again and the captain started tapping at his comm. A three-dimension map hovered atop the table before them, with a mass of blue arrows depicting the American westward drive.

"They know the armored columns would have to navigate along major highways," General Raven said. "I would create ambush points by stacking my forces along these bottlenecks, creating a line of gun bombardment and rocket strikes to obliterate the advance forces. The rest of the columns would be holed up behind them, so I'd let the air force and cruise missiles finish them from the rear."

Kaden nodded. "So we can assume Koch and Lermontov have planned the same, or something similar."

"Agreed," said the general. "As you know, we lost many of our satellites the moment the war started. Thankfully, we were able to take out most of theirs too. So we're all fighting a pretty low-tech war now, but with Koch providing our battle plan to the enemy, our only hope for overco—"

He was interrupted as a distant explosion trembled through the concrete and rock, dust falling through the hologram like silver glitter.

"What was that?" Jack cried, his head tilted upward. Another boom, deeper in tone, struck them all silent.

A soldier ran into the room. "We've got a situation, sir."

"That much is obvious," General Raven said. "And I assume it's not a gas leak."

"Correct, sir. The enemy are hitting the base with buster bombs."

"Where have they targeted?"

"The first strike was on the main entry shaft. I'm not sure about the second hit, sir."

"So they know our weak points," the general spat. "If this keeps up, it'll be like swiping the top off an anthill."

Kaden shook his head. "Now Koch has an even greater excuse to launch his offensive. Or he could use this as a distraction, while he and his moles sneak out."

The general dismissed the soldier and glared at Kaden. But before he could reprimand him for speaking so openly another missile hit, and the faint smell of smoke began to taint the air. In the distance, they could hear shouting.

"General, what if we reverse-ambush them?" Kaden said, thinking back to the WarGames championship. *Lure them in and hit them when they least expect it.*

"Our own ambush?" General Raven asked.

"Exactly," Kaden replied, noticing small cracks beginning to appear in the concrete above them. "Lermontov is expecting us to do one thing. But what if we recalibrate our plans and create a fake attack at the front? The main force could break into multiple prongs and move off the highways, creeping in behind the enemy. Once we get our stealth bombers over them they'll be pinned in front and back, with nowhere to go but down."

The general rubbed his chin, studying the virtual map. He drew his finger along the pathway of the attack routes and considered the mountain passes and plains.

"I'd planned on aborting the offensive altogether, but if we—"

The comm on General Raven's wrist beeped. He viewed the message and then looked up at everyone.

"Gentlemen, it's time."

Eighty

Despite a painful limp, Kaden was the first to stride into the cavernous operations center. The space was filled with large screens, virtual projections, and uniformed personnel—the central command for the combined military forces. The glass-enclosed War Room was filled with people, many over-looking the frenzied activity below.

Kaden scanned the area as Raven Junior and Senior appeared at his side. His first sweep was to locate Katy. His eyes found her in the War Room, busy pouring coffee in the crowded space. He felt his chest expand in relief.

"Look," Jack said from beside him. Koch was standing at the door of the room, only a few yards from the coffee station. They watched the man pause and turn for the door. "He's seems to be leaving. What's he up to?"

A tingling sensation coursed through Kaden, his body taut. "He's making a run for it."

Jack nodded at his father's security staff to follow as they went to confront him. Kaden couldn't help glancing back at Katy. Her back was to him, head tilted as she made small talk with an old White House official who was ogling her breasts. Kaden wanted nothing more than to stride in there and whisk her away—forget the lot of them—but he had a job to do.

"Stop right there, President Koch," came General Raven's commanding voice. Kaden felt a ripple of awareness pass through the center, the murmur of conversation dying around them. A few officers from the Ops Center turned and saluted the general, others blocked Koch with their guns raised.

The door to the War Room was closed and Kaden watched as a woman in a sharp suit tried to open it, struggling with the handle. She held her comm up to the access panel, but nothing happened.

Koch raised his hands slowly, but instead of looking bewildered, he smiled.

"It's over, Koch," said the general. "The entire administration has been informed of your treachery. You're under arrest."

"Says who?" Koch opened one of his palms to reveal a small black device, his thumb depressing a red trigger. The sight seemed to suck the air from the room. General Raven was lost for words.

"You think I'd make it that easy for you?" He laughed. "You can arrest me, Raven, but it will cost you your entire cabinet and military command." He jerked his thumb at the glassed-in room.

The people inside were watching in confusion, Katy's pale face hovering behind their shoulders. The room was soundproof, but Koch's plan was clear even without the benefit of his words. As realization dawned, a group of men started pounding at the door. One guy slammed a chair at the giant window separating them from those outside, but quickly gave up. It was reinforced bulletproof glass, a sledgehammer would struggle to break it.

Kaden's knees grew weak, his injured leg wobbling beneath him. He was beaten, battered, and bruised. But none of that hurt as much as seeing Katy in harm's way, yet again.

"The War Room has been rigged with explosives. I release this little button here and thirty seconds later the room goes… boom." His fingers gestured a star burst for effect.

"You coward," Kaden spat. "Even if you escape, you'll be remembered as the most hated man in our nation's history."

Kaden knew that Koch wouldn't leave without detonating the bomb, he was sure of it. He'd release the trigger the moment he was clear, out of spite alone.

Koch blinked. "Is that you, Sun, under all that blood? You simply refuse to die."

"Let me inside the room," Kaden said, his voice breaking. "If you want me dead, then let me die."

Koch looked at him distrustfully before turning his gaze to Katy, whose face had now joined the others pressed against the glass. She was shaking her head, gesturing for Kaden to stay back.

"Don't do it, Kaden," Jack cautioned.

"Ah, young love. 'Only fools rush in,' as they say." Koch smiled. "It's those kinds of romantic notions that have led to the fall of our great nation, and the rise of the new empire. But that's a speech for another day," he said. "Like tomorrow."

"Not if I have anything to do with it," said General Raven, stepping forward. He turned to the men sitting at the control desks. "Order your units to stand down and await fresh directives. We aren't going to walk straight into Koch's bloodbath."

"*Tsk*," Koch shook his head. "You can try to stop the offensive, but the liberators will still win in the—" A loud, distant boom shook the walls, announcing another missile strike. "See?" he said with a laugh. "They're already here."

"Stand down," General Raven continued. "And await new orders."

"That's too bad," Koch said, lifting the trigger in his hand.

"No, wait!" Kaden cried, his body trembling with fear and fatigue. "General Raven, please. Think of the people inside."

The older man kept his eyes on the command screens, refusing to look at Kaden. "I'm sorry, Lieutenant Sun. I've known some of the people in that room for forty years, but I won't lead half a million men and women to their deaths to save thirty lives."

The man spoke with a cool, hard determination, and Kaden sensed the tension in the room spike further. Raven had called Koch's bluff.

Koch seemed to go red then white in an instant. "Launch at all costs," he cried, two officers at their console standing to attention. One turned to the directing officer watching over them and shot him twice in the chest and once in the head. The man's body flew backward as the shots reverberated around the cavern, sending most of the people in the room to their knees. The second officer fired upon the operators at the terminals around him, the victims' blood sprayed across the screens.

Some people screamed and ran, others returned fire. Kaden scrambled to the glass and pressed his hands against Katy's, wishing there wasn't a six-inch barrier between them. She looked frantic, but at least she wasn't about to get shot.

Jack appeared at his side, firing his pistol as he spoke. "Koch has overridden the door's security system. We need his comm."

Kaden gave Katy a bittersweet smile, his fingers pressed to his lips. A moment later, he was dashing toward Koch, who was firing a small handgun at anyone who got too close. Kaden longed to kill the man, but needed him alive. The trigger could not go off.

He stepped forward with hands lifted to show he was unarmed. Koch turned to him and paused, his gun aimed at Kaden's chest. "You little piece of shi—"

Koch's head jolted back as a stray bullet passed through his throat.

"No!" Kaden cried, lunging forward.

Koch lay on the ground, blood pouring from his mouth. Even as he died his eyes followed Kaden, his lips twisted in spite. In his final spasms he lifted the detonator, offering it to Kaden. But just as Kaden reached to take it, the president sent the small black box clattering at his feet.

Kaden flinched in anticipation of the devastating explosion, before remembering Koch's words. *Thirty seconds...*

The comm!

He ripped at the black device on Koch's arm, but it was designed to be almost impossible to remove without permission. It would take at least fifteen seconds to drag the big, bloated body over to the door. He wheeled around, looking for a solution, and saw a machine gun lying in the arms of a dead guard. Wrenching it from his grip, he pointed it down and released a burst of bullets, looking away as pieces of concrete, flesh, and floor tiles exploded up into his face.

The gun clicked, empty, and Kaden dropped it at his feet. The arm was mangled, but still attached to the body, and it took all he strength to break the final bonds of bone and sinew. At least ten seconds had passed.

He threw himself at the door and pressed the comm to the access pad. Nothing happened. Growling in frustration he jabbed at the green entry button, but still nothing. Then, with a small *thunk*, the bolts slid back.

The door opened inward, but the crush of people trying to escape made it impossible to open. He couldn't see Katy's face among them. "Back!" he screamed, gesturing wildly, "get back!"

A few of the larger men at the front managed to create a barricade, reversing enough for the door to swing inward. Like a full bottle of soda shaken and released, people began tumbling out. There were only seconds left and Katy was nowhere to be seen. It was mayhem.

"Katy!" He staggered through the surging, screaming crowd. "Katy, where are you?"

Time was up; they wouldn't make it. Still, his hope kindled when he saw her. The rear of the room had cleared and Katy was on her knees, trying to get up. A small gash marred her brow and he could see she was disoriented.

"We've got to get out of here," he cried, pulling her into his arms. "Grab my hand!" He began tugging her to the door, but too many people were fighting their way out before them. Only seconds left…

He guessed the bomb was hidden in the lectern at the front of the room, where Koch had been addressing them when Kaden arrived. It was now surrounded by people. There were no other exits, no chance to survive a blast in such an enclosed space. All he could do was close his eyes and hold her in these final moments. Maybe his body would be able to act as some sort of a shield from the devastation to come.

He sunk to his knees behind an overturned table and tucked Katy into his body. Her eyes were slightly glazed, her lips parted. "What happened to you?" she whispered, touching her fingers to his battered face.

"I love you, Katy, so much…" Squeezing her against him, their lips touched and for a brief moment, all was right in the world.

Then the room dissolved into a blinding, earth-shattering light.

After that, nothing.

Eighty-One

The dust settled on the bloodied bodies like icing sugar. All around her were sounds of groaning, choking, and the wet rasp of labored breath. Department secretaries, generals, admirals—death didn't discriminate. Bodies and their parts lay strewn amid the tables and chairs, like dolls tossed aside by some giant, petulant toddler.

The broken oak desk remained pressed against her shoulders. It had been pushed back from the force of the explosion, taking her with it. She now faced the corner of the room. Kaden was gone.

The dust made her eyes water and breathing was almost impossible. Shrill alarms shrieked throughout the space and she knew she had to leave and find fresh air.

"Kaden?" The name brought on a violent attack of coughing. She crawled onto her knees and tried again, louder. "Kaden!"

A soldier rushed to her side and pulled her to her feet, leading her toward the door. "No!" she cried, shoving at him. "Kaden!" Like a madwoman, Katy began stumbling through the wreckage.

She only made it a few steps before she stopped. A one-armed federal agent was bent over a body, his fingers pressed to the limp, bloodied wrist. It was the man who'd been standing beside Kaden as they confronted Koch. He turned and yelled for help.

"Honey?" She sunk to her knees.

Kaden laid face-up, peaceful, his eyes closed. He could have been sleeping. Her hands grasped his cheeks, her thumb tracing his lips and nose, but there was no response, not even the warm, soft brush of his breath.

The agent touched her shoulder. "Katy, I don't think he's breathing..."

She ignored him, hands moving to Kaden's abdomen, where a pool of blood was forming. She pulled back the soaked crimson cloth to find a shard of timber severing the flesh. "Oh my God." The earth started to tilt and the agent tried to pull her away. "Don't touch me!" she screamed, taking Kaden's shoulders and shaking him. "Wake up! Don't you dare leave me, Kaden Sun!"

A young medic dropped to his knees beside her. "I need you to move back, ma'am."

She looked at him in hope and helpless fury. He was a kid, straight out of med school. Katy whipped around to look for someone more senior.

"Whoa, slow down," said the one-armed agent, pulling her to him. "You're going to get yourself hurt."

"No vitals," the medic said. He lowered his hands and started the compressions, then mouth-to-mouth. Katy watched Kaden's chest lift with each breath, only to instantly deflate again. His body was broken.

She lifted his hand, felt the stumps of his missing fingers. "Please," she cried, squeezing. "Come back."

"I need an AED over here!" The young man pumped once, twice, a third time.

Out of the chaos one of his colleagues rushed over with a large gray box. The first medic ripped open Kaden's shirt and placed the leads on his chest and side. At once the machine let out a low monotonous tone.

Katy grimaced as she heard it—the same empty sound that haunted her memories of standing on the wet roadside, watching strangers work over the bodies of her parents. Why did she always emerge uninjured, when everyone around her was hurt?

The second medic pulled out the defrib paddles and placed them over Kaden's chest.

"Take your hands off the body, ma'am!"

"Stand clear. Trigger!"

Kaden's body jolted suddenly.

The monotonous drone of the defibrillator remained unchanged.

"Stand clear! Trigger!" Kaden's body arched again and collapsed, limp against the ground. The medics tried a third and fourth time before shaking their heads.

Murmuring an apology, the younger one explained they had other patients to attend to.

Katy's hand was pressed to her mouth, her eyes slammed shut on the scene before her. Only the tight press of the agent's arms around her shoulder kept her from collapsing.

She heard the men start to get their feet.

"No," she burst out, opening her eyes and grabbing the young man. "Bring him back!" she demanded, flinging the box open and pulling out the paddles.

"Ma'am, you can't tou—"

"Shut up and help me!" She rubbed at her eyes, blinded by the tears and dust. "He was alive a minute ago, he's still with us." When she tried to press the large, red switch, the medic grabbed her hands.

"Stop, it's dangerous." He looked at his colleague. "Can we do one more round?"

The man sighed and he nodded.

"Stay clear."

"Trigger!"

Another jolt, another sudden spasm of movement, and then nothing.

"Again!"

"Clear, trigger…"

Nothing. He was gone.

"I'm sorry." The agent squeezed her shoulder, coughing. "Come on, we need to get out of this smoke." Katy let herself be pulled away, her eyes set upon Kaden.

I'll always be here when you need me.

She remembered his words as clearly as if he'd spoken them. But Katy knew that even the most solemn promises could be broken; love wasn't always enough. Not when faced with guns and bombs and men who didn't care about the people they hurt.

The agent turned her to the door just as the long, sad drone of the machine finally switched off. In its place, a small, sharp *beep*. Then another.

Katy froze, turning slowly. Her eyes leapt to Kaden. He was unmoving, but beside him the monitor showed a blip in the center of the screen. Then another. Peaks and troughs with a semblance of regularity formed. Katy threw herself at him.

"Breathe!" she cried, shaking him again. As if obeying orders, his mouth popped open and his body convulsed, lungs choking for air.

The medics stared at each other in disbelief.

The older man pulled an oxygen mask from the bag at his side and slipped it over Kaden's face. Through the plastic, Katy could see the faintest sign of a smile.

She hugged him, amazed to feel his chest move against hers with each shallow breath. "Oh Kaden, I almost died with you."

Her kisses fell upon his eyes and brow and cheeks. She stopped when she felt him coughing beneath her.

"I love you babe, but you're killing me."

Eighty-Two

Deep Underground Military Base # 2
Medical Center

"You seem to be expecting us," Jack grinned, shaking Kaden's hand and nodding at Katy.

"The nurse said we had visitors, and since my buddy Zac's come by already you're the only ones it could be." He nudged Katy. "She even put lipstick on for you."

They laughed, while Katy flushed at the attention.

"You all right, son?" General Raven approached his bed and took off his peaked cap.

"Yes, sir," Kaden replied. "Especially after hearing the news."

"We trounced them," the general said, face splitting into a wide grin. "Your plan worked well, mostly."

"Mostly?"

"The Chinese and Russians concentrated their forces at about eighty percent of our suspected positions. We were off on a few occasions and incurred some casualties, but we won the battle."

"And prevented a full attack on our base," Jack added. "Bombers took out the main expeditionary force, but the losses were overwhelming, regardless."

Kaden nodded. Katy had informed him half the leadership was gone, including a lot of the staff who'd been most loyal to Cowen and Raven, respectively. "The secretary of defense, our chiefs of staff, and others…" General Raven looked suddenly old beyond his years.

His son patted him on the shoulder. "The young blood is stepping up and doing a fine job of it."

The general smiled. "Yes, they are." He stood straight, his eyes moving to the window and the desert beyond. "Those bastards will be back, but we'll be waiting for them."

Katy's grip on his hand tightened, her knuckles as white as the sheets on the hospital bed. Talk of more violence frightened her—and him too, if he were to be honest. All she'd ever wanted was a quiet life, a small spot to call their own. That was what he'd been fighting for all along and he was determined to give it to her… and his new family.

"Thank you," he said, turning to Jack.

The special agent folded his arms. "For what, Kaden?"

"For believing in me. For…everything."

"Don't mention it." Jack put a hand on Kaden's shoulder. "Take some rest, kid. You've earned it."

"And come back to us when you're ready, lieutenant," the general added. "We need more men like you on our side."

Kaden glanced at Katy, whose eyes were set firmly in her lap. He couldn't believe that in less than six months they'd have a baby to care for. For all his joy at the news, in the early hours of the morning he pondered this new responsibility with sober determination. There were no grandparents to fall back on if something happened to either of them; his child would be left alone in the world. He couldn't let that happen.

"I thank you for the offer, sir, but my days as a soldier are over."

"How about as a strategist?"

"No, thank you."

The steely eyes squinted. "Mr. Sun, you should know by now I'm not used to being rejected."

Jack laughed. "I can vouch for that."

"All the same, sir," Kaden said, "I have to look after what matters most." He squeezed Katy's hand. "As soon as I've healed, we're hitting the road."

The general grimaced. "You've certainly served your country, son, but we'll convince you yet."

Kaden nodded at Katy. "You'll have to convince her first," he said. "And if you think the Chinese are tough, you ain't seen nothing yet."

The four of them laughed, Katy and Kaden's fingers tightly entwined.

Eighty-Three

"**Y**our grand American battle was like watching a child being whipped by their schoolmaster, Mr. Lermontov." The Chinese marshal's lips twisted with dissatisfaction. "I've seen your Russian president on television, trying to make this some great sacrifice for freedom. If your propaganda was as effective as your military strategy, we might not have lost a third of our forces."

Luka Lermontov turned his back on the marshal and strolled to the great window panels overlooking the Hudson.

"Marshal Zhang, I forgive your ingratitude. You forget we have annihilated most of the enemy's leaders and retained almost all our territories. The Russians can't be held to account for the mistakes of your countryman, Li Lei."

The squared-jaw marshal joined Lermontov at the window. The dizzying height and glorious skyline made a man feel like he owned the world.

"My cousin was a sentimental fool."

"Was?" Lermontov asked, brows raised.

Zhang took a silver disc from the breast pocket of his uniform and held it on his palm. "He wanted you to see this and I could not deny him."

Curious, Lermontov peered at the flash of silver. The marshal tapped its side and a holographic video of a man appeared in the air above. He stood alone under the glare of a spotlight, his uniform stained and torn. He was blindfolded.

Though his face was half covered, his mouth was set in a resigned line. A stern voice off camera made proclamations in Mandarin, Lermontov's limited comprehension of the language catching only the words 'crime' and 'shame.'

"He was never the same after losing his daughter," Zhang said, flinching as a series of shots rang out and the figure slumped to the ground.

"You executed him?"

"Our leaders ordered it." Zhang squared his shoulders. "I am now in command of the Chinese campaign and will avenge those who led to my cousin's downfall. Including that American, Sun."

"Kaden Sun? He's a slippery one," Lermontov said. "I warned Li Lei."

"Our intelligence indicates he may be smarter than we realized." Marshal Zhang glanced down at the river below, his eyes sweeping across the hundreds of Chinese and Russian transport ships lining the coast. "He is one of the last descendants of China's most famous war strategists, Sun Tzu. Maybe that doesn't mean much, but he could prove an interesting opponent, even for someone as conniving as you, Mr. Lermontov."

Luka laughed. "You Chinese are so superstitious. All of us are related to someone."

Beneath his veil of amusement, however, his heartbeat quickened. He hadn't felt such excitement since boyhood, planning and killing his father's murderers. These days he found himself bored; even the takeover of the world's greatest nation offered little...*satisfaction*. It wasn't personal enough. It lacked the intimacy of watching your enemy die at your own hands.

"He needs to be eliminated," the marshal said, as if reading his thoughts. "I've ordered our agents take him down at the first opportunity."

"No," Lermontov said, with a wave of his hand. "Leave the boy to me. I'll take care of it."

Marshal Zhang tilted his head. "We don't have time to play games here."

"I don't play games, Marshal Zhang," he said with a smirk. "I win them."

He strode to his desk and waved his hand over his private projection system. A complex 3D diagram of blue tunnels and bases floated atop the table. Above the network lay a satellite image of mountain ranges and rocky terrain.

"What is this?"

Lermontov smiled. "The American underground military bases, delivered by our dearly departed President Koch. It's offered the enemy a key advantage over us throughout the war, as they scurry throughout the highlands and Great Plains, distributing supplies and fresh troops. It's impossible to drive our troops inland when they're fighting and evading us right beneath our feet."

"Like rats in a sewer," Zhang said, slapping his jade-encrusted military baton against his palm.

"That need to be exterminated," Lermontov added. "Tell your leaders, marshal. We need to reinforce your troops. I promise you, within months, the country will be ours. Oil and gas, agricultural land, minerals, timber, infrastructure…the goose with a thousand golden eggs."

A sonic boom rocked the reinforced windows. Luka looked up and saw a swarm of new bat-winged Russian Sukhoi PAK super stealth fighters. They streaked across the skyline, headed for the war front in South Carolina.

Lermontov turned toward Marshal Zhang and smiled broadly. "Let the games begin."

END OF BOOK I

Read on for an advance glimpse of *World War A Book II: The Purge.*

Word War A

Book II: The Purge

Kaden's eyes flickered open, but the swirling sand slammed them shut again. In the distance, he heard a rumble, like the low groan of moving earth.

"Katy?" His hand searched the bed beside him, but all he felt was dirt.

The sound deepened to a roar. Kaden tried to open his eyes, hands shielding them the best he could, but all he saw through the cracks of his fingers was bright light and red wind.

His joints were aching so much that getting to his knees was an Olympic effort, Kaden groaning like an old man on a cold morning. The gale shifted around him, changing direction and offering a small chance to glimpse his surroundings. Through squinted eyes, he could see a spiral of dust, dancing across the desert.

"Katy!" he cried. The mountains to his left were where they'd always been, but everything else was gone. What had happened to the buildings and people?

He began to crawl forward through the rocks and dirt when the ground collapsed beneath him. Arms flaying in desperation, he tumbled down a splintering precipice and into a rocky abyss. He was falling and bouncing against the rock wall, his hands grappling for any hold. When his fingers caught upon a ledge he gripped with all his might, every sinew and tendon stretched taut. His whole body was now hanging above a well of darkness below and he took short, quick breaths to steady himself, coughing into the sand and dirt that streamed against his face. It took everything he had to haul his throbbing body back up to the surface.

By now, the sandstorm had largely passed, revealing a landscape that stole the breath from his lungs. He staggered forward, disbelieving.

Craters pockmarked the desert for miles, exposing large sections of the tunnel network that had once been Deep Underground Military Base #2. Standing at the lip of the void, Kaden looked down into an anthill fifty stories deep, its innards broken and exposed. Throughout the ruined infrastructure were pockets of fire and plumes of smoke, darkened ash floating up from its seemingly fathomless depths.

It was then that he saw them. The twisted, charred remains of the men and women he'd lived with, their blood dripping from the ledges to be swallowed by the soil below.

Acknowledgement

It took two intense years, many sleepless nights, and over ten major revisions (I've lost count) to forge a story that I felt proud enough to bring to readers. This effort was by no means my own and is also credited to my great professional team of editors, cover and interior designers, and those who've provided help along the way.

My deepest gratitude goes to God, Jesus, for His Grace and guidance in my daily journey. And to my family: my wife and kids, for being subjected to the rigor of reading the drafts and for swearing you loved the story (I hope you were telling the truth! ☺)

To my editors, Cate Hogan and Allison Blisard, you are both truly professional and outstanding. Cate, you were patient and delved deep into the subject matter with me, and it was great fun developing the storyboard and going through every aspect of the characters together. Allison, I really enjoyed your blunt yet sharp observations, which helped improved the contents tremendously. To Lourdes Venard, excellent proofreading work. To Clarissa Yeo, thank you for your talented book design and dedication to your craft.

And to Linda, Lilis, friends, fellow authors and so many more who have been a part of this process, I thank you all.